A PASSING ADVANTAGE

"Seeded clouds?" Price asked. "You mean we've seeded these clouds?"

"Yes, sir. We still are. As per General Bengsten's orders."

Said Mackey, "Tell me this, Colonel—the voice on Friday night—he identified himself as General Bengsten?"

"Yes, sir. Code and everything. What are your orders now? I mean, shall I pull in the planes? The Soviets have buzzed them several times already, and the amount of snow we can expect is—"

Mackey nodded and crossed a leg, turning himself away from the others, who were watching him. He wondered if he were being presented a fait accompli, a situation in which he was being availed a passing tactical advantage that would probably never happen again and should not be ignored. And, my God, the possibilities, if enough snow could be put down quickly.

It was probably the only brilliant thing Harold Bengsten ever did or would do. The irony of it— snow, it was usually considered a Soviet medium. They held exercises—or what passed for such—in Siberia every year. But here, if they got enough— Mackey stopped there.

And Patton and his statement at the end of the end of the war? What was it, again? "We are going to have to fight them sooner or later, within the next generation."

"All the ingredients of a superb, exciting novel."
　　　　　　　　　　　　　　—*Houston Chronicle*

"Fiction so realistic it is difficult to distinguish where fact lets off and imagination takes over."
　　　　　　　　　　　　　　—*Ne*

A PASSING ADVANTAGE

MARK McGARRITY

PINNACLE BOOKS   NEW YORK

A PASSING ADVANTAGE

Copyright © 1980 by Mark McGarrity

A Pinnacle Books edition, published by special arrangement with Rawson, Wade Publishers, Inc.

First printing, July 1981

ISBN: 0-523-41441-2

Cover illustration by David Mann

Map by Clarice Borio

Printed in the United States of America

PINNACLE BOOKS, INC.
1430 Broadway
New York, New York 10018

A Passing Advantage

PROLOGUE

The concussion knocked them off their feet. The blast hit them as they blundered through the mud of the trench, and their hands jumped to their ears. The second, the third . . . the entire multiple made them feel thick in the chest and nauseous.

They had seen only a brilliant line off in the distance where the enemy was massing on the eastern plain, but it had been ominous in its length, and the flashes, too rapid to count, had burned right through the clouds.

Then came the screaming, and the earth seemed to render its molten core, cracking open at regular intervals that crept toward them.

Some were disoriented, unwilling and perhaps unable to take their hands from their ears. They crushed themselves into the wall of the trench. Others swore or moaned. One tried to scramble up the far side and run. The officer caught him around the neck and threw him back into the darkness.

It was night and raining, and the officer only just managed to reach the wall himself.

The eight feet of slimy earth grew hot and hard and wouldn't hold their fingers. Dirt and rock fell on them. An arc of the barrage crept into the trench, but off on a flank. The next round overreached, and the entire firegroup, as one, hurled itself against the other wall. But just for a moment. Even now they could hear the high-pitched whine of the diesels in the enemy tanks, wave after wave, that were advancing from the eastern plain.

The officer reached down for his weapon, knocked the dirt from it, and kicked a toehold in the trench wall. But still he waited. Head-on like this, his soldiers had only two targets: the front plates with 85 mm. of armor, and the bottoms of the turrets with 100. And he was gambling. If

3

just one tank breached their perimeter, it could wheel to either flank and roll up their line.

"Aufstehen!" he shouted to the soldiers near him and mounted the wall of the trench. He snapped the weapon into the crotch of his neck. He wasn't used to the helmet that came down and covered his ear. *"Jetzt!"* He sprang up, took aim, and fired.

All up and down their line, flashes, like tongues of fire, darted out at the tanks. The charges smacked into the armor and staggered the soldiers, but every one in the firegroup ran at the tanks that had just been knocked out.

The enemy commander was confused. He couldn't have known where the attack had come from. The regularity of the destruction seemed to indicate mines, but that was impossible, given the artillery barrage that had preceded the push. And no sightings of distant fire had been made.

Now some of the tanks swung around to breach the gaps between the stricken and flaming tanks in the first rows, but the officer and his men, using the wrecks as blinds, were hidden from sight. He bellied past a smoking heap of twisted metal, keeping in the shadow of its track. He hoped the reserve fuel drums fastened to the tank skirt wouldn't blow and that the turret-mounted coaxial machine gun was also knocked out.

Suddenly a tank off to his right exploded, and he was illuminated by the fireball.

The 115 mm. gun of the tank in front of him began to swing around.

He tried to jam another charge down the tube of his weapon, but the second man in his fireteam, standing, took aim and caught the seam of the turret. The blast ripped it off the tank body.

But there were too many for them.

The officer dropped his weapon, turned, and ran back toward the trench.

All up and down the perimeter of II Hill, tanks were ablaze. They reminded him of the smudge pots he had helped his father set out in the orange groves of southern California.

The rain clouds were breaking, and off to the west only patterned wisps, like a veil, kept the moonlight soft on the hillside. The officer could see his men sprinting up the far slope. His plan was to have the entire firegroup over the horizon before the tanks could gain the brow of the eastern hill.

Running through the gouged and cratered basin, he could almost taste the blood in his lungs and his legs felt wooden. He was fifty-two, and he imagined he was fighting his third war. His second man overtook him, and he forced his legs to pump even harder.

His climb up III Hill was more like a prolonged stagger that ended near the top where he stumbled and fell. His face grated into the dirt. Turning, he saw several enemy tanks on the ridge of II Hill. He could tell from the configuration of yellow lights they were British. The beams were working over and back over the basin below.

Then somebody had him by the arms. He looked up. The faces were black. They rushed him over the brow of the hill where the three of them tumbled into the darkness.

He forced himself to stand and move toward the stockpile of longer-range antitank weapons, which had been carried in while the fight was raging to the east. He slid one off the pile and hoisted it on his shoulder. With its charge it weighed twenty-eight pounds.

Keeping well below the brow, he moved toward the left flank of II Hill. Half the firegroup followed him; the other half broke to the right with another officer.

One soldier remained. There were four launchers at his feet.

The soldier waited only until he could no longer see the others or hear their footsteps in the soft earth.

He picked up a launcher and sighted in the lead tank across the basin from him. He felt lucky. Through the cross hairs he could see the looming barrel of the tank. It was a Chieftain. A full 150 mm. of armor protected it all around.

The rocket shot out of the launcher, spiraled in a long arc across the basin, and struck the side of the turret, which had turned to the north.

At first the soldier couldn't tell if the rocket had damaged the tank. He pushed his blond hair off his forehead and kept the sighting device to his eye. But all at once, like a mine, the tank exploded, sending a jet of flame and debris up from its hatch and into the night sky. A large fragment slammed into the American tank to its right and set it on fire.

5

He grabbed for the second weapon and took out another tank. Those off on the flanks began directing fire at him, but he managed to squeeze off a third round. He kept the scope trained on the target until the rocket homed in and the tank coughed a ball of flame, its last.

He then turned and tried to run down the hill, but he was night-blind and fell. The earth was soft and wet and stuck to him, like macerated flesh. It was hot and stank of explosives.

He picked himself up and began running again. He felt the way he had when, as a lad, the gang of them had knocked off the bobby's helmet and had run through the dark, wet streets of Sheffield.

But this time it was different. Even before he had crossed the basin the rockets began falling behind him. Suddenly he heard a shrieking overhead, and he felt a force, like a hot, stinging hand, pick him up and hurl him across the basin, onto the opposite hill.

He tried to lift his head, but the moon and the yellow clouds got grainy and began to dissever. Something was burning his back and legs.

The earth was hissing to the touch of a light rain.

"Bloody hell," he said and hoped the medics weren't far.

The rockets of the firegroup spewed from the hills, like a shower of sparks, and caught the tanks on the floor of II Basin. But the soldiers kept to the heights, jacking shaped charges into their launchers and sighting in the lumbering hulks below. Tank after tank exploded, and thick black smoke and the reek of scorching metal poured from the basin toward the east.

The first mauve blush of dawn had suffused that horizon, and the ragged edge of the storm front was passing, like a curtain, before the moon.

Only the Swedish S-tanks, which had dropped their foldaway plows into the soft Canadian soil and had raised earthen redoubts, remained. And one other.

It had wheeled to the right flank and was now churning up the hill, its turbine screaming. Silhouetted against the burning pyres of the other tanks, it seemed squat, wider than any of the others, and strangely feline, like a massive cat waiting to spring.

First one Dragon and then another slammed into the tur-

6

ret from either side, but still it came on, and the officer only just tackled his second man down into the darkness before fire flashed from its barrel and a round, more powerful than the rest, tore into the brow of the hill.

The second man was tall and black and had two stars on his helmet. He pulled himself to his feet.

The officer scrambled up the slope.

The tank was only 300 meters distant now, and closing. Its lights flashed on. It was a Soviet T-80, their most modern operational tank, with a 125 mm. gun and heavy armor all around. Hydropneumatic suspension insured greater accuracy when the vehicle was firing over rough ground.

The battle proposal had called for the internal computers of the remotely guided tanks to deliver live, but only maingun, fire well below sighted targets. Even so, casualties were bound to occur.

The officer knew it was about to release another round, but its huge, looming shape intrigued him. This was what the tank had been made for, not to be shattered on the floors of the three forward basins, but to shrug off whatever fire man-portable weapons could throw against it and to command the battlefield with speed, mobility, and firepower.

"Jesus, Mike—let's split. We've made our point. They're waiting for us." The second man jerked his thumb in the direction of the helicopters, which were standing off from the action on the flat where the trees began. The other soldiers of the combined-forces firegroup had already boarded them.

Both of the men again hurled themselves into the darkness and another shell ripped into the brow of the hill. But by the time they had scrambled down the hill and had begun running toward the helicopters, it was too late. The tank had gained the top of the hill. Another round flashed from the barrel and nearly caught one of the helicopters, which swung around the margin of the tall pines in an evasive maneuver. The charge bucked through the tops of the pine trees and exploded, setting them afire.

"That was close," said the officer. "That shot could have killed forty men."

The tank turret was turning here and there, the internal optics scanning the area. They could hear the low hush of its turbine idling.

7

"We'll have to hoof it." The officer jerked a grenade off his belt and waited for the turret to swing beyond them. Below its laser range finder they could see the glow of its infrared sensors.

That was when they heard a sound, like the rip before a thunderbolt, and the area in front of the tank was enveloped in flame. The blast blew off the officer's helmet. The second man crimped himself into a ball. A jagged hunk of shrapnel knifed into the ground no more than a foot from them.

When the falling debris had cleared, the officer looked up. The tank was still there, its barrel blown off, the stub twisted as if it had been made of tin.

He lobbed the grenade over the tank, so it would explode on the other side, and they broke for the trees, many of the pitchy upper branches of which were now ablaze, like towering tapers. The two men veered away from the light toward the darkness of the forest.

The grenade went off, and the tank began moving away from them.

The copse extended for about a mile to where it again became tundra plain—open country, tank country—but both men knew the others would be there, waiting at the rendezvous.

At the top of a small hill they turned. The wind had shifted and the flames at the tops of the pines were leaping into the dark forest, setting other trees ablaze. And behind them they could hear the tank pushing through the woods, into and through the trees that toppled before it like so many thin sticks.

It was only then that the officer became aware of the sponginess in his right boot, the numbness in his thigh. He reached down and felt the leg of his battle fatigues—wet and warm. Damn it, he'd caught one. He only hoped it wouldn't keep him from preparing for the winter exercises in Germany.

They moved through open areas where the pink half-light of dawn brightened the forest floor, and by the time they reached the far margin of the forest it had grown hot. On the horizon a crescent of summer sun was phosphorescent and intense.

Moving over the plain, they avoided boggy places that were filled with black, stagnant water and now, in late Au-

8

gust, yellow, greening scum. A hare, frightened, darted before them, and birds, whole clusters of them, rose up out of the short grass and wheeled around, complaining, their nesting areas having been invaded.

The officer thought about how hostile the groups of helicopters and men who had gathered about five hundred meters distant appeared—what an affront they seemed to everything that was naturally a part of the tundra meadow. But yet he was convinced that they and he were as necessary to the survival of his species as the defense mechanisms that had caused the hare to spring now this way, now that, jinking—it was an odd word, but appropriate—before any pursuer, or the birds to break pattern over the copters.

Gnats, bugs, and tundra mosquitoes were attracted by the blood and swarmed around them.

"You trying to be a hero?" The proportions of the second man's body were massive. He was tall and the graying mustache that crimped around his black face like a frown made him seem dour and serious.

He cut a sleeve from his shirt and bound a tight tourniquet around the officer's upper thigh. The pain was intense and he had to bite back his nausea.

The two of them were part of a team and had been together since the early days of Vietnam. It wasn't the first wound that either had treated for the other, but Vietnam was like ancient history now, and the wound, well, it was a cheap shot in every sense—a fragment from a shell that had overreached while they were fighting unmanned machines.

But they were being observed by their troops, and a medevac team near the helicopters set out on foot for them.

And they were hearing the whine of the tank again.

Suddenly, like a boar through canebrake, the tank punched through the trees several hundred meters north of them and came to a stop in the clearing.

It hesitated there, as though wounded and drawing breath, its shattered turret turning this way and that, and again the plain was filled with the shrill howl of the turbine. It shot forward and birds blackened the sky, passing up and away in a desperate rush to escape the noise.

The officer crouched.

The second man pulled him all the way down.

The tank, bucking at full throttle through the wet, uneven ground, sent up sprays of fetid water, muck, and grass, charging one way, wheeling, and churning off in another at the line of men and machines that surrounded it.

The officer saw a small black soldier with a backpack point what looked like a handgun at the tank, and he knew it was only a matter of moments.

Yet the tank came on, its image fractured in the heat that was rising from the many cisterns in the plain, looking even wider and more menacing because of its stubby barrel. The internal electronics had detected the beam of the laser, which was a threat that could not be ignored, and it made straight for the soldier with the indicator.

The soldier held his ground, even took a few paces toward the charging tank.

The officer was struck by the scene and tried to raise himself up to see it better. It was as if he was witnessing a duel between man and machine, or rather, an intergenerational dispute between electronics and mechanics.

And because of the barrenness of the plain and the uneven ground and the distance that the tank had to cross, the event seemed to be happening in slow motion.

The soldier had stopped.

Even the dull rumble of the 203 mm. howitzer back at the firebase beyond the next ridge of hills seemed strangely muted.

Still the bucking, rearing tank blundered on, making up ground.

The officer imagined what the soldier was feeling—fear and panic. If the round fell short, he was dead; if long, he'd be crushed into the swamp by the tank.

But then they felt a sudden force, as though the air near them had rushed up to meet something, and the terminally guided round cracked the T-80 down its length, spewing flames into the early morning sky. Shards of hot metal hissed into the wet grass.

The soldier lowered the indicator, turned, and began walking back toward the helicopters. A shout went up from the other men. They were drinking beer, smoking; their mood was festive. None of them had had any doubts.

The officer eased himself down, back onto the ground. He looked at the blood that had seeped through the dress-

10

ing on his wound. He felt almost giddy, and he wondered if it was only the loss of blood.

"Any idea of the score?" he asked.

"I think we got them all."

The officer looked back at the wreck. Now and again fire licked through the crack in its ruptured hull. Billows of black smoke snaked into the cloudless sky.

The medevac team was carrying a stretcher, but the officer said he'd walk. Using the second man for support and staring down at the leg that was numb and refused to move, he began to remember something, a quote that he'd first read at the Point but had forgotten. It wasn't the first time he'd thought of it over the years. He tried to concentrate, to get it exact.

The grass was thick, but water pooled in their boot prints. And the sound they made, slogging toward the gunships, was the same he'd heard in the rice paddies of Vietnam.

Settling his back against the struts of the ship, smelling the cordite of its armaments, the muck on their boots, the sweat, the gun grease, the special mix of odors that he could tell anywhere—fear, the release of having gotten through (they even had a corpse in a body bag aboard)— he remembered.

It was by von Behrenhorst:

The art of war calls for a vaster amount of knowledge and more inborn talents than any of the other arts, in order to form a system of mechanics which does not rest upon immutable laws, but upon the unknown.

New inventions allow passing advantage, then they become general, and then the whole thing reduces itself to mere base manslaughter, just as it was in the beginning. The art of fighting *en masse*, because it necessarily frustrates itself by its own development, cannot possibly belong to those steps of progress which mankind is liable to make.

The officer closed his eyes and played it over in his mind. Like the steady beat of the helicopter rotors, it had a pleasant sound. He thought of Europe and his command.

11

1

A Zil limousine sped down the middle of the autobahn that led from Kyritz to Viesecke and the sprawling Soviet military complex near Wittenberge, ten miles from the Elbe and the frontier of the two Germanys. The driver honked other traffic from the path of the long, black car, which at times reached speeds in excess of 180 kilometers per hour.

In the back a Soviet officer nodded in and out of sleep, sometimes allowing his eyes to catch the glare of a late afternoon sun on the windows, at other times enjoying the heat that rose from the floor and seeped through his heavy greatcoat.

It was unusually cold for Germany in the middle of October, and the pine barrens they were passing were already coated with snow. Marshal Kork was put in mind of Asia, where with Zhukov he had been rusticated after the war. Seven bitter winters—he opened his eyes again—seven years of nothing but wastelands, ennui, and vodka, when he could have been back here securing the important border and training a truly professional, permanent army, all because Stalin was a paranoiac and had feared Zhukov.

But that was an old story. At least now, finally, Kork was where he should be, even if age was catching up with him. If only they would grant him another year or two. When last in Moscow he had tried to have them agree to four. His request had only met with a silence that Kork had found more chilling as the weeks, now months, had gone by.

The heat and the oscillating whine of the limousine's

powerful engine overcame Kork. He closed his eyes and slept.

When the car came to a stop, Colonel-General Alexeyev opened the door and looked down at the sleeping figure.

Kork was short and squat and his face was florid. Resting against a bright red epaulet, it seemed almost magenta. He had no neck and his flesh lobbed over a tight collar. His nose was wide and bulbous, and there was a carbuncle on his forehead that anybody else would have removed, but Kork was nothing if not himself at all times.

Alexeyev reached across the back seat and shook Kork, who slowly opened his eyes, then blinked and looked around the broad square that the headquarters buildings made. It was dusk, but he could see that Alexeyev had brought out the troops to greet him. Kork had been in Berlin for only a week.

"Vassil." Kork held out his hand. "How are you, my friend. I hope you didn't expect me to stand out there in the cold and watch your tin soldiers strut around."

Alexeyev smiled and, careful of his back, eased himself into the Zil. He closed the door.

Alexeyev was a tall man with shoulders that seemed almost too broad for his frame. Now in his fifty-third year, his light brown hair had begun to gray and was thin on top. The scars on his right cheek and the left side of his jaw made it seem as though his face had been seized by a large bird with talons. Many of the muscles in his back had been destroyed during the street fighting in Berlin in '45. "They'd be disappointed if you didn't."

"Pah! Who calls the shots around here anyhow—me, the marshal, or those noncoms?" He gestured a thumb at the sergeants major who led each column. It had been Kork's program to give noncommissioned officers more authority and encourage individual initiative, as in the American army, but sometimes he thought he'd gone to far.

"*Chief* marshal," Alexeyev said with unconcealed pride, handing the old man a letter, the red sealing wax of which had been slit. He eased himself back into the cushions and watched Kork.

"You're joking."

"I know it's unconscionable of me to read other people's mail, but I thought it might be something exciting, like a letter from your wife."

14

Kork's eyes, which were hazel in color and almond in shape, flashed at Alexeyev, and the smile that revealed a gold canine on the right side gradually grew fuller as he held the several documents to the window and scanned them in the dwindling light.

Alexeyev bent forward and touched a switch that provided interior lights. He then opened a console that was attached to the front seat. He was conscious of the moment, of its importance to his comrade, of how he must be feeling: the satisfaction, the way that the promotion, which gave Kork the highest rank in the army, would put his career in perspective and preserve his importance even in retirement. He'd be consulted, asked to sit in on the deliberations of key committees in the Ministry of Defense, be guest of honor at all important army functions. But more, once back in Moscow, he could continue being Kork—outspoken, a bit rowdy, unafraid, the soldiers' soldier.

The minister's letter was filled with the usual bunk of a promotion. They had never been close, more enemies than friends, and Kork had always come out on the short end of any debate with the man. The first secretary's letter was different, friendly, and he ended by saying that he hoped Kork would choose to spend his Moscow days in Zhukovka. A house was being prepared for him there.

"A *dacha* in Zhukovka too," Kork said, smiling fully now. His face was wide and almost Oriental in shape, reflecting his Siberian ancestry. "What do you know. A goddamn *dacha!* Who would have thought they'd want a peasant like me living in one of their bordellos."

Zhukovka was the Moscow suburb where the *vlasti,* or ruling elite, had estates. Along with the *dacha* went the privileges of shopping in the best stores where the goods were better and cheaper, a set of permanent seats at the Bolshoi, special accommodations in restaurants and hotels, and the Soviet equivalent of servants. Those who lived in Zhukovka had truly made it, and, if only for his wife, Kork was pleased. It was the highest rank in the army, perhaps the most revered institution in the entire country, and she would wear the title like a badge.

But the fact of the promotion—the letter that he could feel in his hands—was ominous too. Voronov's letter seemed a bit too friendly. Could it be they were kicking

15

him upstairs in preparation for retirement? He dreaded the day and had often thought it would be better to be dead.

His eyes strayed to the window, and he looked out across the columns of soldiers, over the buildings, and at the twilight sky. It was leaden, a deep, gun-metal gray that was funereal and spoke to Kork of cold and winter and death. He looked away, back down at the letters, and asked himself how many days he'd had like this, how many promotions, and which had been as sweet.

Only one, and that had been on the battlefield when he had been brevetted adjutant general after the great tank battle, Zitadelle, during the war. The tank columns had made a circle and raised their guns, and when the cap with the single red star had been placed on his head, they had loosed their guns, a volley that had jarred the ground right from under their feet and made them stagger. The battlefield and the war, Kork thought, cocking his head. All the rest had been organization, numbers, formations, emplacements, technology, and politics. To be the country's only chief marshal was a great honor, and it thrilled him, but it was well to remind himself how it had been gained.

"To the Chief Marshal of the 176th Guards," said Alexeyev, raising his glass. "And, of course to the Commander of GSFG."

Kork turned to Alexeyev and smiled. They touched glasses. That was just right. It was one thing to be chief marshal in command of the over 394,000 troops who comprised the Group of Soviet Forces in Germany, but quite another to be chief marshal in command of the 176th and to have been so much a part of its glorious past. There was no more distinguished fighting force in the entire army, if not the world.

"Another?"

"Even if it kills me." Kork eased back in the seat and watched Vassilievich, who was like the son he had never had.

During the war Kork had been commander of the unit to which Alexeyev, only thirteen at the time, had tried to attach himself. Of the eight members of Alexeyev's family, only he had survived the Wehrmacht attack on the Holy City of Smolensk. He had snatched up the weapon of a fallen soldier, a certain Vassilievich, whose name he was then given. All the Moscow newspapers had carried the

16

story with a picture of the young lad riding the back of a tank as it churned across the frozen Dnieper.

Kork only hoped he hadn't ruined Alexeyev's chances to one day lead the army. Alexeyev was both an accomplished field officer and a skilled administrator. Also, he had aplomb, something Kork lacked, and schooling. The old man had made sure of that. He could speak how many of the Western languages? Five or six—and Chinese too, but the politicians in Moscow would sooner select some bootlicker, like Bysotsky, who didn't know guns from galoshes, than a real soldier with guts.

When they raised the glasses the second time, Kork again glanced out the window. There were even soldiers up on the roofs now, their silhouettes black on the dark sky. "What do you think?"

"That it was long overdue."

Kork shook his head. "You know what I mean."

Alexeyev's eyes, clear and blue, met Kork's. "They didn't have to offer you the *dacha*. It's just not done. If anything, they've got you pegged for something in Moscow."

Kork looked away. That was as bad as retirement. Chairman of the Preparedness Committee or the War College, a school. The prospect made Kork shudder.

"But I think not."

No, Kork thought; otherwise they would have promoted Alexeyev himself, given him a marshalcy. It was in the cards and what Kork wanted, but not yet, not just now while he was still feeling . . . fit. It was not the right word, and Kork, who tried to be as honest with himself as he could, wondered if he'd ever be ready to step down. No, down was wrong too. Aside. There would always be Alexeyev to supersede him, and he hoped he would feel as though he was still in command himself.

He turned to his protégé. "What else have you got?"

The colonel-general had another envelope in his hand. "It's just a *svadka*." Alexeyev meant the briefs that were developed by GRU, the intelligence-gathering agency of the General Staff, and were regularly distributed to field commanders.

"Important?"

It was as though Alexeyev had read the change that had come over his old comrade. "Nothing that can't wait."

17

Kork sighed. If his only war had been the Second, so be it; history was filled with other talented generals who hadn't seen as much. He held out his hand. "But you wouldn't have brought it with you were it not, eh, Vassil?"

"After dinner perhaps."

"After dinner I'll be dozing, and you know it, my friend. Hand it over." Kork dug in the pocket of his greatcoat for his spectacles. He then tilted the sheets so the light from the overhead lamp would strike the page directly. Even his much-vaunted eyesight, his capability, when with the artillery, of not having to use field glasses, of being able to call hits or misses, of putting his company's rounds time after time right within the target area—that too was gone, shot.

He glanced down at the page. He was still feeling sorry for himself when his eye caught on one name. "Mackey, General Michael T., U.S.A.," and he knew immediately why Alexeyev had brought the report with him.

Kork pushed the glasses down on the bridge of his nose and glanced out the window.

Over there in the dusk, beyond the buildings and the forest and the river, was where Mackey belonged, and for nearly the past seven weeks the whereabouts of the American general had been unknown to GRU operatives. There had been rumors Mackey had been given a training command in the continental United States and, later, that he'd been given the 8th Army in Asia, but Kork had discounted them.

Mackey's command was based in the 101st Aerial Assault Division, the old Screaming Eagles, which he had restructured immediately after the Vietnam war. The Department of the Army had thought so much of the leaner, more mobile divisional framework that they had made him a full general and had nominated him to become the first American commander of the NATO Northern Army Group in Europe. NORTHAG was multinational and made up of eleven battle-ready divisions of 228,000 men; it included the 140,000 men of the U.S. 7th Army, most of which in recent years had been moved out of Bavaria and positioned along the north German plain.

Kork's eyes ran down the page. What was this? Mackey had been admitted to hospital in Churchill, Manitoba. When? In August. What had he been doing in Canada?

Kork read on.

At first the hospital had reported that *Mr.* Mackey had been "under observation," but inquiries indicated that his right thigh had been operated on, and a nurse on the surgical staff later revealed that the procedure had removed shrapnel from the leg.

Further investigation led to a report that joint military exercises involving combatants from several NATO countries had been conducted in a barren area of Manitoba, which GRU Control Canada concluded was defined by Split Lake and the Burntwood, Grass, and Nelson rivers. Residents said the sky had been illuminated for most of the night. Windows as far away as Thompson were shattered. Several forest fires were started; one raged for four days. But there was no evidence of intense or lingering radiation.

On 21 August fleets of armored transport vehicles departed from the site, their cargoes shrouded with tarps. There was no doubt, though, that they carried tanks. In fact, some of the ballistic shapes of the turrets were definitely those of Soviet T-model MBTs, perhaps even the T-80s that had been captured during hostilities in Africa. Security had been intense, but it was estimated that over 2,000 tanks, assault guns, and mobile rocket units had taken part.

Why the shrouds? Just because they had used tanks?

Alexeyev nudged him and pointed to the bar console.

Kork smiled and turned to the second page of the report.

Turret configurations indicated that over two score of the tanks were M-60s, Chieftains, Centurions, Leopards, and Swedish S-tanks, and Control Canada was under the impression that most of them were badly damaged.

Now Kork's interest was very high. Why would they sacrifice tanks, even if the vehicles were captured or outdated, when NATO was in such an obvious position of inferiority in regard to armor? And then, why sacrifice over forty of their very best? And—what was most important—by what means had they destroyed the T-80s? If the weapon had been man-portable, it could well negate any advantage in numbers that Soviet armor held over the NATO forces. The T-80 was the best tank the Soviets had yet produced.

But wait. Why else would they have assembled so many different-model tanks, sealed off the area, then shrouded the wrecks? And that was why Mackey had been there. He was the U.S. Army's major critic of a heavy reliance upon

19

tanks and armored personnel carriers. Mackey had been present to test his theories and perhaps some of his troops against them. But how had it been done? And a test preliminary to what? To the maneuvers here in Germany this month? And a secret one at that? Why?

Without conscious thought, Kork took the small glass of dark brown *Ghorilka* from Alexeyev and tossed it off. It was an especially strong Ukrainian vodka and only the old soldiers in the Guards drank it. He kept the glass in his hand and Alexeyev topped it up.

Kork kept reading, " . . . most of the tanks had been badly damaged," over and over again. How badly? Knocked out? And why was there no mention of troop movements, the elements and their numbers? Because they had been too few to have been conspicuous among the trucks that had carted the wreckage away? Kork hoped not.

He drank off the refill and looked out the window again at his troops who were standing in the snow, waiting for him. Already it was collecting on their helmets and shoulders, and floodlights from the eaves of the buildings made the white outlines sparkle.

If, say, his conclusions—he corrected himself—his suppositions were correct, what did it mean to the Soviet army? Everything and nothing.

Since '64 they had known that the tank could be beaten. Kork himself had been present when Khrushchev was shown a demonstration of an antitank guided missile system. The Premier had been visibly disturbed by their vulnerability. What was it he had said? "We're spending a lot of money on tanks, and if a war breaks out, these tanks will burst into flames even before they reach the battle line." But three months later Khrushchev was out. Kork had liked him. He had been gruff, but he hadn't been afraid to hear or face up to the truth. Tank production had continued at a torrid pace.

Then, in '67 and again in '72, seminars with top politicians were held in which all elliptical phrasing was done away with. The army—with the exception of Rotmistrov and a handful of others—told Moscow bluntly that guided antitank missiles gave the infantry what it never had: the probability of destroying tanks with one shot before the tank could use its own weapons against them. The Arab-Israeli war of '73 proved it, but Rotmistrov was made chief marshal of tanks, and by '74 the Soviet army had grown by twenty divisions, all mounted in armored personnel carriers that were more vulnerable to antiarmor devices than any tank.

Even so—he turned to Alexeyev and removed his spectacles—he could imagine another scenario in which his army, as presently constituted, could triumph against any opposing force, if only he was allowed certain tactical options. Kork then looked down at the glass. He wondered if the vodka was giving him false pride.

"What about this place, Vassil?" He meant the site of the joint-forces operation in Canada.

"Three basins, four hills, water on two sides, and a forest to the west."

Kork nodded. The Fulda Gap had such features at a point Kork thought ideal for a breakthrough. "And these exercises of theirs?"

"In two series, as scheduled," Alexeyev said. "From the twenty-first to the twenty-fifth, and then from the twenty-seventh to the end of the month."

The proposed NATO action was no usual affair: the NATO signators had agreed—after much public debate—to hold "forward" exercises for the first time in their nearly three-decade-old association. By forward they meant within twenty kilometers of the German frontier. To Kork's way of thinking, there was no reason why they shouldn't have done that years ago. The long corridor had always seemed to him like an invitation to ford the Elbe and strike west. His own forces were—and had been since '45—dug right into the east bank of the river.

Kork's visit to East Berlin had itself been a ploy in the feinting—the implied and other threats—each side had been engaging in since the NATO announcement. Moscow had wanted the West to know that the "Free City," as it were, would be destroyed if push came to shove.

But now this *svadka*. Kork handed Alexeyev his empty glass and smiled. "I wonder, Vassil—could we be getting lucky at last?"

Alexeyev only cocked his head and smiled, wanting to humor the old man, for whom he felt great affection. But in spite of being a soldier, it was Alexeyev's considered opinion that any sort of hostility with the West was unnecessary and ill-advised.

He thought of the vast oil reserves that had recently been discovered in Siberia and the still untouched mineral deposits—coal, magnesium, tin, nickel, uranium, iron ore, bauxite, the list was endless—all over the country. Russia was just beginning to discover how strong she really could be, while the West was exhausted, and not only of resources.

The strategy for at least the remainder of the century could only be one of maintaining such an awesome conventional and nuclear military capability that its sheer potential would deter the ambitions of any adversary. Time was most definitely on the side of the Soviet Union. If they were patient, Europe and much more would be theirs, and without a fight.

And then, Alexeyev too had received a letter, but from Bysotsky alone. The defense minister had hinted that, after a discreet interval, Alexeyev's marshalcy and the command itself would be handed down from Moscow. Six months, a year at most. It was just a matter of bringing Voronov, who was a crony of Kork's, around.

"But I'm too old to believe in miracles." Kork waved a hand to his driver, who opened the door.

Even before he stepped out of the Zil, the first volley of a nineteen-gun salute resounded through the expanse of the complex. An honor guard approached, their shiny boots flashing through the snow. Other units marched in from the avenues at the sides of the buildings, and off-duty personnel appeared in every window.

When the square had filled, the colonel of the honor guard presented Kork with a long black box. In it was the gold baton of a chief marshal. The inscription read, "To Chief Marshal V. K. Kork, our comrade, leader, and friend. From the soldiers of his 176th Guards."

When Kork held up the baton, the division, as one man, roared.

The lights on the corners of the buildings were peach-colored and refracted into prisms in the old man's eyes. He turned to Alexeyev.

The tall colonel-general offered his hand and they embraced.

22

All the same, Kork thought, I've been lucky. All the same.

Sunday
Hitzacker
F.G.R.

Harris enjoyed the feel of the car, an older Porche with rounded lines and narrow windows, especially like this, in snow, when the usual road noise was dampened and he could listen to the engine winding through the gears. Small and quick, the lacquer a deep brown, almost chocolate, the car was like an extension of himself.

He worked a gloved hand over the wheel and glanced down at the clock-face gauges, all business. The Germans knew how to make things, especially cars, and he could feel the precision as he slid the stick into third to pass a line of tanks and APCs that were headed south on the highway from Hamburg to Hitzacker for the exercises. The rear wheels slipped at first and the car fishtailed, but then it seemed to lock on, and Harris shot by the looming, olive-drab machines.

The windshield wipers gave off a furry, muffled sound, and the interior of the small car was warm, almost toasty. Harris was in his shirtsleeves, the three chevrons and arcs of his rank appearing whenever lights passed in the other direction. He was a small man with sharp, almost American-Indian features and dark skin. A trim mustache made him seem dapper, and he took pains to keep himself looking every inch the part of the first sergeant. Harris was from Chicago, and he told himself the snow didn't bother him. But he was tense. It was his first good car.

He swung off the highway, down a steep ramp that hadn't been plowed. Already there was almost a foot of snow on the ground, and the sealed beams—Harris touched the directional switch, flicking on the brights—shot brilliant cones of dense white light, mottled and driving, that stopped a few feet from the car. He switched them down and slowed his speed. He was approaching the outskirts of Hitzacker.

The homes were new but still characteristically German,

23

with tall, gabled roofs, casement windows, and white, lacy curtains. Harris had been in several like that, and he knew they'd be warm, the wood of the sideboards and furniture, the floors, polished to a gloss, the tiles in the kitchen gleaming, and everything would be in its place. Precision. Harris admired that. And order.

He didn't like leaving the Porsche at the side of the road in front of the *Gasthaus*, but the plows had blocked the driveway to the parking lot.

A supply convoy was pushing past. The rasping diesel grind of the ten-ton trucks was familiar to him, but the knobby rubber tires hummed through the snow. It was an odd noise, like purring, but of the sort that came from large cats just before feeding. Lions, tigers; he'd once heard a puma sound like that, pacing in its cage in the Tokyo zoo.

He gave the car another concerned glance. He hoped he wouldn't get plowed in or, worse, hit by some jackass who thought he could drive in snow.

Herr Siebenborn had named his *Gasthaus "Zum Wilden Mann"* after the famous hostelry in München where his wife had been born and raised. It was fairly new but built along old lines with heavy oak shutters and a large front door braced with wrought-iron bands. The sign swinging over the door pictured a man with disheveled hair, crazed eyes, a blue face, and a livid, lolling tongue, the surface of which was now frosted with snow.

But it was wrong, Harris had long since realized: the sign and the name. The Wild Man Inn was perhaps the most pleasant . . . bar, restaurant, tavern, inn—Harris didn't really know what to call it in English—that he'd ever come across, and a couple of times a week he spent the early evening there just relaxing.

Frau Siebenborn was a blond, buxom woman and, on seeing Harris, her smile became just a bit too bright to assure him he was welcome. Harris knew the smile. It was the one used by the people who really didn't want to see them—the U.S. Army, but blacks in particular—there in Germany, and she had greeted him with it (but for different reasons, he supposed), since the night of the fire.

That night too he had been somewhat early, and the bar had been nearly empty. He had ordered a cognac and a beer, and Siebenborn himself had served him and gone back into the kitchen. Later, while raising the stein, he had caught sight of him leaving the kitchen. He had thought nothing of it and had begun reading the paper. He was nearly finished with it when something attracted him beyond the bar—a thin snake of smoke that was working under the swinging doors of the kitchen. In the diamond-shaped windows he could see black, sooty coils, but still he had done nothing. The stein, as he remembered, had remained in his hand; only his head had turned to the door. Why?

He imagined now that it had been the decorum of the place, which he had been trying to overcome, but in his own way—by feeling it in slow steps, a nod to a regular one day, a smile to somebody else the next, a "Nice day," or "Cold out there," or, "You see the Cup finals last night,"—so he wouldn't offend them with his familiarity. It was the same fine line between blacks and whites the world over, the one that determined what would be talked about, how much revealed, and was so difficult to establish, but especially here where Harris knew he was doubly alien. It was the reason he had never brought any of his black friends with him, why he had avoided other Americans at the bar, why he hadn't acted immediately when he saw the smoke.

Until he heard the small, shallow cough of the child and the, "Papa, papa!"

Harris had slapped the stein on the bar and dashed to the kitchen doors, which, when he swung them open, created a draft and caused the fire on top of the range to leap up over the hood, and with a flash, like an explosion, the entire kitchen, it seemed, combusted.

The blast seared Harris's face, singed his hair, scorched his lungs. It knocked him back. The ceiling and wall above the stove were ablaze. He reached back for the door that had stuck open and closed it, dampening the fire only a little.

What to do? The child. "Ulricka!" he shouted.

Nothing.

He found her on the floor, a doll in her arms, half under a preparation table.

Harris snatched her up and rushed her to the door, where the father had appeared, aghast, the pale yellow fire

25

blazing in his green eye. "Here!" Harris thrust the child at him. "With your mouth!" He pointed to his lips and pushed Siebenborn and the child into the dining room and closed the door.

All he could remember thinking was: they live here, this is their home, their business, their lives, and what is burning is not so much a stove, a wall, a ceiling, but a family.

Maybe that was what had brought Harris back to *Zum Wilden Mann* so often, the sense of calm and warmth and competence the Siebenborns gave him, the feeling that life could be good, and not in the way he had known in the army or Chicago. There he had been the first child of a fourteen-year-old mother. In her own way she had been a good, loving, and kind woman, but Harris had always felt cheated.

With the calm he'd forced himself to assume when under fire in Vietnam, he had searched the kitchen for extinguishers or—a grease fire—baking soda, some sort of powder. Flour is what he found, in a barrel that he dumped over the stove. And then water on the walls, from the hose he'd once seen the father using to wash the floor. Finally, when the kitchen was filled with acrid black smoke and steam, he'd found the chemical extinguisher near the door.

But—"What do we have tonight?" he now asked the mother—he'd overstepped himself, gone over the line, not so much with the father or the little child or the other daughters and the son, who now called him Harry, but with the mother. Harris guessed it was because she really didn't know what he wanted, now that he was . . . among them.

"Your favorite, Sergeant Harris—*Kasseler Rippchen mit Sauerkraut und Kartoffeln.*"

"Wonderful," he said gently. His gestures, the way he used his eyes and face, were soft, placating, designed to put her at her ease.

"As you can see, we have hardly any business because of the snow. Paul says you really must try the new Moselle. He's thinking of getting it in. He told the distributor—if Harry likes it, we'll try a case. It's on ice, there behind the bar." Her cheekbones were high, and her smile—that same smile—made them seem too hard, lily-white, and knoblike, as though cut from white stone.

And how to tell her he wanted only to come and watch,

26

how to make her understand that and not be offended or feel as if she and her family were guppies in a fish bowl. Harris put it out of his mind as he made for the bar.

There were multicolored flagstones under foot, but the wood of the booths was still light, new by German standards. A mound of cannel coal was burning behind ceramic tiles in the grate of the fireplace, and at a table nearby three matronly women dressed in dark woolen clothes were gossiping over a tray of sweets. They looked up. One turned to the window, parting the curtains. More trucks were passing and made the teacups rattle in their saucers. She released the curtain and shook her head. The other women looked worried. Harris imagined that they had seen and heard it all before.

In the bar, the swinging door to the kitchen opened and a little girl peeked out. Seeing Harris, she came running to him. He picked her up and whirled her around, then took something from his shirt and handed it to her. It was a miniature rocking chair with an embroidered pillow, tiny and colorful. He lowered it gently into her hands.

She looked up from it to her mother, who had followed Harris. "Oh, mama! Look what Harry's brought me." During the fire Harris had stepped on her dollhouse, which her father had since repaired. Her older sister and her mother before her had played with it. That was the sort of thing Harris admired, the continuity. It didn't matter, the trouble they'd been through.

The kitchen door opened again. "Harry," the father said, "pour yourself some wine and come in here. There's no sense your drinking alone." He closed the door.

"Now you must thank the sergeant," the mother said, her hands clasped at her waist, her shoulders squared.

"Thank you, Harry."

"No, no. It's thank you, Sergeant Harris. We must be respectful, darling."

The girl repeated what her mother had said, stumbling over the *Oberfeldwebel*.

And mindful of his rank and position, Harris thought. He poured two glasses of Moselle, set the towel-wrapped bottle back in the ice, and joined Siebenborn in the kitchen.

Siebenborn was shorter than his wife but big through the chest and shoulders. His hair had turned a gray that was almost white. His features were regular, his eyes pale

27

green, and his upper lip scarcely moved when he spoke. It gave him a thoughtful appearance, as though he was mulling something over. But it also made him lisp now and then.

Taking a glass from Harris, he said, *"Prosit,"* and drank most of it off. "I'm thirsty. This is hot work out here, not like what you've got in store for you. Tomorrow, is it?"

Harris nodded.

Siebenborn went back to his work of kneading pastry dough on a floured board. *"Ja,* that snow—I've never seen so much of it this early. And so cold. It won't be good for your machines, not that I'm thinking of them, but it'll be a little like the real thing this time, eh? Phalanxes," he lisped, "have been going by all day long. British, American, some Bundeswehr contingents. All headed east.

"I read in the papers, Harry, that the Russians have put themselves on alert all up and down the border." He shook his head, then straightened up. His green eyes fixed Harris's. "What's it all about?"

Harris considered Siebenborn. Over the last year they had talked often, and Harris knew that the other man, at the end of the war, had been called up to fight against the Russians in the east. He had been hardly more than a boy at the time, and now he dreaded them. When the currency squeeze had occurred and the GIs had found themselves caught between rising prices and a dollar that was worth less and less, Siebenborn had been one of the first to establish special prices for American soldiers. "Hell, Harry—we need you," he had said. "We're the same people, really." His eyes had shied and he had blushed. "I mean, Hitler was a phenomenon, but the Russians—" he had lisped, looking off. Thinking of Vietnam, Harris had tried to picture what Siebenborn was remembering. He thought he could.

The back door opened and Siebenborn's eldest daughter, Annette, stepped in, the hood of her parka covered with snow. She stamped her boots on the mat near the door before putting her books down, then shook the hood and pulled it off.

She looked up at her father and Harris and smiled. Her hair was the sort of natural auburn that was seldom seen. It was lustrous and wavy, like her father's, and curled around her neck, the skin of which was very white. She had her mother's prominent cheekbones, but her eyes were dark, almost black. Her teeth were large and spaced rather far apart, and she was attractive in an unexpected way.

The young man behind her was tall and solid. A closely shaven but heavy beard made the hollows of his cheeks seem blue. He smoothed his long black hair, which was wet from the snow, along the sides of his head. There was a cleft in his chin, and in all he seemed to radiate strength and health.

He waved to Harris, who nodded and continued with the conversation. "All the stuff you hear about how weak we are—it doesn't help. We need something to perk us up, make it look like we're really trying to defend the border."

"You mean we're not weak?" Siebenborn craned his neck, holding out his cheek to his daughter, who slipped an arm around his waist and kissed him. The narrowed eyes of his smile were telling—she was everything he thought she should be.

Not so the young man. "Karl—go get that bottle of Moselle off the bar and a glass for Annette. Take one for yourself, if you want some."

"A bottle or a glass, Herr Siebenborn?"

Slowly Siebenborn turned his head to him.

"I was just asking. I don't want to make a mistake." Passing by Harris, he tugged his sleeve. "It must be a big bottle. How deep is my thirst?" And then he sang in a bass voice that was mellow and full, "How deep is the o-cean?"

"And no noise in the dining room!"

Annette sat on a table and watched her father cut diamond-shaped pieces of dough with a pastry knife. His movements were deft. A pot of gooseberry filling steamed up from the range behind him and gave off a tangy, sweet aroma. Harris was suddenly hungry.

She was wearing a reddish-brown sweater no different in color from her hair, and knee socks to match. Her skirt and shoes were beige. Harris noticed that her legs were just slightly bowed, down by the ankles.

He looked away. "It depends on how strong we have to be."

"Pretty damn strong with all those tanks facing us." Siebenborn did not look up from his work.

29

Karl Mühling had returned with the ice bucket, the bottle of Moselle, and two extra glasses. "Not so much," she objected as he poured.

"Anything you say." The young man glanced at the father, who pointed to his own glass.

Harris thought of Canada, the time during the NATO exercises in August when he had walked toward the tank, the laser indicator in his hand. The power he had felt on killing it would remain as one of the most vivid experiences of his life. But if the batteries of howitzers back at firebase had stood down, or if the signal hadn't gotten through—. "The tank is a weapon of the past."

"You think so? Not when they've got us—how many is it, Harry? You know the figures."

Harris cocked his head. "Six to one, or about that."

"With APCs? How many of them have they got?"

Harris glanced up at Annette, her black eyes. "Hard to tell. A lot."

"And they've got guns on those APCs, don't they?"

All the Soviet BMP-80s, their newest APC, were equipped with a main gun. "Eighty-eights."

"Just like the Panzers in the last war. So, how many all told?" With a ladle Siebenborn was filling each tart. A flick of the wrist added the precise amount as he moved down the line.

"Thirty, forty thousand, but that's all up and down the border."

"Nonsense. They learned something in the last war. We taught them and then they turned around and taught us—mass the tanks and you can roll over anything. Once you punch through—that's it, you've outflanked the defense and can swing around and pinch them off. Forty thousand tanks!"

"Armored vehicles," Harris corrected.

"*Ja*—all that steel! They're unstoppable."

Harris thought of the 7,000 nuclear weapons in Europe. The tanks weren't unstoppable, but he didn't want to mention that. The setting wasn't right, and he was feeling a little glow from the wine.

"I don't see what you're getting so worked up over," said Mühling, his glass clenched in a fist on his chest. "Those numbers don't mean much."

30

The ladle stopped abruptly. Siebenborn looked up. "And why not?"

"Because we've got too much to lose on both sides. Here in the West we've been fat and happy for thirty years. Now we're going to have to make certain adjustments in our economies, the way we live, and that will bring us closer, as a people, to the East. More than that, we've decided we can't afford war." His eyes were bright. Like Annette, who was his girl friend, Mühling was a university student in Hamburg, and Harris knew he loved to talk, especially about something like this.

"In the East they've squandered the productive capacities of their economies on a war that has never come. The people are sick of it, and not just in the Pact countries. The Soviet leadership knows that. And just now when things are getting so much better for them? It would be disastrous politically."

"Would it now? Would it now?" The ladle was now on Siebenborn's hip. His chest was out, his chin forward. "What if they decide that they've got to go through with it, now that they've thrown down such a big bet, now that they're so much more powerful?"

The young man only shook his head, smiling; his dark hair peaked on his brow. With a long, thin nose that had been broken and was bent, he looked to Harris like a professional athlete, a football player. "They'd have to win in thirty days. Their economy is only just beginning to show its potential strength. The Pact countries can't be counted on fully. Their strategic position is poor, with little access to the seas and with the Chinese and their irredentist ambitions in the East. They've treated them badly." He cocked his head and smiled, looking almost handsome in spite of his nose. "There're a billion of those little fellows now, you know."

Harris could only smile, watching Mühling. He knew how he felt—the talk, the wine, the aroma of all the food in the kitchen, Annette, the way he knew he was grating on the father, how it was a game—all of it gave him a thrill that he couldn't have explained if he had to.

"And the Soviets haven't learned the most obvious military lesson of the latter half of the twentieth century," he went on. "In the words of the greatest military genius of

31

our time"—his eyes darted toward the father—"Mao Tse-tung—"

Siebenborn's head flinched, as if he'd taken a slap on the face.

"—'Wars are won by men, not machines.' " He turned to Harris. "It seems to me, Harry, another industrial colossus was taught that lesson not long ago."

Harris only looked down into the pale yellow fluid in his glass. It was all just talk, and he wasn't about to try to steal Mühling's thunder in front of his girl. That wasn't how Harris got along.

Siebenborn reached toward the range and drew out a ladle of steaming filling. "Let me tell you something, Herr Mühling—it's all well and good to sit back in some history seminar in a university with a bunch of"—he glanced at his daughter—"professors positing reasons why wars can't happen, but"—he raised his other hand—"events—" His curly white hair shook. He had lisped. "—*events*," he repeated, "Don't occur like that. Sometimes there *are* no reasons. *Most* times"—he turned to the American—"there are no reasons, right, Harry?"

"But, sir"—Mühling was almost laughing—"just what do you mean when you say 'events'?"

Siebenborn had had enough of the young man, and he turned to his daughter. "And what do you think of this whole thing?"

She paused, looking down into her wineglass, a wavy lock of her reddish hair shading her eyes. When she glanced up her black eyes had a faraway look. With a hand she pushed her hair behind an ear. "I don't know—with all those guns and soldiers and the night and the snow, it's almost as though you can hear the wings of Valkyrie overhead."

"Exactly!" Siebenborn jabbed a finger at her and looked up at Mühling, his green eyes triumphant.

Annette, Mühling, and Harris dined together in a big booth between the dining room and bar. The weather, far from keeping guests at home, only seemed to bring them out later, and by eight the *Gasthaus* was warm and convivial and filled with people who were trying to forget the gloom of the night, the snow, and the oppressive prospect of an early winter.

32

Since he knew no tab would be presented—or if one was, Harris would pick it up—Mühling ate a great quantity of food and drank as often as another of the Siebenborn children, a son, passed the table. And he talked volubly: about Nordic skiing, which all three of them practiced—Harris because it was part of his training—about soccer, history, Annette, politics, beer, the university, not so much, Harris judged, because Mühling knew very much about any of the topics, but because he was feeling a great sense of well-being. He liked who he had become: his size, his strength, his great good health.

There had been a time, ten years or so earlier, when Harris had felt that way, and it would just strike him suddenly without warning that he had to do or say something and express himself some way—dance, sing, talk, yell, run. It didn't matter what. At such times he had felt almost immortal, as though he'd never change, never grow old, as though the world was his for the asking, although he had always been well aware it wasn't.

With some others Mühling sang, *"I'm Krug zum grünen Kranze," "Keinen Tropfen im Becher mehr,"* and other old *Gasthaus* chestnuts, and was asked on special request to render *"Im kühlen Keller sitz ich hier"* alone.

"Hold onto your glass," Annette advised Harris: both had been watching Mühling, admiring him and the way the vivid flush had risen up on his cheeks, as his eyes grew brighter, his voice louder, and the good cheer that had been building in him seemed to spread out from the booth and pervade the barroom. "It'll shatter on that low note."

Frau Siebenborn only shook her head and moved in among her other guests in the dining room. The father's face appeared briefly in the window of the kitchen door. He too only glanced at Mühling.

The final note was not loud, like an alto's high C, but rather basal and rich and kind of mournful really, Harris judged, something like isolating the purest male tone and making it a curiosity.

But when the others clapped and cheered, Harris thought he heard something else through the din—soft, a clump, like sheet metal collapsing out in the street. He stood, suddenly serious.

"What is it, Harry?" Annette reached out for his wrist. Harris flinched and looked down at the long white fingers on the back of his hand, then forced it forward again, so he wouldn't offend her. "My car, the Porche—I parked it out front. Did you hear that sound?"

She released his hand and followed him to the front door.

Just beyond the Porsche in the snow-filled street, a troop transport had skidded into the back of a communications van, the back doors of which were stove in. There was no damage to the bumper or grill of the other, higher truck. Harris could see that his car was at least twenty feet from the accident and hadn't been touched.

There was a red-maple-leaf logo on the door of the damaged truck. The driver had just gotten out, zipped up his field jacket, cinched his gloves under an epaulet, and walked back. He was a large man, tall and square, with curly blond hair that tufted from under his beret. His wide jaw was set, pink, and pugnacious.

Belgian troopers were piling out of the transport, speaking French.

If anything, it was snowing harder, and Harris knew he had better head back toward Hamburg soon. And it was getting colder. The voices of the Belgians were muffled. Their breaths smoked as they shook out their arms and stamped their feet.

Several began trudging toward the *Gasthaus.*

There were other guests standing behind Annette and Harris, jabbering, pointing, and laughing.

There was only one other soldier with the Canadian master sergeant, but Harris knew there would be trouble. Already the other Canadian was sizing up the seven or so Belgians on his side of the trucks.

For several moments the master sergeant only stared, hands on hips, at the two trucks that were locked together and then at the other driver, who was speaking excitedly in French, gesticulating, taking a step toward him and then backing off.

The whole scene gave Harris the same feeling he'd sometimes gotten in Vietnam, which he'd thought about when they were talking in the kitchen earlier—that you didn't fight for the West or for a country or even for an army, but for yourself and maybe the few others who were with you. And the odds, the numbers, whatever—they didn't matter.

34

Harris now only heard, ". . . goddamn Frog . . . on my ass . . . miles," and the master sergeant's hands shot out, grabbed the other driver, and tossed him onto the hood of the Belgian truck. He swiped the back of his hand at another, knocking him out into the street, where he was nearly struck by a passing car. It swerved, skidded, and got stuck in a snowbank.

Now there were three men on the master sergeant.

The other Canadian had crouched, waiting for the Belgians on his side of the truck. Kicking out, he caught the first on the side of the knee. The man howled in pain and crumpled into the snow.

But there were too many of them, and the other Belgians, who were at the door of the *Gasthaus*, turned and started back.

Behind Harris the patrons of *Zum Wilden Mann* were laughing and cheering, not for either side as far as Harris could tell, but for themselves and the way they were feeling and the spectacle and the night.

He felt somebody push by him. It was Mühling, his eyes bright in the lamplight over the door. He looked at one group of fighting soldiers and then at the other. Harris saw the young man's arms come up and his fists clench, and he knew that feeling too—the need for a test, especially on a night when your blood was running strong.

Harris reached out and pulled him back. "Save your energy. You're going to need it."

Mühling's brow furrowed and he staggered a bit.

"Somebody's going to have to help me dig out the Porsche."

"But there're so many against so few."

"That's all the more reason to stay where you are," Frau Siebenborn said from the top stair. "And I don't want any of them in here with their boots and their blood. If you feel heroic, Karl, I'll let you keep them out."

But a jeep with officers had pulled up. They piled out. A whistle sounded and then a gun.

Harris was told that the police were no longer allowing civilian vehicles on the autobahn, because of the snow, and Siebenborn said he would put the Porsche in the garage out back, after Karl cleared the driveway.

Already Mühling and Annette were out on the sidewalk, shovels in hand.

It was a good idea, since Harris would be involved in the exercises for at least a week, and in weather like this, he thought, it would be best to have it inside. So he accepted a ride in a passing troop transport and left Mühling and Annette to deal with the Porsche.

Sitting in the back of the troop transport, huddled in the cold with some Dutchmen, Harris could almost swear he could still feel her hand on his wrist. But he had been through all that before, in his mind if not in fact, and there was just no way anybody could win.

He forced himself to think of all the things he had to do in the morning.

The snow was fine and still very light. It seemed to spray from the blade of Annette's shovel, as though she were swinging it into powdered sugar. Because of the storm, the gymnasium at the university had been closed, and she hadn't exercised all day. After classes, the train ride home, and the heavy meal, the cold and snow that stung her face were bracing, the contrapuntal rasp of her and Mühling's shovels over the concrete a rhythm that took her back to her childhood when the inn had just been built and customers were few and the whole family had had time to get out and clear the snow together.

Then the snow had seemed to seal off the neighborhood, dampening sound and increasing distances, making every house—the sidewalk, the alleyway, the courtyard—a fiefdom, discrete, with the bastion of the *Gasthaus* itself fronting the street.

Life was good then, she thought, straightening up and watching Mühling, whose body was rocking with each stroke, like a metronome. Not that it wasn't now, but then she had had no cares. The days had passed as in a dream or a fairy tale, where what was expected had been provided, and her world had been so circumscribed that she had been able to concentrate on the changes in things—the world of the inn, its patrons, her parents, herself.

Now everything, everybody was in flux, and change was so rapid and profound that it couldn't be appreciated in its entirety. Only surfaces—the gray in her parents' hair, a death in the neighborhood, a different color paint in the dining room—were noticeable. She had time now only for herself and her studies, and was that selfish? She supposed so, but it was necessary, at least for now.

Mühling had come to the steetlamp, and he turned down the alleyway, stepping in the tracks the Porsche had made when they had driven it into the garage.

Annette fell in behind him and they worked steadily, their backs to the street and the convoys, which were now passing with increasing regularity, a soldier or two shouting or whistling at her from the back of the transports now and then. The frigid gusts down the alleyway ruffled her skirt and stung her thighs, but she wasn't cold. It was too early in the year for that. The chill came later, when the body grew tired of the cold. Now it felt almost good. Her cheeks were flushed, she was breathing rapidly, and her body— her arms, her torso—felt as though she was just getting warmed up, just beginning to feel what she could do.

And it was that which she enjoyed most about her life now—the possibilities. Annette was good at her studies, and she had been assured she could stay on at university, perhaps even pursue a career there. She didn't know. There was so much to do and see, but it was good, the feeling: of strength, of a certain degree of competency, and of having beauty and power in personality. There was that too; she had tested herself and she knew it.

And there they were, she thought, the two of them scraping away at their shadows that loomed down the lamp-lit alleyway, trying to get at who they were, unafraid of what they would find. Her parents had discovered each other and the *Gasthaus* and their children, and she knew they were satisfied, though they seldom said so. It wasn't for her, but she respected what they had done. It had been an adventure for them—they might have failed and lost everything—and it was that which she looked forward to in her own life, the challenge.

Mühling shoveled on, graceful in the way he moved his left leg forward with each stroke, a shoulder dipping and swaying. He had doffed his heavy parka and she noted, and not for the first time, that his waist was nearly as narrow as her own, his hips thin. It added to the impression of upper-body strength. Mühling was a wrestler, and in her mind's eye she saw him after the last match, bearish, having mauled a bigger man, glistening with sweat, smiling his odd, broken-toothed smile, exhausted.

On impulse she cocked the shovel and, when he bent once more, swung the flat of it at his backside.

It was heavy, a coal shovel, and it struck him with a smack. He was surprised, off balance. He turned to her, mouth open, lost his footing, and went down into the snowbank he'd been building.

She scooped up a shovelful and chucked it at him. And another.

"I was waiting for that," he said somewhat drunkenly, brushing the snow off his face. "Ever since that last wolf whistle, I knew you couldn't resist."

She understood what he meant and what he would do, and she glanced around the courtyard at the back door to the kitchen, the snow walls, the storage sheds, the garages. She dropped her shovel as he got to his feet. She began walking, slowly at first, toward the open door of the garage in which they had parked the Porsche.

"They'll never learn," he said in mock resignation. "Why play with the beast?" He shook his head. "Women. Lessons. Perhaps I should become a teacher."

She took a quick step and then another, and then she sprinted toward the darkness and the car, feeling the old, childish thrill of being chased and safely frightened by somebody bigger and stronger but controllable.

He was right behind her, and she only just made the fender of the car and the shadows. With her hands she traced the length of the Porsche and waited at the hood, watching Mühling, whose figure was silhouetted on the lights of the courtyard.

He was humming now, removing his gloves, smacking the snow off his woolen shirt. *"Meine kleine Mädchen,"* he sang. *"Wo ist du, Mädchen? Oh, Mädchen?"*

And he sprang down the side of the car and he lunged over the hood and nearly snagged her jacket. But she was off, down the length of the Porsche and across its rear end, running toward the other cars—those of guests, the family car, the old Mercedes of the woman who lived across the street and hadn't driven since Annette could remember, the *Gasthaus* van with the high sides. There she paused, making sure her feet and legs were concealed behind a wheel, listening for Mühling, who called, *"Mädchen,"* again. He was way off, still down near the Porsche where they had begun.

In spite of the nearly total darkness she took two quick steps across the van and stood close to the front tire. She had played the game often as a child and was familiar with every aspect of the garage, its gasoline and oil smells, where the tools were kept on hooks over the workbench, the spare pipes and drains and ladders that were strung from the rafters overhead. But it was different, this game.

"*Mädchen,* I've got something for you."

Mühling could be coarse, but his strength, his exuberance, the way he moved and was built excited her.

She tiptoed around the van and, stooping, passed by the grill of the Mercedes and nearly bumped into him in the dark. And his presence there was almost palpable to her—the heat from his body, his odor, which was pungent, like that of an animal, but pleasant. He had only missed her because she had stooped.

He had come to rest, listening for her. "*Mädchen,*" he called softly. "*Wo ist du, meine Mädchen?*"

She lunged at him and her hands struck his back. She fumbled lower and her right hand found and slid into one of his pockets. She tugged it down, but it wouldn't give way. Again and again, and when it did rip, a hand grasped her wrist so tightly she shrieked and went at it with her teeth.

He hollered and released her, and she was off again, back down the side of one of the cars and around it. Stooping again, she circled around toward the van that her father used to pick up supplies from the countryside, an old and capacious truck that he had treated with great care.

She knew which door wouldn't squeak, and stepping in, she made sure the lock was set. She eased it shut.

That was when Mühling grabbed her around the waist, his face nuzzling her neck so that the surprise, the shock, the tickling of his beard and breath sent a chill right down to her toes. He lifted her off her feet easily with one hand, while the other ran up under her sweater and pulled up her brassiere. On her breasts it felt almost hot.

She didn't resist. She couldn't really, and he had won, and they seldom got the chance to be alone together, both living at home. She let her head hang back onto his shoulder.

The hand was under her skirt now, on her thighs. It was hard and calloused and seemed almost to scratch her, but as he eased her down onto the floor of the van, which was covered with a thick mat of old cardboard boxes, she turned her head up and pulled his mouth down on hers.

In the dark their teeth collided. She laughed, and they kissed for a long, heady moment during which he moved up on her and centered his weight where she wanted it, rocking forward a bit. Her pelvis moved up to meet him.

He had pulled up her sweater again, and she arched her back and his tongue grazed a nipple. She reached below and seized the head of his penis, hot even through the material of his trousers, wide.

It was almost like a fantasy to her, one that she was reliving there in the darkness of the van where she had played so many times as a child, perhaps always having wanted what was now happening but not having known or been capable of it before.

"Do you have something?" she asked into his ear as he lifted her, one strong hand at the small of her back, the other on the waistband of her underwear.

"I'll be careful," he said.

Her temper squalled. She raised a hand and brought the heel of her fist down on the cardboard matting. "That's not good enough. You can't be careful."

"But I will—I promise."

"Oh, Karl—you can't promise. It's just not safe, and you know why." She tried to push him off her, but he wouldn't move. "I thought we discussed this before?"

She felt his body relax. He shifted his weight off to one side, and she moved from under him.

"Well, didn't we?"

"Yes, of course, we discussed it before." There was anger in his tone. "But who the hell do you think I am, a pimp or a gangster with a condom in my wallet? Or, or—somebody like Schwerin?"

Schwerin was a tall, blond student from a wealthy family who had taken Annette out on several occasions and whom Mühling considered a rival.

"He carries a condom in his wallet?"

"He told me so. You mean"—there was a pause, and she knew what he was going to say. She began to stand. "—you don't know?"

She fumbled for the door, found the handle, and stepped out. "That was low, Karl. And really, it's none of your business, is it? I have some reading to do. Perhaps you better go home and sober up. Thank you for helping me with the snow and Harry's car."

She slammed the door, leaving him there, knowing how he would feel in the dark, alone.

Sunday
12th Panzer-Grenadier Brigade Headquarters
Lüchow
F. G. R.

The building near Lüchow was not quite a castle, but rather a large stone structure that had formerly been a hotel. Turrets rose above the edifice and were toothed with crenelations that against the snowy night sky might have seemed outsized had it not been for the antennas, radar pans, and telecommunications instruments that loomed there.

Curtains were drawn, but tall French windows in the west turret, main floor, glowed with a rich yellow light. There were mostly men in the room, some reading, others conversing in low tones. Beneath a large mantel a fire blazed. A man and a woman stared down at jade chess pieces on a jade and ivory board.

The woman was dressed in a gray-green Bundeswehr uniform, the silver eagle on each shoulder denoting her rank, *Oberst*.

The man wore a civilian shooting jacket of dark brown twill, a green turtleneck sweater, and gray slacks. Only his shoes, cordovan walking bluchers, were remarkable in that the toes had been buffed to mirror sheens. General Mackey had only just arrived. His leg wound had healed more slowly than his doctors had expected, and at the request of the White House he had been kept in the United States—to blunt some of the force of recent overt actions in Germany.

Without thinking, Colonel Kronenberger reached out and picked up a knight. Damn, it was wrong, but she was distracted. Now that she had it in her hand she would have to move. And she could feel Mackey's eyes on her—cold and gray, those of a predator.

41

Kronenberger put the piece down almost arbitrarily and looked back up at the American, who said nothing.

What had always struck Kronenberger was Mackey's bearing. It was as though he was saving himself for something and had been made—short and compact with sharp features and reddish hair that curled back on his head where he let it grow out—to display an economy of means, like a falcon, for speed on a strike.

Kronenberger knew Mackey's record well, having taken time to peruse all the dossiers of generals of foreign armies on German soil, East and West. One had to know the enemy. Who he would be. Well, for her it was an interesting and an open question.

Mackey, Michael T.: too young for the Second War; West Point; distinguished himself in the fighting at Inchon and around Seoul. In Vietnam he became the most articulate, seasoned, and effective field officer in the U.S. Army, and that was an assessment by the Vietminh. After his four tours of duty with American forces, he became, in succession, operations adviser to the South Vietnamese army, senior adviser to the South Vietnamese Airborne, and senior adviser to the South Vietnamese 44th Special Tactical Zone (a U.S. and South Vietnamese composite organization of special forces and Vietnamese Rangers). In that post he had had 56,000 troops under his control, and near the end of the war, when all other ARVIN elements were in disarray, Mackey and his Rangers were still in complete control of their sector. The 44th Tactical Zone wasn't overrun until Saigon itself was falling.

He held two Distinguished Service Crosses, two Silver Stars, four Legions of Merit, eight Bronze Stars, eight Purple Hearts, four Army Commendation Medals, four Vietnamese Crosses of Gallantry, a Distinguished Flying Cross, over forty air medals, and a host of other Vietnamese and Korean awards, all of which added up to one thing—recent experience in depth, something that no active senior officer in any other army on the European land mass could claim.

Mackey picked up Kronenberger's knight.

Kronenberger reached for her bishop.

"Do you really want to do that?" he asked in a German that she had always found remarkably good.

"You think you've got me?"

"If you touch that piece, I have."

"Not until the last man!" she intoned bathetically, and they both laughed.

"Corporal," she said to an orderly, "take this away and bring some coffee, please."

To Mackey she explained, "Now I'm convinced of the true worth of the cellars of Twelfth Panzer-Grenadier Brigade. Not, mind you, that I'm offering an excuse. You planned, as usual, a tactically brilliant campaign, Herr General, and it strikes me that I've never won against you."

It had struck Mackey as well. Kronenberger was a known student of the game, but she seemed quelled in his presence, and Mackey thought he knew why.

Since the war the Bonn government had wanted military technicians, not tacticians, persons who looked upon their profession as a career and not, as Mackey did, a calling. Kronenberger was one such, and her duty with the Bundeswehr was to keep tabs on those who were manifestly military in the exercise of their offices.

And Kronenberger knew Mackey's opinion of the Bundeswehr: that it was a travesty for a government to put 400,000 men and women in uniforms, call them an army, but keep them from learning how to fight. Mackey could only imagine that they were being groomed to function as police *after* a Soviet invasion.

And their potential—it was that which irked Mackey most—time and again Germans had proved themselves to be natural fighters: imaginative, adaptable, hardy, tenacious. He could understand in his mind why Bonn had adopted the policy—the horror of the last war—but not in his heart. "If you desire peace, prepare for war." The advice was 2,500 years old and a warrior's dictum, but to Mackey it was still good.

He watched Kronenberger make the only move open to her, and he thought he saw in it a sort of epiphany. But now, well—in his opinion it was time to forget.

"I put it down to my years in the artillery," he said.

Kronenberger raised an eyebrow. Like her hair, which she wore on top of her head, it was a blond color that seemed almost silver in certain light. Her face was long, her

43

features sharp. Mackey had only seen her in uniform, and she had always seemed to him very Teutonic and severe. She was tall, with long, thin legs and a sure step.

"Yes, I make sure I soften you up with at least several barrages of your own high-caliber wallop, and the rest is like shooting monkeys in a barrel."

"Really? Then we must see what'll transpire when I redeploy my forces and entrench. Hans—where is that coffee? And make it strong!"

Both laughed at the banter, forced as it was.

There was no way of becoming familiar with a person from another army, Mackey thought. He had had acquaintances, even a lover or two, but no friends. There was always the feeling that the other person had chosen or had been born wrong, that one day they'd find themselves on the muzzle side of each other's trench, and so it was like two pugs sizing each other up.

And then, with this woman and the Bundeswehr, Mackey didn't really care. If it ever came down to a scrap—Mackey gathered in his chess pieces and placed those he'd taken from her on the other side of the board— the Bundeswehr would only get in the way. Perhaps they already had.

Mackey thought of the erosion of the American defense budget. In '76 the price of forty-two major weapons acquisitions had jumped by $16 billion, boosting the tab to a record of $146 billion, and those system were absolutely essential to national security. The final cost had actually come in several billions higher, as inflation had continued. Over five years, that had made the cost of any given weapon one-third more expensive.

Something had to give, and what had that something been? Certainly not the in-production weapons systems that had created jobs and profits and had, in effect, established constituencies, but rather the future projects that had been still in the blueprint stage.

At the same time the Soviets had increased their total military expenditures by 3 percent per year in constant rubles and their basic military R&D by one-third. That meant they were working with greater resolve on projects as diverse and essential as—Mackey counted them off as he placed the chessmen down on the board—weather modification, missiles, warheads, fighter planes, submarines, radars, computers, electronic countermeasures, electronic warfare, lasers, guidance and control, unmanned planes, submarine listening devices, and satellites.

In the Yom Kippur War of '73, the Soviet-supplied forces had fielded quality, high-technology weaponry that the Arabs used effectively against the best weapons that the United States had, with only a few exceptions; and if the history of warfare in the twentieth century had proved anything, it was that one key weapon could be decisive.

And throughout it all, our allies, Mackey thought, watching Kronenberger sip from the demitasse cup of coffee, her head back, her light blue eyes regarding him, the tiny cup and saucer balanced in her long, tapered fingers, our allies hadn't contributed as much as a dime to development of the U.S. strategic arsenal, which effectively had protected them for nearly four decades. In negotiations concerning the integration of weapons systems, they kept holding out for deals that were loaded in favor of their own arms manufacturers. It was either accept their proposals or do without standardization.

And then the Dutch, Belgians, and Germans considered unemployment rates of over 2 or 3 percent excessive. Mackey thought of the desperate and poor who peopled America's squalid cities, and how it was their sons and daughters who were over here, protecting the Europeans. And U.S tax dollars, whatever the crippled economy could spare.

Mackey, playing white, made the first move, then leaned back in the chair and folded his arms across his chest. He stared across the board at Kronenberger, her neatly bunned, silver hair, the few loose strands at the nape of her neck, the limpid eyes that gazed upon him as though upon an object that she found diverting but contemptible. If 230 million Europeans didn't have the integrity or courage to pay for their own defense, were they worth defending? He didn't know.

Mackey thought of Lisette, a woman friend of his in Hamburg, and decided that Europeans had style, that was it. There was a certain curve to her hips, which were thin, that was apparent under everything she wore, and it was as though she knew it and dressed to heighten the effect. Her legs were shapely, but not only in that way did she differ from Mackey's wife.

45

She had also, it seemed to him, accepted certain limits of the personality that most Americans refused to acknowledge. It was as though she had said, I can only do and be so much, so I'll choose these several things. What she had chosen—teaching European history at the university, her children, her house, and her friends—she treated with éclat. Mackey's wife tried to do anything and everything. She had had some successes, but a number of salient failures, although Mackey knew it was unfair to blame her.

Kronenberger moved a pawn and crossed her legs away from the board, arranging her uniform jacket over her thigh. She placed a cigarette between her lips, and the orderly rushed over to offer a light. Exhaling the stream of smoke, she gazed across the room, and the entire pose—the intelligent, calm, worldly eyes, her contentment with being an unlikely woman, and now of a certain age, in a singularly masculine profession—communicated to Mackey an almost deterministic acceptance of the way things were.

And how were they? If called upon or even if attacked, most Western European nations would not, because they could not, fight.

Maybe that was it, Mackey thought, looking down at the board: Europeans knew something no American could—that they could live with Americans camped on them, or the Russians, or any number and type of younger, cruder, or more militaristic peoples, and over time prevail. Maybe that was what their sense of style conveyed. Lisette sometimes gave him that feeling. It was as though all his anxieties and concerns, the issues he thought so momentous, were, when viewed with her perspective, trivial. How had she once put it, when talking about some other situation? "Just froth on the waves of history."

Kronenberger herself had been preoccupied by her own thoughts. Monkeys in a barrel, indeed! she had thought after their last exchange. She well knew why she lost to Mackey—it was a defensive game and Mackey played it defensively, without any imagination or panache. He would not depart one move from the posture that he had determined necessary for victory. It was as though he had perceived, a priori, some eternal verity in the tactics of the game, and no matter what offense was mounted against him, he would offer the same sort of cautious defense.

Kronenberger had finished the coffee, and she caught

46

the orderly's eye. She wanted more. While she was waiting, she thought of the briefing that had been circulated after Mackey's purported success during the joint-forces test in Canada. In it Mackey had written:

After any initial clash between infantry and armor, the infantry should give way to the opposing armor and should return when the mechanized columns have moved on. In open terrain this can be achieved by use of the helicopter and/or well-conditioned, elusive foot soldiers.

Once this initial envelopment occurs, rear-guard foot soldiers using man-portable weapons should take a toll of enemy armor and again fade away, thus encouraging the enemy to pursue his drive forward. Again and again elements of the defense should employ this tactic, drawing the enemy ever farther from his source of supply, the lines of which have, in theory if not in fact, been cut off several times.

Meanwhile (once air superiority has been established), interdiction strikes should be aimed against enemy rear areas and bases. The combined attack will readily exhaust an armored thrust before those units can reach decisive strategic objectives.

In a modern context it is to be hoped that the enemy will commit a large percentage of his tanks and mechanized forces to the initial strike, especially if he has a poorly developed logistical capability.

The effectiveness of this approach can only be enhanced by current weapons developments, many of which are being put in place at this time.

There it was, thought Kronenberger, the tactics of a rear-guard action. "An active defense" was the American phrase, but it was the same thing: suck them in, maul them, withdraw, suck them in, maul them . . . , which in some ways might be suited to the game of chess or an ideal battlefield in—she tasted the coffee, which was bitter and pleased her—Canada, but not to the art of war as it would be practiced in Europe. In order to gain victory, Mackey eventually would have to mount an offensive and take back the territory he had yielded. And what territory? Germany itself. And by what means? With tanks and against the Soviets who, by that time, would well understand the techniques of tank defense.

What, then, would be the upshot of Mackey's approach? If he won, both Germanys would be turned into a massive battleground. If he lost, the Federal Republic would first be overrun by the Red Army and then, according to the NATO doctrine of a "flexible response," devastated by an exchange of tactical nuclear and other nonconventional weapons the moment the enemy approached the Dutch, Belgian, or French borders.

The enemy!

Again Kronenberger touched the cup to her lips. The hot brew was making her nose run.

No city would remain standing, the factories that had figured so significantly in the postwar recovery would be gone, the farmlands laid waste and so polluted they'd be unusable for centruies. But most catastrophic would be the human toll—20 to 100 million Europeans would die, the latter figure if cities were attacked, and most of them Germans. Because of genetic damage, those who remained would face the chance of giving birth to monsters.

Kronenberger's hand reached out and moved a chess piece. Again Mackey looked up at her, a damnable, slight smile on his lips. He crossed his arms and looked back down at the board. Cautious, Kronenberger thought, not taking any chances. With his own.

She watched Mackey make another careful move, and she wondered what this small, insignificant man and his President back in Washington could be intending. There was a profound difference between the 7th American Army of old and Mackey's new command. Not only was it significantly bigger—Bundeswehr estimates placed the increments at over 80,000—but its teeth-to-tail ratio (combat soldiers to headquarters and supply personnel) was far different. At two-to-seven the former 7th Army had been a peacetime, defensive force. At eleven-to-four it was now a war machine.

And what was it that he had his men chant? Kronenberger again leaned back in her chair and stared over Mackey's head, at the far wall and the frieze of heraldic figures on it. She didn't have to look at the board to know she was losing again.

48

A prosaic mind, she thought with some satisfaction, is given to sententiae:

"Troopers—why do we prepare for war?"

"Sir—if we want peace, we must prepare for war."

"And why is war like nature?"

"Sir—the judgment on error in nature is death."

Mackey's small hand, the skin of which was freckled, reached out and moved a pawn to K-4. He was becoming bored with the game; Kronenberger just wasn't trying.

Kronenberger forced herself to consider the board. It was as good as over, and Mackey's small, gray eyes were pitying, she was certain. "*Ach, mein Freund,*" she said, raising her palms, the tone of her voice too unctuous to be congratulatory, "you've done it again. I'm afraid I'm no match for your superior strategies. What's more, I'm distracted."

"First it was the Cognac, now the coffee," Mackey replied, teasing. He stood, removed a pipe from the pocket of his jacket, and eased himself away from the chair. He used a cane to approach the fireplace.

"I'm glad you mentioned your first weapon. Cognac, please, Hans. And for General Mackey as well." Kronenberger herself stood and followed Mackey to the hearth. Her Bundeswehr uniform, which had been patterned on the American style but since altered by a skilled tailor, still did not do justice to her angular frame. It made her seem dowdy and sexless.

"No, General," she went on, "I was just trying to be polite in offering that excuse. Actually, I was"—she paused at the fire and faced Mackey—"I *am* preoccupied. In all seriousness, I'd like to know what's in the wind."

Mackey continued to pack the pipe from a tobacco pouch. He well knew who she was and what she stood for. Anything he said to her was bound to get out. If the Germans wanted a paper army, that was their business. But the reality of the situation was that he'd have to deal with them, like it or not, and the NORTHAG command was something he'd groomed himself for throughout his career. And the orders he'd been given in Washington, that had been okayed by NATO headquarters, would have to be issued some time or other, better now, like this, friend to friend as it were.

Mackey reached a bit of kindling into the fire and then lit his pipe.

"After all," Kronenberger went on, "we've been comrades in arms—how many years is it now?"

Mackey glanced at her and again assessed her long, handsome face. Her mouth was full, but her lips had a definite form, as though chiseled, and it was difficult to look at her without considering them.

It hadn't been long. "Years," Mackey said.

"Exactly." Kronenberger was tall enough to rest an elbow on the mantel, and she waited for Mackey to answer her, watching him pull on the pipe and stare at the fire.

Within the building, in the commissary, the dinner bell began ringing.

After a sufficient, patently histrionic pause, Mackey took the pipe from his mouth. "Attack is the secret of defense; a good defense includes assailing the enemy's mental equilibrium. To that end, *meine Freundin*"—he turned to Kronenberger—"I can tell you that I'm about to ask General Beiers to equip all Bundeswehr forces under his command with full complements of live ammunition." The order was just a precaution and reasonable enough, given the proximity of the Pact forces and the border. "And rations for, let's say, two weeks. It's been cleared with your government."

The corporal presented a tray, and Kronenberger reached for a snifter. She had hardly heard the order, the maxim having distracted her. "Sun Tzu?"

"After a fashion."

And not even accurate, she thought.

2

Harris checked his watch. It was six seventeen, and he'd been standing in the snow for nearly forty minutes. Before dawn they'd cleared the parade ground, and now with the other two hundred troopers in his company he was staring out across the windblown expanse at the one row of lights in the barracks compound. Headquarters. Harris kept his eyes on the last two yellow slots. Herz's office.

Harris glanced down at the snow that covered his boots. The company would be airdropped into previously unsecured positions, and they'd have to fend for themselves. Maybe all day and all night and the next day. And it was getting colder by the moment, he could feel it.

"What the fuck's keeping him, Sergeant?" one trooper asked.

"Don't see him out here, freezing his nuts off."

"They gonna call it off?"

Harris only stared that trooper down. Bitching was one thing, quitting another. An exercise in this stuff would be good practice. The snow and the wind and, when night fell, the darkness would promote dispersion and chaos. And they needed a challenge, something to toughen them up, but standing out here like this was stupid, especially after having worked up a sweat clearing the compound.

Harris broke ranks and started through the new-fallen snow, which was fine and sprayed from the toes of his boots. He thought of Chicago and the snow and the cold and trudging to school where it was warm and there was

51

food. And of Hitzacker and the *Gasthaus* and his car, the Porsche.

"Asshole," another muttered.

"Lieutenant, sir." Harris saluted smartly.

"Sergeant?" Reese shifted his weight. He was cold.

"Got any idea when he's going to get it together?"

Reese was tall and gangly, a southerner fresh out of West Point. He was unsure of himself, and Herz, who had mustanged a commission in Vietnam, leaned on him even more than on the men. "He told me to await orders, sergeant. You heard him."

Once again Harris looked in at the headquarters windows. The building was olive-drab, only a shade darker than the sky, but with the snow and the cold, it made the lights look yellow, warm, and inviting.

Harris made up his mind. He was going in there and find out what was keeping the motherfucker. Herz was a hard-ass, but not with himself. "But what're you doing out here, Lieutenant? You don't have to stand out here like this."

Reese looked down at the small first sergeant. Harris knew how to handle himself and had never steered him wrong. He liked Harris, but this was different. Right from the briefing before breakfast Herz had seemed almost like he'd flipped out. He was always severe, but he had spoken only in monosyllables, his voice barely audible, his eyes roaming the room. "No fuck-ups. Not one. Hear me?" Reese judged that the less he had to do with Herz the better.

"The other lieutenants"—Reese motioned his head toward the three other troop formations and the men standing out in front of them, hands behind their backs at parade rest. Snow capped their kelmar helmets and the epaulets of their field jackets, making them look like statues. New boys too.

"They're assholes. You wanna be an asshole? You're an officer. You don't have to take this shit. You can ask, and he'll have to tell you." If it's what I think, Harris thought, we'll spread it around. It would be just one more thing they'd have on him. "At least we'll get ourselves in there."

Reese glanced down at the small, wiry man, the thin, trim mustache that looked as though it had been drawn across his upper lip with a dark pencil. Harris was street-

52

wise and had been decorated several times in Vietnam. But more than that, Harris gave the impression that he'd been places and done things. He never talked about them, but it was enough. People did what he said.

"Sure—we'll go in together. You ask him if he has any orders. I'll take it from there," Harris offered.

Reese thought for a moment. Herz had been down on him since Reese had arrived nearly nine months earlier, threatening him with poor efficiency reports, chewing him out in front of the men, making him a butt for his jokes. The others had gone along with him because that was the army. Somebody got singled out. It was good for you, made you tough, showed you could take it.

But it had just made Reese want to resign. The Point was, well, everything he thought the army would be: tradition, rules; he'd taken some shit, same as everybody, but that was the difference.

"What do you have to lose?" Harris prodded.

Reese knew Harris was playing him, but he was right too. He had nothing to lose with Herz.

Again he glanced at the other three lieutenants, lined up like a bunch of fucking dummies. He thought maybe he should go alone, but he wouldn't know how to handle it without getting his ass in a sling. And if he blew it, Herz would only make things worse. For the men too. That was the way Herz did things.

Reese stepped toward the barracks and the lights, knocking the snow off his shoulders with smart smacks of his gloves. And off his helmet too. He wouldn't let Herz see it.

He stamped his boots and his knock on Herz's door was loud.

"Yeah?"

"Reese here, sir. To see you."

"Yeah?"

"I want to speak to you."

"Yeah?"

Reese looked down at Harris, who pointed at the door. "Inside, if you don't mind."

"Oh, but I do, sonny. I do."

They heard feet hit the floor and a chair pull back. Herz had had his feet up on the desk, just waiting to see which one of them would come in. Reese glanced down at his hands, which were large. The right had formed a fist. Another chicken-shit game. His nostrils had flared; he tried to calm himself.

"You alone, Reese?"

Reese glanced at Harris, and something about his expression, which was quietly confident, or his features, which were clean and well defined, steeled him. Harris was only half his size, had had none of his advantages, but he had guts. "Yes, sir."

Harris's brow wrinkled, questioning him.

Reese pushed Harris back and opened the door.

Herz was smaller than Reese, with a round face and small mouth that made him seem intense, always pissed-off. And his eyes, which were a light blue color, reinforced the impression. They were always glassy, as though he knew he wouldn't like what he saw. His hair was blond and he kept it cut short so the scar on his forehead was more apparent. It was large and pink and shaped like a scythe. He was in his shirtsleeves, leaning back against the front of his desk, hands in his pockets.

"Lieutenant?" he asked, tilting back his head in a manner that said, this better be good.

Reese reached back for the door, which didn't actually slip from his fingers, It closed with a clap.

Reese's heart was beating in throbs. He was breathless and the realization only made him madder: that he had prepared so thoroughly for this career, only to have the man in front of him, somebody he wouldn't care to know in private life, make him quit. "We're out there, Captain, waiting on your orders."

A smile, the thin lips, "And you don't think I know that?"

Reese summoned up all his courage. He thought of a summer day in Aiken with wide fields bordered by white fences and stands of loblolly pine. There were horses in those fields. His father had been in the cavalry. "I'd like to know why we're standing out there."

"Because I ordered you to."

"And you know that the men won't have another chance in a day, maybe two, to get inside or rest?"

Herz cocked his head. "You got something to tell me about soldiering, Reese?" Still the voice was low, a whisper.

Herz didn't like anything about Reese. He was big, sloppy. The way his hair hung down on his forehead and his face was shaped—a long, crooked nose, horse teeth, an undershot chin—it always looked like he was about to break into a silly-ass smile. But Herz knew different; he'd checked Reese's record. He'd graduated eighth in his class at West Point, then volunteered to serve here in Germany. With Mackey. He wrote to him himself.

And when Reese smiled, there was an edge to it. The chin dropped, the teeth showed, the head went back, but it was like he knew too much about you. And the glasses. He'd laughed like that to Herz, first day. And then after Herz had left the room.

Herz was getting old for a captain, and the eyes were on him, studying him.

"I request you pull the men in, sir—until further orders. It's getting cold out there. Real cold."

"You *what* request, Reese?"

Behind the glasses that had fogged in the heat, Reese's eyes blinked once. "My apologies, sir—I *respectfully* request that you pull the men in, sir. Until further orders."

The phone on the desk had begun ringing. Herz answered it but kept his eyes on Reese. "Yes, sir, I was expecting the order. Thank you, sir. And good luck to you too." He hung up and pushed himself off the desk. He stepped toward the windows.

"You come in here alone, Lieutenant?" Herz couldn't see very far across the parade ground. It was snowing too hard.

Reese paused, not knowing what to say, but he wouldn't let Herz make him lie. He decided Harris could take care of himself. "Harris came with me, sir."

Only the blue, glassy eyes turned to Reese. "I thought you said you were alone."

More chicken-shit. The man just couldn't let it alone. "He helped me into the building. You know the way I walk, sir. I think I've heard you telling some of the other officers about it. Harris only wanted to make sure I didn't fall and break something." There—it was out, Reese thought.

Herz smiled, then turned back to the window. "Take the men back to the barracks, Lieutenant. Watson tells me General Mackey wants everybody in full winter gear—foot packs, pants, parkas, wind masks. And skis. Have"—he paused—"Harris and some other troops load them. And fast. I want no delays. We're late enough as it is, but

55

maybe now"—he turned to Reese—"we'll have an advantage." The glaze was still in his eyes, but it seemed like a dismissal, as though he was weary of Reese and men like him.

Reese tried not to feel ridiculous, shambling through the snow toward the men. He knew Herz was in the window, watching him. But his right foot—huge, ungainly—kept hooking in, nearly tripping him. Reese only shouted at the other lieutenants, then threw an arm toward the barracks.

The men broke ranks and, shielding their faces from the driving snow, pushed across the parade ground.

Monday A.M.
Wittenberge
G.D.R.

Colonel-General Alexeyev had left strict orders that Chief Marshal Kork was not to be disturbed. He himself had risen early, had breakfasted with several field-grade officers whom the announcement, putting GSFG on alert, had excited. The younger, less experienced men had kept asking probing questions about the NATO exercises and what Alexeyev thought had led Moscow to order the state of readiness, until a colonel finally pointed out their rudeness.

"No, no," Alexeyev had said, "I can understand your concern, comrades. Whenever you have two armies side by side, anything can happen. That's all this is. It's best to be prepared for any contingency. Just think of the trouble we sometimes have holding joint maneuvers with the Pact countries. Moscow just wants to be ready."

"In case," a young major added.

Alexeyev had nodded. "In case." He knew all too well how little they had to keep them involved.

Looking out into the courtyard where he would take his morning walk, Alexeyev was surprised to discover that the snow was both deeper and finer than he had thought upon first arising. There must be—what?—nearly a half-meter on the ground already, and it was still coming down. The weather report that he had read over his tea had said the precipitation would continue throughout the day and into the night, followed by a period of hard cold and perhaps more snow during the beginning of the coming week.

He raised the tall collar of his greatcoat and noted that his face was becoming more gaunt with age, emphasizing the mottled scars on both cheeks. Even in the hallway near the refectory, his old wounds seemed bluish, like tattoos, and once in the cold outside, he knew his face would ache.

The cold—he wondered if it would matter. But that was foolish. Nothing was going to happen, and, in any case, his troops—all of the officers and most of the men—had trained and lived in conditions much more severe than this. Still, snow and cold hampered the mobility of armor and provided a visual screen for helicopter assaults. It also disoriented troops, especially during night operations, muffling sound and concealing movement. And it provided camouflage too, for anything white.

But again Alexeyev checked himself. Here he was, like the young fellows he had breakfasted with, getting excited, allowing his imagination to speed ahead. Yet the shouts of the sergeants who were directing snow crews across the square were indeed muffled by the snow and came to Alexeyev short and weak, as though miles away.

The other soldiers walking toward him stepped off the path into the snow to let him pass, saluting smartly. Where possible, he used their given names, reaching out to touch their sleeves. It was something he had learned from Kork when he was still just a boy. "Know your troops, care for them, take an interest in their lives. That's all they have to offer, and if they know you don't undervalue the gift, they'll fight all the harder."

Kork—he was an old fox, and Alexeyev judged that in his prime he had been the equal of any modern commander, Zhukov, Guderian, Patton, or Rommel included. In his prime. And the man Kork was facing could only be said to be in his prime.

Alexeyev turned at the corner and continued down the north side of the square, his stride longer now that he had begun to walk the stiffness out of his hip. There was a steel pin in it from the injuries he had received during the war, and, to be honest, he knew that he was no youngster himself.

But this Mackey had experience in modern warfare and

plenty of it. After dinner last night, Alexeyev had gone to his study and had asked a night duty officer to assemble all the information GRU had supplied them on the American general.

There were two thick manila folders, and Alexeyev had found most interesting the fact that three times while Mackey was a battalion commander in Vietnam he had been ordered back to the Army War College—an opportunity that any other colonel would have jumped at—and three times he had refused. Instead, he had remained where the fighting was—and on the ground. He hadn't directed his troops from command helicopters, high above the battle. He had led his soldiers into action, and had been wounded several times. "Iron Mike" they called him. Reading on, Alexeyev found that he had more than iron to offer.

After Vietnam Mackey had written several white papers, outlining a plan for the restructuring of American army divisions. It called for splitting a division into an armored brigade, an air-mobile infantry brigade, and a new group that he called an air cavalry combat brigade. A TRICAP division would mount 162 main battle tanks, the same numbers as a U.S. mechanized infantry division but only half as many as an armored division. The primary difference would be the substantial inventory of antitank weaponry and the emphasis on mobility and Guerrilla-type, irregular-action tactics. Extensive use would be made of the helicopter, but seldom at the forward edge of the battlefield. The strength of the standard TRICAP division would be 13,000 men.

Mackey had gone on to state that, contrary to general opinion both within the U.S. Army and without, Vietnam had not been a debacle. It had been a learning experience in every way. What the United States required militarily was a flexible ground force that was capable of short-notice, in-depth defense, but that could strike if necessary. He welcomed the new, all-volunteer army and said the modern battlefield required highly trained professionals, not doughboys and grunts. Volunteers could be trained, regardless of their backgrounds, and should be rewarded.

He himself was. The report came to the attention of Meisenzahl, President Harper's Adviser for National Security Affairs. Macky was given the 7th Army. Nearly all of it was now structured under the TRICAP plan.

Alexeyev had then begun reading through Mackey's other writings, in an assortment of Western defense perodicals.

"War depends on three things," Mackey had written, "courage, ground, and climate." He had then gone on to outline the effect of those conditions on commanders who had faced overwhelming odds but who had, by means of superior tactics, timing, and daring, won great victories. Alexander, Scipio, and Cromwell came in for special praise. None of them had ever been defeated, and Mackey observed that none—as far as was known—had ever made a direct approach, that is, they had never confronted the enemy's strength. Rather, they had always managed to concentrate firepower upon some weak point and then, like Napoleon later on, had sent a force in to drive across the enemy's rear.

But the battle he admired most was Cannae, where Hannibal, facing better-equipped and supplied and vastly superior Roman legions, had thrown his forces into a crescent, had let the Romans push back his center, and had then wheeled in his flanks to complete a double encirclement. Seventy thousand Romans had died, ten thousand were captured, and it was a perfect military victory with no loose ends. It wasn't repeated, Mackey had gone on to observe, until Napoleon's victory at Austerlitz and the Russian encirclement of German forces at Stalingrad. Twice he spoke of Kork, both times praising the daring of the then-obscure tank corps commander.

And here they were, Alexeyev now thought, facing each other—Kork at the end of his career and equipped with the most powerful striking force ever assembled, Mackey just having attained the prominence necessary to direct a major clash and with perhaps more experience in the techniques of modern warfare in spite of his youth.

Alexeyev stopped and walked back to the entry that led to the strike center, a super-hardened bunker deep in the basement of one of the buildings on the square.

One wall was a map of Europe that showed the dispositions of Soviet ground forces and their Warsaw Pact allies to the east of the Elbe and the frontier, and the NATO contingents to the west. The elements in flux—the British

Army of the Rhine was moving into Saxony and for some reason French units were being grouped near their border with Germany and Belgium—were lighted, as was any air traffic of interest at a given moment. Quite a number of planes were being tracked now.

"In addition to their five AWACS, they've put two other reconnaissance craft over the river. At least, we believe their mission is reconnaissance, but neither had rendered a signal nor have they the configurations of the E-two-a, E-three-a, or the British Nimrod variety. Air Command is sending up interceptors to check."

"When did that start?"

"Well, it's been going on since Saturday morning, sir, but with all the other air activity, we only determined the pattern last night. Each team is relieved at three-hour intervals. It looks like they plan to keep at least two planes in the air at all times."

Alexeyev hardly heard the colonel. The planes were probably precautionary, put there to make sure that none of the NATO contingents strayed toward the frontier. He was concentrating more on the British Army of the Rhine, which seemed to be pulling in behind the forward concentrations of the Bundeswehr forces, as though positioning itself as a reserve unit. "Does that disposition match the information we have concerning their intended battle groupings for their maneuvers?"

"Within acceptable parameters, sir."

Alexeyev eased himself against his desk and wondered how much the army could rely on the information GRU supplied them, much of which had been gleaned from their over 13,000 ferrets in Western Europe. With such numbers it had to be assumed that the West could feed any information it wanted to GRU. And then, what was this business with the French, who were not a part of NATO and were not taking part in the exercises? What had they been told to cause them to begin a build-up on their borders? Probably nothing.

No—Alexeyev didn't trust GRU's ferrets or those of the KGB and MVD. He trusted more the surveillance satellites, the tall radar towers that had recently been erected to guard against cruise missiles, and the aircraft that the air command still sent up. Hard evidence in black and white—

Alexeyev removed his hat and overcoat and placed them in Kork's command chair—that couldn't be coopted easily.

He watched the red dots that represented the surveillance planes and thought about all the sensors—seismic, audio, chemical, and infrared—that had been placed all along and on both sides of the frontier to monitor troop, truck, armor, and supply movement. Could he believe in the information they supplied? He thought so, since the devices had been built to resemble twigs and leaves of grass and even small pine trees, and the West certainly couldn't afford to sweep an area hundreds of kilometers long and ten deep. And, in case of hostilities, more would be dropped.

But still, they were American inventions that had been devised whole decades ago, and GRU was unsure of what advances the Americans had made in recent years.

Alexeyev picked up his cap. "Keep me informed, Colonel. Anything extraordinary, no matter how slight, no matter the hour. And leave a standing order to that effect."

"Chief Marshal Kork called earlier with the same request."

"Really? He's up?" That surprised Alexeyev. Usually the morning after was disastrous to the old man. Only a portion of his liver was still functioning and his kidneys were shot.

"At least since"—the colonel glanced down at his notepad—"five twelve."

"Good for him!" But Alexeyev's step was quicker as he moved toward the stairs.

When he entered the study, Kork was smiling over a mug of tea, staring down at a map that was laid over his desk. And Alexeyev could tell from the creases that it was the old one Kork had kept as a souvenir, the one they would have used if they'd been allowed to push beyond Wittenberge back in '45.

"Nikolasha," Kork said affectionately, his face an alarming shade of red, "do you know what I've been thinking?"

Alexeyev closed the door. "No, Volodya Kirill, tell me about it," although he well knew and in detail.

61

Fowler placed the tray of coffee on the table. General Price looked up and thanked him with his eyes.

Fowler straightened up and moved away toward the door, where he stood at ease, his hands clasped behind his back. As usual he'd been up since four fifteen, but his morning had been filled with details far different from his normal assignment as General Mackey's orderly.

. While the general had been showering and shaving, Fowler had again scoured the rooms, ceiling to floor, for the sort of devices—*Kleinhören* D IIs; microminiaturized and sensitive—that he'd noticed in other areas of 12th Panzer-Grenadier headquarters, and had even checked the bottoms of the cups, the tray, poured the sugar out of the bowl, the milk out of the pitcher; then he had gone through the general's clothes, which had been cleaned and pressed during the night, and his shoes, which had been shined.

Afterward, Fowler had taken up his post by the door, just to make sure his sweep wouldn't be burnt. He now rested his fingertips against the wall and glanced at General Mackey, who was using the light through tall French windows to read the disposition report that Price had brought.

Mackey was still wearing his bathrobe. Below it he had on a T-shirt and his uniform trousers. There were slippers on his feet.

What had always struck Fowler was the way Mackey appeared ageless, even, like now, after having been out most of the night. Sometimes—when he was doing the battery of exercises in the morning—he looked maybe forty-five, but at other times in his thirties. Late thirties, but he looked young, definitely not whatever age he was; fifties or sixties.

Fowler had known Mackey for a long time. He'd been his paperboy, gone hunting with him on the general's farm outside Honeoye Falls, which was south of Rochester. It was actually his wife's family's place. They had no kids, and she ran it herself when the general was away, which was most of the time.

A bitch, some said, but that was because she made them work. Fowler could still see her now, sitting in the rocker in the den, pushing the shiny point of the needle through the drumlike top of a crewel frame, some bright pattern, waiting for the paper. A tall woman—real busy with the farm and groups in town and the philharmonic, he'd heard; she had tipped well because it was a long road down to her house—with silver hair she kept tied back and glasses with metal frames. She looked older than the general, by much.

When Fowler had screwed up—in school, mostly—the general had come to see him, to hunt, he said, but they sat on a fence and he gave him the pitch about the new army. He said he needed somebody he could trust, somebody he'd known for a long time and liked.

Fowler had always thought the general had been quiet when they were hunting because that was the way you got the most game. But he had been wrong. It was as though Mackey was always mulling something over. He only really came alive when they were fighting, or about to, like now, which was as close as they'd ever come to it. Then his eyes—they were gray—came alive. And he was different, and Fowler didn't know how to approach him.

Price was something else, like a rock, always. He pulled the whole command together. All the other blacks could see he wasn't just another up-front nigger, that he and Mackey were a team. And Price, with the deep lines in his face and the white mustache that curved around - his mouth, looked watchful and tough. He was huge, maybe bigger than anybody in the command. Fowler hadn't really served under anybody else, but he'd heard stories, and he was glad he was where he was.

Mackey closed the folder and had Fowler carry it back to Price.

Fowler returned to Mackey with a cup of coffee.

Mackey had had trouble concentrating on the memorandum, not only because he could see at a glance that Price had positioned Blue Team, his command during the exercises, as he would have himself, but also because he was distracted by the way he felt.

He parted the curtains and looked out beyond the parking lot where, in a wide field that was bordered by a forest of tall pines, half-tracks were clearing a mustering area.

It was the onset of winter, he supposed, when he tended

63

to evaluate himself, to reckon the pluses and minuses. And what had he to show? A few victories and some stars. His marriage had been a failure. He'd had no kids, nobody to follow him, no personal life. He'd been a loner, preoccupied, driven, and it had been folish, ultimately.

Mackey now heard several car horns and, turning to look in the other direction, saw through the driving snow a cordon of automobiles with their lights on and small flags waving from the fenders. Bengsten, the SACEUR. Mackey knew what he wanted.

He looked away, at the snow and the trunks of the pines off in the distance.

The exercise, Reforger—what number was it this time, X or XI? And did it really matter, pushing it forward like this? Mackey thought not. Bengsten had arrived to deliver the caveat.

The bark was black, and the trees looked like columns of soldiers under a tall white tent.

He was hearing voices in the hall.

When the door opened, Price lumbered to his feet.

"Mike," Bengsten said to Mackey. "And Howard." He moved toward Price first and shook his hand with both of his.

Like Price, Bengsten was a tall man with a square frame. His face was broad and so weathered it looked as though the creases and lines had been added to make him look tough. The skin was leathery, and Mackey wondered where Bengsten had been to get a tan at this time of year.

Bengsten was an administrator and not a soldier. In Vietnam he had distinguished himself by leading the weather-modification effort during the Tet offensives. But he had found Washington more to his liking. Mackey believed Harold Bengsten got along well with politicians because he was one of them.

Bengsten now asked after Price's wife and family, naming them, inquiring about their schools, their activities.

Price smiled, flattered that Bengsten remembered. They talked on for a moment and Bengsten then turned to Mackey, making sure their eyes engaged.

Bengsten smiled, his teeth seeming very white against the tan. "Got a mess out there, don't we, Mike?" He reached for Mackey's hand and then turned both of them to the window and the snow. "But it'll make things more interesting, I'd say." He released Mackey's hand and his smile fell. "You probably know why I'm here."

Mackey eased himself against the desk and glanced down at his slippers. He was a shy man and Bengsten's patronizing manner embarrassed him, gave him the feeling that he was childish and there were aspects of the world—power and relationships between the powerful—that he would never understand.

"The President thinks we've made our point, now he just wants us to go through the motions. No"—he paused and Mackey glanced up and studied Bengsten's features—saturnine, the tan permanent, somebody said he dyed his blond hair except for the gray along the sides—"incidents. Everybody stays in place."

Again the smile. "That's it, I guess. I could have called, but he wanted me to come in person."

Mackey nodded. "Thank you, General. It's good to see you."

But Bengsten's eyes had again focused on the scene beyond the window. "Let me ask you something, Mack—what do you think of this place?"

Mackey frowned.

"I mean Germany."

"I don't understand you, sir."

"As a country."

"Well"—Mackey thought of the Bundeswehr—"they could be stronger."

"You're right, but would we want that?" Bengsten's tone had become patronizing, didactic, and out of the corner of his eye Mackey saw Price's head go back and his legs cross the other way.

"I don't know about that, sir. Wouldn't it run counter to the foreign policy we've been developing for the last thirty years?"

Bengsten's voice went lower still; his tone became more confidential. "You're right, Mack. Certainly. But could that policy be wrong for the future?" He paused, then went on. "After all, it's not as if we can afford to be here anymore. Perhaps—" He glanced toward the windows.

They could hear shouts, short and sharp, from the barracks complex behind the headquarters building.

"—perhaps we didn't realize we never could." Bengsten knew that was wrong. "Well, that was clearly impossible

65

immediately after the war, but now?" Bengsten shook his head, and Mackey was struck by the theatricality in the gesture.

Mackey asked, "How would that be accomplished without yielding the continent to the Soviets, and without hostilities?"

"My question is, Mack, would we not *want* a war? Limited, of course."

Mackey's ears went back. He had not expected that. "But how would that help us in the long run. It'd only make our problems worse—oil, capital; we'd lose our major trading partners, at least for a time.

"And if we won, I don't see Central and Eastern Europe being much of a prize. We'd just have to sit on it, to keep the Soviets from taking it back, and we wouldn't want to invade Russia."

"And then—I hope we're just talking here?"

Bengsten's golden eyebrows knitted. "Of course, of course, Mack. Just a few 'what ifs.' " He glanced at Price and smiled.

Price kept his eyes on Bengsten's face.

"And then, Harold—what if the whole thing went nuclear?" Mackey looked away, hoping he hadn't said too much. "I don't know. I could be wrong."

"No, not at all. You're right, General, as far as you take it, but it seems our thinking has been static too long on Europe and the Soviets. We've been content with the way things have been. But things have changed enough to show us we can't go on as we have since the war. We need another approach."

A Panzer column was moving away from the complex and Bengsten had to speak louder. "Look, all we ever hear—in the press, the media—is how big Russia is. Hell"—he turned back to them, his large body silhouetted against the light through the window—"we all know that's a crock. They got—what?—two hundred and fifty-seven million people. Only fifteen million are communists, only one hundred and thirty-six million are actual Russians. The rest? Some of those places we think of as monolithically Russian weren't conquered until the turn of the century or later.

"And then, we alone in the States have two twenty, with Canada, two forty or fifty. The NATO countries and

France about the same. The Chinese? That's anybody's guess. A billion?"

Bengsten came forward again. "If I were a Soviet general, Mack, I don't think I'd get much sleep at night wondering what would happen if I had to fight a two-front war. Given the Chinese threat, the Soviets really need those Eastern Bloc satellites and all their"—he waved a hand—"national minorities, and they're not very firm, believe me. Not very firm at all. They'd bolt the moment they thought we were going to stand up to the Soviets. Hell, they hate the bastards. How can they help it? The Reds have been camped on them for generations."

Sure, Mackey thought, but those countries and minorities feared and consequently respected the Soviets, who would always be there when the West, out of weakness or loss of will, pulled out. But he said nothing.

"A fluid situation there," Bengsten went on, "wouldn't be all that bad for us. I'm privy to the facts, Mack—you know that—and I can tell you we got big, long-range problems. And the cards"—Bengsten opened his hands and closed them again—"just seem to keep falling for the Soviets. We're going to have to scramble and we better start now."

Price cleared his throat, then said, "And you can imagine a scenario that would remain strictly conventional? I don't see the Soviets getting beaten and not resorting to their nuclear stockpile."

Bengsten checked his watch. "We better cut this short. I just stopped in to see if you guys were ready. Let me just ask you this"—he looked up at Price and smiled—"General. Would such an eventuality be all that bad for us? Would we *want* it to remain conventional?"

Price and Mackey only stared at the man.

"Look, I better get going." He turned toward the door. "You probably heard we got a lot of observers for this one. I'll be watching you guys hard. Don't try to look too good." At the door he winked. "They might write something off."

"But, General—" Mackey pushed himself away from the table and moved toward Bengsten.

He'd heard the argument before; that just stinging the Soviets and letting them fall back wouldn't do much for the long-term problems, only make them worse because of the inevitable hardware and resource wastage; that if they could be hurt bad it would take them decades to recover and by then alternate fuel sources would be in place and delivering; that, given the Chinese threat, if both the Soviets and the United States resorted to their intercontinental missiles, both countries would be decimated, but the Soviet Union would be overrun. It was just not a realistic option for them. Not rational.

And if the United States lost a European engagement, the only strategically viable course would be to yield the Soviets a devastated continent. Otherwise, it would only be a matter of time before the world was theirs.

Bengsten had opened the door, and Mackey eased it shut. "Did you speak to the President about this, Harold?"

Deep wrinkles appeared on Bengsten's forehead. "No, of course not, Mack. Nor Meisenzahl. It's just"—his eyes moved away, toward the window once more—"that I get so damned fed up with these people. You know how it is."

Mackey nodded.

Bengsten waved to Price. He offered Mackey his hand. "Good luck, boys." He left the room.

Price was looking down at his hands.

Mackey again approached the window and parted the curtains.

The morning sky was dun, like tarnished pewter. The wind had changed, and the snow, which was fine and hard, was shivering the panes. He watched a Bundeswehr company tramp out across the parking lot, the gray and forest green of their uniforms blending with the diminished tones of trees and sky.

Mackey wondered just how cold it was and what that could mean. "What's the name of the major, Howard—the guy who's the ski-mobile hobbyist, who prepped the sleds for us at Fort Drum? A motor pool officer."

"Werbiskis," Price said.

"Yeah—that's him. Could we get him on the horn?"

Price nodded.

"And then I wonder if we could get a report on the thickness of the ice in the river. You know—where it might be forded, where it was frozen over last, how long, what weight it can bear—that type of thing?"

"The Ilmenau?" Price set down his cup and reached for the sheaf of documents on the table.

Mackey wondered how much the snow and the dark sky

and his mood and Bengsten's visit had to do with the decision. He glanced up into the roiling storm clouds that were just visible above the snowy tops of the pines.

The sound that came from him was one of speculation— he was weighing the situation, the issues—but it also had the timbre of a stifled moan. "Well—I had the Elbe in mind. It's closer."

Price thought for a moment. It was only reasonable, given the situation. He nodded once. "Yes, sir." And stood.

Monday, A.M.
Hamburg
F.G.R.

Annette had caught an early train, and having fifteen minutes before class, she had stepped into the commons for a cup of coffee. But it had been a mistake. Schwerin was there, studying, and on seeing her, he hadn't hesitated. He had smiled at her, gathered together his things, and joined her in the line.

She had wanted only to take a seat by the window and stare out at the *Platz* that lay between the several academic buildings of the campus. Usually the neo-Bauhaus structures were severe, but the gun-metal gray light of the skies contrasted with the snow that covered ledges, roofs, balconies, and the *Platz*, and seemed to seal off the university, making it a world unto itself.

It was a day on which the heating pipes were clanking, when doors got shut in a hurry, when students rushed through the open spaces to get under an archway or into a building, their footsteps muffled in the snow, when concentration was most intense and people—university people—tried to wrap themselves against the onslaught in a mantle of knowledge. It was a day when the coffee, a cup of which she now held in her hand, tasted better, and reading, especially in a big chair by a radiator or anyplace that was warm, became a pleasure for itself, and it was here at the university that it was done best.

But it was the irony that interested Siebenborn most— that the snow, in covering the buildings, had revealed the university's flaw. How much, she asked herself, could really be learned like that, by curling up, by burying yourself, by escaping into a library, a body of opinions any one of which could only be more or less objective and all of which could only relate to the truth of an event when considered as a whole. And what that meant to her was death—a conscious decision to spend the rest of her life there or in some other or in a concatenation of universities in Germany or abroad, when life outside the walls, in the city, nearly anyplace else could be more immediate, more personal.

But what sort of life? In an office dealing with even drearier detail. No, not there. Then where? She didn't know. Certainly the *Gasthaus* was nothing but detail that became more complex the better the meals they laid down, the more service they dispensed, but it was different in kind and could be felt, seen, and tasted. So, what would she do? She didn't know, but the uncertainty alone was thrilling. She had confidence in the future and herself. Everything would work out.

She had moved out onto the steps of the commons, hoping that the cold would drive Schwerin away, but he had tossed his winter coat over a shoulder, as though immune to the bitter breeze. He smiled down at her, making sure she could see his white, even teeth, running a hand down the sides of his head where his hair—the color of yellow gold—swept back, the part precise. He dipped one shoulder, then the other as he spoke, parrying with her.

He wanted to take her to a concert and afterward to late dinner in a Hamburg restaurant that was overpriced and ostentatious.

"And then?" she asked, knowing that he knew she would miss the last train, that she'd have to stay in town with a friend or with him.

"Well"—he blushed—"we can see how the evening proceeds."

But she knew how it would go. She'd disappoint him, and she didn't want to be coy or a flirt. Life—at least as she perceived it at the moment—was too short for that, and she was ashamed to have made herself appear available to him.

And glancing over at an archway on the other side of the *Platz* where Mühling was conversing with some other students, talking too loud, making his deep staccato laugh echo around the buildings, his nonchalance obvious, she felt sad. For the first time in over two years they hadn't sat together on the train. Mühling had taken another compartment, not even looking in at her when he had passed, and had remained in his seat, supposedly reading a paper when she had waited for him. They'd been playmates, companions, and friends since childhood, and lovers after a fashion, but all that was about to change.

Last night had made things plain to her; they just couldn't go on blithely—as Mühling seemed to want—avoiding the hard decisions and the responsibilities of being adults. Mühling had an invalid mother and would have to remain in the Hitzacker-Hamburg area. Siebenborn wanted to go someplace different—it didn't matter where—and as for marriage, to which he had alluded on several occasions, she didn't think she'd ever marry. Just the idea of it was too confining, too permanent, especially now when change seemed so imminent and inviting.

Annette now saw Mühling spin around—light on his feet for all his size—and wrap his arm around a tall blond girl who was passing and pull her into the lee of his shoulder. The girl laughed, then looked at him quizzically, her eyes running down his face to his lips. He began walking her across the open space, toward the academic building in which the history seminar would be held, right past Annette and Schwerin. The blond girl was Erika Mählmann, and she was easy, Annette had heard.

What he was doing was childish, she thought, but at least it was a beginning and would make things easier. She glanced down at her shoes as they passed. She couldn't, she wouldn't look at him. And in a way it hurt her too, but she would recover.

Once again she thought of change and what the future would hold, and she wondered if maturity would be better or only different. Better, she decided: the paring away of the many people, things, and prospects that interested her now, until she found only certain pursuits and certain people fulfilling. Or until the contingencies of life decided those things for her. There was that to consider as well.

"I'm sorry," she said to Schwerin, "but I really must return home early tonight. Because of the military exercises my parents are expecting many guests at our inn. I have to work."

71

She stepped down the stairs of the commons and Schwerin followed her. She decided that it was necessary to confirm what was happening between Mühling and her, just so they wouldn't have to go through it again months later. "Now, I can see you've got two arms and two legs," she said. "It's still an open question as to whether you've got a head on those shoulders, but if you'd like to help, you're welcome. I can promise you only a good meal and a bed"—she glanced up at him—"in my brother's room.

"And then of course"—she smiled, looking down at her bookbag—"you can meet my parents."

"Do you really think I could help?" he asked insouciantly.

Her eyes fell from the sharp, chiseled features of his aristocratic face, to the cashmere sweater and tweed coat, to his thin, nearly delicate hands. "Of course. We'll put you in charge of the silver."

The seminar discussion dealt with the establishment of civilization in Central and Eastern Europe during the sixteenth and seventeenth centuries, how such colonies had been thwarted by the many nomadic tribes in the deserts and steppes of Europe and Asia: the Nogais, Kirghiz, Kalmyks, Tartars, Afghans, Bashkirs, Turkomans, Mongols, and Manchus. Whenever an increase in population, a drought, an internal squabble, or war drove them off their grazing lands, they struck toward the areas of nascent civilization.

Mounted on horse and camel, they used speed and mobility to effect surprise. Frau Professor Doktor Froben, in her prepared remarks, outlined a succession—five hundred years long—of Tartar onslaughts in Poland, where the mere hint of a raid caused mass mobilizations, the erecting of barricades, the stockpiling of weapons. If the Tartars were victorious, they wintered over and ravaged the countryside, leaving it in spring a wasteland, barren of any exploitable resource.

Because Eastern Europe acted as a buffer, Europe proper was saved from the scourge. It wasn't until the end of the seventeenth century that the nomads were put down by means of firepower, but effectively their presence stunted the growth of civilization in the east for centuries.

At the end of a seminar hour it was Froben's practice to

attempt to relate whatever they were discussing to some current subject, if only to provide a sense of the continuity of history.

"Did anybody read the article in last week's *Der Spiegel?* The one about the Red Army?"

The frost on the windows was mounting and made the light in the room crystalline and sparkling, an effect that Froben found pleasing. It had been a good class. Everybody had been prepared, but then again, the reading—about exotic peoples and places and speculations concerning unrecorded history—had been engaging.

The newspaper article had been an analysis of the demographic makeup of the GSFG, the ranks of which, increasingly, were being filled out with Asiatics and recruits from the Soviet Union's national minorities, many of them the progeny of the very people they'd been discussing.

"Are we now faced with the possibility of a modern invasion by these nomadic hordes, one that would begin here on the Elbe without the advantage of an Eastern European buffer? The Czars, of course, made use of the Cossacks in just such a way, to put down any sign of restiveness to the west."

Froben sat back. Her part was over. In a postgraduate setting, of course, it wouldn't work, but she could see the eagerness in their faces—to test themselves, to prove their minds.

Mühling's large shoulders twitched. It was as though he had to fight to keep his hands in his lap. His dark hair, which he wore very long, peaked on his brow. With the cleft in his chin and the long, thin nose that had been broken and was bent, he looked to Froben like a professional athlete, a football player. "I don't see how the Red Army differs from most armies of ruling nations, down through the centuries. Napoleon's army, at least his imperial army of conquest, was replete with 'foreign' troops. The British armies throughout their long history of rapine and exploitation were stocked with Hessians, Scottish, East Indians, Irish, and other subject peoples. The American army—the present one—is nearly half African."

"*African,* Herr Mühling?" Froben asked, frowning.

"Well—black, then. We"—he glanced at Annette, and Froben rejoiced to see the large young man blush—"I mean, we from Hitzacker," he corrected in a small voice, "have an acquaintance who is a first sergeant in an air-assault unit. He's black. We"—again his eyes moved toward the girl—"talk some.

"He's serving in that army because of an accident of birth. In another age he might have been a gladiator or a mercenary. He says he's thought of retiring and going to Africa where at least he'll be close to the issues."

"He's fooling himself," said Schwerin, his arms folded across his chest, his smile defiant, superior.

Mühling's head snapped to him. "How would you know? Are you acquainted with the man?"

"I don't have to be, but he's got a good point that contradicts yours. The armies of declining empires throughout history have been filled out with just such men—paid, professional, but alien soldiers. You have to fight for yourself to be truly free.

"And another thing"—Schwerin turned to Froben and bowed slightly, not taking his hands from his arms, his blue eyes glinting with pleasure—"it was omitted that the article also said most Soviet recruits do not know Russian, they come from rural hamlets or the steppes or Siberia. Most have never driven an automobile before, they have little or no mechanical aptitude. The purposes of things as simple as lubrication, why weapons must be cleaned and thoroughly, spare parts, rpm ranges, and so forth are lost on them. The technologically adept, native Russian speakers are needed in industry. They cannot be spared for the army and what amounts to the long *Sitzkrieg* since the last war."

Schwerin glanced at Annette, who was doodling in her notebook and hadn't looked up at him.

"During Pact exercises last winter," he went on, "over a third of their tanks did not even start. Those with minor problems, like a thrown track, had to be pushed aside. The soldiers treated the entire affair as an outing, a break from the usual routine. They sent runners into all the *Kneipen*. Some ran off the road. Others looted. Still others passed out or fell asleep.

"The article concluded that they don't care for Germany, for Germans, or for soldiering in a foreign country. It questioned how hard they'd fight if called upon.

"Certainly, Frau Professor Doktor, if these men who are poised against us are Cossacks, then they are unlikely Cossacks indeed."

74

If only, Froben thought, Schwerin could learn to mask his handsome face, he'd go far. All his emotions could be read in his features. He had firmed his lower lip smugly, and the ball of his chin was white.

"And what do you think about this, Annette?" Froben asked.

Annette did not look up from her notepad, only turned her head this way and that as her pencil worked over the page.

The competition between the two young men had embarrassed her, especially since Mühling was no match for Schwerin intellectually. And she had been thinking about how brave and forthright Mühling had always been, how in his bearish way he had always taken things head on, regardless of the setting, and how it had worked when they were children and he'd been facing down the bullies from the next block, but now, well, he'd have to moderate his approach, perhaps learn more about himself, if he weren't to meet with further set-backs. And—she glanced up at him, the bent nose, the single, lateral furror on his brow that she had only noted a few times before—he seemed almost desperate, but she couldn't help that.

And also she remembered the conversation of the night before, the one with Sergeant Harris in the kitchen, and how inane all the patter in the seminar would seem if any sort of fighting broke out. For Hitzacker, for Hamburg, for Germany.

"The only correlation I can draw," she said, "is that uncertainty and weakness, not strength, mark both periods.

"By weakness I mean that here in the West we no longer know where strength—economic strength—resides. It has moved up from Venice, through Europe, to London, and during the last war it shifted to New York. But the center of capitalism is now fractured, shattered, in flux. The situation is"—she glanced up and pushed a wavy lock of her reddish hair behind an ear—"chaotic. It's a transition period in world order. Things are up for grabs."

She looked back down at the pad. "I personally don't like standing armies, massive machines, and all the might of the armament we keep hearing about on both sides. They are another sign of weakness—some debility or rot or perceived insufficiency. In the East it may be because the hierarchy of power is too narrowly based. In the West because the capitalist system has never been stable. It relies on confidence and growth. We have neither now.

"And then—look at wars. They're initiated and waged by the weak, who believe they have something to gain, not the strong. In the last war both this country and Japan felt themselves to be weak and were, relative to the other powers. They became stronger through early victory, but it wasn't enough."

"But how does that explain the present situation?" Mühling asked, his head back, his eyes assessing her.

She did not look up at him. "Again weakness comes into play. After the last war Western Europe chose—and I don't mean this in a pejorative sense—'wrong.' We opted for weakness. The Russian army won the war, but the other combatant nations decided to ignore the fact. Instead, we erected a myth of Western superiority and relied on a partner, the United States, which from a strategic, military point of view alone could not be much help to us in an emergency. The other problems, perhaps, could not have been foreseen."

Schwerin spoke up. "And so you think the Red Army could have defeated the Wehrmacht if no fight had been carried out in the west?"

She turned the pad to get another perspective on what she was doodling. She did not want to debate either of them, but she would not truckle. "Yes. Certainly. Without a doubt. It was the Allied hope that Russia and Germany would chew each other up. They waited until the final year of the war to make a direct assault on Europe. Even then the Soviets had our forces on the run. It would only have taken more time."

"We're getting off the track now," Froben said. "What is your point, Annette?"

Annette placed her pencil on the notebook and straightened up. "That we're experiencing a period of uncertainty. It's too naïve to say that in the future no one nation will be able to establish a global hegemony, but—given the spread of technology—I don't think there'll be any 'world' wars anymore. There's too much to lose.

"But I'm not so sanguine about human nature as to believe that there won't be flare-ups, conflagrations, brief, horrible clashes in which the hierarchies of power will at-

76

tempt to establish new structures by testing each other's wills."

She glanced back down at her pad and picked up the pencil. "As I said—now everything is in flux. Uncertainty and weakness prevail."

Froben glanced around the table. The others were quiet. She smiled, "That's all for today. See you on Wednesday."

Placing her outline back in her briefcase, Froben noticed that neither Mühling nor Schwerin tried to leave with the girl. "Annette," she said, "may I speak to you for a moment about the matter I mentioned?"

Applications for a graduate fellowship in history were due at the end of the week.

Annette shook her head and gathered up her books. "I'm sorry, Doktor. I haven't decided. I'd like to think about it further."

Froben cocked her head and looked up at the frost on the windowpanes. It would be a shame if she passed up the chance.

Monday, A.M.
East of Uelzen
F. G. R.

Mackey was cold. He stamped out his snow packs before opening the door and stepping into the mobile command center, a complex of inflatable shelters that had been air-dropped into a pine clearing fifteen kilometers east of Uelzen. In the distance diesel generators roared.

The interior of the shelter was warm and dark. On CRV consoles his staff scanned the changing dispositions of the contingents in the Reforger exercises. Mackey himself had only just returned from an onsight tour of the battle area.

He placed the clipboard on a table and nodded when Fowler asked him if he'd like some coffee. He then moved toward a heating register, again wondering about the weather and the problems it could make for his forces on the ground.

Even from the air, it had taken Mackey over three hours to locate the contingents of his Blue Team. A strong northerly wind off the Baltic was driving the snow in gusts that had blinded them momentarily, made the windshield of the helicopter opaque, caused the pilot to pull back on the stick. Only now and again had trees, farmhouses, roads, and a few small towns in the battle area appeared, and Mackey had waited for open places, like the last they had reconnoitered, before having the pilot approach the action.

Mackey had glanced down at his clipboard:

2nd Arm. Reg.
75th Panz-Gren. Brig.
4th Canad. Mech. Brig. Group
1st Bat., 75th Rangers
1st Inf. Div.
101st Airborne
8th Inf.
2nd Bat., 16th Belg. Inf.
2nd Bat., 75th Rangers
10th Arm. Canad. Reg.
12th Panz-Gren. Brig.
4th Mech. Brig. Group, BAR

He had touched the pilot's sleeve and pointed down.

"Will I put her down, sir?"

Mackey had said no. As at the other sites he had just wanted to get a look at the action, especially there where the Chieftain, NATO's heaviest tank, was operating.

The helicopter had begun its descent toward the patchwork of winter fields, windbreaks, farmhouses, and barns below when another gust struck them and they seemed to plunge through a milky white void.

Mackey had felt pressure on the back of his seat. Fowler. Mackey was reminded that his orderly had not had any Vietnam experience. Like most of his troops he'd never experienced fire.

Blue Team tanks had been attacking across a wide farming basin bounded by lightly forested marshes that were frozen over. Still, Mackey judged, the water wasn't deep enough to form thick ice, and the brigade commander had chosen to avoid them. It was from there that Red Team had launched its antitank defense.

But the tanks churned across the field, the purplish smoke of simulated fire puffing from their guns and quickly dispersing in the wind. A laser pulse projector, mounted on top of the gun barrels, shot beams of light. Other projectors were carried by the antitank forces. A hit on a tank cut out the engine and radio and ignited smoke generators on the back of the turret. It was a whiter smoke and enveloped stalled tanks and some units of APCs behind them. The field commanders complained over the side band, which Mackey's helicopter monitored, but the field judges were firm.

In the distance, beyond the marshes, Mackey had caught fleeting glimpses of air-assault units that were being dropped in to envelop the Red Team forces, and whenever the lead tanks struck open, wind-swept areas, they rushed forward. Front-line Red Team units were abandoning positions, slogging through the snow and the ice of the swamp toward their gunships.

Again Mackey had touched the lieutenant's sleeve. Mackey held out his hand, wanting him to keep the ship where it was.

Holding his binoculars off the bridge of his nose, Mackey had peered down at the Chieftain.

The squat, olive-drab machine had become mired in the deep snow on the lee side of a wall. There, like a stranded tortoise, it had churned, rocking, its tracks spitting back snow and loose rocks until its teeth struck ground and sprayed the deep brown earth across the field. Only then had it moved forward. Slowly, haltingly.

And then at the Elbe, Mackey had had the pilot put the helicopter down. He and Fowler had gotten out and walked toward the bank of the river, down a short, steep hill. A copse of linden trees stood like tall, mottled sentinels on the banks. There, protected by the hills, the branches were heaped with fresh snow.

Only a thin stream of black water had been visible in the middle of a bend in the river. The rest was covered with snow. Mackey couldn't even see a melt-line of softer, wetter snow near the stream; and then, farther east where the river straightened out, one long drift seemed to cover it, shore to shore.

Mackey raised his glasses.

A plow had appeared on the opposite bank and was pushing a load of snow into the river. That wasn't unusual in itself, but the Soviet practice had long been to wait for a storm to end. But they were on alert, Mackey reminded himself, or so he'd been told. Kork. He had to be following every move that Mackey was making.

But how much could he know—Mackey again scanned the lights on the other side of the river, the moan of the tractor motor weak and intermittent—in the snow, like this? A fair amount electronically. Mackey thought of all the sensors—chemical, biological, smell, sight, sound—that the Soviets had scattered along the frontier.

And he thought of the Jasons, the group of scientists—America's top minds from the best universities—who had been assembled during the early days of the Vietnam war. In brainstorming sessions they had come up with those sensors which, when linked to computers, could detect the movement of men and machines, could even detect bicycles and count them. Minelets and bomblets were theirs, and many of the electronic devices that were now standard to the modern battlefield. But since the war no academic worthy of the name was willing to devote time to military topics. The entire defense effort was under a cloud that, perhaps, would never lift.

Mackey had squatted down and dug through the snow until he struck ground. "Call that yard, Fowler?"

"And some, sir. It's a lot of snow and it's got that . . . winter feel to it. Don't look like it's going to let up neither."

Snow. Mackey thought about Napoleon's retreat from Moscow, and how the snow and cold had decimated his forces but had provided the screen without which Marshal Ney could not have succeeded in his rear-guard action. With only 7,000 men, no cavalry, and a few guns, he had been completely cut off, but time and again he had slipped through, stinging the Russians badly and keeping them off the main army.

"Can you check that ice, Corporal? If you fall in, you're on your own."

Fowler had smiled and scrambled down the bank.

Ney's action—all the way through western Russia, the Pripet Marshes, and Poland—was a brilliant military feat, but it had been no real victory.

Fowler, cautious at first, had stamped one foot on the ice. It held. Then the other. Two, three cautious steps. A few more. He jumped on it. "Solid," he had shouted up to Mackey. "Want me to go out farther?"

Mackey had only waved him in and turned toward the helicopter. He'd gotten the picture.

Now he wanted a forecast.

At a desk in the mobile command center, he picked up a telephone. "What's Colonel Dimauro's first name, Howard?"

Price looked up from a monitor that he and several other officers had been studying. "Bob. Robert. He's called here twice already. Says he'll only speak to you."

Mackey frowned.

A communications sergeant put the call through to Bremerhaven, where the meteorological command was located.

"Sir, I've been trying to contact you. I'm afraid the seeding has triggered the Bergeron-Findeisen process. I hope it's all right, but there's nothing we can do about it now anyhow. Pulling the planes down might help."

Mackey eased himself into a chair and undid the straps of his snow packs. "I don't understand."

"General Bengsten and his order to commence a seeding operation. On Friday. He told me he was issuing the orders in your behalf, since you were out of the country.

Mackey stopped what he was doing and looked up. He could hear static and the overlay of many voices—on the phones, in Dimauro's office, in the command center.

Mackey thought for a moment, about Bengsten's visit and the whole process of moving the exercises forward. Now this. He clasped his palm over the speaker. "Howard, could you pick up on this line, please?"

Price turned to him, not wanting to leave what he was doing, but he could see from Mackey's expression that it was important.

Mackey held up four fingers to indicate the button and waited for Price to pick up.

"Now, let's get this straight, Colonel," said Mackey. "Harold Bengsten called you on Friday night."

"Yes, sir."

Price had been scanning a report. His eyes flickered up and met Mackey's.

"And you talked about what?"

"The weather, sir." Dimauro almost began to laugh. He was young for a colonel, and his voice sounded boyish, enthusiastic. "General Bengsten said you knew about it. You did, sir—didn't you?"

81

"I just want you to run through it again."

"Yes, sir. I tried to give the SACEUR an estimate of the amount of snow that would fall and the conditions—temperature, wind, chill factor, and so forth. I mentioned the Bergeron-Findeisen effect, sir."

"Could you explain that, Colonel?"

"Well, he seemed to be interested in putting as much snow as possible on the ground. For the exercises."

Mackey waited and Dimauro went on. "I didn't go through it, because the general, he— Would you like me to now, sir?"

"Yes, please. If you don't mind, Colonel."

"Well, within the clouds the heating effect of the sun sometimes causes an even greater transfer of water vapor to seeded ice crystals, thereby increasing precipitation."

"Seeded clouds?" Price asked. "You mean we've seeded these clouds?"

"Yes, sir. We still are. As per General Bengsten's orders."

Price's hand came down. The papers he was holding thwacked on his knee. "Butler," he said to one of the men he'd been conferring with, "I've got it."

"Go on, Colonel," Mackey said.

Dimauro's voice lost some of its insouciance. "But in cloud masses with preexisting ice crystals and minute solid crystalline particles call ice nuclei, the temperatures within the formation could descend—and the reason I was calling is that they have, sir—could descend to zero degrees Fahrenheit or lower without the droplets freezing and falling. Then a phenomenon called the Bergeron-Findeisen process is triggered. The amount of snow to be expected is increased at a coefficient rate. A factor of two, maybe three."

"You mean a blizzard," Mackey said.

"Well, yes. A blizzard."

"He then advised me"—there was a pause—"*ordered* me, sir, to commence seeding operations."

"Three planes, you say?" Price broke in.

"Well, I didn't, but, yes—three planes, sir."

"They've been up since?"

"Saturday morning, sir. May I ask what this is all about?"

Said Mackey, "Tell me this, Colonel—the voice on Friday night—he identified himself as General Bengsten?"

"Sure did. I mean, I served under the general in Vietnam and I'd recognize—" There was a pause. "Could you tell me what this is all about?"

"Please answer my question, Colonel."

"Yes, sir. Code and everything. Sir?"

"Yes, Colonel."

"What are your orders now? I mean, shall I pull in the planes? The Soviets have buzzed them several times already, and the amount of snow we can expect is—"

Mackey motioned to Price, then lowered the receiver into its yoke.

Price did the same. "Bad connection?"

Mackey nodded and crossed a leg, turning himself away from the others, who were watching him. He wondered if he were being presented a *fait accompli*, a situation in which he was being availed a passing tactical advantage that would probably never happen again and should not be ignored. And, my God, the possibilities, if enough snow could be put down quickly.

Mackey grasped the back of his neck and rubbed it and almost laughed out loud. It was probably the only brilliant thing Harold Bengsten ever did or would do. The irony of it—snow, it was usually considered a Soviet medium. They held exercises—or what passed for such—in Siberia every year. But here, if they got enough—Mackey stopped there.

But the ploy, Bengsten's—one discrete act, but timed perfectly. He hadn't mentioned it, of course, during the visit earlier, but that was Bengsten. Nevertheless, it had taken guts and didn't detract from the elegance of the effect. A small move, as with a pawn, *en passant*.

Kork. What did Mackey know about him? A Russian to the core, Kork could be bellicose but imperturbable, pugnacious but conciliatory, angry while happy, and cunningly blind. He could be hateful, loving, cruel, and forgiving, a martinet one moment, everybody's friend the next, and all in a morning, an hour, a mood. Kork was unpredictable, and therefore not really controllable. But Mackey was convinced he'd jump. He'd have to. The snow was a threat that couldn't be ignored.

The phone—the fourth line—had begun ringing again.

83

Price picked it up and listened. "No, Colonel—the general's busy." He listened for a moment, then said, "You have your orders. Follow them." Price hung up.

And had Bengsten been prompted or directed by Harper? Directed, no. Prompted? Maybe in the same way Mackey himself was being.

Harper. A politician. And deft, from all Mackey knew of him.

Maybe—Mackey reached down and refastened the buckles on his snow packs—a President or a Western leader couldn't plan and initiate a war here in Europe, no matter how necessary, because of the horror of the last war, because of all the nukes on both sides, because of the risk of an all-out engagement. But then again, wars were like women. They had to be wooed. Consent was required, whether engineered or not, and not only in the West. The whole nation had to say yes, or at least a solid majority. Even Stalin had had to deal with that.

Once again Mackey nearly smiled thinking of Bengsten. He also thought of the Ems dispatch.

And Patton and his statement to McNarney at the end of the war? What was it, again? "We are going to have to fight them sooner or later, within the next generation." And later in the conversation, ". . . just let me handle it down here. In ten days I can have enough incidents happen to have us at war with those sons of bitches and make it look like their fault." And then to his aide, Harkness, after he hung up. "I really believe that we're going to fight them, and if this country doesn't do it now, it will be taking them on years later when the Russians are ready for it, and we'll have an awful time whipping them." It had been a mistake, though. Patton should never have opened his mouth.

Mackey looked up at Price, questioning him.

"Me?" The large black man shook his head. "I try not to think too much. I run an army, I got to stick to the facts." He glanced down at the reports in his hands. "Right now we've got on the average of thirty-eight plus inches of snow on the ground. And then for some as yet unexplained reason we've got the contingents of the BAR that aren't involved in the exercises moving into Saxony."

Mackey turned to him. He hadn't known that.

"We've got the French staging some sort of build-up on their borders with the Federal Republic and Belgium."

Nor that.

"And finally"—Price took a step toward Mackey—"from what I know of those guys on the other side of the river, we've got one pissed off old man who'd sooner fight than eat. He's got a mighty big club in his hands, and if he's going to use it, it's got to be soon."

Mackey thought for a moment. It would be wise to pull the tanks back, say, into a crescent just beyond Uelzen and the Ilmenau, but he didn't want to do anything extraordinary. And perhaps they were best where they were, as a kind of bait.

And the Blue Team units, attacking from the west. He'd sent the air-assault elements in wide arcs, running down the flanks of Red Team and along the banks of the Elbe to the north and the line of the frontier to the south. Maybe he should call them in? But again that would be deviating from the battle proposal. Bengsten would call. The observers with him would be put on notice.

"Let's just make sure the units in the field remain dispersed and resupplied. I want all fuel tanks topped up, wherever possible, and all weapons stocks at a hundred percent.

"And let's declare a mini-truce at"—he glanced at the clock; it got dark early—"fourteen hundred hours. For a hot meal.

"After that I want the tanks to remain wherever they are. The more snow that builds up on them the better. Skeleton crews, two men at most. The rest are to be lifted to Uelzen. Have them report to Werbiskis. Did he get what we wanted?"

"So he says."

"And we better get this thing out of here, Howard." Mackey meant the mobile command center. "Meet me in Uelzen in, say"—he checked his watch—"three hours."

Mackey had opened the door and was about to step out.

"But, Mack—what if he's just sitting there?"

"Who?"

"Volodya Kirill."

Mackey turned up the collar of his field jacket and tightened his cap on his brow. It was the question he'd been avoiding—what if Kork didn't rise to the bait, what if he just sat there?

Mackey looked down at his hands as he fitted on his gloves. But he had decided already, hadn't he? Years ago. Or it had been decided for him.

He looked out at the driving snow. "We'll blow him a kiss." He stepped out and closed the door.

Monday, A.M.
Bonn
F.G.R.

The Defense Ministry's Hardt Höhe complex was a modern steel and glass structure that had been built on a rise just outside the capital.

Kronenberger swiveled in her office chair and looked out through the wall of glass, across the sloping fields of Rhineland farms, toward the river in the distance. Already snow had covered the roads and the riverbank. The water was black and inky, out past the ice and snow where the current was strong. A stiff breeze was mottling the surface with whitecaps. Cars along the esplanade passed in a hush that was chilling, like death.

While she listened to the tape that was being played to her over the telephone, Kronenberger removed her glasses and placed them on the desk blotter. All morning long she had been trying to make up the work she had ignored during the past week, memoranda in Dutch, French, and Italian, and she found she had to concentrate on the flow of English words, the assonantal slur of the American accents.

But Mackey's voice was familiar to her, and once she understood the gist of the conversation and recognized the other participants, she leaned back in the padded leather chair, turned herself away from the desk and crossed her legs.

She massaged the bridge of her nose where the glasses had been riding and promised herself she'd arrange to have contact lenses made. She was tired and the reading in her present post, which she'd held now for only eight months, was enormous. Her predecessor had told her most of it was worthless, but she suspected that was why he now occupied a cubicle in a drab office building in Stuttgart.

What was it about the SACEUR's particular tone that she found so off-putting? It was irritatingly patronizing when he was speaking to less senior officers, obsequious when in the company of heads of state. If for no other reason, she considered the man untrustworthy.

Now this.

When the tape had finished, Kronenberger began rubbing her eyes, slowly, gently. She knew it was wrong; the doctor had told her so. But it felt good. If genius was an infinite capacity for detail, then she was no genius, she decided. Her head was swimming with facts, German facts mostly, but French, Dutch, British, Italian, Canadian, American—"And where are they now?"

"General Bengsten has retired to the observation center near Uelzen. A command post will be established for him there. Generals Mackey and Price are at Blue Team headquarters, which—"

"I know." It was a mobile command shelter that could be repositioned on short notice and was presently located fifteen kilometers east of Uelzen.

Kronenberger thanked the contact at 12th Panzer-Grenadier headquarters and rang off.

She did not reset the glasses on her face. She sat there in the deep cushions of her office chair, rocking slightly, her fingers moving slowly over her eyelids.

From the new insight she had into Mackey's personality, she judged that he had only been drawing Bengsten out. But Mackey's request to ascertain the thickness of the ice in the Elbe—well, it was just a precaution and perhaps necessary from a military point of view, but it was provocative as well, now, during the exercises.

In the distance she heard three low drones, of a tug or a barge signaling for a bridge to open. When she looked up she saw it had pushed right up the channel and shattered the ice. Snowy plates roiled in its wake.

And Bengsten—maybe she could make a case against him. For the present, at least, the man should be watched. But with caution. If her people made themselves obvious, she would be in trouble. Her career would be on the line. She tapped a button on the control panel near her right hand. "Hofmann—may I see you for a moment, please?"

An hour later Kronenberger took the elevator down to the subterranean computer center of the Hardt Höhe complex, which was a series of long rooms that glass walls divided. She proceeded to the lounge, asked for, and after some grumbling received the assistance of several data-processing officers who had been playing cards there.

Their attitude neither surprised nor angered her. Spit and polish and yes-sir-no-sir nonsense had no place in a modern military setting where two-thirds of the soldiers were technicians, not infantrymen. And in a nuclear age such spirit was excessive, if not downright suicidal. Kronenberger believed that the reaction the West German people had felt toward any manifestation of militarism after the war was justified and appropriate.

But she wondered if all the complex electronic gadgets before her would count for much if the Soviets released their tank armies.

A captain volunteered to carry some of the large, print-out sheets into a conference room, and he held the door for her. There they could hear only the hush of the air-venting system. The light was intense and achromatic.

She opened the information out and read the individual sheets all down the length of three long tables. She then reached into her uniform jacket for her glasses. Her hand automatically went to the other pocket as well, for the package of cigarettes. But she had stopped smoking three weeks before. It was at times like this—quiet moments in which judgment was required—that she missed them most.

The captain had not left the room. She turned to him.

"May I be of any further service, Colonel?" he asked. He was younger than she, with curly, graying hair. His eyes were playful. Vogel. He had asked Kronenberger out on several occasions, and, when she finally accepted, the evening ended in heated combat in the back of a taxi and his telling her that she deserved the epithet of Ice Maiden, which some others of his age and rank had given her. She had laughed, but the comment had stung her. It wasn't that she was indisposed to him, but that the nature of her commission and her plans for herself required circumspection and discretion.

"No, thank you, Captain," she said, fitting the bows of her glasses under her long blond hair. She then removed her uniform jacket.

Vogel was still there. "Shall we give it one more try?" he asked.

She glanced down at all the paper on the tables. Back on her desk an entire stack of memoranda awaited her. "I have a dinner engagement tonight."

"May I ask with whom?"

"*Bundesminister* Ludeke," she said, matter-of-factly.

It quelled him. She only heard the door open, and then all was quiet.

She began to wade through the print-outs, wishing somehow they could devise more legible computer characters, some that hadn't been designed with toothpicks by children in grade school.

But she found nothing in Bengsten's many public statements to support the view he had expressed at 12th Panzer-Grenadier headquarters. Nor in the private conversations to which the Bundeswehr had had access. He had been thoroughly cautious until this morning, she concluded, and she disliked him all the more for his stealth.

Not so Mackey.

As NORTHAG commander he had been asked on numerous occasions to speak to German civic groups and other audiences, and each time it had been as though the American had been trying to educate them about the Soviets. Or was it something more definite than that? Kronenberger thought so.

For instance, he had begun one speech with a quote taken from a text by Sokolovskii, the architect of modern Soviet military strategy. ". . . in a just war, which can only be waged by our state, Soviet military strategy will have a decisive, active, offensive character." Mackey went on to characterize the three main elements of such an offensive: shock to stun the enemy; power to crush the initial defenses; and speed to seize key strategic positions so that the enemy could then be beaten in detail. Sokolovskii predicted advances of up to seventy miles in a twenty-four-hour period. The Weser was only seventy miles from the Elbe, the Ems seventy more, the Rhine seventy again.

Mackey then examined the statement with the sort of detail that Kronenberger found refreshing: Sokolovskii's contention was based on a campaign in Manchuria when Soviet forces had been operating over barren ground and facing light resistance. During the Yom Kippur War, even

89

the highly regarded Israeli tank army was stopped cold by a properly organized defense. Mackey cited numbers and types of tanks and the armament that was employed against them in a manner that must have been boring to his audience but Kronenberger thought informative.

He then went on to question the logistics infrastructure necessary to support a pace of seventy miles per day. He noted that even in East Germany the GSFG was supplied by rail; and a depot that served three of twelve Guards divisions, which represented the "army within the army" (that is, their elite forces), was twenty miles from their post. Goods had to be off-loaded and trucked.

He wondered if they intended to resupply their advancing army by rail. If so, he judged that it was impossible to put down seventy miles of track per day, especially if a retreating force destroyed bridges, other railbeds, and made the establishment of any communications links difficult. Consequently, much reliance would have to be placed on over-the-road transportation, which even in the most heavily industrialized areas of the Soviet Union was often sporadic.

Railroads were vulnerable to interdiction strikes, as the Soviets had proved themselves during World War II. The gauge of Soviet rails was broader than that of European track.

Facing no armed resistance in Czechoslovakia in '68, Soviet armor ground to a halt. Tanks stood defenseless in Prague. There simply was not enough available road transportation to keep them in fuel, food, and essential equipment. The tank formations had passed by filling stations and gas pumps without knowing what they were. Elements had become lost; map reading, it seemed, was also a problem.

"Their experience in Czechoslovakia points up two other traditional weaknesses in the Red Army: command and control in small units, and the need for a loyal *and* skilled officer corps. The communist movement is doctrinaire and revolutionary, but ardent revolutionaries do not always make good officers.

"If after twenty-four hours NATO had chosen to step into Czechoslovakia, we would have found a Red Army that was unable to prosecute an engagement, much less a battle or a war. Only a massive airlift of needed goods salvaged the operation." Mackey then went on to critique the Soviet air resources, which were vast but of poor quality and not really suited to blitzkrieg warfare, as outlined by Sokolovskii.

In conclusion Mackey returned to the three major elements of Soviet military strategy.

Could they shock us by a surprise attack? Perhaps, but not likely. Could they overpower our initial defenses? That's an open question, but I think not. Do they possess the speed to seize key strategic positions and hold them until the mass of their army arrives? On that score I think my doubts are well founded, and—ladies and gentlemen—it is my contention that once you deny the Soviets any one of those three elements, you deny them the continent. And they themselves know this.

Then why the massive army that's facing us? Simply stated, the Soviets have and still are increasing their military power in Europe to give us the impression that they can dominate Europe and consequently the world. They seek to undermine our resolve and, perhaps, provide themselves an opportunity.

We know that the Soviets have imperialistic ambitions, but we also know that they now lack the economic diversity to become an imperialistic power. While they build themselves up, they have raised a threat—it's like a big bluff—over there in East Germany. But if we give them a chance, I'm firmly convinced that they will seize the moment and drive their tank armies across Europe.

After the speech somebody in the audience had asked Mackey if he was suggesting that the Soviets could and should be beaten.

He said that he didn't think it appropriate for him to address that question.

But in his private talks to his troops—Kronenberger glanced at her watch, nearly lunchtime and she was suddenly ravenous—Mackey had been more open. She would lose her table at the restaurant she frequented, but she admired Mackey's easy command of history. His dossier said that he was an avid reader. On leave he traveled to scenes of former battles and studied the terrain. He had learned Chinese in order to read Sun Tzu and Mao.

In speaking to a group of recently arrived junior officers, he cited Leonidas's victory at Thermopylae in 480 B.C. Three hundred men had stopped ten thousand Persians for three days.

"During our Civil War, gentlemen, the Union army was victorious only because more boys in blue marched down the road with guns, bullets, and blood. It was the most costly lesson that the U.S. military ever mislearned. We got the idea that numbers alone could win. But Vietnam showed us different. All the numbers in the world can't beat an inspired enemy.

"Now, those three hundred Greeks knew what they were fighting for: not just their wives and homes and families, but for all those things we consider best about Western civilization. In a word, they didn't want to be slaves."

Well put, Kronenberger thought; Leonidas and his troops, all of whom had died to a man, had been Spartans. They had had their own slaves.

"And that's why you're here in Germany and make no mistake about that. Those men on the other side of the Elbe represent the dark side of our tradition. Individually they're no different from you, but together they are a cancer. You're here to make sure it does not spread. I want you to pay attention. We're going to show you how to fight outnumbered and win."

Again Kronenberger checked the clock. This really wasn't getting her anywhere. Standing, she began to skim the rest of the information, but every once in a while she was stopped.

"The only good army is an active army." It was a quote taken from one of the Ottoman Sultans, she thought.

"The defensive form of war is in itself stronger than the offensive. We must make use of it only as long as our weakness compels us to do so." That was Clausewitz.

Then she read, "When the necessity of war is once recognized by a nation, nothing further is needed than the resolve of a leader to conquer or die." Von Scharnhorst.

Finally, her eyes caught on another statement. It was part of a drill chant used by the 101st Air Assault Division, the pride of Mackey's command.

"Troopers—is there an enemy?"

"Sir—there is an enemy."

"Troopers—is the enemy threatening us?"

"Sir—the enemy is threatening us."

"Troopers—what must we do?"

"Sir—we must meet him and defeat him."

Kronenberger straightened up and removed her glasses. She wondered if she had put Hofmann on the wrong man.

3

For several hours Kork had been sitting in a wingback armchair. It was an old item and ponderous, with claw feet and deep, stuffed cushions that had long since assumed the shape of his body. He had had the orderlies carry it over to a window. There he had taken up his position. In a vast field a single BMP-80, the GSFG's primary APC, was churning back and forth. Twice already it had traced the full length of the expanse without slowing.

Alexeyev pulled up a chair and sat. He glanced out at the dark green wedge of the APC, then back at Kork. "Frankly, Volodya Kirill, I don't think we have anything to worry about. It's all just smoke and shadow, something to restore their confidence, make them feel they're on top again.

"And then—what can he possibly do that we can't? The snow is the same for him there as it is for us here. He won't attack us, he can't. Public opinion—"

"Mackey?" Kork's laugh was short and sharp. "Do you think he gives a damn about public opinion? My good friend, you may have studied the West, but I have studied men like Mackey. He is a warrior. Only victory means something to him."

"But he's constrained, Volodya Kirill, as we all are. He by NATO and Washington, we by—"

"You think so? Under whose auspices are those exercises being held over there? And who pressed to have them moved up? And what about these other provocations?" Kork dug in the pocket of his khaki cardigan sweater. He

95

was sitting with one leg folded under him. There was a cup of tea on the left arm of the chair, a telephone on a small stool near it. He glanced down at the memoranda, his eyes small and hard. "The British, the French—they're all in on it. The bastard—he's got something up his sleeve and his sleeves are"—he flourished his hands; his face was getting redder—"copious." Kork pushed himself back in the chair and looked back out at the APC.

"But what would they have to gain here in Europe?"

Kork leaned forward. Had the APC slowed? He thought it had. "We have a saying in Siberia, Vassil—'No cur as fierce as the cur of a cripple'—and that's exactly what a new reunified Germany, allied with the West, would represent—a big dog at the portals.

"No"—Kork pushed himself back in the chair and wrapped his hands around a knee. The wry smile had not left his face and his eyes were shining. He did not shave high onto his cheeks, which were bearded with fine, curly hair—"and this Harper, this President of theirs, is no *boy*—" He said the last word in English and snapped his fingers.

"Scout," Alexeyev supplied.

"That's right. He's not at all what he appears." Kork thought of how it all dovetailed: the peculiar Western stealth that Harper had used to mask the build-up, coming right out in the open with the question, debating the forward exercises with the Dutch and Germans in public, even going on television to explain it to his people. And Kork could not help admiring that. It was nothing short of brilliant, and right under Moscow's nose. "Waltzing us two steps forward and one step back. The son of a bitch has already even made his excuses, before"—Kork's face suddenly flushed an alarming shade, nearly vermillion—"*before* the fight!"

An orderly had approached them. "Excuse me, Chief Marshal, but perhaps you haven't noticed the phone."

"What?"

"The phone, sir." The young man pointed to the telephone. The small red light was winking.

Kork waved him off.

"But it's Moscow, sir."

"Tell them I'm busy."

"It's the first secretary, sir."

Kork hesitated before picking it up. Once more he looked out at the APC.

Alexeyev began to stand, as though he would leave, but Kork grasped his sleeve and pulled him back into the chair.

Kork wasn't religious, but he was superstitious and he said a small prayer. He picked up the receiver, closed his eyes, and rested his head against the soft cushion of the tall chair.

"Volodya Kirill?" a smooth voice asked. "How's my chief marshal this afternoon?" Voronov's voice was clear and Kork was thankful for that. Intonations, inflections, stress—it would all matter. "Been napping?"

"Oh, well—it's that sort of day, sir," Kork said in the bumptious, self-effacing manner he always adopted with important politicians. To them he was a character, but he was old army, the strike force that had beaten the Wehrmacht, and Kork would do nothing to detract from the image. "It begins to snow and I curl up."

"And the fireworks, haven't they disturbed you?"

Kork could picture Voronov in his long office in the Kremlin, sitting at the desk that never had anything on it, looking as placid as ever. He was a stout man with silvery hair that he combed back in precise finger waves. He had a small mustache, also gray, and his skin always looked freshly talcked.

"It's a new kind of war they're fighting over there. Quiet. Nothing but snow and cold."

"So I understand. And how much have you gotten?"

Kork thought for a moment. Voronov was proud of his own war record. Unlike all of the other, older Politburo members, he had not been a political commissar. Voronov had fought in the Guards with Kork. Kork's eyes flickered open. Once more he glanced out to the APC. "As a tanker I know you'll understand when I say nearly too much."

There was a long pause. When Voronov began speaking again, his tone had changed. "Volodya Kirill," he began, "I'm here, and you're there. We can talk, but it's not the same.

"There are some here with me now who consider their seeding of those clouds a provocation, direct and undeniable. There are others who say they had no way of controlling the process, that perhaps their general merely wanted to put down a little snow to make their excercises interest-

97

ing, but as you can appreciate, other issues must be considered."

Again there was a pause, this time longer. Kork thought he heard the sound of a cigarette lighter clicking open. That would be Voronov's way—slow, steady, sure. He had good judgment.

"Are we being tested?" Voronov asked in a rhetorical manner. "Oh, yes. Doubtless. But my question to you, comrade, is if we have been provoked?"

Kork too waited. He did not want to seem overly eager, and quickly he reconsidered all he had been thinking about since he had received the air command report concerning the cloud seeding. Was he being rash? He thought about Mackey and what he knew of him, and he looked out the window yet again. He didn't think so. Could he win, if push came to shove?

Unhurried, enunciating every word clearly, Kork said, "We have been provoked."

"Ah."

In the background, on the Moscow end of the line, Kork could now hear other voices speaking rapidly, some nearly in anger, and he held the receiver tightly to his ear, trying to make out what was being said.

"Then I want you to respond, Volodya Kirill. Something . . . appropriate, so that they'll know."

"Well, I could—"

"No, no. We have confidence in you. So far this is just between army and army. I wonder if we could keep it that way?"

Kork felt a rush, a kind of elation. "I'll do my best."

"That's all we ask. Keep me informed."

The line went dead.

Kork tried to set the receiver in its yoke, but he couldn't seem to get it right and an orderly rushed to help.

"Tea. Please," Kork said. "Vassil?" He glanced at Alexeyev, who only shook his head. And in his expression did Kork read a kind of resignation? He thought so. "Then I've got some things for you to do.

"We'll begin with the place they convene, the number again, Vassil?"

"Twelfth Panzer-Grenadier headquarters."

Kork laughed. "Yes, that's it. Panzer-Grenadier headquarters. Sounds like something, doesn't it? Very romantic.

Let's wipe it right off the map. Throw them some heavy 'grenades,' make it a target. We'll put the Heinies on notice about who they are dealing with and who'll be the first to get burnt.

"And those planes, the ones with the crystals." Kork swiped his hand, like an angry bear batting away flies. "Use their own missiles, the ones the ministry sent us for demonstration.

"And then"—the APC was again having trouble with a drift—"jam their radios, their navigational instruments, anything, everything that they've got."

"But if we do that now, then later—"

"There isn't going to be any later," Kork snapped. "This is it, now."

"But I can only say—respectfully, Chief Marshal—that I think it's a mistake. It won't take them any more than a few hours—"

"Then, it'll be my mistake, Colonel-General. When you're in command you can make your own. Until then, please carry out my orders. If you don't, I'll replace you, and that's a promise."

Kork stood, feeling ashamed to have treated his protégé so harshly. "Now then, you'll find me in the strike center, watching the"—he again waved his hand—"pictures.

"Vassil." He reached out and took the other man's hand. "Never take counsel of your fears." It had been said by the American Confederate General Jackson, and Kork knew Alexeyev would appreciate the irony. "And did we start this?" Kork's eyes were nearly almond shaped. Oriental. They were yellow and sagacious but hard.

"No, Volodya Kirill, we did not start this," Alexeyev said, although he thought it was hardly the point.

Monday, P.M.
A GSFG Tank Park
Eldena
G.D.R.

The half-track carried Colonel Mikhaylov and Lieutenant Bukhara only as far as the edge of the tank park where the armor was lined up, row upon row. There was room for the vehicle to pass through the columns, but the front wheels sideslipped where the snow had drifted over the tank skirts. Mikhaylov had the driver stop. The two officers got out.

Mikhaylov was still in his thirties. He was nearly bald and his nose was short and bulbous and red. He had stomach trouble, abetted by all the tea he drank and tobacco he smoked. Whenever the temperature fell below freezing, he caught colds. Already he could feel one coming on, the first of the inevitable concatenation.

Standing orders on alert required at least one crewman to be in each tank around the clock, but Mikhaylov could see lights through the drivers' slits in only a half-dozen, and he knew what was going on. It was like an icebox in those tanks, especially after three or four days of hard cold. The chill rose straight up from the ground and was unbearable. Then, in every fourth or fifth tank the men got together with some coals in a bucket and a few bottles of bootleg vodka they bought from German farmers or made themselves.

"But this—?"

"Berezniki." Bukhara said the name precisely, as though trying to make Mikhaylov remember it. "*Conscript* Berezniki."

"He could be back at his barracks." They were trudging through deep snow toward the engine Mikhaylov could hear running deep within the park.

"No, sir, I've checked. He's the man and he's out here. It's his tour."

The turret hatch was open a crack to vent their tobacco smoke, and Mikhaylov could see four men clustered around the tank commander's seat. Over it they had placed a board. They were playing cards, and—Mikhaylov allowed himself a thin smile—the man whom Bukhara had described was among them.

He had taken off his greatcoat, his uniform jacket, and shirt, and was sitting there in his long underwear. Indeed, he looked dwarfish, almost like a child. His chest was tiny, his shoulders thin. He had set his leather tanker's cap at a rakish angle with the flaps dangling loose, and he was chatting with the men, his voice loud, having to overcome the oscillating roar of the diesel.

But it was his face, which was pale, haggard, and old,

that made him seem so odd, like a . . . puppet, that was it. A caricature of a woebegone soldier with his oversized boots that he'd also taken off and set on an ammo hatch, the suspenders, the cigarette stuck in the corner of his mouth, the little hairy line that was his attempt at a mustache, his child's body and old man's face that made him seem eternally weary but willing to put up with a dozen armies, if need be.

Mikhaylov prised up the hatch. The downdraft blew some cards off the table and one of the men shouted, "Hey, asshole—you live in a barn?"

But Berezniki had stood, raising his hand in salute, his eyes wide. It was a ludicrous gesture, the way he held out his palm, the thumb clutching the cards, more like an extended wave.

The others craned their necks to look up. Even the pair of legs stirred.

"Oh, Colonel—" the captain said, slipping his cards in his pocket and motioning the others to get rid of theirs. "Welcome aboard."

"Don't get up. Don't move. I want all of you just as you were." Mikhaylov's snowy boots made the metal slots slippery and he nearly fell. When the lieutenant closed the hatch behind him, the tank, which had been designed for four, was crowded.

Mikhaylov pointed to the engine. Gerasim reached for the cutoff. The harsh pinging softened to clicks and then all was quiet. The interior lights dimmed. One man unhooked the lead wire to the electric fire, another switched off the cooker.

"Do I come out, sir?" There was a man who had crawled right in over the engine.

Gerasim was a blond young man with broad features, yellow eyes, and prominent canines that looked like fangs when he smiled. He glanced at Mikhaylov. "Just continue on, Stiva. I don't think the colonel would want to disturb you.

"We're replacing seals in the pneumatic system, sir," Gerasim went on, somewhat sheepishly, his eyes moving around the tank to see what else was out of place. "It's a tough job out here, like this, with—" When his eyes met Mikhaylov's he stopped speaking.

101

"You have a work order for this?"

Gerasim took it from a pocket and handed it to Mikhaylov.

The colonel looked at both sides, as though to make certain of its authenticity. He could well have signed it, but he couldn't remember, given all the scrambling they'd had to do for the alert. It was either his signature or a damned good imitation. "Who requested this?"

"The tank commander, sir."

"And he is—" Mikhaylov looked around at the other two.

"Back at his quarters, sir."

"And these men?"

"Mine, sir. We were playing a game of cards, sir," Gerasim confessed. "Conscript Berezniki has volunteered to remain with us here, as long as it takes."

Volunteered! Mikhaylov thought, to stay inside here where it was warm with—he had to bend to look into a pot that was still bubbling; there was a thick ham bone in it, two leeks, some slices of potato and the water was green, probably peas—a little luck in the pot. He was probably being paid for it and had arranged the whole goddamned thing.

Mikhaylov felt suddenly tired, overwhelmed by it all. He glanced down at the cigarettes on the playing board. They'd been wagering with them, but Mikhaylov himself often played cards with Gerasim for stakes far higher.

He glanced up at Lieutenant Bukhara, who was examining his cap. "Ask him where my magazine is," he said in a low voice.

"Are you speaking to me, sir?"

Mikhaylov only nodded.

Bukhara asked the question in Kazakh.

Berezniki did not turn to him. He was still smiling and his eyes were fixed on Mikhaylov. In them the colonel read fear and awe but innocence too, as though he couldn't understand a word of what was going on, as if the complexity of the situation were too great for him: that if he were just to hold the pose of his initial reaction—the salute—on seeing Mikhaylov, all the trouble might blow over.

Bukhara asked him again, this time louder.

Berezniki only turned his head to him. His brow furrowed. He turned to Gerasim, questioning.

"Does anybody here speak Uralian?" Bukhara asked.
Nobody replied.

"This man"—Bukhara indicated Berezniki—"was speaking when we entered. Certainly he wasn't speaking to himself."

One of Gerasim's men cleared his throat. "Sir," he said to Mikhaylov, "it's not as though he tries to make himself understood. It's just babbling."

Mikhaylov turned to Gerasim, and in a low, steely voice he explained. "Yesterday afternoon a magazine—*my* magazine—disappeared from the officers' day room. This man"—he pointed at Berezniki—"was in that room. He was under no orders to be near the building, in the building, or in the room. He had no business there. For somebody who doesn't understand what's being said, it seems to me he makes out quite well. I'll have no thieves in this command, and no liars. If he doesn't produce that magazine, I'll have him taken to the guardhouse, court-martialed, and shot. Perhaps somebody can make that clear to him."

As Mikhaylov had spoken, Berezniki had cocked his head this way and that, like a bird turning an ear to the ground.

. Bukhara stepped toward the command seat and reached for the maintenance manual. He showed it to Berezniki. "Book," he said in Russian, "but soft. Soft. Paper."

Berezniki only looked up at the others, terror in his eyes. Bukhara slid the book back into its holder.

"Let's see if we can find it," said Gerasim. He and his two crewmen simply turned and looked around, opening lockers, looking under the command seat, up overhead where, in nets, the personal effects of the tank crew were stored.

Bukhara reached for Berezniki's greatcoat, his uniform jacket, and finally his boots, which he turned to the light and peered into. Haltingly at first, he began to pull every type of cloth and paper out of them—a soiled engine rag, felt from the print shop, an old newspaper rolled into a ball and stuffed into the toes—as though the man had made nests for his feet.

Mikhaylov wondered if the man had been issued those boots and decided he had not. He had traded for them. He had wanted them big. For heat.

Still, Bukhara found no magazine, not a trace of it.

"Get your clothes on," Mikhaylov said to Berezniki. "We'll have some of your own people question you." He straightened up.

Berezniki looked at Gerasim, who pointed to the coat and boots. He looked at the others, each in turn, his eyes now pleading, wide with fright, and then he reached for the top button of his long underwear.

"No, no," Gerasim said, glancing at Mikhaylov and wanting to smile, "on. *On.*" He picked up the little man's jacket and tried to hand it to him, but it fell to the deck.

Berezniki was unfastening the other buttons deliberately, one at a time. His hands were shaking, his chin was on his chest.

And uttering a small sound, like a whimper, he raised his head. There were tears in his eyes. He opened the underwear.

There, pinned neatly as a liner, were pictures of nearly naked women in absurdly suggestive poses: one on a bearskin rug with her back arched and legs splayed; another, seen from behind, her head between her legs; yet another licking a phallic bedpost as somebody with hairy arms, who was out of the picture, was mounted on her back. Berezniki began undoing his belt, as though he would step out of his trousers.

Gerasim turned to Mikhaylov. "Is that your magazine, Colonel?"

The other men wanted to laugh. It was a story that would be told all over the tank park. Eventually it would get back to headquarters.

And then—Mikhaylov sighed and forced himself to consider Berezniki's face again; the deep creases of a man who had lived out in the open most of his life, who had not eaten well, whose one thought for most of his life had been, and continued to be, mere survival.

The army. Mikhaylov felt suddenly bleak. And the cold. He could detect a definite tightness in his chest now. "No." He motioned Bukhara toward the ladder and the hatch. "That's not my magazine."

Bukhara did not look at Mikhaylov. He turned and fitted on his cap.

"But," Gerasim asked, his eyes too wide, "don't you still want Berezniki to accompany you?"

Mikhaylov didn't—he couldn't—answer him.

It was snowing harder than ever, and the wind was soughing through the fir trees on the margin of the park.

Or was it something else? He stopped and cocked his head. The attack siren? It was hard to tell. Mikhaylov had always heard it back at headquarters where it was louder, and with the wind and now the noise overhead he couldn't be sure.

Helicopter rotors. Dozens of them. Mikhaylov looked up, heedless of the snow that stung his eyes.

They were right overhead in the snow clouds, and the men in the tank—Gerasim and the others—had lifted the turret to look.

It seemed to come right out of nowhere, an odd-shaped craft with stubby wings that were laden with rockets. It was dark, lightless, and the two cannon barrels in the fuselage were large and gaping, like nostrils.

It only hovered there for a moment and then veered off, almost rolling right over, and was gone, back up into the snow.

That was when the SAMs lashed out, and above them, like a fireworks display, brilliant orange fireballs appeared.

A concussion off to their right knocked Mikhaylov against the turret.

Bukhara had gone down. There was something odd about the way his hat had been knocked back.

But standing right out on the front of the tank shaking a fist at the sky was Berezniki, still wearing only his long johns and tanker's cap.

The concussion of another blast knocked Mikhaylov off the tank body into the snow.

And a good thing too. Debris was falling everywhere. Hunks of hot metal hissed into the snow. An entire tail section of a helicopter fell on a nearby tank, engulfing it in its fiery mouth. The stabilizer rotor kept spinning in the wind.

And bodies—pieces of men—were all around him.

And Bukhara. Mikhaylov scrambled around to the other side of the tank, on top of which Bukhara was still lying. He was just about at Mikhaylov's eye level, but the colonel waited for what seemed like a break in the firestorm overhead.

He raised himself up, grabbed Bukhara, and pulled him down into the snow.

The hat was sodden and it seemed to stick to his hand. He jerked away but it came with him. He looked down. The liner was vermillion, a red, wet hole.

And Berezniki was by his side. He raised Mikhaylov up, and with an expression that the colonel couldn't read—maybe pity, but a kind of joy too: for the wind and the wailing and the explosions that were occurring now in the distance—clasped him to his thin, wretched breast.

Harris hadn't known what had happened, what could have caused it. Nothing in the helicopter—the radio, the nav aids, radar, even the infrared systems—seemed to work; they were all jammed and out, and the windshield was a wall of white driving snow. Even the compass. Something was making it spin and catch and spin back.

Harris had gone forward into the cockpit where Herz was sitting with the pilot. Herz had that same thin smile on his face, mechanical and goonish.

"But I don't know where anybody else is," the pilot complained.

"Fuck 'm, they'll take care of themselves."

Harris didn't think they could. The company had rendezvoused on the Elbe and waited until the signal had arrived from headquarters. They had then proceeded down the bank of the river, slowly, tree-top level, jinking down into clearings, using whatever terrain cover they could find, and in single file. The snow was too heavy for anything else.

And then they had kept losing sight of the river in treeless areas or wherever farm fields ran down to the water. Everything was covered by snow—walls, sheds, roads, the river itself. There was no water.

"This is dumb," Harris said.

"What?" Herz had to remove his earphones.

Harris only pointed down. "Us."

"Not a chance." Herz's eyes were glassy, calm, as though he knew what he was doing.

"But what's that, Captain? Where's that?" Harris swept his hand across the gauges on the control panel. "It could be due north."

From the rear of the helicopter where the troopers were huddled with their skis, Lieutenant Reese appeared.

Herz turned and, seeing him, said to Harris, "That's up,

Sergeant." He jerked his thumb. "And that's down. And that's straight ahead. This isn't going to stop us. We're following the river."

"What river?" Harris had demanded. "Can you see a fucking river down there?"

Herz had only looked away, out the window he was sitting by.

"Really, sir," Reese had begun to say; he had a small compass in his hand and the needle was flicking and jumping, "I don't know what's doing this. I don't think it's our capability. Even if it is, I can't imagine our using it here so close—"

Herz turned on Harris instead of Reese. "Look it, you little bastard—you fucked up once already today. You wanna make it twice?"

Harris had searched the captain's bulging blue eyes that had not looked real, but like pale blue marble that stopped right there.

"Motherfuckin' robot," Harris had muttered.

"What?"

Harris had only looked away, trying to catch sight of something.

"What? What did you say, Sergeant?"

Reese turned to go.

"Stay here, Lieutenant. Did you hear what the sergeant said?"

Reese had said nothing, only looked back down at the compass.

"You want to repeat that?"

Harris had wondered what the helicopters behind them were doing. Were they following, and at the same speed? The terrain below was flat, a plain. If the others hadn't panicked and had proceeded . . . Maybe Herz was right, he had thought for a moment, but he had known better.

Given their flying time and speed, they already could have overflown the border, violated the frontier. And they couldn't know if the other ships were behind them.

Harris turned to Herz. "You're an asshole. You call me a little bastard again and I'll kick your ass. You got that?" He kept his eyes fixed on Herz until Herz looked away.

They'd both been in battle before. There was no rank or position when it came to dying.

And the pilot had understood what was being discussed.

He had begun easing the ship down, still maintaining some forward flight. Three hundred, two fifty. At two hundred, Harris caught something—a shape, huge and looming—out of the corner of his eyes, or at least he thought he did. When he glanced over it was gone. Nothing. What was that tall, out here in the country?

Radar pans. The massive, tower-mounted devices the Soviets had erected to counter the threat of cruise missiles.

But they had just passed over the snowy tops of a forest of pine trees and had broken into an open field that was bordered by a high wire fence.

"Are those tanks?" Reese asked. He was still standing between Harris and Herz.

And there were men in them. Two standing on a tank, a couple more in the turret hatch wearing the soft, dog-eared tanker's caps of the Red Army.

Harris' eyes met Herz's, briefly. Just a flash.

The pilot jerked the stick back and away, giving the rotors all he had.

Reese was hurled down into the darkness, toward the men.

The ship heeled over and fell off, the blades nearly clipping the turrets of the tank columns.

The pilot jerked it back and they just cleared the fence and the trees. He kept his eyes on the low windows that had been set into the fuselage below his feet. A clearing, anything, a road—they had to get down. The SAMs would be sent up in clusters.

A house. There it was. A guardhouse near a road.

The pilot laid the ship right over it.

They weren't there more than a few seconds when a missile, then two more streaked overhead. Too fast, too high. But sensing the helicopter, they sank. One caught the top of a tall tree and ripped into the forest, tumbling and exploding.

Soldiers had run out of the house, carbines, automatic weapons in their hands.

"Defensive fire," Hertz shouted.

The pilot didn't hear him. The ship lurched down and forward, right at the men, who scattered. And he followed the road where he could, not much farther off the ground than a tall truck.

Mühling had stopped into the café of the railroad station long before the first evening train back to Hitzacker.

There was a coin bank statue of a Negro on the back of the bar—an "African," he thought, bitterly remembering his embarrassment in the history class. A pfennig was placed in the palm of the outstretched hand, and when the lever was depressed, the arm sprang up at the elbow, the jaw dropped open, and the coin was slapped into the wide red mouth. As the arm came down some device inside said in English, "Thank you, sir. I is a hungry nigger." The voice was raspy, mechanical, and the laughing which followed sounded like the grinding of gears.

Yet Mühling had been standing in front of it for nearly two hours, drinking, throwing pennies into it, although he could really afford neither. Like the exercises, the calisthenics and weight lifting, he had performed in the gymnasium after the end of the class, the simple repetition seemed to calm him, help him to forget, but every once in a while it came back to him with a pang—what had been happening between them, not just the night before, but for many months now, ever since she had spoken of the chance of her winning the fellowship for graduate studies.

And he knew her too well not to realize that there had been much more to the seemingly minor incident in the back of the van. A year before, a half-year, they would have carried on somehow, had some fun, enjoyed the night and themselves. But it was as though the fellowship, the offer, had hardened her, made her definite about things, made her into somebody who outwardly—it was that which hurt most, her auburn hair, her smile, her large teeth that were spaced somewhat too far apart, the way she tilted her head to the side to watch him—was the same, but behind the dark eyes things were different, he could tell, and he knew the change would be permanent.

And the fellowship just pointed up the differences between them; she, the pretty one, the brilliant student, honored and admired, with a world of opportunities before her; and he, big and ungainly, just slogging through, a dummy.

He glanced at the statue. Yes, he'd be a wage slave the rest of his life, or at least some sort of slave. If he ever got out of the financial hole that his father, who was dead, and his mother, who was crippled, had been in, it would only be through plain dumb luck.

And to have seen her there in the Platz with Schwerin, who was everything Mühling would never be, to see him bend to her and that smile of his with the perfect teeth, the thin, definite shoulders, the way he always looked like a little pimp, the way she leaned back to watch him caused an anger that was deep and immediate and he'd never felt before. Like nausea, it had beaded his brow, made his vision blur, and his right leg had begun to twitch spasmodically, the way it always did after a wrestling match.

Mühling had to grasp the hand of the dummy to place the pfenning in its palm. He depressed the lever and then pointed to his glass.

He thought he heard, "Thank you, sir. I is an angry nigger."

"That's right," Mühling said through the raspy laughter. "That's right, that's right."

The bartender looked at him hard, assessing him before he filled the glass. Steinhager—he seldom drank it. Crazy juice. Mühling was waiting for it to work.

"Train soon, Karl?" he asked.

Mühling didn't answer, and the sting of the liquor didn't seem to help. As when he had jumped down from the rings in the gymnasium, too tired to go on, gasping for breath, and had looked up into the icy sheen on the grated windows, he now saw in a brilliant, silver flash a scene in which Annette and Schwerin were in some sumptuous hotel or at his house or on his boat—that was it, Mühling had heard the story of the boat and the shipbuilding father—on a bed that was as wide as a van, doing every manner of thing to each other. And she was loving it, throwing back her head and howling and shrieking. But the worst part of it was that he himself, Mühling, was somewhere about, up on deck at the wheel or performing some function as a navy.

No! he almost said aloud. I don't know Schwerin. He's probably just a little mouse. And I don't know that she really knows or cares for him. It's just that I've been drinking, I had been last night. She wanted to sit with me this morning. I'm being a fool.

But in turning away from the bar, trying to nurse the hollowness in the pit of his stomach, wondering how he could have known her for so long and not realized that it never could be, that she was hard, a bitch, that she had been playing him along because he was available, handy, that had it been anybody else—Schwerin, say—she would have been just as happy, just as agreeable, he saw them passing by the windows of the café. At least he thought he did—the wavy, dark red hair, the back of Schwerin's head combed down like he'd just been to the barber.

Mühling started forward but stopped. What was happening to him? he wondered. Everything—the snow, the confusion that the military exercises had caused with the trucks and tanks and soldiers on the road, in the café, the station, the way Hitzacker had seemed like a confusing, bothersome dream last night, a kind of nightmare—was different, changed, and beyond his control.

He slipped another coin into the dummy's hand and depressed the lever. He turned to the door.

"Karl—your tab."

"I is an *angry* nigger!" Mühling shouted with the dummy. His shoulder glanced off the jamb and struck the door, which popped open as though it had been held by a spring.

The air of the station was cold and laden with an ozone stench from the power lines overhead. It was his smell, their smell, the one he associated with the train ride home when they talked or simply sat together, jammed in by all the other commuters, reading. But he saw them again, stepping into a compartment.

Mühling headed for the club car, the one with the bar, knowing there he could get credit.

"Déjà vu," Schwerin said when they had seated themselves in the compartment, and Annette could tell that he was excited by the prospect of Hitzacker and the inn, and she smiled, giving herself over to his mood.

Schwerin was really quite handsome, perhaps too handsome, in a usual north German way, with a long, thin, but perfectly straight nose, a narrow face, clear blue eyes, and

111

a dimpled chin. But he also had a peculiar way of using his head, snapping it in one direction or another as, it seemed, his thoughts changed, or as he spoke.

The compartment was hot, and he stood and pulled down the window to look out. "Nineteen forty or forty-one, wouldn't you say, Annette?"

She stood and looked out with him.

His head went back as he scanned the crowded platform, the Bundeswehr soldiers with carbines clasped to their chests standing at every fourth compartment door. His eyes were slightly closed, as if trying to recall a scene, and he was smiling, the skin pulled taut over prominent cheekbones. "It's October, just as it is now, and we've extended our lines as far as the Caucasus, but the cold, the snow is just beginning, boding only ill. Still we go on with the same high hopes. It's only a matter of time before all of the Ukraine is ours and we're in Moscow, and the feeling is still in the air, the sense of victory, the invincibility, although there's been an"—he raised a hand and crimped his fingers, as though turning a dial—"adjustment, a subtle change.

"Things were bigger then, better."

They heard a whistle, and she touched his sleeve. The train was about to depart.

An old man and a woman who was carrying a small baby, well wrapped in an open wicker basket, had stepped into the compartment from the hall side of the train. The man had thick glasses that made his eyes look splayed. He nodded to the priest, who was reading a breviary in one corner, and sat.

"I'm serious," Schwerin went on, pushing up the window and then examining his hands after clapping off the dirt. "I have a theory about that."

Like many people of wealth or position, Schwerin's voice was too loud, as if he didn't care who overheard him, since any offense wouldn't alter his circumstances. Annette glanced at the others, hoping they wouldn't listen.

"You see," he tilted his head to her, but spoke more to a point on the wall, above the heads of the people on the other side of the compartment, "because war is a societal endeavor to which every available human energy must be relegated, it is the highest form of human experience. It is an adventure, a gambling game that offers the greatest rewards—territorial expansion, the promise of wealth, the lure of enhanced power, maybe even world domination and godhead." His eyes strayed briefly toward the priest. "And, of course, the losses can be total and irremediable.

"But more than that, war is participatory and directly appreciable by the masses. Nobody is unaffected, in one way or another, but for most people—those who actually get to pull a trigger or who are close to the action—it becomes the central event of their lives, more memorable because more is to be won or lost in a shorter span of time."

The priest looked up from the breviary.

The old man had closed his eyes and rested his head against the cushions of the seat.

The baby had begun to cry, and the old woman was trying to quiet it with a rubber pacifier that looked to Annette as though it was shaped like a penis.

"As such, war is theater—a tragedy, to be sure—but on so vast and encompassing a stage that its grandeur cannot be denied.

"And let's face it," he went on blithely, "we in the Western world have placed all bets on science and technology. It's the new god. A war, well"—he snapped his head to her—"is the most total form of technological expression. It was with the Greeks, the Romans, in the Middle Ages with armor and the crossbow, and it is now with all the terrible weapons of mass destruction."

"Then because of science, are we doomed?" the priest asked, his eyes troubled under heavy black eyebrows.

Schwerin blinked several times. His eyes fell on the priest's collar. "I wasn't aware we were speaking to you."

"There seems to be much of which you are not aware. War, for instance. And science. And God. It occurs to me that you don't believe that man is perfectible. In God's image."

Schwerin looked down at the backs of his hands. He breathed out as though he found the priest's question naïve and tiresome. "I think I know what you mean when you say God, and in such a way individual man *is* perfectible. But when we speak of war, we are not speaking only of individual man."

"Then what are we speaking of?"

"Oh"—again Schwerin canted his head and looked away—"societies and forces."

113

"Then societies are not perfectible?"

"Some have proved themselves to be. Within parameters."

"And these 'forces' you speak of, can you name them?"

"I'd prefer not to try, there are so many."

"But which man can't control."

Schwerin eased himself back against the cushions of the seat and crossed his legs. He looked away from the priest, up over his head, as though bored. "It depends on the mix. I'm sure many wars have been avoided by manly intervention."

"Which is to say, it depends on the men?"

Before he could reply the old man on the other side of the compartment cleared his throat and straightened up. He reached into his overcoat for his tickets. "Here we have God, or at least one of his minions, and he brings war with him."

The conductor, a large man with a handlebar mustache and bags under his eyes, stepped into the compartment. Usually he joked with the passengers, called Mühling and Annette, *"Herr Und Frau Universität,"* and made pleasant fun of them for the amusement of the others in the compartment, but tonight his eyes were worried. And with the hall door open, Annette thought she again was hearing reports, like distant thunder, over the rumbling of the high-speed train.

Looking beyond the broad back of the conductor, who had stooped to take the tickets from the old man, she saw flashes toward the northeast that briefly illuminated the dense snow clouds—first white, then gold and a deep crimson that dwindled and disappeared. The report that followed seemed to rock the train.

"Lightning?" the old woman asked, having taken the baby in her arms.

The conductor only shook his head and turned to the priest.

"It's the military exercises," Schwerin said in a loud, confident voice. "We'll have almost two more weeks of that."

The conductor's eyes only flashed at him once, when he punched his ticket. To Annette he said, "Your *brother* is in at the bar, Fräulein. He doesn't look so good, if you know what I mean."

114

When the door had closed, Schwerin asked, "Is your brother older than you?"

Another concussion seemed to stun the train or frighten the engineer. It slowed.

"Younger."

"Does he work in Hamburg?"

"No." Annette had taken a notebook and a pencil from her bookbag. She drew a line that represented the Elbe and then the border of the two Germanys. She made a circle and put a cross in it to signify Hamburg, and then another line which she marked to indicate the railroad line, down the southeast bank of the Elbe.

Watching her, Schwerin asked, "The university? Does he go too?"

Annette made an X at a point not far beyond Boizenburg. "We're here. That"—she pointed to the window—"is someplace in here."

Schwerin looked up and blinked. "Perhaps the Soviets have decided to put on a little show of strength? The 'God of the artillery' and all that Red Army bunk."

The priest had closed the breviary. He was holding it across his stomach, and his eyes were closed.

Monday, P.M.
Bonn
F.G.R.

The study of the defense minister's private residence in Bonn was lined with books, from the floor to a very tall ceiling. A ladder mounted on rollers and a rail enabled the browser to reach the topmost shelves. And the volumes seemed to be well used too, the bondings wrinkled, the pages thumbed.

On a table near a window, the curtains of which were drawn now at night, was a globe with a wooden base. It was quite old, the sort that might have graced a philosophe's study. So too had the desk literary overtones for Kronenberger. It reminded her of an etching she had once seen of Goethe at his desk, forehead in one hand, pen in the other. It was flamboyantly a 'writer's' desk but tasteful

115

and spare and made out of black, durable wood. Could it be ebony?

Kronenberger got up to examine it and wondered why she was going over these details so carefully. Had she in fact developed a detail-oriented, occupational epistemology, one that was—she lowered her head toward the desk—unnecessary, idiosyncratic, and exhausting? Was she becoming just a uniformed civil servant?

Thus Ludeke caught her flatfooted, her face only inches from the wood.

"Colonel. I mean, Katie. Sorry to keep you waiting."

Kronenberger straightened up and smoothed the sash of her pearl gray dinner dress that made obvious her stature, her wide shoulders, and narrow hips. The skin of her upper chest was very clear and white.

After dinner she had asked Ludeke if she could speak to him in private. To mask his essential shyness he treated her cavalierly, like a man of the world who could pooh-pooh her paltry, feminine interests and efforts. But they'd been to bed together, and she knew he worshipped her. Although she had encouraged him, he hadn't had the *virtu* to continue the liaison. He had a brilliant mind. He was astute and would continue to occupy high office, but he couldn't deny his origins, she had decided. At base he was a petit bourgeois.

"I apologize for pulling you away from your wife and other guests, *Bundesminister*. I hope you realize that only a matter of state would cause me to ask you for this conference." She waited for his eyes to meet hers before she added, "At this time."

Ludeke closed the door. "I suspect it has to do with the incident over the Elbe." He moved toward the desk where he sat, forcing her to take a straightback chair yards away.

Ludeke's hand strayed toward a crystal ink bottle. In it was a quill pen.

He was a man well past fifty, but he looked far younger, forty at most. He had curly brown hair and the sort of blue eyes that always seemed to have a twinkle in them, even, as now, in a time of crisis. Never did he seem grave or angry, and on television he had the aplomb of a master of ceremonies. And it was perhaps because of his calm that he had been given the defense portfolio.

"It's a shame about the men who lost their lives, but"—

he leaned back in the chair and allowed his eyes to fall on her—"I can understand the Soviet position." For the briefest moment his expression changed. Was it wistful? She thought it was.

Kronenberger crossed her legs and stared down at her ankle. She placed one hand on the seat of the chair and leaned into it, arching her shoulder. She looked up at him. "Not to make an argument, sir, but I would consider it the most serious—the *only* serious—incident since the erection of the Berlin wall."

She then went on to explain the conversation among Bengsten, Mackey, and Price that her contact at the 12th Panzer-Grenadier barracks had played her over the phone and her own discoveries about Mackey.

"Frankly," he interrupted, "I find their candor refreshing, Colonel. I can tell you from long experience it's not very often that Americans are so forthcoming." He removed his cigarette case, which matched his wristwatch. Both were gold and ostentatious.

He knew she had stopped smoking, but he took a long time lighting it. After dinner she missed them sorely.

He tapped the cigarette on the desk, then examined its end. The match was waxed and flared like a child's sparkler before rendering its flame. "Excuse me—what are you getting at?"

Kronenberger added the bit of information about the Soviet jamming of NATO communications and the report—still unconfirmed—that a U.S. air-assault unit was missing.

Ludeke only nodded. She watched him draw on the cigarette, some Turkish brand of toasted tobacco, the smoke from which was mellow and rich and enticing; she had smoked one once, when they had been together in Paris.

"I'm here because I think you should file an official complaint and press to have both of them removed and immediately, given the situation. This is only day one of the exercises and already—" She stopped speaking.

Ludeke had raised the cigarette and was staring at it, his eyes distant, concentrating more—Kronenberger imagined—on the smoke curling from its end than on the rather desperate matter at hand.

"I would say that we should be concerned more with why the Soviets, after nearly forty years of more or less peaceful coexistence, have chosen this moment to provoke us." His tone was speculative, offhand, and slightly nasty.

"Perhaps they really haven't," he went on. "After all, we have two massive armies facing each other . . ." his voice trailed off. "And Kork—have we considered him?"

He turned to Kronenberger. "You know, Colonel, it strikes me that those should be our concerns at this moment and not the patriotic and bombastic maunderings of the American martial mind. And—correct me if I'm wrong—you've rather overstepped your area of responsibility, have you not?" Ludeke drew on the cigarette, the head of which beamed at her briefly, like a red, dying eye.

Kronenberger glanced down at her hands. They were long and thin with neatly trimmed nails. She played the piano.

Ludeke was contemptible, really, and weak. He was allowing his personal feelings—the taunt that she posed him, the fact that he liked her too much and disliked himself for it—to warp his judgment.

"Your thoughts?"

She looked up at him. In a way she was sad that she had discovered how narrow were his concerns, how paltry his prerogatives. Somehow the realization made all the hours they had spent together, which formerly she had considered memorable, odious.

"Kork wouldn't have done something like that without a go-ahead from Moscow."

"Ah"—he raised the cigarette and looked down at it—"now there I think you're right."

Kronenberger had the taxi stop at a café. There she purchased a package of her last brand of cigarettes. Inhaling, she thought about the passage in the *Divina Commedia* where in hell thirst is slaked with dust. The low-tar tobacco burned the back of her throat like caustic powder.

She had the man stop again. She bought several other brands. They were all the same.

If only he had offered me one, she thought.

118

4

On paper all Allied intelligence had been made to interface
with the system in the mobile crisis-management headquarters were Bengsten was sitting. In that way the SACEUR
could communicate with all subordinate officers right
down to individual tank and aircraft commanders in the
field.

But at best the system was a patchwork of conflicting,
redundant, and often antiquated equipment. Instead of
adopting digital systems with common software formats for
computer language, cockpit displays, and interfaces,
they'd only updated bits and pieces of the oldest parts of
the network. The many British and German devices that
broadcast in the C band could be permanently jammed or
chafed and were not—Bengsten shook his head, he had the
proof right in front of him—secure. The newest elements,
which operated on K_u could respond to ECM and were
superior.

Bengsten scanned the gallery of observers: a senator,
two congressmen, several members of Parliament, and rep-
resentatives of almost every NATO nation and France. He
hoped he had made it clear. Mackey had had the capability. He could have overriden the Soviet jammning. Now the
whole thing was on his head.

Only moments before, Bengsten had placed on full red
alert all Allied forces in Iceland, North Norway, South
Norway, and the Baltic approaches, the United Kingdom
air forces, the Land, Naval, and Air Forces Southern Eu-

rope, the Naval Striking and Support Forces Southern Europe, and the Allied Land Forces Southeast Europe.

Bengsten's eyes followed Lieutenant General Herder, who was no longer at his command post, one tier down from Bengsten, but rather walking through the dark, sloping room, talking to this one and that, shaking hands, patting backs. Young for his rank and position, he was Commander-in-Chief Allied Air Forces in Europe, and rather like Mackey in the ease—was it simple-mindedness? Bengsten thought it was—with which he approached his profession. Mackey wasn't unintelligent, Bengsten well knew, nor was Herder, it was just that they both seemed to have come to their profession without an overview, with no concern for larger issues, with a childlike acceptance of purpose and duty.

Bengsten wondered if Herder would maintain his aplomb if the Soviets threw their 4,500 aircraft at him. Herder only had 1,400 planes at most, and many of them were no longer superior in speed, maneuverability, and firepower to the newest Soviet planes. Perhaps in avionics and training he had the edge, but he would have all those numbers to overcome.

Numbers which just could not be ignored.

He watched Herder's head come up and his expression change. Bengsten followed his gaze to the display screen that pictured a red alert all along the FGR salient that was defined by Neetze, Gartow, and Bergen. Along that frontier all the sensory devices had suddenly become activated, as if a massive pincer attack into the salient had been launched from across the river.

Bengsten punched several buttons on the console in front of him. Neither in Finnmark nor in the southern sector were the surveillance mechanisms showing any activity, nor in the south central region. Only there along the Elbe.

Bengsten again stabbed at the console.

The room was still. Nobody moved. Everybody was staring at the board.

A congressman, the fat one who smoked cigars, approached Bengsten, but the SACEUR waved him off. One of Bengsten's aides rose to placate the man.

Air activity seemed normal.

Bengsten checked his watch. 8:01. "Get me Mackey," he barked to the man by his side.

"I just tried, again, the moment— And General Price too, sir. Somehow the links to his mobile command center appear to be jammed."

Bengsten again went to the console, tapping in the code that was one of NATO's most closely guarded secrets and pieced the NATO surveillance capability into the GSFG security grid.

They too were showing massive armed incursions, but along the entire German frontier from Travemünde in the north to the Berchtesgaden in the south.

Bengsten pushed himself away from the console and tried to keep the surprise off his face. But he was overjoyed. In spite of the odds, Mackey had taken the bait, and in typical Mackey fashion. Somehow he had gained access to the Soviet security grid.

Bengsten recalled Mackey's absorption in all facets of electronic warfare. With the snow and the cold perhaps he had a chance, but—Bengsten glanced down at his hands on the edge of the desk; he forced himself to relax his grip— he hoped it wouldn't be slow going but rather clean and surgical. Washington and Bonn would try to interfere, but maybe he could handle it himself on this end.

He wondered how the Soviets would react. With the grid negated they had only their eyes and ears, and it was night and the storm was worse than ever.

Herder reached over Bengsten's shoulder and punched several buttons. The original picture appeared, the one that showed the Soviets advancing into the salient. He began to laugh, slowly at first, but it was picked up and carried around the room, first by Herder's staff and then by the American, Dutch, Belgian, British, and Canadian officers. Only the politicians did not smile. And Bengsten.

He knew he was being watched by the others, that they were waiting to see how he'd react. He stood.

He could do nothing there but watch and wait, and he didn't want anybody to think he was a party to Mackey's action. That would only remove him from the scene. And he didn't want to get caught in the middle—between Washington and Bonn and the fighting, if there was any. Not yet.

And he had something to check on.

Bengsten, his expression concerned but stony, began making his way to the door.

"Could it be a mere electronics failure, a diode, a transistor?" a Dutch defense assistant asked him.

No, it couldn't. The computers were self-checking. The failure would have registered, had there been one.

Off in another part of the room, an officer with a decidedly British accent was saying, "Brilliant, absolutely brilliant."

And Herder. "With all this snow—it almost makes me want to go skiing, doesn't it you, Senator?"

Monday, P.M.
East of Uelzen
F.G.R.

After Price and he had conferred one final time, Mackey had gone straight to his quarters, where he had showered, shaved, and put on his newest winter uniform. He had left word that he was not to be disturbed and, turning off the lights, he had opened the curtains and had drawn the rocker over to the window.

There he had sat and watched the snow fall out across the expanse of the parade ground, coming down in heavy, windblown sheets that appeared to have wrapped the landscape in thick, layered gauze. Everything seemed so quiet and tranquil, and he wondered about the venture and his plans. He turned them over in his mind, this way and that, trying to be objective, looking for flaws.

He had failed in that, as he knew he would, and he could think only of chance and luck. They needed to have things break for them, and, like a lyric in a tune or a fragment of a poem, a Clausewitz quote kept recurring to him.

"From the outset there is a ploy of possibilities, good and bad luck, which spreads about with all the coarse and fine threads of its web, and makes war of all branches of human activity the most like a gambling game."

If so, he had wondered, what were his odds and on which bet? That theater nuclear devices would not be called in on either side and the clash would remain conventional from the outset? He didn't know, he couldn't, but it was what worried him most. He was banking on Soviet restraint, and he would issue strict orders, once the strike was

122

under way, that under no circumstance would he allow any of his command to resort to nukes. The weapons were supposed to be cleared through the SACEUR and the White House, but in battle little occurred according to form.

And on the other side—would the Soviets use them? He didn't think so. On a chaotic, open battlefield already heavily armed with precisely guided nuclear weapons, they'd surely lose their army. If they seized Europe, there'd be some question of their holding it, given the losses and the trauma.

Kork. Considering the impedimenta of the Soviet bureaucracy, his career had been a concatenation of herculean efforts to strengthen and defend the Red Army from every sort of onslaught. And Mackey had come up with an interesting fact about him that he hoped was revealing. Kork, even now in his middle seventies, collected tin soldiers. The Sotheby galleries sent him notices of sales and sometimes sought his advice. He was an expert in the field, and Mackey wondered if, perchance, he thought of his command in the same way. A collection. To be protected and not wasted.

If so, Mackey faced the perfect adversary. He'd disarm him, tooth by tooth, until the GSFG was a harmless mass of terrified, routed peasants or until Kork was removed.

That too was a real possibility. Kork's age was a factor. At the first sign of indecision, his first lapse of memory, some little gesture, some vague sign of senility, they'd begin to question his ability to carry on. There were those on the Politburo—Bysotsky, the defense minister, for one—who didn't trust him, if only for personal reasons. Kork was old army and did not fit in with the young officers who believed in high-technology weapons.

Again Mackey had played the Clausewitz quote over in his mind. And the von Behrenhorst statement, the one that had come back to him in Canada, the need ". . . to form a system of mechanics that does not rest on immutable laws, but upon the unknown."

The unknown.

Still sitting in the dark, he had reached for the phone and had asked to be connected with Bremerhaven. Dimauro said that it was a fact now, the Bergeron-Findeisen process had indeed been triggered.

"Then how much more snow can we expect?"

"I couldn't say, sir, but a lot."

The unknown. Mackey had thought for a moment and then decided. "I want all we can get."

There had been a pause. "You mean, you want me to send up another team, sir?"

"That's right, Colonel."

And another pause. "Well—I mean—shouldn't we consider—?"

Mackey had known what Dimauro had wanted to say: that they should consider what had happened to the other two planes, that he'd have a hard time getting crews, and if not, at least a hard time deciding who to send, knowing that he'd probably be sending them to their deaths.

"Let me ask you something, Colonel. Why do you think I'm ordering you to do this?"

There had been yet another pause. Obviously Dimauro had been trying to gauge Mackey's tone. "To provide a—a variable for the exercises?"

Mackey had said nothing, only watched the snow strike the window and fall onto the shrubs nearby.

"Or to maybe foul up the Soviets in case—"

Still Mackey had waited.

"Sir?"

"Yes, Colonel."

"Could we have something else in mind?"

"That's right, Colonel."

"You're not kidding. Sir." The question had gone from his voice.

"You have my orders, Colonel. I understand your position." Mackey had thought for a moment, then added, "General Bengsten and I think you've done a first-rate job with this, and I commend you." Mackey had hung up and had asked to be connected with another command.

"Dave—Mike Mackey here. Is your squad standing by?"

"Yes, sir. According to your orders."

"Good. Eight o'clock sharp I want all ECM activated and the Soviet system—the entire grid—coopted."

"But won't that tip them off that their measures are no longer secure?"

"I'd say so."

"Begging your pardon, sir, but do we want to do that? I mean, they'll just scrap the entire thing, and we'll have to scramble to breech any newer grid. I'm not sure we could do it."

"Hopefully we won't have to, Dave. You're certain we have them coopted?"

"Positive." Was it fright that Mackey detected in Byrne's voice? "If I understand you then, we—"

"I think you understand me, Colonel."

In the background Mackey could hear voices going through some sort of numerical drill. It sounded like a chant.

"Well—can I wish you luck, sir?"

"No, Dave, you can wish *us* luck."

"Sir—I wish us luck."

"Thank you, Dave, and thanks for your help."

Mackey had tapped the cutoff button and checked his watch. Six thirty-eight. He then asked the monitor to alert the men in two minutes. "I'd like to speak to the men."

He had placed the phone in its cradle and reached gingerly into the darkness, feeling for the microphone on the table. He had turned it to him. Still he had not switched on the lamp but had remained in the darkness watching the snow fall through the funnel of light that illuminated a flagpole close by.

But yet again he had picked up the phone and asked for a connection. "Jake," he said when the call had been placed through, "do we know the exact location of One seventy-sixth Guards headquarters power station?"

"Of course, Mike."

"At eight sharp I want you to take it out."

"What about their reserve system?"

"I'm not thinking so much of their juice as I am of their internal lines of communication. It would be nice to have their phones knocked out." Mackey had almost added "too," but he had decided to blur things as much as possible. That way, if it went badly, machines might be blamed, not men.

"It can be done. They'll have to resort to their third system. I've got a guy here who can jam that one down their noses."

Mackey had hung up. He had known how it would be accomplished: a cruise missile with its terrain-contour-matching system would hug the ground, jinking this way

125

and that to avoid radar detection and elude all the missiles and antiaircraft fire the Soviets would put up against it. Still, Conlon could put it right in a window, if he chose.

Mackey then heard the voice of one of his aides calling the men to attention through the intercom.

He went over the checklist that Gustavus Adolphus had devised for a commander:

1. painstaking planning
2. a thoughtful accumulation of supplies
3. celerity on the march and in maneuvers
4. sure firepower
5. taking and holding strong points, when they can be resupplied
6. a secure base and precise communications
7. strength through sober morals and good morale
8. discipline
9. the idea that a calculated risk is not the same as foolhardiness

Mackey decided that at least in the care and training of his army and in his plans for and expectations of them he had fulfilled the demands of the seventeenth century warrior-king as well as, if not better than, any modern army commander, but they'd soon see. Battle was the only real test. Still, given short notice and the necessity of surprise, he had prepared his troops as fully as possible. All depended on his conception of how, with modern arms and their attendant systems, victory could be gained there on the north German plain. With nearly all other factors fairly equal, that was the question. The Soviets had tanks and one theory, he another, and the issue would be decided shortly.

Mackey had reached into the darkness and tapped the button on the microphone. "May I have your attention, please," he said in an even voice, as though he were speaking to a person on the other side of the small table. "This is Mike Mackey." He waited for a moment so that the others could finish whatever they were doing. His voice was being transmitted throughout the camp and to the Lüchow base as well. Earlier in the day Conlon had set up the system and had made sure the signal could not be jammed or unscrambled and was consequently secure.

"Tonight we are going to strike—I repeat, *strike*—east

across the Elbe. That is what the snow and the cold and all our weeks of training on the sleds at Fort Drum and earlier today and every other effort we have made for the past three and a half years had been about."

He waited for a while, wanting them to accustom themselves to the idea. He moved back and forward in the rocker, as though pacing himself. The room was almost cold, the way he preferred, and he wondered how the new men, the ones who'd never been in battle, were taking the news, perhaps glancing around their quarters, seeming to see the ordinary things of their barracks for the first time as though the news had suddenly brought everything into focus. It had been like that for him in Korea and when he read the telegram that had at last given him a divisional command in Vietnam.

"This is not a premeditated attack. As you know, this afternoon the Soviets jammed our electronics capabilities. What you don't know is that it caused an air-assault unit to stray into their territory. We lost nearly an entire company. Our men, following standing orders, did not fire a shot. Once they realized their position, they only tried to leave. The Soviets did not let them."

Again Mackey waited.

"Now then, I have reason to believe that our actions are sanctioned in the very highest circles of our government, but the onus of this strike rests solely with me. I'm sure, if you think about it, you'll come to understand, as I do, that there are very good reasons for it. But I'll get to that.

"First, let's ask ourselves what we face. There are five Soviet ground armies in East Germany. Even counting their East German allies we are, because of the Reforger exercises, roughly equivalent to them, except in five categories.

"They have four times as many tanks, six times as many APCs, and a decided advantage in numbers over us in aircraft. They have superior surface-to-air missiles and anti-aircraft gun systems. Their artillery is also not to be underestimated. With their mobile rocket batteries and with the other weapons standard to their arsenal they have both more tubes and more rapid rates of fire than we. As soldiers, they are not to be treated lightly either. They are hardy. In their own way they are resourceful. Their officers have insisted upon rigorous training schedules, and the

127

troops are seasoned to hardship, but like most of you, they are inexperienced in actual combat. Their commander, Chief Marshal Kork, and some of his subordinates saw extensive action in World War Two. Kork is considered a highly skilled tactical commander, and I respect that estimate.

"So much for their strengths."

Mackey rocked a bit more.

"Their weaknesses are several, both in planning and personnel. First, they are prepared to fight a more total version of their last war. By that I mean their being in tanks and APCs is to our advantage, as we saw in Canada and elsewhere, but even more so with the snow on the ground. Second, their air capability, while greater than ours in numbers, is less sophisticated overall. Their pilots are not trained as rigorously as ours, many don't have a tenth of the flying hours of our average pilot, and almost none has any direct combat experience. When they sent up Soviet-trained pilots against us in Vietnam and the Middle East, the kill ratio was six to one. Also they don't have many tactical support craft similar to our A-tens and Harriers. Those planes should help us against their tanks, if we need it.

"Personnel. They don't like it here in Germany. The average Russian soldier feels lost away from his culture. He is hardly paid anything, not allowed much leave and then usually chaperoned. His barracks are spartan, to say the least, and alcoholism is rife. Many are not Russians, that is to say, they speak Russian only as a second language. Many come from regions that were only added to the Soviet Union in this century. And most are not communists. Also, the average Soviet soldier has little affinity for things mechanical.

"Finally, the Soviets were placing all their bets on the tactics of a no-warning, quick-strike, lightning war that would put them in Paris in a week. I say *were*, because now the advantage of surprise and mobility is ours."

Mackey let that sink in. He was rocking faster now.

"That brings me to our advantages, our strengths. They too are several. We have more antitank devices than they, in particular the man-portable rocket launchers armed with the new RDX and HMX chemicals and fragmentation shapes. As we saw on the practice range, the T-sixty-two-

128

A-, -seventy-two, and even their new T-eighty tank cannot stand up against us, if we adhere to our training. What's more, we will be on the defensive, eventually. I won't tell you more than that for security purposes, but terrain and predeployed positions of enormous firepower will be brought to bear on their tank armies. Surprise, the weather conditions, your sleds, and air power I've mentioned."

If anything, the snow was falling harder now. It was as though it had created another medium, neither air nor water. Mackey only hoped it hadn't gotten any warmer. They had to get those sleds across the river. From a tactical standpoint, that was the biggest "if" he could think of.

"Notwithstanding what happened to our men this afternoon, we must ask ourselves why we are doing this. Over the last seven years they, the Soviets, have been steadily adding to their military capability, and few increments have been defensive. What they have been building is an offensive war potential—land, sea, and air—that has never before been equaled in peacetime. That force across the river is an army of conquest, and make no mistake about that.

"What we have come to learn in this century is that such a military build-up is not without a purpose, sooner or later, and already we've seen how they've been probing our weaknesses in Asia, Africa, the Middle East, and even South America.

"In short, it is incumbent upon us to seize the moment—while we have a chance, and I think we have a good one—and in such a way that it does not spell disaster for all of mankind."

The pipes leading to the radiator began to ping and twang.

"Some would contend that the task facing us is too great, that they are too strong in arms, men, and will. But any estimation of the Western world, from Japan through the North American continent to Western Europe, shows that we have twice the industrial base of any combination of Marxist-socialist states and one and half times their manpower. We produce sixty-five percent of the world's goods and conduct seventy percent of its business.

"But mostly, what it all comes down to is the way they conceive of human nature and the way we do. Theirs is a dark view—that a few people at the top should control the

129

destinies of the world's people, because we need to be led. Ours is that people need to be free of such encumbrances, as fully as the necessities of organization will allow. Our system is far from perfect, but in my opinion it is more just and worth fighting for.

"Soldiers of the Northern Army Group"—Mackey's voice did not rise in tone, but only became more intense; he eased forward and clasped his hands across his chest, as though praying—"you with whom I will fight and win or die, know this: we are the strong right arm of a tradition that is at least four thousand years old, that evolved from men of good will who believed that freedom would allow reason to triumph over passion, that beautiful things would be built and made, that lives would get better year by year. In spite of many set-backs, the tradition has continued, but the darkest days are upon us, and it is only you and I who can turn things around. Tonight. Across the river."

Mackey had paused.

"The nature of the war, I believe, will be determined in the early going, perhaps the first few hours, or at least the first few days. If they don't use weapons that contravene the spirit of the Geneva accords, we won't, but I want you to know that, rather than make use of a nuclear device, I will step down as your commander.

"Specific orders, your assignments, and maps of the sectors you'll be operating in will now be passed out. Study them closely. Know that you are the best—in training, in arms, and in worth. And may God go with you and may we gain the victory that we seek and our people need."

Mackey had groped in the darkness for the button of the microphone and then eased himself back into the rocker. He clasped his hands again. Now he had only to wait, but only for a while, there.

Monday, P.M.
Wittenberge
G.D.R.

Kork has been dozing when the monitor in the strike center had gone haywire. They didn't dare wake him. He only knew that the room had suddenly grown quiet, and Alex-

130

eyev, who'd been sitting by his side, had risen and discussed something with the others, down by the display screen.

Then a stunning explosion off beyond the square rocked the building. Kork opened his eyes. The lights flickered off, then on again, then off for good. The emergency system went on and both lights and the display board were once again illuminated. But something was wrong. The ground sensors showed a massive assault in progress, along every sector of the entire German frontier, which was impossible.

Alexeyev left the other officers and calmly walked back up the steps to the topmost tier. He sat beside Kork. "Well, it seems they've responded."

"The generators?"

Alexeyev reached for the phone on his desk. "I think so." He put the receiver to his ear, listened for a moment, and then stared down at it quizzically. He handed it to Kork.

Dead.

"One shot?" Kork asked.

"That's all I heard."

Kork began to smile. What he had been feeling in his old bones, the special sensation that all the maneuvering in the West, the statements and denials, the snow, the ice crystals, the little argument that he had heard in the background, bits of which had been coming back to him—they were going to get their test. Of that he was now convinced.

What to do?

Kork glanced at the board, then straightened up in his chair.

The more junior officers, glancing up and seeing Kork smiling and animated, were heartened, but they didn't know what to do. Their gameboard, Kork thought, was busted, and now they weren't even soldiers, just out-of-work technicians.

"Tell you what you do, Vassail. You round up some trustworthy officers. Not that bunch down there. Tell them to put together several teams of runners. They're to have helicopters at their disposal, mechanized ski sleds, or whatever light, fast machines will go through this stuff. They'll comprise our internal lines of communications.

"And then"—Kork reached in his pocket for the old and

131

tattered ordnance map and carefully spread it out on the desk—"I want you to tell me what you think." On it Kork had already drawn in the deployed NATO forces and had circled Hitzacker and Lüchow. He pointed to both places. "That's where our fox will jump. Where do you think he is now?"

"Who—Mackey himself, or his army?"

"His army, of course. I don't give a damn where the son of a bitch is," Kork muttered.

"There, where you indicated, Marshal. If he strikes, it'll be preemptive. He'll try to catch us"—Alexeyev paused; something Mackey had written recurred to him—"en masse."

Kork patted his sleeve. "My thinking exactly. Let's try to keep him from that.

"And now"—he glanced up at Alexeyev—"we must respond ourselves. As soon as we can, with whatever we can."

Alexeyev's eyes worked over the map; it was all too obvious how much the salient in which the NATO exercises were being held resembled one big pocket. A bag. Had Mackey planned it that way? Kork's words came back to him. Our fox. "If we could—"

Kork nodded. "I've thought of that."

An officer approached them. "Sir, everything—all the radios—are jammed."

Kork nodded.

"What are your orders?"

Kork cocked his head. "Go sit on your hands. That's what I intend to do."

The officer left.

"What about Moscow?" Kork asked.

Alexeyev didn't know. He signaled to another officer and asked him. "Out, Colonel-General."

"Then we're on our own." He thought for a moment. "It's bait, I'm convinced of it, but have we any choice, Vassil?"

Alexeyev only turned and hurried toward the exit. Now it was speed that mattered. He who would or could strike hardest and fastest—well . . .

Kork's eyes were closing again, but he forced them open enough to see the strike center staff talking together down in the first rows. Kork knew he couldn't last whole nights

132

and days without sleep, and it was better not to try to conceal his age. Still, it wasn't smart to let those technocrats hang around with nothing to do.

"Tuchin," he called without opening his eyes. He motioned his head slightly.

When he felt the colonel's presence by his side, he said, "What are the chances of getting your Ouija board operating again? I sort of miss the"—he waved a hand—"whole show."

The man squirmed. "Well, Marshal—we've confirmed that it's not merely an electronics problem. It's the generators too. They've switched over, as perhaps you've noticed, but the power is low, too low to override the jamming, if—"

"If you knew what was jamming you," Kork completed.

Tuchin was flustered. He shifted his weight again.

"It seems to me," said Kork in a voice almost thick with sleep, "you should solve the first problem—the power—and then proceed to the other. I don't claim to know much about it at all, mind you, but could I be right?"

"Yes, of course, Comrade Marshal. That's exactly what we'll do."

"Thank you, Colonel."

He hurried off.

Kork thought about Mackey. He wasn't a son of a bitch by any means, merely a worthy adversary. In fact, Mackey intrigued him. How *would* he get across the river in sufficient strength to wield a telling blow. More interesting, however, was another question that then occurred to him: how Mackey would fare with that very same river at his back?

Monday, P.M.
At the Elbe, Northeast of Dannenberg
F.G.R.

At the river Price had had his driver stop. He had flicked up his infrared goggles. They hadn't been much good, even with the beam on, but he figured the Soviet night-seeing capability had been negated as well. The snow again. Maybe Mackey was wrong and they could get too much.

Price could see only a steep defile, one long bank of

133

white sloping down into the darkness where the Elbe lay. Was the ice frozen thick enough, out in the middle where the current was swift?

He glanced down at the small screen, only one of the many command devices on the long sled. On another they pulled a mounted TOW antitank missile system. Behind that was a skid of reserve missile and rocket rounds.

All up and down the riverbank sleds had come to a stop. He could hear the low popping of their idling engines, and every so often the breeze wafted him the slightly sour stench of hot, spent oil and gas. But yet it was quiet there, as though he were riding some special vehicle—a time car or a lunar lander—the deep and falling snow having created another, perhaps a better world. At least one that offered enhanced possibilities, or so he hoped.

As in Korea and Vietnam, Price forced himself not to think of home and his wife and children, to consider only the task that lay before him. At such moments he lost all sense of self and became solely and purely what he was, a soldier, no different from the millions who had gone before him down through the centuries, who had died without the thoughts of death that arose in other situations, although he did not think and hoped he would not die.

And he waited for the signal from Mackey—that Reiner and the other brigades were in position beyond Lüchow and the attack could be coordinated.

Major Plodeyev was cold and angry. He could see the sense in alerting them, putting them out in the frigid, bone-chilling bunkers all up and down the frontier, because of the threat the NATO exercises posed, but they'd been there eighteen hours now without relief, and long ago—six, seven hours at least—some of the men in his section had begun handing around their canteens that were filled with whatever they could find that passed for booze.

And how could he stop them? he thought, and why *should* he? Eighteen hours without even so much as a cup of soup. They were supposed to be hardy, and they were, but not foolhardy. The cold—he'd only experienced its like in Siberia, but he knew the toll it could take on men. One needed food, and often, to stave off its effects.

But he was just making excuses for his own failure to keep them in line. The vodka only made them feel better, warmer, made them think they could stand it, when with no food in their bellies drink was exactly the worst thing they could take.

And where was their relief? Plodeyev could understand how the snow could make things difficult, but what an excuse. What if they were attacked in the snow? How could they respond if they couldn't even funnel relief to the forward positions. And the communications being on the blink—that was an outrage. Kork would have somebody's ass for that, Plodeyev was sure.

But then again, how could the enemy attack under such conditions? No—he stamped his feet and thought of his wife who was alone with their only child in the flat in Wittenberge. She too loathed Germany, but she was a good woman and never mentioned it.

Sergeant Lobachevsky came up to him. "The water's frozen and the propane ran out, sir. Maybe you'd like a little of this?" He offered his canteen, the cap of which was off.

"I can't," said Plodeyev. "Even if I wanted to."

Lobachevsky stepped away, a bit too fast to make Plodeyev believe he had really wanted to offer him some. "I understand, sir."

Plodeyev moved toward the periscopic binoculars. "But thank you, Sergeant. I appreciate the sentiment." He did not touch his eyes to the viewing ovals. He could feel the cold radiating off the metal. No wonder it was so cold in the bunker. He wondered how long the propane had been out.

What was that out in the river, a boat? Plodeyev could only see now and then, when the snow abated slightly. "I wonder if you could dig up something to burn in the stoves, Sergeant? It will give the men something to do. I'm fairly sure we'll be here for a while longer. And have them break out the cots and the hot rations. I want everybody to eat something, even if it has to be thawed out. When we get the place warm, we'll get some shut-eye in shifts. I don't think the people on the other side of the river are fool enough to be out in weather like this." Again he eased his eyes into the scope.

The boat was there again but larger, probably approaching the lee shore for deeper water and less ice. But it became obscured again, and Plodeyev lost interest.

He stepped back from the infrared device and wished he had accepted the sergeant's offer. A good stiff one would do him nicely right now, but he was an officer, a party member, and had his career to think of. With little to do, soldiers gossiped like fishwives.

But once more he looked through the scope. What was that thing out in the river? Nothing. It was out of sight now, and really he didn't give a damn.

Outside, Lobachevsky and the men he'd rounded up girded themselves against the cold, bitter wind that howled around the low sides of the bunker. They slogged out into the snow that was in places up to their hips.

"He's a fool," one of the soldiers remarked. "What difference will a wood fire make in that goddamn tomb?"

"You don't see him taking the air, do you?"

"He's probably got a little flask on him somewhere. The good stuff."

Lobachevsky said nothing. He'd heard it all before, and the major wasn't responsible for any of their trouble. It was headquarters and the snow.

First there had been the alert, then the attack gong had gone off, then they'd been told it was just some sort of fuck-up, someplace at headquarters. Scuttlebutt had it one of the generators had blown up. No phones. The radios sounded like they were being ground to bits. Now the propane was gone, and piss could freeze before it hit the snow. The major was right about the fire. Just the sight of it would cheer them and they could melt some of the ice and get something hot going.

Suddenly Lobachevsky stopped. What was that he had just smelled? Something hot and sour, and had he heard something? Yes—there it was again. A whine, or was it a scream? A scream, shrill and loud, but not a scream. It was something mechanical, like jets.

He told the others to go on. "Anything that can burn. Be resourceful."

"You don't see the old man having to be resourceful," one of them said. He meant Marshal Kork. "He's probably all gassed up right now, and not just on propane."

The others laughed.

Lobachevsky turned back. If it was relief, he wanted them to relieve his section first. He started back toward the bunker through the tracks that they'd made. He'd get a flare and direct whoever it was in.

Sergeant Harris was surprised. He had expected at least small arms fire and maybe rounds from the heavy artillery he could see looming from the emplacements to his left and right, but nothing. Not a shot.

But here, up on the east bank and beyond the bunkers, he could see lights behind the glass-enclosed slits and he was hearing shouts now and again. Way off to his right, maybe four or five hundred yards, he could see an open door and some figures against the light. And somebody was walking toward them, slowly, laboriously, through the snow.

On the river the sleds had bucked and vaulted through the deep, windblown drifts, and the ice had creaked and moaned. The very center was bare and glassy and from a distance looked like black, still water, deep and cold. On it the tracks had slipped and the towed sections of the tandem had slid with the breeze, so he had nearly jackknifed when he hit the drifts again. But Harris was experienced and had plunged on with the others to his left and right, spreading out down the river, dispersed to penetrate the perimeter, lurching and diving with the powerful sleds, as though teamed to wild, mechanical horses.

Harris had scarcely noticed the screaming of the engine, the snow and ice that had stung his cheeks even with the wind mask and the grease they'd coated their faces with back at camp. He had been locked to the machine and, strangely, he had felt sweaty and his mouth had been dry as his sled had vaulted off the river and plunged deep into the snow.

Howling, it had scrambled up the steep grade, staggering from side to side because of its load, hot and something frazzled and sounding weak at the top. But, as General Price had said, the Soviets had never dreamed they'd be attacked and their defenses weren't much. As it was, the blowing snow had covered over most of the barbed wire and the tank- and man-traps. In any case, they were only token snares that seemed even less in the night and the snow.

Now Harris and the four men in his team worked quickly. They detached the final two sleds, unstrapped the skis, loaded them on the next one, and secured them to the sides. At first one of the small engines on the ordnance sleds wouldn't start, and, Harris noticed, the figure approaching them was drawing closer.

As he had learned in Vietnam and they'd discussed in tactics sections, surprise was usually available only once in any given battle. Lacking tanks, their exit from the east bank of the Elbe would be impossible without first destroying the fortified positions on the way in. Harris had been given five such assignments, more than any of the others, before he would reach the tank park at Eldena. And—he glanced up and looked out across the snowfield—the man would be upon him any moment now, before they had primed the charges in the demolition sleds.

Harris rose from his crouch over the hatch of the sled and turned toward the man. The others did not even look up, only went on with their tasks.

Lobachevsky had wondered what they were up to, leaning over their machines like that, and he wondered where they had come from and why they were so far from the main road. They'd probably gotten lost in the snow, but where was their track. Lobachevsky had been looking for it to walk in, knowing that heavy supply sleds would have pushed down the snow and made a hard path. He wanted to know where they'd gotten them, because a notice had gone out that Moscow hadn't expected the forbidding weather so early and deliveries of artic gear would take six to eight weeks.

"It took you long enough to get here," he said, "We're even out of propane. I hope you brought some of that."

The man did not answer and looked strange, because of the wind mask over his face. And why had they detached the two final sleds so far from the bunkers? Ah, there it was. Lobachevsky heard another engine start up and saw a puff of smoke blow away from the tailpipe of one of the sleds. It was then turned and pointed at the bunker.

Lobachevsky had come beside the other man now, the one who had walked out toward him. "What are they doing?" Lobachevsky asked, seeing that none of them had gotten into the sled but only watched it move away from them, slowly at first, but picking up speed so that within fifty meters it was hurtling toward the array of bunkers there on the bluff. The other one was sent the other way, toward the emplacements to the west.

The man only glanced at Lobachevsky, touched him on

the shoulder, and turned back to the other men who were assembling and mounting a strange-looking cannon on the body of the middle sled. They moved through the work with great precision and in almost no time the man who had met Lobachevsky stepped behind the scope and trained the gun on the woodshed, which was about 600 meters distant.

Suddenly a long missile jumped from the barrel of the gun and, when well away from them, its rockets ignited and it streaked toward the woodshed, the fireball fading off into the snow and darkness until it struck the woodshed and blew it up into the trees and set them afire. That was when first one sled and then the other struck the bunkers in front of and behind Lobachevsky. The combined concussion knocked him off his feet, into the deep snow near the sleds.

Through the binoculars Plodeyev had watched the sled approaching him with the same dispassion with which he and watched Lobachevsky conferring with the five men. It wasn't until the sled was almost upon him that he realized its significance, but he felt he had known all along. He'd seen vehicles like that before and the snow parkas and wind masks, but the gun was curious and the round that they had fired off convinced him.

But it was too late. Plodeyev neither crouched nor said anything to the others. Through the lenses he seemed to get a vision of his wife back at their flat. She was sitting close to the kitchen stove, reading a book, eating a large green apple. Her feet were up on a hassock. She was wearing the woolen booties his mother had knitted for her. And the baby was in his crib across—

Lobachevsky didn't move from the snow. He lay on his back and watched the four men mount the sleds. The engine snarled and whinned alternately as they left, moving off at a clip and bucking through the drifts as if they were nothing. And through the ground, in his back and spine he could feel other explosions, many of them and in rapid succession. North and south a dull glow, like dawn, had appeared, and he thought he heard helicopters overhead, but he doubted it. The weather—

But he didn't doubt it either. He didn't doubt anything. He still thought he could feel the man's hand on his shoulder. The enemy's hand, the hand of death. And that horrible white mask with holes for eyes and a mouth, like a mummer's mask at Christmastime.

Lobachevsky opened his mouth and something came out, like a wail. He had never been in battle before. He had been spared but he didn't know why and he was lost. And the calm with which those men—the enemy—had gone about their jobs. And had they considered him not significant enough even to shoot? No—the hand on the shoulder, it was a gester of— Clearly they were after something else, and at that moment Lobachevsky didn't care what is was.

He gathered in his legs and squeezed his hand and arms between his thighs. He turned his face into the snow. At least there he couldn't see the flames or smell the pitchy wood smoke of the burning forest. And he felt safe, there in the cold cocoon.

Monday, P.M.
Near Hitzacker
F.G.R.

Mühling was waiting for the train to come to a stop. It had been slowing now for several minutes, issuing only short bursts of power that jarred the several dozen men who were grouped around the small bar.

It was the snow, some speculated, the exercises, said some others. One man, glancing out the window, said he thought he had seen what looked like a ski-mobile club. "But there are hundreds of them."

"They've probably been sent out to save the army," another opined, and they laughed.

Mühling himself was seeing only a blinding silver spot, the exact size and shape of the pfennigs he had been feeding the coin bank dummy in the café earlier, but right in the center of his vision. It had been getting more definite and brilliant with every Steinhager he drank, and now he had to turn his head to the side to catch a brief glimpse of anything he wanted to see. Slowly, inexorably, the spot would move toward it.

At first it had intrigued Mühling, but now it was just making him feel nauseous.

With the final burst of the train that brought them to a

halt, the conductor banged down his glass and wiped his mustache. He pulled out his pocket watch and checked it, then began to move through the men toward the door.

"Don't need a watch to time this train," one man said. "A sun dial would do."

Somebody began laughing, and for no particular reason Mühling felt his anger rise.

"Could have crawled this far," another said.

Mühling tried to say, "In a moment you're going to have to," but he couldn't get it out, and the conductor turned to him. "You keep still, and no more of that." He pointed to the glass and then waggled the finger at the bartender.

Mühling lunged for the conductor, but some of the men who'd been watching grabbed at his jacket and pulled him back.

He felt as though he'd been set upon by a pack of dogs. Even in his condition he was stronger than any one of them, maybe stronger than all, and he had only to toss his shoulders and arms to knock them away. But they kept picking at him, saying things like, "Watch it, boy!" "Push him back." "Jesus, Karl—relax." "He needs a spiked collar and an iron chain."

Nor could he see them, really, and now his drink was gone. Spilled. He had raised it to his lips. It clicked on his teeth but was empty.

He slipped it in his pocket and pushed toward the door.

"Hold it. *Der Führer* told me that you're to stay put. He means stay put." When the man reached out to grab hold of the hood of the parka, Mühling spun around and grasped his wrist and hand in one of his own. He could feel the bones roll over. The man shrieked and went down.

Mühling's power thrilled him. He felt giddy, like grabbing up the next man and crushing him, breaking his goddamned back.

The others cleared a path for him, but once out in the cold air between the cars he wondered why he had left the bar, where he would go. There was some reason, but he couldn't remember what, and all he could see was windows: the hall windows and the dark, snowy night beyond; the compartment windows filled with the good, the moral, the sober who were rushing in and out to their little jobs in the city, who couldn't afford to get drunk. In a year he'd be among them, if he was lucky.

141

The hall in front of him was a brilliant silver burst, and now a soft phosphorescent nimbus had begun to spread out into the periphery of his vision, as though he were seeing through smoke or mist or—he tried to glance at the windows—snow, that was it.

And then he saw them, or he thought he did, and he knew why he was there.

Schwerin was reading, and she had rested her head, all those dark red curls, on the back of the seat and closed her eyes. And was her head lolling toward Schwerin's shoulder, as it had toward Mühling's the night before? He couldn't be sure, but he thought so. He'd only caught a glimpse.

He fell against the blinding silver spot that was the door. The people inside the compartment looked up.

Mühling could see Schwerin, if only he didn't look at him. His hand fumbled for the doorknob, which he wrenched down and pulled to the side.

"Karl?" Annette said, straightening up.

With his other hand Mühling reached out and grabbed up a handful of Schwerin's cashmere sweater.

The book fell to the floor.

A baby began to cry.

Some man in a black suit stood, and Mühling lurched into the compartment and struck him in the chest with the heel of his left hand. The blow sent him sprawling back into the seat.

But Mühling had Schwerin up now, wriggling like a rat.

Annette had hold of one of Schwerin's arms and was trying to pull him back. She was shouting, but it only made Mühling more sure of what he wanted to do.

"Get your hands off me. What do you want?" Schwerin asked in such a calm voice that Mühling relaxed his grip for a moment, and Schwerin batted his hand away.

"To talk to you," said Mühling, chagrined at how drunk he sounded.

"Why didn't you say so?"

He could see only Schwerin's pant legs, his shoes, and his blond hair. The rest was the pfennig and its snowy penumbra.

"Out here."

"No, don't."

"I'll be all right," said Schwerin with the sort of self-confidence and the precise accent that was everything

Mühling hated about him. "Where would you like to *talk*, Mühling? Between the cars? Perhaps outside? The train has come to a stop."

He stepped by Mühling, out into the hall.

"Karl—you're being a fool," Annette said. "You're drunk. You're vicious. If you ever had a chance with me, you've lost it."

Mühling staggered, his anger making him dizzy. There she was again, holding it over him, thinking she could control him, that he would do what she said, refer things to her for judgement, even—even make love, if that's what it was called, when she said and in her way so she wouldn't be sullied by him.

"Will this do?" Schwerin said when they had gotten down the length of the hall near the rest rooms. "Now—what do you want?"

Mühling had to think. He didn't rightly know what he wanted, and then out of the corner of his eye he saw the windows flare up—silver, like the spot, and then yellow and a deep red color—and the report of some explosion nearly knocked his legs from under him. The train seemed to jump off the tracks.

"Get off the train," he said to Schwerin, low and thick.

"Get off yourself. And I must warn you, Mühling, I have studied the martial arts."

Mühling tried to laugh but he couldn't. He reached out for Schwerin, but another blast made him miss, and two fists, lashing out from behind the brilliant silver spot, smashed into his face—his mouth, his nose—and he lost his footing and slammed into the side of the car. He fell.

For a moment only. The blood in his mouth, hot and soft, like gravy, was something he knew well, and he charged, hurling himself up and forward, trying to tackle the shiny silver thing in front of him, to wrestle it down onto the floor where he could crush it out.

But something—a shoe from the feel of it—again struck him in the face, across the bridge of the nose, the eyes, the forehead, and it knocked him back a bit.

He looked up. It had cleared his head, the blow. And his heart was pounding, his body responding to the attack.

Schwerin, looking down at Mühling's bloody face, was filled with revulsion—for the way Mühling looked and who he was and how he was acting, but because of what he himself had done too. Yes, he had studied the martial arts, but he had never had to use those skills, and he'd thought that the first two blows he had delivered the pitiful drunk would have been enough. But the kick, well, that had been something he'd been taught, but it had been low, dirty, and he was ashamed of himself.

But Mühling was getting to his feet.

Schwerin lashed out again. Once, twice, a flurry, until his arms were tired and his hands—his knuckles, his wrists—were stinging and raw. There was a pain in his right elbow that went right up his arm to his neck.

And Mühling had nearly caught one of his hands, and if he had—He remembered having seen Mühling in a wrestling match with a huge man even bigger than he, and—

Schwerin turned and fled toward the door that led to the next car.

In it he found the conductor and two other rail employees. The conductor only pointed to the next car. Closing the door, he could hear Mühling's laughter, deep and rich, as though he'd only just begun to pull himself together.

Mühling could see him, the face and shoulders framed by the window of the door of the next car. He slid it open and rushed into the darkness.

But somebody pushed or kicked or tripped him. There were hands on him everywhere, fists, a knee that was driven up into him when he had his legs apart, and he felt himself sinking.

They threw him out into the snow, which was soft and cold and felt good on his hot face.

"It's not far. That's the road up there, Karl," the conductor said, having followed him out to make sure he was not hurt.

The train's whistle sounded.

"No more drink for you on this train. Another night like this and I'll see to it you're banned, and that'll be a fine kettle of fish for you."

Mühling couldn't get up. The pain was too intense and had just begun to form a knot in his lower stomach. He'd have to wait.

But after the train was gone, he got to his knees and tried to take a bearing. He could see the highway beyond a field. In the other direction, across the river, explosions

144

were mottling the sky, sounding like distant thunder in August.

Even the red rear lights of the train had dwindled into the snowy night, and he was cold. And angrier, but mostly with himself. The night would help him out, drive the booze away, and he was ten, maybe fifteen kilometers from Hitzacker, not much really, if he could catch a ride.

The little bastard had taken advantage of him, but Mühling would only let that happen once.

5

After dispatching the reconnaissance units, Alexeyev hadn't returned to Kork in the strike command center. He had stopped a tracked vehicle that was pushing snow out of the headquarters square and had ordered the driver to take him to the helicopter hangars. The machine seemed to move at a snail's pace, and he could hear dull rumbling off to the west.

"Thunder?" the driver asked his mate.

"Not in this weather."

"Look over there." The driver pointed out the side window above the trees where a dull orange and yellow glow was forming, getting brighter by the moment. "And over there." He pointed to the south.

The man who handled the wing on the plow turned right around in his seat and stared at Alexeyev, who said, "The situation calls for calm. And speed."

The driver tried to get more out of the tractor, but it was already straining to its limit.

And the colonel in charge of the helicopter wing tried to talk Alexeyev out of going up.

Alexeyev took him by the arm. "Don't you have ears, don't you have eyes?" He pointed to the horizon. "You and your men should know this terrain like the backs of your hands. I want your best pilot. You and the others are to ferry men to the tank parks, then resupply them. They'll need—" Alexeyev didn't know what they'd need, he didn't even know by what means the enemy had breached their perimeter. "—everything. Now, tell me this—could they have come by air?"

"I don't know," the Colonel stammered, "everything's—" He motioned to the sky and the snow. "I don't think so."

Alexeyev didn't either. The radars were inoperative, foiled somehow, but not the missiles. And he had read an article by Mackey that described how vulnerable the helicopter had proved in Vietnam. Mackey thought it only good for resupply, occasional tactical support with their TOW and Hellfire missiles, and emergency operations such as medevac.

Then by what means?

Alexeyev thought of Kork, dozing in his chair, and tried to summon his own calm.

At the forward tank parks, those nearest to the confluence of the Elbe and the Havel, he was already too late. From afar they saw the glowing pinpricks of light, tiny dots way below them and arranged neatly, like the bulbs in a marquee. They were the new attack tanks that had been pushed right up to the riverbank for the alert. And Alexeyev had been forced to group them. There were just too many of them and too many APCs. If they had lined the roads with them under these conditions—

Suddenly something roared through the clouds and nearly struck them, then knifed back into the darkness, its two jets like the eyes of a cat, now here, now there, as it maneuvered evasively, down toward the tank park.

"What was that?" Alexeyev asked the pilot, whose face was ashen.

"An A-ten or a Harrier," meaning the NATO all-weather, close-support aircraft that could fly tight patterns at high speed and treetop level and thus foil radar and missile-and-gun combinations.

Could the entire thrust be airborne? Alexeyev wondered. He didn't think so. NATO wasn't well enough equipped.

"We'd better get out of here," said the pilot. "If it comes back for us, we're cooked."

"No—take me to Lenzen. If they've got their planes up, we must get ours."

"But—"

Alexeyev knew what the pilot wanted to say. The Soviet all-weather air capability did not include aircraft that could contest the low-level air space that the A-10s controlled, and it was a moot point, since when they got to Lenzen the airfield was in flames. Even through the snow Alexeyev could make out the shapes of the shattered planes on the ground.

The pilot let out a sob that sounded like the cough of a horse.

"Easy, son," Alexeyev said. "Easy."

"But shouldn't we attack?"

They were circling the air base's tower, the control room of which was ablaze, like a massive torch.

"With what? As you can see . . . And where?"

"Their—their airbases, their cities."

"Whose cities?"

"The Germans'."

"This is not the Germans' work. The Americans are doing this."

"But—" Tears of frustration were rolling down the pilot's cheeks. His name was Urtuchuk, and he had told Alexeyev that he was from the steppes. "But where are they? They didn't do all this with just planes."

It was a good question. Strangely, the young man's venting of his emotions had calmed Alexeyev. If the enemy was anywhere, he was farther north and east and—Alexeyev again thought of Mackey and his writings, he would never have attacked in one place alone—south as well. "Take me to Eldena."

Halfway there, dropping down as close as the pilot dared to the pine forests, Alexeyev saw the enemy surging through the trees in open snow sleds. A soldier jerked an unguided antitank gun to his shoulder and fired at them, nearly catching the landing pods on the belly of the ship.

"We'd better go up," the pilot said. "If they throw those TOWs—" He didn't wait for Alexeyev's concurrence, only banked the copter off and away into the clouds.

But it was a telling shot nonetheless, for the man would not have taken a chance on hitting his own craft. Obviously they had none in the air.

At the Eldena tank park, Alexeyev discovered, as he had supposed, that there was too much snow for the tanks to move. He ordered all guns to be turned to the southeast. Drivers were to dismount and with all available mechanized infantry were to advance south into the woods to meet the enemy. If they had any portable antitank weapons they were to take them too. They'd know the enemy. They were in snow sleds, the sort that were used in Siberia.

Lastly Alexeyev ordered the artillery to begin firing, "walking" their rounds out from the south edge of the woods.

Now they'd see what the Americans were made of, Alexeyev thought. "No retreat," he said to the Colonel in command of the tank park. "You'll fight to the last man."

"Yes, Colonel-General," the man snapped. His name was Mikhaylov, a heavy young man with a red nose. "You have my word."

Alexeyev suspected, however, that it would not be good enough.

Monday, P.M.
Along the Frontier North of Salzwedel
F.G.R./G.D.R.

Brigadier General Reiner hadn't stormed the frontier, like Price, for the Elbe veered away from the border at Schnackenburg and the fortifications between Wustrow and Salzwedel and Pretzier were extensive and well manned. Instead he opened up with a rocket and artillery barrage.

Initially Colonel Gurchenko, who was in command of the sector, thought NATO was merely responding to the attack on their aircraft, which had been all the talk in the officers' mess, and that, as on the Ussuri River against the Chinese, where he'd served from '69 to '73, they'd probably lob some shells at each other for a few months, at worst fight a limited engagement or two that the Soviets would dominate because of their firepower and the numbers of their guns, and then the statesmen would put the matter to rest and things would become quiet once more.

And Gurchenko had returned to his command post in a hilltop bunker overlooking the Jeetze in good spirits. It was the sort of training, he had found, that was most valuable to his gunnery teams—when they had real targets to fire at and especially in adverse conditions, such as these, and when their fire was returned and there was an element of risk in the entire proceeding.

But even from afar—two, three kilometers—he could

tell things were different this time. It seemed, somehow, that the NATO gunners couldn't miss. And whatever they were using was chewing up the fortifications at a rapid pace. Whole sections of concrete and earth had been moved, woods toppled over and set afire, roads knocked out, less well-protected gun emplacements already gone, as though some gigantic shovel had scooped them out and tossed them into oblivion. Nothing was left of them but a steaming crater and the reek of cordite.

And the men inside his command post were frightened; Gurchenko could tell from their eyes. And he couldn't help himself either, when the barrage continued. Unlike Soviet artillery, they didn't fire thousands of rounds per second, they fired only a few shells or rockets at a time, but their accuracy was deadly, their payloads immense.

The whole bunker was shaken, as though having been hit by a meteor. Men were knocked right off their feet. The next round jarred the concrete slabs out from under them, and they came down hard on their hands and knees or their backs. In a corner one young soldier was vomiting. Lights went on and off. Bulbs in the battery-operated packs shattered and had to be replaced. Another man had become incontinent. He was staring down at his pants and crying hysterically.

What could they be using? Some new type of explosives? The Geiger counter was passive, only the usual radiation. And how was it they never seemed to miss? Could they be throwing the iron bombs he'd read about? Were the rounds aerially directed? How, in this weather? It was a possibility, and clearly he had to do something.

"Contact Air Command. Throw up some SAMs," he ordered. "They've got spotters on us overhead. We've got to knock them out," he shouted during an interval, his ears so fuzzed he could scarcely hear himself, his whole body tingling and jittery. "Haven't you fools been returning their fire?" They knew where all the NATO defenses were located, and Gurchenko had always thought he could silence them whenever he pleased. It would just be a matter of time.

"Communications are jammed," the major shouted in his ear. "Anyway, they hit the SAM emplacements first. The mobile units—"

A round fell on them and from a flank of the bunker

they heard men screaming and a cloud of dust and debris billowed from the passageway and pushed into the command center.

"—the snow—" was all the major could manage. Another round fell squarely on the roof of the bunker and the lights went out again.

In the dark somebody scrambled past Gurchenko, and another person ran into him, falling heavily. When the lights returned, he saw it was a captain. Something had fallen on his head and the side of his face looked as if it had been crushed. It was a pulp of flesh, blood, and dirt.

"But haven't we been returning their fire?" Gurchenko demanded.

Now it was a rout for the doorway.

"Take your weapons!" the major shouted. "Take your weapons! And your overcoats. Proceed with calm."

But nobody heard him.

Gurchenko grabbed his arm and spun him around. "Haven't you been returning their fire?"

The major blinked and passed his tongue over his lips. In an oddly clear and calm voice, he said, "Obviously it wasn't effective, sir." He reached for his hat, which lay on a radio console.

"Where do you think you're going?"

"To try and regroup the men, where else? You'd be wise to follow me."

Gurchenko spun around and grabbed a soldier who was rushing by them. "Stop. Stay. It's an order. We—"

The man shrieked in pain.

Gurchenko had grabbed his arm. The sleeve of his uniform jacket was hot and sodden. The man sank to his knees and looked up at Gurchenko, his eyes terrified and pleading, his expression anguished.

Gurchenko stooped, wrapped his arms around the man's back, and hoisted him to his feet. "Go," he said, placing his own cap on the man's head. "Take my tractor. Tell the driver to take all the wounded back. Don't stop until you get to a dispensary. See if you can reach somebody at staff—" He had been speaking more to the major, but when Gurchenko turned around he was gone.

The man fled after him.

Gurchenko could still hear moaning, and then there was a special coldness in the bunker. He tried to decide what it was as he gathered up his night-seeing binoculars, a radio pack, and a carbine. Where were his gloves?

Others rushed by him, some being carried, one crawling. Yet another round fell on them.

Death—that was it. It stank like a morgue in there.

Gurchenko rushed toward the doorway. He was too late. The bunker collapsed on him, like a shoe box hit by a boulder.

On the margin of the pines, a kilometer south of the bunker, there were several men who were dressed in parkas and had a number of snow vehicles near them.

Major Nasgin hallooed at them and, gathering his men to him, began to trudge through the deep snow toward the figures who were visible because of the contrast of their white parkas against the dark trunks of the pine trees. Those others seemed either not to have heard them or were distracted, erecting some sort of guns on four of the sleds.

But one of them turned to Nasgin. He had something like a handgun in his mitten. He held it at his waist but pointed the barrel at them.

Nasgin stopped. The man seemed so relaxed, his other hand on his hip while the men with him worked unconcerned. And he was tall, this man. Much taller than most Russians. That was when Nasgin noticed the cord that ran from the butt of the gun up to a pack that was strapped to the man's shoulders.

My God, Nasgin suddenly realized, that was how they were putting so many shells— He spun around. "Run!" he shouted to the men near him, pushing the wounded man he'd been helping so he fell into the snow.

Nasgin reached down to pick him up, but he heard a screaming overhead and turned his head up into the black sky. The blowing snow stung his eyes but he didn't blink. He straightened up, knowing that this sky was the last he'd ever see, the snow the last he'd ever feel.

Reiner hadn't wanted to waste even a round of the weapons stocks, which they'd carried with them, on the soldiers from the Jeetze battery. Later he'd need everything he could muster.

Harris knew they'd meet resistance at the Eldena tank park. The helicopter, the one that had dipped down to get a look at them, had been the tip-off. If only the shot had hit the thing, but the angle had been poor and both it and they had been on the move, and they'd only seen it for an instant.

What would they find? he asked himself as he followed the tracks of the faster reconnaissance sleds, the dashboard of his snowmobile lightless except when viewed through the infrared shield that was attached to the bill of his parka cap—his fuel was down only a quarter of a tank, better than expected. Tanks? Yes, tanks, but immobilized tanks. Infantry? Yes, he suspected they'd find infantry. The enemy would know by now what had happened at Kaarssen, Dömitz, Neu Kaliss, and Lenzen, and perhaps at the other depots and storage facilities along the salient, and he'd be out to meet them in force. But how? On foot? Harris hoped so.

They were sprinting through the pine forest, which, he remembered from the maps they'd gone over back at base, was only a few miles from the Eldena tank park. They were using the woods for cover, since the surrounding countryside was open farms. But he wondered how valuable it was on a night like this. Still, they were out of the wind here and the snow was falling straight down through the branches in fine, coppery snakes that glistened in the infrared beams and then, as they roared past, in heavy clumps that fell from the upper branches like bombs. And they didn't have to worry about mines in these conditions— the snow and the relatively light weight that was distributed over the length of the sleds had taken care of that.

From in front of them Harris heard the report of heavy artillery shells falling and, slowing, he glanced through the gaps in the trees and saw bright red fireballs to the north. The Soviets were trying to catch them in an artillery screen.

Without pausing to consider, Harris and half the platoon of sixteen vehicles cut sharply to flank left, the others with Reese to flank right. Harris pushed from the woods into an open field where the snow was so deep they had to slow to catch sight of potential obstacles, but in no time, as expected, they came to another woods and Sergeant Truscott, who was running point, turned his recon-attack sled to the northeast again.

And they didn't stop when they approached the eastern arc of the barrage, but Harris could hardly keep his eyes on the track or his hands on the bars of the sled. The Soviet artillery barrage was "walking" across the open field and through the forest, which they had recently left, in such a way that no single inch of the attack line was not covered and nothing—tanks, trenches, APCs—would have survived it. Even here on the periphery the sled seemed to sidle right out from under him with every concussion of the Katyushas.

It was almost as though the field had been mined, sown regularly in tight rows like a garden that blossomed in vivid orange fireballs, first one line and right after the next and the next. And the snow, Harris noted, did not survive the attack either. It had been immolated or atomized or something. It simply was not there anymore. Behind the barrage lay a gouged and cratered, steaming field across which any tank could rush. Harris wondered if Mackey had considered that, but realistically, how many tank paths could the Soviets clear like that? Still—how many would they need?

Nearing the southwestern perimeter of the tank park, Truscott and Corporal Fuller cut away from the five other vehicles, across the field that the barrage had turned into a slushy, muddied hole.

Truscott could hear the dirt grinding over the rollers, and he hoped the fields had been well tilled and he wouldn't pick up a stone. Even so, soil was no good for the sled. It'd go over the field, all right, but—

Truscott was from Kentucky. His family had been soldiering for the United States since the War of 1812. He had been in Vietnam. He had been wounded, taken prisoner, and had escaped. He was thirty-six years old now and was thinking of retiring. Assing around out here like this wasn't his idea of fun anymore.

Fire. Off to the right. A bullet struck the cowling and twanged off into the darkness. He crouched down into the cockpit that had been lightly armored and he twisted the grip of the accelerator, veering away from the direction of the fire.

Fuller's sled was on his left.

Another burst.

Crouched down, Truscott could hardly see where he was going, but he'd taken a compass bearing before ducking and he kept the machine on it.

But this time they'd opened up with tracers that raked down the side of the sled, piercing the armor, he could tell, and a flare went up, dim above them in the still-falling snow.

Again and again bullets hit the sled. There were at least a dozen guns on him, he guessed. He had to do something about them. He couldn't go on like that. Sooner or later those tracers would hit something—an antitank warhead or the engine—and it'd be all over for him. And they had to cut in sometime, the whole attack depended on him and Fuller drawing the tank fire.

Truscott threw the latch that unclasped the cap on the muzzle of the cannon that had been fitted to the nose of the sled. Truscott and Fuller had machine guns there too, two apiece. He wrenched in the grips of the sled sharply and bore down on the nest from which the tracers had come. He armed the cannon and loosed its rocket, firing the machine guns at the same time.

The rocket jetted up through the snow, low and straight, and struck a tree in back of the enemy's firing position, cutting it right down, spraying the area with lethal shrapnel that could pierce even armor.

He fired again.

Fuller fired.

A bazooka round from deep within the woods nearly struck Fuller's sled.

The trees were ablaze.

Truscott twisted the handle that controlled the direction of the machine gun fire, and his tracers saturated the position that the antitank weapon had been shot from.

Through the flames he could see soldiers fleeing, trying to slog through the heavy snow.

Fuller's next round struck another tree and caught a whole bunch of them. The shrapnel seemed to spew them into and through other trees, tearing their bodies and uniforms in shreds.

Something fell in front of Truscott's sled. He tried to veer away from it, but it went up and nearly flipped the

156

sled, which fell into the gully it had created. The engine coughed and sputtered and refused to climb out.

Fuller plunged his sled into the dark woods, his nose gun rapping. The tracers swept a wide area, cutting down the routed Soviet soldiers. Three times more his cannon fired.

The woods were ablaze and already they were drawing tank fire from the park, which was about a half-mile away.

Truscott was stunned and dizzy, but he knew what he had to do. He tossed as many portable antitank weapons out into the snow as he could.

Fuller had swung back for him, and they placed them aboard his sled. Grabbing Fuller by the waist, Truscott crowded onto his seat. They'd be slower like that, but not by much. The sled Harris drove towed three others in tandem with three men and a mounted TOW.

With his second man crouched down inside the tandem sled, Campbell led the fireteam that was to breach the tank park perimeter and attack the stranded tanks. Cautiously at first, he probed the nose of the sled into the dark woods, around the pine trees that were dense there.

Campbell was from Houston and his father had promised him a hack's license and a new cab if he'd make this his last hitch. But there was no chance of that. Since before he could remember he'd thought the cab and the other jobs he'd had—hauling beef in a meat factory, loading boxcars, as a diesinker's helper in a steel plant, even a stint as a salesman and he'd been good at it—lacked something, and that something was adventure. Maybe he'd watched too much television, seen too many movies, but he'd rather go down out here with a bunch of other guys doing something exciting and—like the old man said—necessary, than adding sixty bucks a week to a savings book and hoping his wife didn't get knocked up too soon. And after this, when he did get back home—

They'd come to the fence that Lieutenant Reese told them would be electrified. They didn't know if there'd be mines, so none of them dismounted. Campbell only ducked down into the cockpit while his second man rose and took aim with a rocket launcher.

It was quiet there in spite of the tank guns they could hear firing off toward the south—Truscott and Fuller and the two others with Reese's half of the platoon; Campbell wondered how they were doing—but somehow the moment that he crouched down and waited for that first shot seemed to take forever. There were birds in the woods, either frightened by the tank fire or confused because of the brightness in the sky where the forest was on fire, and he heard the barking of dogs too, from beyond the fence. Guard dogs—they'd been told about them too.

The rocket struck the base of the concrete pillar of the fence and blew it away, leaving a low hole with charges snapping and arcing from the only slightly severed wires at the top.

Within the compound a siren had gone off.

They didn't pause to make the hole in the fence larger. Already Morin and Lynch had charged through the gap, running the sleds into and through a thicket of larch saplings that had been allowed to grow on a small rise overlooking the tank park below. The branches whipped about the sleds, scraping the cowlings and windshields. They had to duck.

Suddenly they broke through the thicket and found themselves on a small rise above the tank park. They stopped.

Below them were perhaps five hundred tanks and APCs, many more than they had been told the yard contained. To the south maybe a dozen were on fire, but across from them to the east where Lieutenant Reese's squads were operating, many more had gone up. And all guns were turned away from them, even those of the infantrymen on the backs of the tanks and the tops of the APCs. They represented the greatest threat.

Before fanning out, all six of them snatched up antitank tubes and fired off at least three shots apiece, casting the spent casings into the snow. Eleven connected, blowing turrets off, hitting the diesel drums that were mounted on the rear of the tanks. Shrapnel and flame spewed over a wide area, setting some of the enemy afire. The tankers fell and jumped off the tanks and rolled in the snow, but it too was burning. And the surprise of being hit from that flank threw them into confusion. Many began running right at them. Tank commanders swiveled their main guns here and there. Still, personnel farther away from them knew what had happened, and they turned their guns on them.

Campbell and the others fanned out, charging the sleds

down the bank at the tanks. Some guard dogs—large Alsatians—charged through the deep snow at them, their jaws snapping, but were knocked aside. But just as they had in Canada, Campbell and his team used the tanks that had been knocked out as blinds. And this time it was different. The sleds were too fast for the fire they were receiving. Each one selected a gap between two knocked-out and flaming hulks and breached it, sliding to a stop between them so the two men could sight in the targets in the next row.

The twin explosions were stunning, and except for the tank blinds they might have taken shrapnel themselves, the Soviets having grouped their tanks so close together. But at that distance they couldn't miss and the charges could pierce any armor, even the T-80s'.

Campbell's only conscious thought was that they wouldn't, they couldn't, have enough. There were too many tanks, there had to be.

Second row, third row, fourth—if they ran out, if they got caught inside there, it was all over. Had to be. All they could do would be to try to escape, but to where?

And in the rows, when they shot across the gaps between the next two wrecks, they received little fire, strangely. Out of the corner of his eye Campbell thought he saw the Soviets standing on the tanks, hands on hips, some even with binoculars to their eyes, trying to see where the attack was coming from.

Other tanks were firing south, where Fuller and Truscott and the other two were.

Still other tanks were rocking back and forth, the tracks hot and stinking and digging deep ruts in the earth, the drivers trying desperately to pull them out of formation into the rows.

Colonel Mikhaylov was up in one of the radar towers at the top of the hill to the north, his night-seeing binoculars clasped to the bridge of his nose. Goddamn the radios being out, he thought. What were they using that could foul them up so? And right here within the park, from tank to tank, the sets were useless.

But in a way the scene fascinated as much as it sickened him, for the way those little sleds were passing between the mired tanks reminded him of the story of the German wolf packs, passing up and down the convoy lanes in mid-Atlantic during the war, picking off defenseless freighters with their deck guns.

But these were not defenseless freighters, goddamn it. They were the backbone of the most powerful tank army ever assembled, and they were *his* tanks.

And hell, *he* had seen the small burst of fire at the fence off one flank where the three sleds had entered the park, but there was nothing he could do about it. He had an aide fire off a flare in that direction, then several more, but they didn't carry far enough, and the snow made them dim. And then—then!—some of those fools on the tanks closest to the impending attack had actually turned around and stared up at the flares. It was a disaster, that's what it was, and Mikhaylov couldn't stand idly by and watch them grind up his tanks. "To the last man." Alexeyev's words were still in his ears, and it would be that too. Soon. There was only one solution, and that was sacrifice.

Mikhaylov turned to descend the stairs and personally direct the gun emplacements on the hill to fire right at the enemy in those little sleds, wherever they were and without regard for whatever tanks were nearby, but he only took one step and it was his last.

Harris and Johnson and their crews had stopped well away from the north entrance to the tank park. There were two guardhouses at the gates with pillboxes on either side and radar towers farther on. Beneath them were two large-bore artillery emplacements that commanded the brow of a small hill. The complex was the last of the five strategic positions that Harris had been assigned to take out.

He and Johnson, seated at the scopes of their TOWs and maybe a mile back from the towers, waited while the others advanced on skis toward the fortifications.

The moment the first rocket struck, Harris sighted in the farther tower and loosed the TOW, keeping the radar pan and the observation cupola firmly fixed in the axis of the cross hairs on the scope.

The fins of the missile corrected for the drift that the wind caused and responded precisely to Harris's targeting. It was over in two seconds, maybe three. The missiles were swift and sure.

Back on the sleds they bolted through the burst gates,

the pillboxes on either side in flames, the towers above ravaged and smoking. Devoid of the pans and twisted, they seemed like a kind of modern sculpture.

And the whole scene—the flaming tank park below, the snow, the light from the blazing pillboxes flickering over the drifts, the way the two gun emplacements, when struck from the rear where the magazines were, took off half the hilltop—was special to Harris and unreal. It was almost as though, having caused it, he wasn't afraid for himself anymore, as though he had squeezed the rest of his life into a few brilliant, spectacular, horrible, but beautiful moments, and whatever came beyond this night could only be less.

Johnson had been killed, and two of his men. Harris had liked Johnson. They had partied together, soldiered, fought, and—who knew?—maybe they'd been meant to die together. The thought didn't bother Harris, and in a way he was almost glad Johnson was dead. It gave Harris less to worry about, made it easier for him to get out.

And then the tank park was below them and theirs for the asking. As General Price had said, the tanks would light things up, and wherever there was a dark shape among the burning tanks, he sighted it in and squeezed the trigger. The system was accurate within three miles. Its rocket burned out quickly, making it hard for the tank commanders to see where they were coming from.

Harris received fire from time to time.

He moved twice, not closer, but off to the flanks.

But they didn't have enough, not nearly enough.

Reese had said the Soviets had probably moved up reserves at the beginning of the storm and increased their strength in the park. It had been to their advantage, of course, but it was a shame they hadn't attacked with more men, more sleds, and more munitions.

Reese thought so too. He had stopped his sled deep within the tank park. Wrecks were blazing on every side of him, sending up blinding, searing sheets of exploding munitions and diesel fuel. It was hard to breathe. Gusts of snow and smoke and flaming air blew down the windows between the tanks, choking and blinding him.

Reese's man-portable rounds were spent, only one TOW missile remained, and he couldn't see a target. Of the three men in his fire team, only he was unhurt. One was dead, or so he thought, and the other wouldn't live. He had strapped them into the sleds and the blood had soaked right through his mittens.

And Reese himself was shaking uncontrollably, not, he told himself, because he was scared—because he was but he wasn't—but because of all that had happened, what he had done, seen, felt—the men he had killed, the tanks he'd blown up. It was then that the sled began to receive small arms fire.

A shot smacked into the engine cowling, and then two more, and looking up, he saw a man charging down the back of a shattered tank at him. He had a carbine in his hands, firing wildly; his coat and tanker's cap were aflame.

Reese only had a chance to raise his arms before Berezniki dived on him. They went down into the snow and the idling sled, with nobody to brake it, moved off into the flames.

The little man was enraged, cursing and flailing at Reese with his arms and legs, the burning coat hissing in the snow. He knocked off Reese's glasses, his knee came down and caught the American in the groin, but Reese managed to get a leg under Berezniki and he thrust the little man, like a rag doll, away from him. Berezniki rose up into the air and to Reese it seemed almost as though he paused there, arms out, head thrown back, figured against a sky of golden flame, before falling back toward the tank, where he struck his head and crumpled into the snow.

Reese scrambled to his feet. He could hear shouts from other men and more shooting.

He looked around for his glasses but couldn't see them. The carbine, the Russian's. He snatched it up and began running back the way he had come, through the tank park, pausing behind each wreck before darting across the gaps, keeping his eyes ahead of him where occasionally darker figures appeared and he threw himself into the snow.

They took him for wounded and dying or dead once, coming upon him before he had a chance to scramble up and trudge on. He got a kick, a good one, in the ribs, and the shot scorched down through his parka and snowsuit and burnt his back. Otherwise, however, he was uninjured. But he couldn't find his thick glasses.

Reese could see only banks of burning gases, walls of

flame, and dark shapes—smoldering tanks, the Soviets when they appeared, and finally what looked like a building, with sheds and fuel tanks nearby.

There were lights in it too, but Reese avoided them. Being taken prisoner—Reese was more afraid of that than death. Newspaper articles. His name. Reputation. He fumbled for a door handle and stepped in.

He could hear engines, two-cycle engines down the long expanse of what he guessed was a repair garage. There were tanks and tank parts all around him, disassembled, turrets hoisted up on chains, and the place smelled like grease, diesel fuel, and oil.

He thought of hiding himself, but there was no point in that. They'd find him eventually. If only he could get back to the rendezvous, to the river where Price and the others would be waiting.

He moved toward the lights, but with caution and stealth, reaching down in the dark places to feel what was in front of him. A wrench. A piece of sheet metal. The bed of a narrow-gauge track.

Using a stack of cartons for cover, Reese peered at the Russians, who were working frantically over a half-dozen or so snowmobiles, lashing weapons to them, piling in anti-tank rounds, a recoilless rifle, ammunition. The area was filled with thick blue smoke and the blatting din of the engines, on which mechanics were working.

Suddenly one of them shouted something that Reese, whose Russian was limited, made out as, "That's enough! Take them out as they are!" He was a stocky blond man with a crew cut, a motor officer.

The lights went out and a large bay door was cranked up. Snow and cold billowed into the garage.

Reese again thought of escape, of maybe . . . but there were too many of them.

He remembered where the tank mines were stored, on a massive tier of skids near the bay door.

He snapped the carbine to his hip and squeezed the trigger.

From afar Harris thought maybe a nuke had been called in. The explosion was white, phosphorescent, and seemed to burn a path through the snow clouds and sparkle. But then other stunning reports followed at intervals and were punctuated finally by the long, rumbling roar of the fuel storage tank going up.

Price had said it was stored underground, but he didn't know where. Under the tanks marshaling yard, just outside the garages.

None of Reese's unit made it to the rendezvous with Herz south of the tank park. Truscott, Fuller, and Campbell couldn't be found. Herz spent twelve precious minutes waiting for them, drawing tank and artillery fire, but they just vanished, it seemed, in the rubble and flames of the forest.

Monday, P.M.
Hitzacker
F.G.R.

Under the canopy of the railroad station, Annette waited until all passengers had debarked from the train. It was difficult to tell who was coming and going with the crowd that was present. Never before in her life had she seen so many people in that small place, and they distracted her.

Some had gathered to hear news, an explanation of the explosions to the east, since all communications were still disrupted. Most, though, seemed just to want to be out among people, to gossip, talk, and derive a modicum of support from the proximity of their townsfolk, friends, and relatives. But a few, most of whom were older and claimed to have seen it all before, were trying to catch the return train. They were fleeing to Hamburg or beyond.

But all, she judged, understood that something big, something important, something that could change their lives radically was happening. And it had little to do with rumors of the sled force, which some of the train passengers had seen, or the howling which some of the townspeople had heard, but with the bitter wind, the storm, the fire in the skies, and the thought, which had occurred to her several times, that perhaps it would never cease. The whole tenor of the scene made her think of Armageddon and the end of things.

"Why are we standing here?" Schwerin asked.

"We're going to wait for Karl, if you don't mind. He's—" She thought of who he was to her; if nothing more, her best friend, and to have seen him so distraught, so out of control, had pained and made her feel guilty. "I grew up with him."

"Then we'll have a long wait. The conductor threw him out, back there where I—" Schwerin only looked down at his knuckles, which were swollen and still quite sore. The open cuts prevented him from putting on his gloves.

Annette turned and moved off through the people, exasperated with Schwerin, with Mühling, with the crowd and the chaos. "How far back was it?" she demanded when they had gotten out into the street at the end of which the *Gasthaus* was located.

"I have no idea, but not far. Don't worry about Mühling." Schwerin had cast his head back to look up at the windows of the buildings they were passing—shops, businesses, cafés that were thronged with civilians—the apartments above, and the steep, gabled roofs covered with snow. There was a face in nearly every window. "He's a survivor, if I ever saw one. Too bad he has to drink. Some people just can't and shouldn't and he's one."

Annette only hurried on, knowing that Mühling's situation was infinitely more complex than that, that he was having to face a life as an adult that would impose far more demands and restrictions on him than those which she and Schwerin would encounter.

"Are you going into your father's business, Alex?" she asked as they passed the side street on which Mühling and his mother and maiden aunt lived, not wanting to look down the shadowed lane, at the lighted, yellow bay windows in which, invariably, one or the other of the women could be seen behind the lace curtains, waiting for Karl to come home. He was due; the train was in; they would have heard the whistle, to say nothing of the other noises.

"Well, we must have a talk, father and I. It was understood, when I first enrolled at university, that these years were my own. But the whole world isn't just exports and imports, tonnages carried, and so forth. And—" he glanced down at his feet, at the snow that was spraying from in front of their boots—"I thought I'd apply for the fellowship. Are you thinking of doing the same?"

Annette couldn't help herself. Her head turned to the

alleyway, her eyes looked up. Both of them were there, the aunt with her high pile of snow white hair handing the mother in the wheelchair a cup and saucer. Soon they'd be worried. The aunt would put on her hat and coat and boots and trudge over to the *Gasthaus*. Annette's mother would be busy and therefore short, more probably rude, to her.

"I don't know," she replied. "I haven't decided. I don't think so." Did she see him smile? She thought so. "Could you wait here a moment, please, Álex? I have to leave a message."

"Certainly. Nice town you have here," he replied as she moved off down the alley, trying to run but unable to because of the snow, knowing she was wanted at the *Gasthaus*, wanting to tell her father of the people who were leaving on the train and what she had seen, hoping that he had heard something else and could put it all in perspective and calm her fears.

And she felt like some sort of interloper—a housebreaker, a traitor—knowing where the latch key was, where the empty coal scuttle would be, and just how much coal they'd need for the night, where the shovel was, how full the bin, the light behind the entryway, the number of stairs, the cooking odors of good, plain food that pervaded the hallway as she trudged up the stairs.

"Ah, Annette, my dear," the aunt said, opening the door. "Frieda said that couldn't be Karl's step on the stairs. He makes a racket, that one."

Annette couldn't look into the old, careworn face that would be powdered and rouged now at suppertime, the neat plaits of white hair held by a net, the neat but worn housedress, some flower pattern, with a scalloped collar and a full skirt. She hustled the full scuttle toward the bright, tiled stove that was as tall as the room and nearly as long and heated the flat. On the hob were the dinner pots that would remain unserved until Mühling arrived.

"And where is he?" she asked.

"Annette—is that you?" the mother called from the living room. "Where's Karl? Is it true what's being said?"

Annette opened the grate and reached for the poker to ash the stove. "What's being said?"

The aunt crossed herself. "That there's fighting across the river. The Russians—"

Annette straightened up. She had known, of course, that

166

there had been firing and explosions of such force that it could only be military, but fighting? Between whom and whom? And if so, then the Soviets would have had to have been attacked. And then she remembered the sleds, the ones she had heard the man on the train talking about.

The ashing completed, she dumped the clinkers into the pan and carried it across the kitchen to the chute in the hall.

"Not so rough, please, Annette," the aunt complained. "You'll get dust all over."

Annette opened the chute. "Karl won't be home for a time. The train was having trouble getting through the snow. He and some other men got out to help. They asked him to stay on awhile longer, to make sure the train will get back.

"Of course, he'll be paid for it. It was an opportunity he thought he shouldn't pass up."

"Really?" The aunt's eyes, which had seemed to crystallize, like two blue agates, with age, were worried. "But *how* will he get home and *when?*"

"What is it, Frieda? Where's Karl? Come in here, Annette?"

"I can't. I've got to get home," she explained to the aunt. "I don't think he'll be long. An hour or two. Maybe three. But I must rush. Work." She turned the handle of the ash pan to the aunt. She could not again look at her eyes.

On the way down the stairs, she heard the aunt say after her, "Are you sure that's all, Annette? This is highly unusual. And Karl—I know he needs his food, especially on a night like this."

After closing the door, Annette remained in the shadows of the building. She felt miserable—having lied, having caused the disruption. Certainly she had known enough about Mühling to have realized that he could not be dealt with so peremptorily, and had she really wanted to? She didn't know. Was there something she could do, some way she could go get him? Not with all the snow on the roads, and she really would have to work—that or help her family evacuate.

She waited a few more moments. She wouldn't let Schwerin see her tears.

6

Not long after Alexeyev had left, Kork had reached for the
phone. Still dead. Somebody had come up to his side.
"Sir?"

He had opened his eyes slightly.

Medvenev. A captain. His mother was Kork's wife's second cousin. An old cow's last calf. "Got your snowshoes
handy, Captain?"

Medvenev had only smiled and cocked his head. He was
handsome, with dark good looks and that tailored appearance of the old regime.

"Can you do something for me and keep it between us?"

"Certainly, sir."

Intelligent too. Kork had gone over his record closely.
Nepotism and playing favorites had no place in his army,
but Kork would have trouble at home if anything happened
to the boy. "I want you to get yourself to the river, to
where we've got those hovercraft located."

"Schnackenburg, sir."

Kork nodded. The hovercraft were new and Kork didn't
think much of them. Huge and ungainly, they'd been designed for the naval infantry as a means of debarking from
seagoing ships. Kork hadn't wanted them but Moscow had
insisted. From his own sources he had learned they had
made too many of them. Kork now wondered if they'd
prove a felicitous mistake.

"I'd be interested in knowing what they can do in this
weather. If they can move, I want you to keep an eye on

the snow—what it looks like after they've passed. Can you drive a tank, Captain?"

"Of course, sir."

"Then take one for a spin, right behind the behemoth. But you're not to engage the enemy. What you're doing is more important than killing any Americans. Have I made myself clear?" Kork opened one eye and perused Medvenev. Suave, with polished manners and the ability to make himself get along with all types, he'd already proved useful.

"Take care of yourself." Kork gave him his hand.

A little later, perhaps a half hour, one of the staff officers placed a note on Kork's desk and stepped back.

Kork read it slowly, carefully. It was from Alexeyev, from the field, and worse than Kork had expected. He wagged his head. It bothered him most that he could think of no clear response, at least none that wouldn't play into Mackey's hands, beyond widening the conflict—taking Hamburg perhaps and sweeping south, or striking through the Fulda Gap and wheeling north. But he would have thought of that too. The bastard.

A clear response. Moscow would want that and would be calling for it soon.

"Tea."

"Pardon me, sir?"

"I said tea. Have somebody bring me some tea."

The phone rang and startled Kork, but at least it was something. He picked it up. Tuchin. "Now that you've fixed the phones, I want you to see if you can override the jamming somehow, even if you've got to use different radios. And Tuchin—you're performing well. There's a generalcy in this, and that's a promise."

Kork handed the phone to the aide. "Get me Forward Air Strike Command." He sipped from the teacup, letting the dark brew burn down his throat.

When Pelche came on, Kork said he wanted him to bomb the Elbe. "Right along the salient from Boizenburg to Schnackenburg."

"But—the river?"

"You heard me. Big bombs. I want no bridge and no ice left. I want you to keep doing it until I tell you to stop."

"But are you aware of the conditions?"

It struck Kork as funny. He began to laugh. He had

170

been trying to forget about Alexeyev's description of the airfield at Lenzen. It all came back to him in vivid detail.

When he had quieted, he said, "They've got their airplanes up. I think we should have ours. I'll add to that any and every military target within the salient." The tone of Kork's voice was too pleasant and Pelche got the message.

Kork began to slide the receiver back in its brace, but the aide said, "Colonel-General Alexeyev is on another line, sir."

Kork kept the phone. "Where are you now?"

"Beetzendorf."

"They've gotten that far south?"

"Not yet, but soon."

Kork's mood became glum. More than having had their noses bloodied, they'd been knocked down, and hard.

"And their losses?"

"Minimal. Then again, they didn't have much to lose. It strikes me—" Something went wrong with the telephone. When Alexeyev's voice came back on he was saying, "—hold what they've won."

"I didn't catch that. The phone." Kork clasped his hand over his left ear.

"I say I don't think they're planning on holding what they've won."

Nor did Kork, now. At least for the moment, Mackey's objective seemed to be to smash the GSFG, to maul Kork while he appeared helpless, and then to let the cards fall where they would. Kork would counterattack when he could, and Mackey would be waiting. Again.

And Kork wondered what he could do about that. The losses—the lure that they represented, Moscow's undoubted insistence that they carry the fight into the F.G.R.—would prove too great. Then the conflict would widen. Or it would be taken out of his hands.

"Have you heard from Moscow?"

Kork didn't answer him. "Tell me what you saw, Vassil. In detail."

Somewhere there was a key to the whole thing, and Kork only hoped he could find it.

Mackey sat in the near darkness of the mobile command center that he had positioned at Himbergen, staring down at CRV screens that were monitoring both fronts. Every once in a while he would strike a match into the ashes of his pipe, take a puff or two, and allow it to go out.

The myriad flecks of light to the south represented Reiner's force that was comprised of two of the five brigades of the 101st, the largest division in the U.S. Army. To the north Price had attacked with two others. Mackey had withdrawn the bulk of NATO force to beyond Uelzen and the Ilmenau.

He tapped the buttons of the computer keyboard to the right of one of the screens and the force equivalents appeared below the field of dots. Reiner's strike group was just shy of 8,000 men, riding a motley assemblage of 1,000 requisitioned and newly commandeered sleds that had been armed with 500 TOW mounts and a substantial supply of antitank rounds. Mackey had dropped in reserves immediately after the attack had been launched.

The strength of the enemy facing Reiner was assessed at over 80,000 men and some 5,000 tanks and 4,000 APCs, and the odds were even more disadvantageous than the figures suggested. The Soviets had been camped on that terrain for forty years. Just in sheer numbers of carbines they could stop the sled force, if they could engage it properly. Mackey couldn't think of an important engagement in modern times that had been prepared for—granted, on short notice—and fought from such a position of inferiority. He wondered how Reiner felt.

Confident. Perhaps it was the snow and the cold, the way things seemed to happen slowly and fluidly and were falling right into place. Or the gliding of the sleds, the ease with which they had driven through the gaps the artillery had blasted in the border fences and armor traps, but Reiner was elated. He felt . . . different in a better way. He couldn't find words, nor did he try.

Placing the laser indicator back in the holster on his hip—after having dispatched the Jeetze artillery bunker

172

and command post and the wounded Soviets who had come running toward him waving, as if they had expected help—Reiner felt almost omnipotent. The planning, the timing, his crews, everything was just right.

Reiner had been an army brat, and his earliest recollection was of wearing his father's steel pot with the single star on it. He had his own star now, and after V.M.I., Korea, and Vietnam he was finally being allowed to do with his troops what an army should—take the issue to the enemy and beat him on his own ground. He had never thought snow and cold would be his conditions, but tonight they were.

Reiner was a half-inch short of the six-foot-six cut-off for the army, and he had to ease himself and the communications man-pack that was strapped to his shoulders into the sled.

They bolted again, off through the shadows and the blowing, drifting snow. But Reiner kept his eyes below him, staring into the deep darkness that the cowling made around the CRV screens that were monitoring his sector. A-10s, Harriers, reconnaissance copters, surveillance planes, and even satellites were feeding information to the computers at Mackey's base, which then beamed the signal to Reiner, and it was there in the darkness where he would command the many elements of his widely scattered operation. It was there his duty lay.

A third of his force had been assigned the task of wiping out the Salzwedel tank park and as many of the enemy as they could meet. The object was to smash them again and again, inflicting losses as great as possible, and then flee back across the frontier, drawing the enemy with them.

"Emil," a voice said through the earphones that were connected to the man-pack.

"Yes, Mack."

"The picture's changing at Salzwedel. Somehow they've got some of their tanks moving. They're forming a reverse crescent, tanks in the center, APCs on the wings. They'll probably throw their men in front. They did that at Eldena. But you've got a problem—the town itself will have to be skirted."

"Can do," said Reiner, and for a moment he thought there wasn't any problem he and his men might not overcome.

173

"They could bottle you up easy."

Reiner thought it unlikely. Surprise and mobility were on his side.

"Call for air cover if you need it, but remember—we still want little collateral damage."

Reiner contacted his other platoons, apprised them of the situation, and modified their tactics, before they got too close. He knew how Mackey wanted it to go. If they could keep the East Germans out of it, maybe they might refrain from fighting or at least from throwing the bulk of their considerable forces against them. In the beginning, like this, any diminution of Soviet strength was to be courted.

He glanced up—they were racing across an open field, and through the infrared goggles he could see on either side of him the surging orange lights of his sled army, like a field of fiery eyes, beating through the drifts. Overhead an A-10 passed low, no more than 100 feet.

"You're about two miles from the perimeter, Emil," Mackey said.

Reiner didn't have to be told.

The A-10, banking suddenly, issued a deafening squeal that sounded like steel maws ripping sheet metal asunder. It powered up into the snow clouds and the night, then cut back over the tops of the pines to the north. A whole battery of SAMs streaked after it, only the low-level missiles visible as their guidance systems struggled to follow the jinking plane. Antiaircraft batteries had begun firing too; their flak clouds blossomed pale yellow and orange.

That was when the Katyushas began raining down on them, and overhead other planes, MiGs, swooped low, dropping cluster bombs that took out at least a dozen sleds.

But the defenses weren't coordinated. Again the SAM batteries lashed out, seemingly with hundreds of missiles this time, and deep in the clouds a flurry of explosions—twenty or thirty—occurred. Seconds later shards of shattered planes—MiGs, they had to be—fell to earth.

Down below the cowling, in the shadows of the sled body, Reiner could see the blips off to the north that were his A-10s, none together, moving back and forth in evasive maneuvers, waiting to be called in. He counted them quickly: thirty-six. All there. The Soviets were confused and that was good.

But Reiner was impressed by the rocket and artillery

barrage. He knew Stalin had called artillery the God of War, and he had read about how the Russians had directed the fire of over 27,000 guns on Berlin before they had attacked, but this—a scepter of fire striking the ground, regular and paced—was awesome. It pounded and moiled the earth—walls, a farmhouse, a barn, animals, machinery—blowing all into scraps and bits and burying them with the next round and the next and the next.

There it was, Reiner thought—the East Germans were involved in it now. They had to be; it had been inevitable.

Already the driver had pointed the nose of Reiner's sled toward Salzwedel. There, moments before, all lights had gone out, or so one of Mackey's technicians now told him.

Reiner no longer wondered if they'd be waiting for them. The question was how many of the 19,534 inhabitants and those in the police and border forces would fight. And the G.D.R. military presence, in the small camp south of the stadium—would they fight? If nobody else, Reiner was counting on them.

Monday, P.M.
Salzwedel Tank Park
G.D.R.

Alexeyev had arrived in the Salzwedel sector an hour earlier.

It was almost as though most field commanders had been stunned or mesmerized by the jamming and the phones' being out. Even some of those who had been attacked hadn't responded. They had been routed, and no attempt at regrouping and counterattacking had been made. Alexeyev put the failure down to the concept of the "total offensive" and the unignorable fact that few of them could think of any military action that did not directly involve tanks.

And yet Alexeyev found only skeleton crews on the perimeter of the Salzwedel tank park, standing "guard" near bonfires while the rest of the tank army and their mechanized infantry escorts were comforting themselves, either ensconced in their barracks or lounging in their machines. And the vodka—long the special curse of the Russian army—was being passed around: Lights were on, not simply the bonfires, but electric lights everywhere: in Salzwedel, at the Volksarmee garrison, and throughout the Soviet camp.

Alexeyev had had the helicopter pilot put him down directly outside the front door of the commander's living quarters, a low wooden building with a wide porch. The lights had been out, but the hubbub of the descending machine brought them on. The general, a certain Andropov, threw open the door, his figure silhouetted against the lights, hitching up his suspenders, his face maddened and belligerent at having been disturbed from his sleep, until he saw who it was.

He closed the door and stepped out into the cold, but Alexeyev caught a glimpse of the woman tying the belt of Andropov's bathrobe as she walked toward the toilet.

Alexeyev relieved him of the command summarily, and then, pausing to consider, elevated a young Georgian colonel, Gamsakhurdia, to the post.

With Gamsakhurdia, Alexeyev trudged through the snow to the first bonfire they could find. Thick brands—as Alexeyev had noted from the air, one a complete tree trunk with its limbs still on—were lying in heaps, blazing, and the men were drinking. The arrival of the two officers filled them with a sort of drunken propriety. They glanced at each other sheepishly and didn't meet Alexeyev's gaze when he asked them where they'd gotten the logs.

"C'mon, speak up," Alexeyev demanded. "The enemy, the *real* enemy isn't far off and you'll all be dead in moments."

They only glanced down into the soft, ash-strewn snow and the pool of water that had formed a glassy, bright halo around the fire.

Gamsakhurdia spoke up. "Sergeant Kostova—tell the Colonel-General."

Another Georgian, thought Alexeyev, wondering if such a diverse army, in which officers and men observed special relationships based on region, ethnic background, or simply—as in the case of his own secretary—hailing from the same home town, could be galvanized into an effective fighting force. Well—the warmth of the fire was comforting—the Americans were little different in their diversity. "Speak up, man," Alexeyev roared. "Hear those guns?"

The men listened to the dull, irregular reports in the distance. It sounded as though the earth was being struck by some massive metal instrument.

"Would they be ours?" Alexeyev asked.

Only if they were firing across the frontier, they all knew, and that meant war.

"The JS-threes," Kostova said sheepishly, meaning the old postwar Joseph Stalin-model tanks that they used as tractors now, they were heavy and powerful and could pull mostly anything, "but we only used one, Colonel—honest."

"They'll go through this snow?" Alexeyev asked. He glanced around at the others, their eyes bleary from drink and frightened because of his anger.

"We—we got the trees over there," another soldier volunteered, meaning to the west. He staggered. "In the woods, Colonel-General, and that's the truth." He began nodding his head. "Ain't it, boys?"

But Gamsakhurdia knew the man wasn't telling all of the truth. Too lazy to cut their own kindling, they'd gotten the shorter lengths of wood he could see stacked near the tank by raiding the Volksarmee wood stocks at the garrison south of Salzwedel. "You mean you went all the way over there and back?" He jerked his thumb toward the east.

Kostova only lowered his eyes and said nothing. His face was fleshy and the tight earlaps of his tanker's cap, cinched under his jaw, made it seem as though his cheeks were bound by butcher's string.

"When?" Alexeyev demanded, trying to summon his patience. His countrymen were like mules—they'd sooner suffer a drubbing than vary from their own pace.

But he noticed that beyond the pale of the fire the tank tracks were fresh. Several of the brands on the fire were only smoldering.

"How about the Germans," he asked, "are they drinking too?"

One of the more drunken tankers answered up. "No, Colonel-General, they're sleeping."

The others chuckled and glanced at Alexeyev shyly.

"Then at least they'll die in their sleep." He turned to Gamsakhurdia. "These are your orders." Alexeyev told him to bring all available JS-IIIs and T-10s, another older-model tank, to the northern perimeter of the tank park. Weighing fifty tons and powered by 700-horsepower diesels, they had great mobility. Combined with heavy armor and a 122 mm. gun, the T-10 was one of the most difficult tanks to defeat on any battlefield.

Half of them were to knock down the snow and form paths for the other tanks. Alexeyev wanted the tanks spread out at hundred-meter intervals in a concave line. The other half of the T-10 force was to advance north to meet the enemy, with T-80 units following in the rear, using the paths of the heavier armors' tracks. BMP armored personnel carriers—500 of them—would advance last.

But it also occurred to Alexeyev that the JS-III tank body had been used as the chassis for antitank batteries. Fully armed, their weight had to be greater than the forty-six tons of the JS-IIIs. He didn't know if the anti-tank missiles would be effective against the small targets the Americans would present, but it was worth a chance. Again, tanks and APCs would follow them. He ordered Gamsakhurdia to divide the force of sixty missile launchers into two groups, each moving off on the flanks to a distance of—Alexeyev could only guess at the range of the sleds; they were fast, but how wide would they swing?—twenty kilometers, through and by the Volksarmee garrison south of Salzwedel on the right, as far as the frontier on the left.

What else? All lights out. The immobilized tanks were to be covered with snow, once in place. Minimal gun crews. The rest of the tankers and infantry were to equip themselves with whatever man-portable antitank weapons were available. Regrettably those stocks were low; they had never thought they'd have to pit mere men against a mobile enemy, what with the preponderance in armor.

He filled Gamsakhurdia in about the Americans: how they would fight, what to expect. And Alexeyev then made the fateful decision to loose SAMs at whatever was in the sky. It was a guess, but based upon the only evidence he had at hand.

And fire, beginning immediately. Everything they had, "walking" out from the perimeter until all available munitions stocks in the tank park were spent.

Anything else? Alexeyev didn't know. He was cold, tired, and hungry, and where was he himself to go? Not up in the helicopter again, for he had just made that impossible.

"I'll need a T-ten myself." He felt slightly foolish, but he really didn't have an option. An old war horse, Alexeyev had thought—one sound of the bugle and his head came up.

Keeping his eyes on the monitors, Mackey had watched Reiner's force become smaller and smaller as it approached Salzwedel, platoon-sized groups dropping off to complete the bag he planned to catch the Soviets in. And losses. They were taking those as well.

The streets of Salzwedel were lightless, and the snow that capped abandoned cars, storefronts, the gabled roofs of tall, three-story houses, and the spired church made it seem empty, as though the residents had been evacuated or were hibernating through a cruel winter.

But Reiner saw other signs too. The Germans had been alerted. There were footprints leading from the police station to the air-raid warning center in the town hall across the street, a half-timbered medieval structure with tall windows on the second floor that reached to the eaves, the panes leaded and diamond-shaped, a building it would be a shame to lose.

And the other tracks—a single tank's track that led right down the main street to the square where it cut south.

It was there, suddenly, that the Soviets opened up.

Klieg lights from the tops of buildings were flashed on them, and down every street, every alleyway, pushing into the square and firing, came huge, lumbering antitank vehicles, their missiles lashing out at Reiner's sleds, the flashing, roaring rockets blinding them, deafening them, striking sled after sled, the warheads, designed to defeat tanks, gouging craters from the square and hurling men, shrapnel, machines, paving stones, and the earth below into the homes and shops that fronted the square. Small arms fire rained down from the roofs. Then tank fire began, from behind the antitank vehicles—stunning, disorienting, lethal.

The foremost contingents of Reiner's sled force were caught, stymied, unable to move, but from behind him he heard the special howling sound of the two-man mobiles on which the nose cannons had been mounted, staggering as they fired. And then other men from other sleds began firing the man-portable weapons, first at the tanks and missile platforms and then up into the roofs of the houses, at the lights and the snipers there.

It cnly took seconds, it seemed, and the square was an inferno.

Women and children were screaming, houses aflame, tank hulks blocking every passage but the one to the north down which Reiner and his men had come, and he heard fighting behind him now too.

"Need help, Emil?" the voice asked.

But Reiner was out of his sled, using it as a blind. Only the tanks remained. One had just fired over his position, the round punching through a store façade and exploding within the building.

But the sleds with the TOWS had swung into the square, firing on the move, first one and then another striking the tanks, and again and again, shattering the huge, boxy tanks—what were they?—knocking chunks of them back down the streets and alleys.

A turret was blown off in one piece and struck the side of a building. The wall toppled, exposing the tiers of the apartments within. People fell into the rubble. A man had a child by the arm, trying to pull it back up into a bedroom, when the building itself collapsed.

Reiner jerked an antitank launcher to his shoulder and fired it at a mass of people, some of them Soviet soldiers who were bottled near a shattered missile launcher. The round bucked through them, striking the hulk and spewing shrapnel over a wide area.

Sleds had sprinted in close to the buildings and the troopers fired up, across the square at the snipers. The antitank rounds smashed gaping cavities in the roofs. Slate tiles, chimneys, bricks, stone, and rafters tumbled into the square.

A plane dipped down into the narrow, flaming air space and a battery of rockets streaked from its wings, the cannon in its nose barking steadily. Beyond the square to the south, other explosions, other fire was heard, but already Reiner and the men who remained had begun to retreat, the sleds whining through the northerly entrance onto a street filled with the litter of other vehicles and tanks, its houses aflame, its people mired in the snow, struggling to flee out into the dark, snowy countryside, wearing only bedclothes, blood, and terror.

Reiner pointed and his driver took them across back-yards, over fences covered by snowbanks, through gardens and leafless shrubs, and they swung around Salzwedel—perhaps as they should have to begin with—and toward the south.

"I count thirty-seven of ours down," said Mackey. "Are you okay, Emil?"

Reiner had to force himself to think about the act of speaking. He wondered if he'd been hit, if he were in shock. Off to the west he could see three tank columns of perhaps a hundred vehicles, and he realized what it was—only some of the tanks could move through the drifts and then slowly, laboriously, the others following.

Above the city an A-10 was overwhelmed by SAMs and the flaming wreckage fell into a factory, which exploded, the fireball turning the countryside a vivid, brilliant yellow that muted to orange and then red and was followed by lesser bursts.

Reiner tapped his driver's shoulder and pointed to the tanks. Already other of his men had sighted in the targets. Like a field of sparks the rockets shot from the darkness.

"I'm calling in some more support," said Mackey.

"Don't. We've got them canalized. SAMs," was all Reiner could manage.

He pulled off his mitten and in the shadows of the cowling he tapped a code on the keyboard. In his other hand he held the laser designator, aiming it at the rear of the columns, where his men had not reached.

The sleds drove straight for the tanks that had just been knocked out, using them as they'd been taught, as blinds for their continuing attack on the interior rows.

It seemed like only seconds later that the terminally guided, eight-inch mortar shells began falling. Reiner held the designator on one tank, then another, and then the next in the row, and the powerful rounds immolated each in its turn. Shards of hot metal slammed into tanks in other rows, the puff balls of flame and smoke blinding.

The Soviet tankers, not knowing how or from where the attack was coming, seeing one after another of the tanks utterly destroyed with hardly anything left but scorched snow and twisted tracks, knowing that the path of destruction was creeping toward them, unable to move, having no targets but their own tanks in front of them, piled out of

181

the hatches and began fleeing, off into the snow and the deep, impossible drifts south of Reiner.

Without being ordered, Reiner's driver climbed out of the sled and fixed skis to his boots. With an M-16 he advanced on them. He didn't like what lay ahead of him, but he knew his duty. There were just too many of them, and only a few tankers with small arms and grenades could block their push to complete the double encirclement or, later, could punch a hole through which the tank could escape.

Huggins was from South Carolina, and until joining the 101st he'd thought of snow only as a curiosity. Now he set off with long, powerful strides, quickly propelling himself up to the gliding speed on an angle that would enable him to cut them all off.

Some couldn't even reach their sidearms, the snow was so deep. They just stared up at him, their faces, which were lit by the flaming tanks, orange-ish masks of hopelessness, not pleading or begging, only frightened beyond resistance, their eyes round with fear, like headlights. And Huggins tried to think of them like that—things no different from the tanks, things that had to be gotten rid of, but he couldn't. He merely pointed his weapon at them and squeezed the trigger, the jarring, repetitive sputter from the barrel a familiar sound that seemed almost pleasant to him. In a way it relieved him of the burden of the strange and horrible situation.

Back in his command center, staring down at the monitors, Mackey could see the the rush on the Volksarmee garrison was different. The men never left the sleds, only tore down through the nearly empty camp, firing to the left and right into the dark buildings, warehouses, garages, fuel depots, and bunkers. They met some resistance and took further losses, but Mackey imagined it was in one exhilarating charge, and about four miles south of the tank park they completed the linkup, and that was that. The bag was closed.

But in it Alexeyev found that the T-80s could move across the fields and forests where the artillery and rocket barrages had been laid down, could operate on their own, free from the paths of the T-10s, only occasionally becoming stalled in the odd drift that remained.

Standing in the open turret, like old times, Alexeyev waved them on.

The T-80s, lighter and faster, sprinted ahead, saving their munitions for sighted targets, but the enemy was elusive, here one moment, gone the next, lashing out at them from the flanks and then fading into the woods and shadows. The silhouette of the sleds was too low, the configurations of the cowlings and windshields too sleek and difficult to locate, and their speed was surprisingly fast— seventy or eighty kilometers an hour, Alexeyev guessed.

The T-10s had no chance against them, especially against the sleds that fired the TOWs, for the older, heavier tank had to stop to fire accurately. Its barrel lumbered and would not swivel a full 360 degrees. It could only get off four shots a minute under the best of conditions.

But even the T-80s with their complement of wire-guided antitank rockets had trouble scoring on the fleeting, deceptive sleds, and with only eight rockets apiece they simply did not have enough.

Thus the turret-mounted gun became the main means of defense against them, although the toll that Alexeyev and his men took had to be balanced by the fact that the tracers, arcing out into the snowy night, seemed to help the Americans sight in the tanks.

Losses were light at first, and then, when they approached the frontier, the sleds turned and attacked.

Standing in the turret, Alexeyev only heard the howling—an oscillating, frightening wail—of the many sled engines, and suddenly over a rise they jumped, fanning out in a long line, and in a moment they were on them, coming from all angles, from behind and from the flanks, fearless and seemingly contemptuous of the firepower of the tank army.

A shot screamed by Alexeyev's turret and then a second shot right after caught the T-10's undercarriage and stopped it dead. The turret gunner jerked the barrels down and tried to follow the sprinting sled as it howled by, but he was too slow. It was gone in the snow and the smoke.

But another gunner in another sled had something in his hands. A machine gun. He sprayed the turret and the turret gunner fell back into Alexeyev's arms. There was a gaping, bloody wound in his neck. Alexeyev released him and he slid down into the darkness and smoke below, with the others. Alexeyev seized the handgrips of the turret gun.

But down through the field of tanks, echeloned in depth as the commanders had been taught, the sleds flitted in and out, coming at them from every angle, never relenting, and their antitank weapons were deadly at close range. But in spite of the noise and the flashes, the concussion of tank guns, the sickening crack of armor being breached, the explosions when fuel tanks and magazines were struck, and the steady, staccato rasp of the turret guns, the men on those sleds seemed to go about their task with a practiced and lugubrious calm, as though administering a *coup de grace* on a massive, monumental scale.

Alexeyev himself had fought with soldiers like that—experienced soldiers, hardened soldiers, soldiers who knew that a battle was not over until the last enemy was dead.

And then, when the A-10s swooped down from over the trees to the north, he knew it was all over.

Yes, his SAMs went up in groups and ripped into the wing of planes and the T-80s hit the sleds again and again, but Alexeyev knew he'd been overmatched.

Below him in his own tank somebody was sobbing, calling for help, but Alexeyev turned his attention to the sleds. He thought of Mackey's statement about war, that only three things mattered: courage, ground, and climate. Regardless of training and expertise, Mackey had been gambling. He couldn't have known for sure that his few men in open sleds could steel themselves to front and defeat armored columns. And then the north German plain was some of the best tank country in the world, and the climate—well, he had forced that too, but he couldn't have been sure.

Climbing out of the turret onto the body of the tank, Alexeyev picked up a rocket launcher. His bare hands seemed to stick to the aluminum barrel, and he felt old and tired and hopeless. He snatched at the collar of his greatcoat and drew it across his neck. But then again, he thought, would Mackey have attacked if he hadn't been sure?

Perhaps. He thought of something else Mackey had written about. A calculated risk—it wasn't the same as foolhardiness.

Alexeyev jumped off the tank, into the deep snow.

Away from him, perhaps two or three kilometers to the south, he could hear further fighting, but the sleds were gone from the forward sector, even though a good number of the tanks were still intact.

And the snow too had eased up, only to be replaced by thick black smoke from the wrecks and the stench of burning, scorching metal, flesh, rubber, and blood. Pyres, the flaming tank bodies reminded Alexeyev of.

Or were they? Again Alexeyev glanced up into the sky. Climate. Only a few flakes were coming down now. It wouldn't always be snowing. And after all, the battle hadn't tested their offensive capability, had it?

Nearby, the engine of a T-80 coughed, then sputtered, and its turbine ignited, a whine not dissimilar to that of the sleds, although lower, more powerful, and menacing.

7

People were gathered outside Zum Wilden Mann: Bundeswehr officers, reservists, the mayor, two reporters from the local newspaper, and others whom Annette did not recognize. They were looking down the street toward the river and the G.D.R. beyond. Few of them were speaking, and their eyes were solemn.

And the hallway of the *Gasthaus* was crowded, the cloakroom a jumble of hats and coats and boots.

Annette could tell from the brittle smile that was frozen on her mother's face and the near-panic in her eyes that she'd been working without letup all day long, that she was close to losing control, either forgetting something or having a fit of temper or breaking down and crying from the strain.

"We'd better go around through the back."

"Do you mean—in through the kitchen?" Schwerin asked. "My God, the place is packed. And big. You didn't tell me that it was a—"

"*Gasthaus.* Yes, I did, and that's all it is."

"You know, I must tell you that I've dined here before, with my mother and father. It was a few years ago, before we"—he paused, then blurted out—"met, of course, but the food was very good."

"My father will be pleased to know that. Tell him, when you get the chance."

But the chances would be few.

When the back door opened, her father looked directly at them but did not see them. His eyes were glazed. He

187

was working at the ranges and ovens. Two waitresses and a waiter were standing on the other side of a steam table, waiting to pick up orders.

"Come this way, Alex. We'll wash up. I'm afraid we'll not get a chance to eat until later, but by then you'll know what you want."

In the lavatory that was used only by the *Gasthaus* personnel, Annette and Schwerin shared one bar of soap and a sink.

She watched Schwerin's face as she dried her hands, the bemused expression on his handsome features, how the prospect of becoming part of the work crew in the inn delighted him. He was really quite childish, and she again thought of Mühling and of herself and how it had been equally childish for her to have invited Schwerin back here, and on such a night.

"Here, you had better put this on. We don't want you to ruin your sweater." She slipped a bib apron over his head and arranged it around his collar. She had to reach around him to tie both ends, and their bodies came together, her hair touched his face. "This way, when you threaten to quit, you don't have to fumble for the cord. You can pull the whole damn thing off in one enraged gesture and fling it in the chef's face."

"Have you ever done that?"

"I've wanted to, many times. But this chef spanks, and hard."

"You know, Annette"—Schwerin looked down at the bow on his belly—"you really are a beautiful woman, so"—he searched for a word, suddenly embarrassed and at sea—"pretty. I mean—"

She was watching him: how the blush had been instantaneous almost, how befuddled he had become. And she realized how his Prussian bluster, his outspokenness, was the way he masked an essential shyness. "Go on."

"No, I mean it. You have no—no flaws. You're beautiful."

"You said that. I like it." She fitted another apron over her own head. "Because it's true, but, please, Herr Schwerin, I'm beginning to think less of your mind, your vaunted powers of observation, your objectivity. Just what is it you like so much about me?" She turned her back to him so he could tie the apron.

His fingers fumbled with the ends and his breathing was troubled.

She reached behind her and tied it herself, then opened the door.

"—your mind. It's—"

"Ah, you disappoint me, Alex. I was hoping you'd mention the total me. Out here in Hitzacker we observe no Cartesian split. In all things a great congruity obtains, but don't misinterpret that."

"Annette." He reached out and took her wrist.

She turned back to him.

"May I kiss you?"

She felt her head move to the side, the way it did when she was assessing something or somebody. Why? she wondered. Did she really think she could control people and events, that she could direct every aspect of her own life, when she herself was often perplexed at who she was?

Maybe that was it—that the civilization had no essential flaw, that there was no knowing who you are, saying I am thus and so, that only after having lived (and that was an active state, involving other people over whom one had little choice and less control) could one see the trends, the successes and failures, the drifts.

She thought of the snow, the guns, the explosions, and soldiers. "Of course you may kiss me."

He closed his eyes and leaned toward her. He flinched when their lips touched, but he did not put his hands on her, so she pulled him close and felt his thin, hard body against her. She wondered how he'd be in bed and if he'd loosen up. It was plain he adored her, and it diverted her to imagine how such devotion would be actualized. There was competition present in their relationship as well, but that, she judged, might only spur him on. He would—

She broke from him. "Don't let that muddle your brain. You're about to use it in a way you never have."

She took her father's place at the range, not simply stepping behind the steam table, but reading the duplicate slips that had been slapped down by the others, learning where he was, and how she could slip into his rhythm.

"What have you heard?" he asked her when she put a hand on his shoulder and moved him aside.

"Where?"

"On the train, of course." He stepped out of her way and

then pulled over a carton and sat on it, easing his back against the wall.

She thought for a moment that she would downplay all the explosions she had heard, the rumors of the sleds, the direction of the reports, but again that would be wrong. The truth was what he wanted, and she told him while instructing Schwerin how much and in which bowls to place the vegetables or apple sauce or gravy, what types went with what entrées, how the plates should look.

And it was a great relief to her to give herself over to the complexities of the kitchen. She fell into the movements that had been familiar to her for many years, the details that were difficult but challenging too, the hot and often tedious labor that was central to her life and that of her family.

The news had disturbed her father. He got up and moved to the back door, which he opened and looked out of. "I don't know. That firing. And it all seems to be coming from the east."

"Ah, the Ruskies," her brother said, who was waiting tables and had just entered the kitchen. "They're coming for us tonight. Scratch a Russian, get a Tartar."

"Scratch a German," one of the girls behind him replied, "get a Prussian."

Schwerin's head came up.

"Make fun, you two," the father said, closing the door and moving back to his seat on the carton, "but it could be serious. With everything else that's been going *kaputt*—the radio, the phone, the—"

He left off. His wife had entered the kitchen, and her eyes found him sitting there.

"We've only got food and drink, right mama?" her son said.

"You hear anything out there, Gretta?" the father asked.

"Out where?" She eased a heavy tray of dirty dishes onto a table by the sinks and began slapping duplicate order slips on the counter for Annette, who said, "What's this?"

"Veal."

"Are they saying anything?"

"I can't read your writing."

"You'd better learn."

"Did you?"

She turned on her husband. "Did I what, Paul?"

190

"Did you hear any of them say anything, there in the dining room? The reporters, the soldiers."

Her eyes widened. She started for the door. "Left and right. Give me another glass of beer, please. More wine. When do you think my dinner will be ready? Maybe never, with papa on his backside." She pushed through the swinging door.

"Marital bliss?" Schwerin asked Annette in a low voice. "Do you think we could be as happy? Considering what Frau Professor Doktor Froben thinks about you, we might open a university together. Just think of it—you could take care of the students and I the boilers."

Her father had been watching them. He stood. "Now, who's your friend here, Annette? He must be from good stock. I've been watching him closely and he's a rare man with a ladle."

Schwerin blushed and forgot what he was doing, what came next. He didn't know if it was a compliment.

Tuesday, A.M.
Mobile Crisis-Management Center
West of Uelzen
F.G.R.

Bengsten looked down at the phone that would connect him to Washington. Before picking it up he considered his options.

With the other heads of state, Schleymann and Van Wijk, he'd kept the report low-key. A clash, minor so far from all that he could know. The storm and the jamming had made communications with the forwardmost units impossible. They hoped to rectify the situation soon, and he'd be in touch.

But now Bengsten wondered if the time was right to piece out the situation in detail.

He pulled the sheet with the latest estimates in front of him and stared down at it. There was no doubting Mackey had ability as a field commander, that he'd understood his opportunity perfectly. The "worst case" figures that had been compiled by Bengsten's staff listed Soviet losses in the fourth and ninth sectors at over 5,000 armored vehicles, counting APCs. Over 2,000 planes had been destroyed, most on the ground and many of them the advanced MiG-23s and 25s. Human losses were placed at nearly 30,000 men, not counting Volksarmee and civilian casualties. And all the figures were undoubtedly more advantageous than these.

But the weather was changing, and if Bengsten read the situation right, Mackey intended to lure the Soviets into the salient, which he'd sacrifice, perhaps along with Hamburg and Hannover, on the premise that if he could maul them badly enough, they wouldn't have the strength to hold whatever they had taken.

But it was naïve. The Germans would never tolerate such a lengthy engagement on their soil, and the opportunity of completing what Bengsten believed he himself had set up would be lost. There would be no clear outcome, and even the status quo that had obtained since the war would be gone. The Soviets would be bitter and would demand concessions, and the Europeans, who were weak, would cave in.

Bengsten reached for the receiver.

"Harold—I've been trying to get you for hours. What the hell is going on over there?"

"In a nutshell, Mr. President, I think General Mackey overreacted."

"To what?"

Bengsten paused. The others around him were listening. Bengsten would need them later, and he hoped he could cozen their support. He had to choose his words carefully.

"The Soviets started it, as far as I can tell from the information at hand. They shot down three of our reconnaissance planes. I assume Mackey had put them up, just to make sure everybody would stay in place. They then jammed and chaffed our command-and-control capability for—let me see, I've got the figure here someplace"—Bengsten fanned the stack of memos on his desk—"about four hours. One of our air-assault units strayed across the frontier. The Soviets put up their SAMs. Only two copters got back. None of our ships returned their fire.

"And that was when"—Bengsten paused again, raising a hand and furrowing his brow—"Mackey jumped."

"Jumped how?"

"He attacked them—the tank parks, their airfields—right across the river and the frontier."

There was silence on the other end. Five seconds. Ten. Bengsten waited.

Nobody in the crisis-management center moved.

"Well—how does the situation look now?"

Here was Bengsten's chance. Mackey was popular with the others and that was a fact he could not ignore. And Harper—Bengsten thoroughly believed that the President had wanted what had happened so far. "Good, from a tactical standpoint. It was a brilliant maneuver. He caught the tanks in the parks, the aircraft on the ground. Their losses are sharp and continuing."

More silence. He then heard Harper saying something to somebody with him, probably Meisenzahl.

"How sharp, Harold?"

Bengsten ran through the figures.

"Where's Mackey now?"

"I don't know. Part of his response was to jam them. The Soviets. It's been going back and forth electronically. It's chaos really. Those figures I gave you are only approximate, but if anything they're low."

"What about our losses?"

"Well"—again the hand and the furrowed brow—"as I said, it was a brilliant move. As far as I can tell, Mackey has only used the Hundred and first, so far. He's got everybody else in reserve, waiting. So—let me see—that's thirteen thousand men. I don't think he could have lost half of them yet."

"But you think·he will?"

Bengsten nearly smiled. It was the question he'd been waiting for, the one that told him Harper really didn't mind what had happened, that he was thinking of continuing the action.

"I don't know what to think about General Mackey, sir. It could be there's something we don't know that caused him to act. So far it's a textbook exercise in tactical acumen, but the weather's changing to the south and the Soviets are massing along the river and frontier. This is only a guess, sir, but I think he's trying to lure them into the salient. And they'll have no other response without opening the thing up either here or someplace else.

"But you know, sir"—Bengsten was putting himself out on a limb, given his position as SACEUR, but it was worth the chance—"it's my perception that the Soviets don't know or won't recognize they can be beaten. Here on the plain."

"Who else have you talked to?"

"Bonn and the Dutch sir, but some time ago. The entire picture was different then."

Somebody close by shuffled his feet. It was a lie, Bengsten had only just put down the phone.

"And Mackey could contact you if he wanted?"

Bengsten glanced at the others. They hadn't heard the question. "I believe so, sir."

"Harold—why has it taken you this long to contact me?"

Bengsten looked back down at the several memos and wondered if he'd gotten in over his head this time. Harper knew what he was doing. All crisis calls were recorded, and he was covering his own tail.

"Sir, we weren't really sure of what was happening. As I said, the Soviet ECM played havoc—"

"Harold, I want reports every half-hour. Is that understood?"

"Yes, sir."

"And if anything should come up, I'll be right here."

Bengsten put down the phone. His palm was sweaty, and for the first time he felt tired. He only hoped he could hold out.

Sitting at the other end of the long, darkened room, Herder had found it impossible to keep his seat. The display board in front of him looked like some special stellar configuration—a milky way or a collision of two galaxies—with red and white celestial bodies moiling together along the parabolic axis that was the salient. Herder was a commander, a leader, but he was not an armchair warrior.

When the A-10s had been up, he had sat calmly there near Bengsten where he belonged. Given the strictly tactical role of those machines, they were merely an extension of the ground army, but the mix on the screen was different.

Nearly an hour before the radars of the AWACSes had picked up a rendezvous of hundreds of planes over western Russia where there was little or no snow. The NATO computers had processed the configurations and had determined that not only Blinder and Badger medium bombers were to be thrown against them, but also Flogger and Foxbat air-superiority craft as escorts, and behind the first waves, variable-geometry Tupelov Backfire bombers. Given their speed and rates of ascent, all craft were fully armed, but with what and where they would strike were still open questions.

Against them Herder had called for all available planes with air-defense capabilities, but the backbone of his force were the new Panavia Tornadoes, F-15s, -16s, and -18s. It was a match-up about which Herder had only dreamed, and all of the craft, on both sides, he considered things of the spirit, creations of men who in former times would have been world-class artists or thinkers or philosophers. To Herder's way of thinking, applied science was the focus of the twentieth century, and nowhere had time, money, and genius been so subtly applied as in the field of aeronautics. And to fly those planes, to feel the thrust of their engines, to know what they could do, and to learn to make them respond to your slightest whim—it was that which Herder missed most.

He turned away from the screen. He didn't know if he could merely watch.

Tuesday, A.M.
Bremervörde
F.G.R.

It had taken Luftwaffe Oberst Krauszer, Commander of 2nd Wing, 2nd Allied Tactical Air Force, fourteen minutes to get himself out of bed and into the tornado and to put the new multirole fighter of German-English design up, into, and past the clouds.

There to the east the pale mauve glow of dawn was familiar to him. On countless other mornings, especially during exercises, he and his wing and all other air-defense forces had scrambled and had flown for days at a time, returning to base only to refuel and rearm. It had been part of "surge" training, an attempt to simulate the conditions under which they'd have to fight outnumbered and outgunned both on the ground and in the air, but he knew from the start this was different.

Krauszer had been expecting to be awakened. The night before he and his air wing had readied themselves, even to the extent of a point-by-point check-out of each airplane with ground crews. Krauszer had wanted no losses or inefficiencies because of malfunctions or attrition.

But from the moment he was admitted to the super-hardened concrete hangar and saw the Tornado on its rail, he put things together. Not only had he gotten a call from General Herder the night before to be expecting the unusual and perhaps one or more direct orders from him personally, but the laser pod that would simulate hits or misses was gone from the brace along the underbelly of his aircraft and the real thing with its two missiles was in its place. Spaced out under the wings with ECM modules were six others, two radar-directed and four infrared. And then the final package, a kind of box, had been inserted in its holder near the tail. It was top-secret and almost never used.

And not only were the snow clouds a curious shade of yellowish-green, tufting there near the first pale streak of sunlight, but his radars picked up bevies of Soviet configurations at the range limit of sixty miles. They were many and fast-closing.

Herder's voice came to him through the headset. "I gather you've concluded this is no ordinary alert, Colonel." He went on to explain the circumstances of the Soviet air attack.

All the while Herder spoke, Krauszer kept his eyes on the CRV screen in the cockpit. His air speed was just over Mach 2 and the Floggers, which were leading the Soviet strike force, were doing 2.3. Thirty-seven miles, thirty-one, twenty-eight. In only moments they'd be upon them.

A red warning light began flashing on the radar console. A plane that the computer dubbed F1-2 had locked onto his aircraft.

Krauszer selected F1-1 as well and loosed the two radar-directed missiles at them. The plane rose slightly, suddenly lighter and swifter, and the missiles knifed toward the blinding chrome-yellow smear in the eastern sky that was the rising sun. Automatically every other plane in the defense force as well as the mobile crisis-management center and NORTHAG command headquarters were sent the information that F1-1 and -2 had been sighted, selected, and challenged. Other information on other challenges kept appearing on another, larger screen.

Nineteen miles, fifteen, eleven.

Krauszer then went to the small box attached to the belly of the fuselage and altered his radar configuration. Soviet screens would now be showing information that Krauszer's aircraft, some F1-?, was ahead of them and flying at them. If the missiles they'd fired had discrimination capability, the pilots would now have to override the internal computer system. Krauszer was betting they had. They'd put up their best at first, but the pilots would be too busy.

Krauszer had been through it all before, at the Nellis Air Force Base complex called "Dreamland" in Nevada. There, on dozens of occasions, he had had to tack back and forth through simulated Soviet ground and air antiaircraft defense in order to deliver suppressive fire on ground-based targets. Now he had only planes to worry about. The traffic was too thick and conditions too poor for Soviet SAMs, and anyway, the intelligence briefing he'd read on the monitor had it that many of their batteries had already been knocked out.

Krauszer knifed down with the rest of the air wing, hurtling into the clouds and hitting the afterburners that knocked him back into the padding of the seat and drove the Tornado to its Mach 2.2 maximum speed. At the same time he activated the radar jamming device and initiated a chafing procedure. Then he ignited the infrared jammer that burned fuel in a combustion chamber to produce an infrared energy source that was modulated to deceive the guidance systems of Soviet air- and ground-based missiles.

Throughout these procedures Herder had kept speaking to him, and Krauszer felt strangely detached. He had expected battle to be some special thrill, an excitement, but here he was up in the netherworld of cloud and bright, limitless sky that had become so familiar to him, going through the drills that were now second nature, as though nothing had changed. He couldn't optically sight the enemy yet, and the missiles directed at him passed unseen, they and he were traveling so fast. Only the computer registered hits. The aggressor craft designated F1-2 simply disappeared from the screen. F1-1 survived for a time, but then faded out as well.

"They've put up seventeen hundred planes," Herder said.

Now that was something that hadn't appeared on Krauszer's screen. It meant that—

"You'll be busy," Herder concluded, his voice surprisingly clear, as though they were seated close together, only having to speak in low, dispassionate tones.

But Krauszer's body suddenly tensed.

Out of the sun, in blinding silver flashes, the Floggers appeared.

Krauszer jerked the stick down and to the right and again hit the display screen to note that the computer had picked up a radar lock and was changing his configuration in rapid succession to optimize confusion. Through his flight boots he could feel the infrared jammer emitting bursts of fuel, and his hand snapped out and flicked the toggle of the computerized laser designator.

He came up under and marked one of the Floggers, and a missile dropped off the other plane, passing down below him before igniting, burning down through the clouds where it would circle and come up at him.

But the beam had a firm fix on the Flogger, and the computer activated the 30 mm. quad cannon, which rapped out a burst at the Soviet plane.

Krauszer didn't pause to sight the strike optically. He pulled back on the stick and swung away, his eye on the radar display screen. The sky was teeming with planes, with strikes, with losses, but yet seemed as tranquil to Krauszer and as beautiful as ever.

"Good luck, Colonel."

"Thank you, sir."

"You'll need it."

In a way Krauszer wished they could have music— something light and gay and schmaltzy by Offenbach or one of the Strausses, but he knew his world would change. In a few minutes his missiles, which had provided such sure kills, would be spent, and he'd have to rely on the cannon, the ECM, and other evasive measures, and the ballistics guns, which were virtually useless in these conditions, and already the Soviet bombers had dropped off his radar screen, down to treetop level, flying blind through the snow clouds toward their target.

What could it be? Hamburg? Bremerhaven?

Without more missiles or more planes Krauszer and his force were overmatched, even if they had the opportunity and the time to rearm.

Monday, P.M.
West of Hitzacker
F.G.R.

Mühling had been right about the cold and the snow—the combination sobered him—but wrong about the highway. He had gotten up onto the crown of the road only moments too late. A road crew in a team of trucks had just passed by and they didn't hear his shouts. And he could tell from the depth of the bite that the plows had taken, from how much the trucks had sideslipped and how hard their engines had been laboring, that they wouldn't be back until morning, if then. Too much snow had come down and too much was falling. In an hour or so they'd get stuck too.

Mühling had worked for the highway authority during emergencies and would in the winter to come. He enjoyed it—the back roads, alone in the truck at night or sometimes with a wing man, just them against the storm, the special taste breakfast had with the knowledge that he had worked all night, made things usable for the others. And the money. That was important too.

He had cinched the parka hood around his chin and remembered that he had his gloves on him somewhere. His books? The conductor would take care of those. Or the bartender, if he had left them in the train. He wondered how large his tab was there and at the café in the Hamburg station, and how he'd manage to pay it off. Work again. Mühling was good at that—putting in the hours. He'd better get used to it, he told himself.

Almost all the traffic was moving toward the west, and the eastbound drivers wouldn't stop for him. They honked and swerved and fishtailed by. The trucks didn't bother to move. Lights flashed and the beams jumped over the packed snow beneath the drifts, the bullhorns throbbed, and Mühling had to move off the road into the drifts that were often hip-deep. Military convoys, mostly. Mühling had to turn his back to the eddies of snow and wind in their wake.

But then even that traffic ceased, and Mühling thought he knew what had happened: the authorities had closed the road, declared it impassable. Or—he turned and looked toward the northeast where the distant fire had become a continuing obbligato to the storm during his now three-hour trudge—something else had occurred.

By his reckoning he had covered only half the distance to Hitzacker, and he was more than just cold. His feet and hands were now numb and with every breath the damaged membranes in his nose, the tissues in his mouth stung him. He had a steady, throbbing headache at the very back of his head. He was slightly nauseous but quite hungry too. He had fallen heavily and was bruised. He was paying, he supposed, and he would go on paying. It was the way things were and would be, for him.

That was when the lights flashed on and something—a car—shot by him, the shape black and darting and canting off at an angle.

Mühling tried to throw himself out of the way, toward the bank of snow by the side of the road, but the rear fender of the car caught his legs and sent him flying, up, into, and beyond the bank, where he came down, head and shoulders first, into a deep drift.

He knew he should wait for a moment or two until any pain would tell him if and where he had been injured, but he couldn't breathe. With his first breath, a gasp, he had sucked in a mouthful of snow so cold it tasted almost dry.

His hands came up to his mouth and tried to bat it back, but it was as if he was drowning, and he was disoriented. It was everywhere—below, above him, to every side.

Mühling panicked. He began flailing, and only the report of an explosion, some stunning tremor that continued, told him where the ground was and the sky. He knifed down his legs and thrust himself upward.

The entire river, it seemed, was ablaze with billowing bursts of liquid fire that towered up into the night sky, making the falling snow glow, like dust or sparks, making all the snow too brilliant to look at. Mühling cowered and turned his back. He crouched down in the hole that his body had made in the drift until his eyes would become accustomed to the brightness, his ears to the roaring.

He wondered, looking down the road and seeing the car that had struck him nose-first in another drift, if he could walk. The ground beneath the snow was heaving, jumping, and the car looked like a blur.

But then the fire began to move down the river. The bombs from the planes that he could hear now and then in the clouds, the one that came hurtling out of the sky and crashed on the road maybe a half-mile behind him, burning like a massive, twisted pyre, moved east on the river, toward Hitzacker, and the shock waves became less severe.

The driver of the car was revving the engine, snapping the gears from forward to reverse, trying to rock the car out of the drift.

When Mühling opened the door, a hand came up with a gun in it. He stepped back.

It was a woman dressed in a uniform. "What do you want?"

"To help you."

Her blond hair was just visible between the brim of the winter cap and the raised collar of her storm coat.

"I must get to Hitzacker myself. That bombing"—he looked off, at the clouds of fire that still could be seen in the distance.

"You're an oaf, you know," she said, lowering the gun. "Walking out there in the middle of the road. I could have killed you."

"And you're a fool, madame, if you don't mind my saying so, to be on this road, now"—his eyes again flickered toward the fire—"and to be gunning the engine like that. You'll only dig yourself in deeper. When I tell you, take it slow. Do you have a shovel?"

"In the trunk." She handed him a key.

But when, after fifteen minutes of shoveling, the old black Mercedes—some sort of antique, he guessed—would not extricate itself from the snowbank, Mühling, in a fit of pique, thinking about the bombing, his mother, his aunt, Annette, the Siebenborns, even Schwerin, set his feet and grabbed up the back bumper; he both freed the car and ripped the chrome guard from its underpinnings.

"Rusted through," he explained to her when he was in the warmth of the large car. "I hope it can be fixed."

She did not reply. Her eyes were on the road and she had again switched out the lights. With the brightness to the north and east and along the river it was easier to see through the snow without them, but—

"At least you can turn on the parking lights," he said. His right side, his buttocks, his back were hot with pain.

She glanced at him and complied, but it made little difference. A pedestrian would have to be watching for them, and the snow was like a porous white wall in front of them that only the fireball of a blast could penetrate.

"You're in the Bundeswehr?"

She nodded.

"Can you tell me what's happening?"

She shook her head. "Your guess is as good as mine, but it looks like war, doesn't it?"

"Why the gun?"

Her eyes, which were a light blue—like Schwerin's, Mühling thought—met his briefly. "Why the war?"

When they neared the Hitzacker/Uelzen crossroad, down which she said she would turn to head south, Mühling told her not to stop. "You might get stuck and we're not traveling too fast. I can hop out."

"Hitzacker will be one of the first towns overrun," she said. "It won't be defended. You may stay with me if you like." If she got stuck again, she thought, he'd come in handy.

"I can't," Mühling said, trying to see the insignia on her epaulet, "Colonel. My family—"

When he opened the door, she reached out her hand and grasped his. "Good luck."

"Same to you."

Mühling launched himself out of the car and tumbled into the snow, this time falling as he wanted, rolling with the direction of his body.

When he got to his feet he could see the spires of the town, the taller buildings, even some of the houses silhouetted black against the firestorm in the river.

He tried to run but stumbled and then moved on.

Tuesday, A.M.
East of Uelzen
F.G.R.

On the monitors, Mackey had watched the Soviet air attack. The objective was to destroy the ice in the Elbe and catch Price with his back to the river.

Price was almost a mile from it in a woods that had been partially destroyed during the night and was still smoldering. The ordnance and the heat from the ensuing fire had turned the ground into deep slush and muck, and the sleds had to labor hard to push toward the weapons and fuel supplies that had been helicopter-emplaced.

And not all of the stocks were still there. Bands of Soviet foot soldiers on snowshoes and skis—whatever they could scrounge from the Germans—had been moving out from the destroyed tank parks and from the barracks and headquarters area that Price and his men had by-passed. They destroyed the caches and waited for the Americans to return. Resupply was haphazard, and Price couldn't tell if he'd have enough.

With the thin, grayish light of daybreak came gusts of warm air pushing up from the south. Banks of fog rose off the snow and made the dark uniforms of the Soviets black against both ground and mist. In groups of two or three, in platoon-sized aggregations, even in great masses the size of battalions, they pushed toward the river, knowing only that the Americans had attacked and were somewhere to the south. They trudged relentlessly through the deep, now sticky, snow, still not knowing if the sleds were friend and relief or foe and death until it was too late.

Price and his men had only to follow their tracks to run them down. They swept out of the fog and right in among them. Chaos, terror—after a while Price became sick of the slaughter. It was too easy and perhaps not necessary from them, for it seemed that the Soviet commanders had consigned anybody with his back to the river, their own foot soldiers included, to certain death. With the bombing, yet another artillery and rocket barrage had begun, but this time coordinated in a continuous line and presenting a firetrap—the holocaust on the river, the Katyusha attack pushing them toward it.

Price divided his forces into two groups, sending half west toward Boizenburg, the other half east toward Lenzen in an attempt to break through the firescreen and wheel around the advancing Soviet forces.

Overhead now, seemingly at every altitude, there was a continuous roaring. Scraps of planes kept falling, pilots in parachutes, whole burning masses of metal and glass. It was as though the feathery soft fog and the warm air had been created by some celestial fire, the coals and ashes of which were plummeting to earth.

Price and his men stopped for nobody, neither for their own wounded nor for the Allied pilots who called to them from trees and heavy, sodden drifts. They had to force a breakthrough north or they too were dead.

"Any luck, Howard?" It was Mackey.

"Not yet."

Price's sled had come to a stop. There was something in front of them. It was huge and bulky and seemed to be leading several long columns of tanks toward the river. Price tapped the driver and pointed toward the front of the sled column.

Only from time to time through the fog could they get a sharp visual sighting of the thing. It moved quickly over the snow in short, powerful bursts, then waited for the tanks to catch up. But through the infrared goggles it seemed terrible, a huge glowing object that was giving off great heat.

Inside the Soviet hovercraft the commander had made it plain that he didn't want Medvenev around, and it had been Kork's fault.

After the helicopters had dropped in the new radios, Medvenev had been able to contact the chief marshal instead of having to climb aboard the old tractor and push back toward Wittenberge the way he had come.

But Kork had said, "Stay where you are. The whole area is in turmoil. Make yourself useful there," and everybody had heard. Medvenev blushed. The radio operator had to take the microphone from him.

After a while the commander, a lieutenant colonel, said, "I wonder, Captain, where your turmoil is?" They were within three kilometers of the river and all they'd seen was their own fire ahead of them. Every available tank within the radius of ten kilometers had been added to the force, and knowing that made the commander feel invincible.

Price's sled force took them head-on. Price himself had swung his own machine around the small hill, where from the top he'd observed the twin columns of tanks that stretched back as far as he could see through the drifting fog. He didn't know how many there were, he couldn't tell, but the opportunity was plain, both to inflict another severe loss on them and to break through to the north.

The sleds howled out of the fog and mist, and the TOWs, striking the front of the hovercraft, seemed only to stun it momentarily, but a trooper on a point sled fired low, under the skirt of the craft, and the explosion lifted the wide, looming shape up where yet another round seemed to get sucked right into the rotors. It was thrown back, almost vertical. It balanced there, its other engines roaring, then came crashing down. Only the rear end would rise off the ground, and moments later a cruise missile silenced it, though the hull remained intact.

By then the sleds were beyond it, taking out the tanks two at a time down the length of the columns.

The Soviets called in tactical air support, but the V/STOL aircraft had little opportunity to suppress the attack. The sleds hugged the sides of the tanks, and only those near the flaming and knocked-out hulks could be targets, and then there was fog, flame, and thick black smoke from burning oil and diesel fuel. Price's troops were white on white and any visual sighting had to be taken at speed.

Medvenev, who'd been standing in a niche out of the way, thought the entire hovercraft would flip over. The commander fell from his perch near the main gunner onto his back and neck, his legs raised in the air, then crashed into and snapped off the periscope and other jutting, barb-like appendages of electronic gear, one of which caught the collar of his fireproof uniform and hung him for a while. But when the angle increased he was dropped into a nest of wires near the turret and electrocuted, his body frazzled by the power that the many turboengines provided.

The interior was filled with thick black smoke and a rank, burnt odor that choked them.

Medvenev had fallen to his knees to catch whatever air remained when something else struck them with great force on the other side. Chunks of metal cut through the interior, through the apparatus and even the armor, leaving gaping holes in the shell. There was no fire, only the stench from the commander's corpse, and Medvenev then heard the whining sound, oscillating but continuous, that passed by on both sides of the wreck.

Not immediately, but after a while—when he could forget the moaning of the injured and dying, the stink, the sight of the crewman near him whose stomach looked as though it had been turned inside out, and the mumbling, the praying, the other one with the icon in his hands who'd turned his face to a blank wall of metal and wouldn't turn around—Medvenev moved to one of the holes and looked out.

At first he didn't notice the strange white masks until he heard the praying crewman mention devils and it came to him that the men hurtling by on the snow sleds really did resemble mummies, effigies of death. And Medvenev was suddenly cold, shivering, unable to control the quaking of his body in spite of the two greatcoats he found to wrap himself in.

Long after the sleds were gone he thought about climbing out of the wreck and trying to make contact with some Soviet contingent, but his last glimpse through the hole had shown him only a long line of flaming tank hulks, stretching back into the fog and mist, and other individual soldiers, such as he, wandering aimlessly through the snow, some calling out, others lying down, still others struggling through the deep drifts toward the woods.

He knew that, as an officer, he should go out there and round them up, but it was just not in him. Something had happened to him, some change—shock or fatigue or fear.

Nine miles to the northwest Price gathered his sled force. The break-through had been effected with heavy Soviet losses, but weapons stocks were again low. Nevertheless, he had no choice but to swing west, to search out and destroy whatever formations he could find.

Into the breach Mackey threw a reserve brigade from the First Cavalry. They crossed the river in waves of helicopters. Sleds were dropped and they too pushed west, hoping to strike another hovercraft and tank columns behind it or, failing that, any concentrations they could find.

To the south Reiner was quiet. Mackey hadn't heard from him in five hours and he wondered why.

Tuesday, A.M.
South of Salzwedel
G.D.R.

Since near dawn Reiner had been waiting and now with the rain he knew he had to act. Soon the sleds would have to be abandoned, and his men, armed only with what they could carry, wouldn't stand a chance against the massive concentrations of Soviet ground forces that had been moving past his position at a large farm near Brunau.

It had been the sheer size of the armies that had made Reiner seek refuge in the barns, outbuildings, and the house of the farm and had kept him from establishing contact with Mackey. He was afraid that in any encounter with even a portion of those troops his small force, which he estimated now at fewer than 4,000 men, would quickly exhaust its weapons stocks and would stand defenseless against the enemy. As it was, they had been fortunate to have come upon the farm at daybreak, when the snow had stopped and the fog was clearing, entering it from a woods that nearly reached the house on the east and concealed them from air observation. The sleds were still there, under the trees although the men had moved into the buildings for warmth and to rest.

Reiner lowered the curtain in the bedroom on the third floor and glanced around the room, noting the gilt-framed photograph of a teenage girl with blond hair and rosy cheeks, a blush that had been added, of course, but probably had been there in real life. She lived in Köln now, a doctor. "Medical," the old woman had added with pride, "although we wanted her to find a husband and take over the farm. We've got no others, you know, and it's too much for the two of us. Now."

And her dolls, eiderdowns, mementos, and childhood collections that had been left on the dresser, the bureau, and along the ledges of the windows—a gymnastic trophy, a toy car, a tennis ball, even a cast iron replica of the Brandenburg Gate and a Soviet tank with a bright red star painted on the side.

They weren't political, the old woman had said. "We just want to go on doing what we do—farming."

"What about the Russians?"

She had only hunched her shoulders and turned back to the stove.

Her husband was a tall, timid man with a blond mustache, a long, bony nose, and watery eyes. He hadn't said a word when Reiner had opened the kitchen door and stepped in. He'd been packing a pipe. He looked up Reiner, then back down at the pipe, as though he'd known him for life. He had walked into the pantry and asked his wife to put on a pot. He had thought—perhaps he still did—that they were Russians and drank tea.

Down in the largest barn Reiner now told the troop leaders, "As soon as we make contact with the enemy, I'll call for air cover, but we'll try to get as far west as we can first." He was standing near the final stall of the barn and could feel the heat rising off the black-and-white Holsteins that turned their heads now and then, eyes wide and worried but their jaws working steadily on the hay that the farmer had spread in the feeders to distract them while the milking machines relieved them of their burdens.

"No sense in painting a pretty picture," he went on and thought of the photograph in the bedroom and of his own children and wife. "We're cut off both in the way we planned and in another way." He straightened up and placed his hand on the soft, warm flank of a cow. "To be honest, we never expected them to have as many men or machines in this sector. Our munitions are low. And we've got the rain to consider.

"As I see it, we've got two courses of action—to surrender or to continue on with what we've planned, hoping the rain and the overcast skies"—he gestured to the open barn door, beyond which they could see the wet snow that seemed purplish, like lilac, against the muddy barnyard and the wet stucco walls of the outbuildings—"will shield us some, as the snow did last night.

"Surrender is out. It looks bad for us now, but we could make out okay. And we've been given a job to do and I'm for doing it right down to the last man.

"Second, I'm not sure they'd recognize a surrender. We've hit them hard, and they weren't big on taking prisoners in their last war, especially from the units that had made them smart. I can only think it would be better to plow right through them as far as we can west, hoping we can throw them into confusion and break back through the frontier to our own lines."

Only then did Reiner glance around the group, face to face, and he was gratified to see that to a man they all wanted to go on, but then one and then another of them looked beyond Reiner and toward the doorway. Turning, he saw the old man standing there in the rain, and then one Soviet soldier with a Kalashnikov in his hands, and then another and another.

The old man only managed to take the pipe from his mouth and raise it toward Reiner, as though calling him, when a burst of fire from the many guns blew him forward and then rolled him toward the cows, which froze, panic-stricken at the din and the smoke and the men who stormed the doorway, firing all the while.

Reiner threw himself down and scrambled between the cows, into and among the black rubber hoses and the stainless steel suction cups that had been fitted over the nipples of their bags. His only thought was to get back to the sleds and put through the call that he'd been delaying since dawn, to Mackey, to tell him of the concentration of forces in the sector, the formations and reserves that they'd considered the Soviets incapable of moving up on such short notice. Tanks, APCs, artillery, rocket and SAM batteries—

The cow above Reiner caught a burst, the concussion of the bullets thrumming against her ribcage like a drum roll. She rose up in the air, hopping front hooves to back as though running in place, and Reiner tried to roll over, under the legs of the next cow, but the tubes, the hot milk that gushed from them, the terrified screaming of the animals—had he ever heard that sound before? he asked himself with strange dispassion as the cow fell to her knees and began to topple onto him—the cascading hooves of the other cow prevented his escape. And anyhow, there were guns at every door and window now, and none of Reiner's men had more than sidearms with them.

Reiner doubled up and tensed his body and saw only a black-and-white flash, a blur, of the cow falling on him.

At first he felt little. He had heard something snap inside of him—in his chest or back or ribcage—and then he couldn't see or hear anything. Or breathe. He couldn't breathe, as hard as he tried, and he stopped trying.

When the pain began—in his hips mostly—he relaxed his muscles and the cow's immense body only crushed him all the more. He had—what?—a minute, two or three, and he tried to keep himself calm, but all his life he'd been terrified of the water for just that reason: his most memorable and recurrent nightmare was of drowning or suffocating, of the choking, searing sensation he got when water entered his lungs or the panic of a pillow over his head and the consciousness of trying but being unable to make his lungs fill with air.

Reiner began struggling with all his might, trying to kick and flail and moved his neck and head free—a Soviet bullet would be better—but it only made the panic more severe, and the only other sensation he had left, taste, had now become apparent to him—hot milk and blood and muck. He tried to cough but couldn't. He began gagging.

And a new kind of sensation, a numbing, began to eat into the pain. Suddenly he felt as though there were two of him—the Reiner who was dying there, crushed by the cow, and another Reiner who was dissociating himself from that husk, moving away, up, to some small place where all would be tranquil and free from pain and care and duty.

The army could take care of itself. It'd have to. And what was it all about anyway—being Reiner or Mackey or the Russians who had appeared in the doorway and had killed him.

After the battle of the Salzwedel tank park, Colonel Gamsakhurdia had found himself far forward of the main action, almost on the frontier where, from time to time, American shellfire threatened his immobilized tank and the few others that remained, the sled force having struck them and moved on. But he could hear fighting to the south, and he became convinced that the enemy had not attacked in force and would not follow up and annex the sectors that they had as much as won.

And he had been watching one of the American sleds idling slowly where it had become lodged against a shattered tank, its track spinning slowly, futilely as it endeavored to move forward. It seemed like some blind, ignorant mote, struggling vainly to complete the impossible task of moving the fifty tons of iron and steel from its path.

But he had approached it cautiously, not so much because he feared the dead and wounded soldiers who lay all about the battlefield, but because he respected the U.S. military experience since the Second War. They had suffered greatly from booby traps and antipersonnel devices and had applied their vast technological expertise to making any potential enemy—the Soviets in particular—suffer more severely because of their experience.

But Gamsakhurdia had doubted the driver or gunner of the tandem sled had had time to activate any devices, and could such a system be automatic? If so, it would have to be negated each time somebody climbed aboard, and in the heat of battle . . .

Aboard, he studied the controls and found it to be little different from the Soviet sleds he'd been trained on in Siberia. He put it into reverse, worked it away from the wreck, and collecting a few tankers who had survived, headed south.

"Strike and fade away." It was something by an American general that Mackey had quoted in one of the pieces Gamsakhurdia had had to study, and it kept recurring to him as he searched the many, confusing tracks at the edge of the battlefield to determine where the enemy had vanished to.

It wasn't until two A.M. that Gamsakhurdia caught up to them, three fifteen before he'd contacted Alexeyev, and dawn by the time the airborne and helicopter attack was coordinated.

"No real need for hurry," Alexeyev had said. "They're probably waiting for an opportunity for a surprise strike from the rear. And it's probably better that their command think their southern force is in place up until the time we launch our main strike. Then you can put your plan into action."

"Shall we try to take prisoners?"

Alexeyev had thought for a moment. His own forces needed a full victory, the knowledge that they had beaten tough, experienced soldiers. "Did they?"

And for Gamsakhurdia it had been as though all the proscriptions had been cast aside and anything was game and only the results—blowing the white-clad bodies across the barn—mattered.

8

Tuesday, A.M.
The White House
Washington, D.C.

Harper lowered the receiver of the white phone into its cradle, glanced at the translator, and picked up the red one.

The woman, a professor from Georgetown, lifted her phone. The wires led to a tape recorder, a black box, another tape recorder, and finally entered the wall.

Meisenzahl, his adviser for national security affairs, was the only other person in the room.

A small red light on the black box went on and Harper could hear static on the line and several voices, all speaking Russian, a language he did not know.

Harper was in his shirtsleeves and he hadn't slept or eaten since getting word of the situation on the Elbe. He was a beefy man whose formerly handsome face had fallen to jowls. He needed a shave. The woman, the translator, had been startled on seeing him. In public Harper always made it a point to look well turned out, but it was a pose. He only cared about his personal appearance insofar as it affected his career.

He again heard voices, and the translator, who was sitting next to him, turned the yellow legal pad so he could read what she began writing.

"Voronov's voice: 'Is that on?' Another voice: 'Yes, sir.' 'Then shut it off, Dimitri, please. Give us a moment.' Odd slurring of vocals; sounds tired. Yet another voice: 'A moment is all—' "

The line went dead and Harper eased himself back into his seat. Collective leadership, he thought, but he wondered

213

how different the minds of those on the Politburo could be. Harper was hoping for difference, indecision, dissension, and strife.

Harper rumpled his graying, curly hair and wrapped an arm around the back of the translator's chair. "What's your name again?"

"Rubin, Mr. President." She was a thin young woman with large, dark eyes that glanced up at him and then again fell to his beard.

"But your first name."

"Maxine."

"How old are you, anyhow?"

"Does it matter?"

Harper liked the reply. Long-time mayor of Boston, he had become governor of Massachusetts and President in rapid succession, but he tended to view his present involvements on every level through his early experiences as a Boston ward heeler: politics was people; some were good, bad, or indifferent, but everybody had a handle. Harper had always made it his business to find out as much as he could about everybody who could enhance or diminish his power.

"You know your stuff?"

"I must, you hired me."

Harper smiled and glanced up at Meisenzahl, a liverish old man who kept his hands folded in his lap. His eyes were bright and watchful, but he was mindful of his position. There was no phone in front of him. Harper, although he had just called an emergency meeting of the National Security Council, was an unlikely politician. He did not believe in collective leadership. The meeting would be strictly *pro forma*.

The room was cool, almost cold, in the way that Harper preferred. Heat brought ennui, torpor, and he wanted to be sharp. "You've been briefed, but let me tell you what I want, Maxine." The small red light was blinking again but Harper did not reach for the phone. "Atmospherics. As much as you can catch from any background voices. We'll have you go over the tapes, of course, but I'll need as much as I can get while we're talking. You've studied these men, listened to their voices before, so if you think they're angry or tired or"—he paused, searching for a word—"resigned, I want to know." Again he glanced over at her, and she returned his gaze without any diffidence. She was confident.

"Okay"—Harper reached for the phone—"let's see what they have to say."

"Mr. President—felicitations."

"Voronov," Rubin wrote.

"I hope my phone call finds you and your family and the people of your great country well and prosperous. I call concerning certain incidents that have been occurring along the border and in the sovereign territory of the German Democratic Republic, a beloved and sister state of the U.S.S.R.

"I've prepared a statement about these events. I'm tired, as perhaps you yourself are, and I shall have my assistant here read it. Then we can talk."

There was a shuffling of papers, and then the translator's voice said, "I'm sure you're aware of the present, precarious state of world peace, and of the fact that the armies of the Warsaw Pact nations are poised to strike deep into the heart of West Germany, having been attacked and provoked for the past eleven hours. Soldiers of the G.D.R. and the U.S.S.R. and many thousands of innocent German civilians have been killed, maimed, and injured, their property and possessions laid waste by marauding Western armies led by elements of the One hundred and first Aerial Assault Division under the leadership of NATO Northern Army Group Commander, U.S. General Mackey.

"Through heroic valor and the force of superior arms, the combined brotherhood of socialist armies has driven the invaders from the Republic, and only through humanitarian restraint and a concern for the peoples of Western Europe have they come to a stop within their own territory.

"I hereby demand that you order the withdrawal of all and sundry military personnel from within fifty kilometers of the border and agree to the indemnification of all aggrieved parties, including the U.S.S.R., for damages, deaths, and indignities you have caused. I further demand that you relieve from command all and every officer who has engaged in this unprovoked onslaught, and apologize to the G.D.R. and the U.S.S.R. in a public forum, namely before the convoked body of the United Nations.

"If not, the combined armies of the Warsaw Pact nations will take appropriate punitive action and will decimate the assembled NATO armies in Central Europe." The man had stopped speaking.

Harper placed the point of his pencil on the yellow pad and drew a circle. He put a square inside it, connected the diagonals, and then bisected the center with perpendiculars. It reminded him of the gun sights of an antiaircraft battery, the logo of the old Panamerican Globemaster stratocruisers, and of the world.

Fifty kilometers would surrender Lübeck, Hamburg, Hannover, Brunswick, Kassel, and perhaps Bremen and Bremerhaven, should the Soviets decide to occupy those areas until reparations claims were settled.

And apologize? For what? For having recognized the Soviet threat in Central Europe and having done something about it? It would be political suicide for one thing, and a national disgrace for another.

And it just wasn't Harper. He may have accommodated powerful interests in his time, but he had never groveled and was not going to start with Voronov.

What it all came down to was will. Meisenzahl and he had talked about it before, that at some point he'd have to confront Voronov and his iron-willed cohorts. The moment was now. "Bullshit," Harper said evenly.

Meisenzahl smiled.

Rubin looked up at Harper.

There was static and a voice asked, "What was that?"

"Bullshit," Harper said again.

The Moscow translator paused, then made a sound as though searching for a word. What he said met with silence at first, and then somebody began laughing. It was low and gravelly and contagious.

Harper drew a question mark on the pad.

Rubin shook her head, then wrote, "Perhaps Bysotsky." He was the minister of defense.

"You must be joking?" Voronov said, but obviously to the translator. Rubin wrote it down on the pad.

Her hand kept moving; somebody else was speaking. "Shouldn't we consider that if he seldom or never swears, then perhaps he means what he says."

"My friend," Voronov began, his voice manifestly unctuous, "after our meeting in Helsinki last year, I thought we understood each other, but this . . . colloquialism, it disturbs me. Could you please explain what you mean?"

216

"Your armies struck our army. General Mackey struck back. You are now, as you've said, prepared to strike again. That's your decision. I'll make no threatening projections about the outcome, but if you want battle we'll meet you strike for strike, make no mistake.

"Earlier today you sent your northern fleet out into the Atlantic. There is not a plane, a surface vessel, or a submarine the whereabouts of which is not known to us. All are being followed and have been targeted. We have the capability of counterposing any attack that you may be planning.

"The same goes for your fleet in the Indian Ocean.

"And finally, bullshit means that the United States will not be bullied by you or by anybody else. If you want a fight, mister, you've got it."

Meisenzahl closed his eyes and leaned back in his chair.

Rubin's voice was strong and clear, her face impassive as she spoke into the receiver. She paused only on the last sentence, weighing how best to render its street-tough informality, then said it through.

Even to Harper the sound of her voice palpably conveyed his meaning. He nodded.

There was a long pause and silence on the other end. Somebody then coughed. More silence.

Fnally Voronov said, "So—we have a problem, you and I. A big problem, no? I can't rest easy with the blows you have rendered me, and you can't allow me to assuage the pain. Is there no way out?"

"That's for you to decide."

Somebody else began speaking in a low rush, and Rubin wrote, "He wants to make us seem—"

Then Voronov's voice returned. "Tell me—do you plan to keep this line open?"

"I don't see why not."

"Well, perhaps we'll be speaking again."

"Perhaps."

Voronov hung up.

Harper dropped the phone in its yoke. He hadn't eaten in so long he felt almost nauseous. He said to Meisenzahl, "Full global alert. All elements, all weapons."

He picked up the white phone. "Get me the SACEUR."

Bengsten came on almost immediately.

"Harold, I've just spoken to Voronov. He says he's going

217

to go through with the objectives of their build-up, and he's left no doubt in my mind that he plans to throw everything at us he has."

Meisenzahl cleared his throat. "But do we know that?"

Harper lowered the phone and cupped his other hand over the speaker. His eyes met Meisenzahl's, which, Harper noticed for the first time, had begun to cloud with age. "When I want your opinion, General, I'll ask for it."

"How do things look there?"

"No change, really, since we last talked."

"Have you heard from General Mackey?"

"No, sir."

Harper smiled. He himself had. And his handle on Mackey—he had read the man right.

"Keep me informed."

"Yes, sir."

Harper hung up.

Meisenzahl had left the room and an aide entered.

"Are you hungry, Maxine? I'm starving."

Rubin couldn't think of eating—she had butterflies in her stomach. He frightened her, but she thought it best to say she was.

"Sandwich?" he asked.

She nodded. "Roast beef, please."

"Hard roll or white. Hard roll, I'm betting."

She nodded again and he laughed.

"Bring us a bunch of them, Bob, and some coffee. Make it hot."

Tuesday, A.M.
Near the Elbe
F.G.R.

Mackey knew it was foolhardy to be so close to the river, to have had the helicopter drop him here three miles upstream from Boizenburg, but somebody had to see how the Soviets would cross the river—at a few points or several or many—and the arc of the rocket barrage had long since passed beyond him.

Now the concussions off to the south were dull, hardly trembling the earth, which was still hot and sticky from ordnance. He had been watching the flashes, like distant lightning, rising in staggered rows from the launching positions that were wrapped in mist and darkness across the river, and finally that had stopped too.

After a while he began to hear low whining noises, a few shouts, and the occasional sound of a tank hatch being dropped into its collar and tightened down. All that came to Mackey clearly and seemed peaceful, like the sounds over a quiet lake, and in fact the water had again become placid, with only small chunks of ice and slush around the shore. Out in the middle it was still and black and deep.

And then all was quiet again and Mackey thought he knew why.

He looked around, all up and down the bank and through the tangle of toppled and splintered and smoldering trees, for a more secure position that would provide him cover from the tank fire, but he decided that his present spot—a rock outcropping on a bend in the river that commanded a long view in both directions—was best. It was covered with low bushes and no mechanized vehicles could climb its flanks. A flat area on top would allow the helicopter to drop in for them after the tanks had passed.

He ordered his radio man to seek cover behind a large boulder behind them, and Mackey crept to the edge of the outcropping that ended there in a cliff. He found a sort of natural sink completely enclosed on three sides by rock, and he began to wait, but not for long.

The whining increased gradually to a shrill, high-pitched roar, and then it seemed as though the other bank of the river exploded, the fire white all up and down its length. Mackey ducked and the rounds from the tanks slammed into the outcropping and jarred the rock out from under his hands and knees so that he had nothing to hold onto and came down hard with each thunderous blast.

Mackey flipped over onto his backside and crouched in the lee of the tallest shelf of rock, hands to his ears, elbows between his knees, which he squeezed tight, trying to contort himself into a tight ball, one that would bounce easily on the rock and present the least area to the shrapnel and shattered rock that was knifing through the darkness. The concussions were blowing back the trunks and stumps like chaff before a stiff breeze, and in brief lulls between rounds he could even hear waves washing through the slush and ice on the shore, the fire over the water having created turbulence.

He heard the radio man moan or cry out.

"You all right, Tompkins?"

"Yes, sir."

Scared, Mackey thought, like the Soviets themselves. If they weren't, they wouldn't be wasting their fire. The sleds had surprised them, and they didn't know if they might not be surprised again. Mackey would have preferred them to be confident, but that was war. In fact, he indeed had another surprise for them, but it all depended on the rain holding and Price disrupting their rear.

A lull, then another sound—grinding, pinging, straining—diesels. Mackey twisted around and eased his head above the shelf, holding the heavy, night-seeing binoculars to the bridge of his nose. He thought of Napoleon listening to the guns of Austerlitz, how he had noted that it was never good practice to engage the enemy in force until he had committed himself too far to withdraw.

Mackey would lead the attack north with the objective of linking up with Price, who had succeeded in swinging around behind the Soviets. Once that was completed, Mackey would call for the marine force that he'd placed in Bremerhaven to take defensive positions from Lübeck up the eastern coast of Schleswig-Holstein to protect his rear, and then he'd wheel the entire northern contingent of the 7th Army and drive south across the salient and isolate the main body of the remaining Soviet armies on the North German plain.

Without fuel, ammunition, or ready reserves, cut off in hostile territory with changing conditions—great, glorious torrents of rain that had been falling through the early dusk—the mud would pose an increasingly severe problem to the Soviets, and the destruction of their army would be assured.

The operation had proceeded not in every way that he had planned, but rather within the parameters of his expectations, and he'd been able to exploit opportunities. And of the three essential elements for victory—courage, ground, and climate—the latter two would again be working for him, and soon. Of the first he was now assured.

And how would Moscow rapidly replace their elite forces, their "army within the army," and all their tanks, guns, and planes? Their industrial base wasn't as strong as the West's and given their air losses, it was now vulnerable to preemptive strikes.

And he thought about Harper and the phone call he'd gotten only a few hours before.

He had been in the mobile command center that he'd moved again to Adendorf, and he had glanced down at his maps.

Somewhere down the length of the long command trailer a phone had been ringing, its tone more that of a buzzer than a bell. Only when it was answered did the sound penetrate Mackey's consciousness.

He had straightened up and glanced away from the maps, into the dark corner in which a module was displaying the continuing air battle over the sector north of Boizenburg where Price was supposed to be, and Mackey had had a feeling that the call boded ill.

And his leg had been bothering him again as he weaved his way through the rows of machines and gadgets that had helped him monitor, regroup, and resupply the sled brigades for the past half-day. It was dark and the electronic gear made the interior of the trailer warm, the only direct lights being those over the few desks that were spread far apart.

"General Mackey?"

Mackey's eyes had shied, down and to the left. He had recognized the voice. Harper.

"This is the President. I've just received a long, urgent phone call from Chancellor Schleymann. He says there's fighting going on along the border between your troops and those of the Soviet Union. A Bundeswehr general"—there was a pause—"no, a Bundeswehr colonel by the name of Kronenberger has reported to Defense Minister Ludeke that you started it by provoking the Soviets and when they retaliated in a fairly minor way, you attacked them. What do you say?"

Mackey snapped the light out over the desk and eased himself into the aide's chair; he pincered his temples between thumb and forefinger, rubbing them slightly, and breathed out. "There's fighting, sir, but I didn't start it."

"That's what Harold Bengsten just said."

Mackey looked up. That surprised him.

"Tell me—how much fighting?"

221

Mackey thought for a moment. Bengsten would have put Harper in the picture. "I hit them hard."

"How hard?"

"Hard enough to knock them back." Harper didn't respond, so Mackey continued, "They're stunned and reeling. Do you know the terrain, sir?"

"General Meisenzahl and I have a map in front of us."

Mackey went over the situation and his plans.

"It strikes me that you took a lot of decision-making upon yourself, General, and now you're taking more. I wonder if you understood the consequences of your actions."

Mackey thought he knew why Harper had to ask him that, but he wasn't solely responsible for the fighting by any means and would not be made the goat. "How do you mean, sir?"

"That lives and property would be lost, that the Germans might have to give up some territory, and that"—Harper breathed out—"I'd have to relieve you of command."

There it was.

"Tell me," Harper went on, "could you stop this imminent invasion?"

Mackey quickly considered his options. If he was going to be relieved, and blamed, then he had nothing to lose, and they—Mackey and NORTHAG—had come too far for that. "I think General Meisenzahl can tell you why I wouldn't want to stop it, sir. They won't be able to hold the salient, and if the opportunity is seized—"

"And which opportunity is that, General?"

Mackey thought about Reiner and his troops and the others and he hoped they hadn't died in vain. "Without the GSFG here on this plain, they'll be unlikely to take any offensive action anyplace else in the world."

"And you think that's an opportunity?"

"Yes, sir. I see it, I saw it that way."

There was a long pause. Finally Harper said, "I wonder if you remember the chain of command."

"Yes, sir, I'm familiar with it."

"From this moment on I want you to follow it."

Harper hung up.

Mackey had stood. To his aide he had said, "Where's the equipment that controls this thing?"

The same phone had been buzzing again; it would be Bengsten.

The aide had pointed to a radio console.

Mackey had kicked the feed line from the power supply. The buzzing had stopped. "It happened in the dark," he had said to the aide. "Not that it matters."

Now, from his perch on the rock above the Elbe, Mackey could see only the guns, turrets, and front hoods of the tanks, but he noticed that there was a gap after every tenth tank, and slowly he began to discern huge, lumbering shapes that became more distinct as the roaring of the diesels increased. And the shapes appeared to grow, to rise up as the carrier platforms approached the river, to tower above the tanks on the other bank, like silhouettes of tall, narrow buildings.

Suddenly the engines stopped, the dark shapes that loomed up into the sky swayed in place, no tanks fired, and then the shapes began to fall across the river toward the south bank, slowly at first but then more rapidly until they clanged down, like iron claws reaching out to pull the other bank toward the tanks. Bridges—dozens of them.

The firing commenced again immediately, but Mackey only crouched, for what he'd been waiting to see now occurred.

The tanks lining the banks did not used the bridges, but rather with snorkels raised they churned down the defile and forded the river. Other machines—mobile SAM and Katyusha batteries, older APCs and large artillery pieces that were towed behind tracked vehicles—clattered across the steel bridges.

Mackey waited there, watching wave after wave of tanks slide down the far bank, enter the water, and then crawl out, black and gleaming wet, like wide, mechanical rats pouring in from the east. Thousands of them.

Once the first rows had passed, the firing there on the riverbank ceased and he could only hear it in the distance, from the vanguard of the tank force. Clearing the river, some of the tank commanders opened the turrets and appeared in the hatches, confident now that no opposition had been encountered. Europe lay before them, or so Mackey hoped they were thinking.

It was difficult, but he waited nearly an hour while other Soviet forces—reserves and trucks with supplies—

appeared on the other bank. He did not think of the attack, his defense, his plans, his army, Harper, Bengsten, Kork, or himself; he merely crouched there, one man alone in the rain on a bitter night, a hunter who was concentrating all his acuity on one sense, his hearing.

And then from far off in the distance and across the river to the north he heard a rumble and a pause, and then another and several more. And planes, A-10s, jinked overhead, having been dispatched, not to attack the tank force that had struck south, but to fly north and aid Price, who by now had to be low on munitions and would need their help.

Soviet SAM batteries streaked from positions throughout the area, and only then did Mackey leave the sink, using the rocket flashes to scuttle through the tangled brush to his radio man.

If now he could stall the Russian advance, if the rain would only hold, and if Kork and Moscow would see that they had too many tanks and men already within the salient to make the use of more drastic measures a tenable option, then Mackey felt there was a chance he could complete his victory his way.

Up over the trees to the east he could see a large ball of flame that flickered up into the clouds and the dark night. Hitzacker: compensation for Salzwedel, Lenzen, Eldena, Dömitz and the other G.D.R. towns that had been taken out. That was war.

Tuesday A.M.
Hitzacker
F.G.R.

Immediately before the bombing had begun hours earlier, all activity in *Zum Wilden Mann* had ceased. Diners had looked up from their meals; the mother, who had been ringing up a bill, stopped with her fingers on the buttons of the cash register; a waitress held a tray inches from a stand and looked up.

In the kitchen Herr Siebenborn had stood and called for quiet. "Annette, Annette, please—just for a moment. Listen."

At first she mistook the sound for wind but realized that she had been hearing it now for several minutes without its becoming part of her consciousness. It was a howl, low and basal, that might have been mistaken for wind, but her father had gone to the back door and opened it.

The sound kept increasing, becoming impossibly loud and then louder still until it was a terrible, deafening rumble that seemed to slide the floor from under her feet. She rushed to the door and with her father and Schwerin pushed through the snow to the end of the alley and looked up into the sky to the north and east.

There were planes in every direction, but mostly coming in from the east. Multiple explosions were occurring, again to the east.

Then the bombing had begun. The buildings shook, the river turned to fire, pots and pans in the kitchen fell from the racks on the walls and cascaded over the floor. In the dining room people shrieked and panicked and trampled each other trying to get out the doors. Others slumped off their chairs and crawled under tables. There was crying and shouting. A heavy oaken chandelier shaped like a wagon wheel, its hub and fixtures wrought iron, crashed down and splintered three tables. A man was caught beneath the rubble and began to bellow for help.

Lights went on in every window all over the village and then flickered out. A heavy Soviet bomber already in flames dropped out of the clouds, caught the steeple of a church, and plummeted into a public housing complex on the eastern edge of town.

The air-raid siren began wailing, the fire alarm followed.

Then Mühling appeared among the figures at the end of the alley. He rushed toward them, and Annette thought Schwerin, who was standing beside her, would turn and run.

"We must flee," Mühling said. "I've just spoken to a Bundeswehr colonel. War has broken out, and"—his eyes passed over their faces, which were blank, dumbstruck; he wanted them to do what he said—"and she says Hitzacker won't be defended. They'll yield it to the Soviets. It's only a matter of minutes before they'll attack."

Still none of them moved.

Mühling turned his head back toward the fire. Much of

the town was now in flames and an oil storage depot down by the river now went up and made him cower.

He stepped toward Annette and took her arm. "You must come with me. We must get out of here."

She was tired, exhausted from all the events of the day, the five hours that she had spent behind the steam table, working over the hot ranges and stoves, and everything seemed surreal to her, horrible but fascinating, the clouds of fire that were burning up into the night sky so terrible and towering that it all seemed as though beyond escape. "Why?"

"Well—because I love you."

"What does that mean?" Even her own voice, the strange dispassion in her tone, contributed to the feeling of dissociation. It would only be a matter of time before the bombs fell on them and everything would be gone—destroyed, immolated—and she would be dead and it didn't matter.

Mühling again looked up at the cloud of fire. "It means I won't let you die." And to the father he said, "I'm taking your van. I want you to come with me, but I must get my mother and aunt first."

He released Annette's arm and turned back down the alleyway, to the street and the people and his house beyond.

Annette glanced at her father, who looked suddenly old and exhausted and unsure of what to do. She remembered what he had said to her many years before when she was still a small child and he had been building the inn on top of the old cellar of a burgher's house: that they had built for keeps then; that those walls could withstand any bombing; that he had wanted to keep the cellar not just for wine storage, "but in case the Russians should return."

"Take the family down to the sub-basement, papa. Just for now. I'll go help Karl and come get you when everything is ready." She reached behind her for the cord of the apron, but Schwerin took it and undid the bow. She pulled it off her head and handed it to her father.

"I'll come with you, Annette, if I may," Schwerin said.

She glanced at him. He seemed calm, different from how he usually appeared, chastened somehow, but composed. Yes, she thought, he'd respond to a crisis. He wasn't big and strong and manifestly brave, like Mühling, but there was something soldierly in his bearing. "Good."

"But with all this snow—" her father said after them. "And you should have on a coat, Annette. Don't be long. I'll be waiting." He turned and rushed back to the kitchen door.

Inside he tripped and fell over the litter on the floor and couldn't get his footing on the stairs because of the jarring. The others—his wife, the children—were frantic, terrified. He brought them down to the wine cellar where the concussions were, if anything worse. Wine bottles had been worked loose and lay shattered all around the floor. A large wooden keg had cracked and was sodden with white wine.

Annette found the streets in disorder, clogged with frantic people on foot and in cars that kept getting stuck. The tops were piled high with goods that had been lashed to the roofs. In their panic people were quarreling with each other. One man had drawn a gun and was threatening another driver.

She thought of what she had read and heard about war: what had happened to those people who had fled and those who had remained, and there was really no option, no proper course. All was chance, but she would go with Mühling, if only because he seemed to know what he was doing, and he was strong and he loved her and at the moment it meant very much to her.

Across from Mühling's alleyway several men from the fire brigade were trying to extricate a NATO pilot whose parachute had snagged on the façade of a burning building. There seemed little point in it, though, for the man's face was charred, but the eyes—large, white, and hopeless—turned up into the clouds, searching them, as though he heard the screaming long before the curtain of fire began raining down on the riverbank at the end of the street.

With the others Annette and Schwerin stopped and watched the wall of flame, a continuous line of fire that was at least a hundred meters away and was advancing on them at the pace of a fast walk. And they ran, all of them, the others back to their homes and families or simply away from the fire, with Schwerin following Annette down the alleyway to the entry and stairs up to Mühling's flat.

Karl was in the apartment doorway with his mother over his shoulder and his aunt holding the door.

"But I don't understand where we can go, where we can stay."

"London, Paris, Rio de Janiero," Mühling replied in a jocular voice, though Annette could tell from his eyes that he was as frightened as she.

"But what will we use for money?"

"I'll rob a bank. Two banks. One for each of you."

"But, Karl—all our things."

"We'll buy new ones. As I explained, we'll probably have to anyway."

"Hurry!" Annette called up to him. "We'll have to run."

But they only made the entry when the barrage line fell on the building. Annette looked up and thought she saw the roof coming down, the stairs collapsing, Schwerin and the aunt falling right at her, but her back was against the wall and then all was black and she smelled smoke and felt pain so severe that it began eating into her consciousness and she passed out.

At the *Gasthaus* Herr Siebenborn had dashed up the stairs, but already he knew it was too late. Through the leaded glass windows he could see the line of fire immolating all before it, chopping down buildings and houses and turning the roadway into an avenue of fire. He only just made the shelter himself before the house fell in on them. The passageway up was heaped with rubble and debris and the air was filled with plaster dust, smoke, and gas.

Siebenborn paused in the doorway, shining the flashlight up at the wreckage. They had plenty to eat and drink, and, given any air and no fire, they could last for days.

But his wife was whimpering, his youngest crying, and his son asked, "What about Annette?"

Siebenborn wrapped his arm around the boy's shoulder. Nothing could have survived the attack, although there they were themselves, alive.

Siebenborn hung his head. "Annette," he said.

When she came to she could find none of the others—Mühling, his mother, Schwerin, or the aunt—in the rubble of the building. She had crawled out through a gap in the wall, her back bruised, her scalp bleeding. She was dizzy. She fell trying to climb over the heap of stones, trying to locate them. She kept calling, but she could hear only the

228

crackling of the fires, the awful screaming of the rockets, and other fire, back down toward the river.

And she was disoriented. Nothing was recognizable. All the buildings were down or on fire and streets were gone. In their place were fields of rubble and mud riddled with holes gaping down into the sewers, wires flashing, and screams and moans and shouts for help from what looked like piles of shattered rock. Even the snow was no longer there, it had vanished from the ground. It was just dawn and a thin, bitter drizzle was falling on the wreckage.

She recognized only the large slab roof of the garage behind the *Gasthaus*. It had fallen like a lean-to.

She began trying to pull away the rubble from what she thought had been the back door, but she remembered the descriptions of the digging out during the last war, that one had to take care lest the rubble shift.

Looking around for a lever of some sort to prise up a large chunk of concrete, she saw the tank stop and the man in the turret point to her.

She tried to run but her foot punched through a hole and she went down and they were upon her, one of them ripping off what remained of her skirt. "Wait," she said in Russian. "Help me find my family and you can have what you want," but they dragged her across the courtyard and into the garage, where they threw her onto the low back of the brown Porsche.

They took turns holding her ankles on the fenders, her wrists on the roof, and the weight of their bodies pressing her back against the car made her think she had broken something.

But gradually some defense mechanism she had never needed before allowed her to distance herself from the event. The Annette who mattered, the one who thought, had retired from the physical scene of her body's being violated, probed, and inseminated by the seven laughing, chuckling, leering men to a very quiet place in her mind, one which, when she allowed herself the peace it provided, shielded her from the indignities or the horror of whatever else would unfold with the event. All was tranquil there, painless, and nearly pleasant.

Only the little one with the mustache, the bandages around his head and one of his hands, and the large, sad

229

eyes, was gentle. In her dizziness and the strange unreality of the scene, the laughing of the others, she hardly noticed he had returned. He even wrapped his greatcoat, which stank, around her, as though trying to keep her warm, and he lowered his head and nuzzled her breasts.

And that was how Mühling found them.

She saw him over the soldier's shoulder, dark against the fire that was visible beyond. He had something in his hands that rapped out at the others, who hollered and were knocked back into the shadows of the garage, their bodies jumping and twitching and falling.

But the little one remained where he was, on top of her, inside her. And he whimpered once or whined, before Mühling snatched him off her and seemed to break him, like a rag doll, in two, so that stuffing, some kind of paper, popped out from beneath his underwear when his body struck the wall. The bullets from the gun pinned him there, nearly upright.

Annette could move only her neck, it seemed. Mühling had to pull her legs together and help her up. He wrapped what was left of her overcoat around her, and placed first his mother, whose eyes were rolling back into her head, and then Annette into the car.

It didn't, it wouldn't start.

Mühling grasped the wheel with both hands and shook it as though he could bring the engine to life that way. He turned to her.

Annette was having difficulty returning from the quiet place, the peace that it had brought her, and she didn't understand what the black fluid was that had seeped from the corner of his mouth and covered his chin. She wanted to remain cowering there, miles, perhaps even a world, away from what had happened to her body, to her family, to Mühling, his mother, his aunt, Schwerin, the *Gasthaus*, Hitzacker.

But she began to smell herself: the odor of their many bodies, the stink of their seed, their blood, the reek of the gun smoke and hot metal and death, and her eyes wavered toward the heap of rubble where her parents were. It brought her back. "I must wash. My family—"

Mühling only shook his head. He had wiped away whatever had been on his chin.

And the car started.

9

Several hours before, Kork had picked up the Moscow line.

"Volodya Kirill," Voronov had said in his most saccharine tone, "I have before me a map indicating the present dispositions of our forces and those of the aggressor NATO nations. The information was supplied us by your staff, and thus I assume it is accurate and up-to-date.

"I'd like to go over it with you and then discuss with you the"—he paused—"extent of our losses. Please don't hesitate to correct me where I'm wrong. I'm not a soldier, only a poor administrator."

Kork looked down at Alexeyev's large, furry cat, which was sitting in his lap. Kork liked the way its muscles bulged under the light yellow coat and the green eyes, some turquoise shade, that closed and opened regularly, as it was being stroked. Little Bear, the staff called it; Kork realized he was trying to distract himself.

It was Voronov's tone that bothered him most and the bit about being only an administrator. Before his recent elevation, Voronov had been minister of defense. During the war he'd been an able and tough soldier. An officer, Kork corrected himself.

But Kork listened attentively as Voronov outlined the present picture—the fact that Soviet forces were now flooding the salient, poised to strike Hamburg and Brunswick and to pour through the Fulda Gap farther south—and corrected the figures only twice.

"And what do you make of it, my friend? From a military standpoint."

Kork liked that even less. What other standpoint was there, now? Political? Kork thought he knew what was in the back of Voronov's mind.

Alexeyev entered the room, and the cat only turned its head to its master. Comfort, Kork thought—something he, as an old man who was now very tired, could appreciate too.

Kork sorely desired to emphasize the positive, the retaliation, that the army was on the move and carrying the fight deep into the enemy's territory, dominating the battlefield, and all the other clichés of tactical parlance, but those reports were not yet in, and Kork would not sacrifice his credibility with Moscow. Once he did, it would only be a matter of time before they replaced him.

Alexeyev reached down and patted the cat, which began purring now that it had two hands on its back.

"Well—we've suffered losses."

"So we've noted. Why?"

"We could not have known how or when or with what they would attack, or if, in fact, they would strike at all. I understood from our last conversation, Comrade President, that the opportunity of striking across the frontier with a significant body of my forces was not being availed me, at that time. Could I have been wrong, sir?"

He could hear Voronov drawing on a cigarette, and he could imagine him looking up over the desk and the heads of the others, who would surely be with him now, his eyes placid and clear. Once again Kork glanced down at the cat.

"No, my friend, that's right."

"And, to be honest, under normal conditions we could have responded. As has been confirmed, however, they altered the climate. Given our tactical posture, we have now responded in the only way possible."

"Do you think, then, they planned this attack long in advance?"

Kork sighed. He was being used as a sounding board. If, say, he had planned the attack himself, he would have included many more sleds, thousands more. And the reports said that the sleds were different in design, power, color—obviously a force that had been assembled on the spur of the moment by requisitioning or commandeering or outright purchase. Kork also thought about the aerial assault unit that had strayed across the river. Kork didn't think that

Mackey was the sort of commander who would knowingly sacrifice even one of his men, especially considering his overall disadvantage in numbers.

"No—it was impromptu, I believe, and felicitous. For them."

Alexeyev had tapped Kork on the shoulder.

"Then what are our prospects, my friend? Are we now faced with a protracted struggle?" It was not Moscow's opinion that Pact forces could win such a conflict, conventionally.

Kork glanced up at Alexeyev, who was holding his hat over the cat, upside down. He tapped the liner and the drumlike crown of the hat showered water on it. The cat lit out, jumping down into the shadows of the desk.

"Rain?" Kork questioned silently.

"Torrents, cloudbursts, monsoons," Alexeyev said, flourishing his hand.

"And the temperature?"

"Rising, but not too fast."

"Pardon me, Volodya Kirill—we didn't catch that."

"I was speaking to Colonel-General Alexeyev. He reports that quite a bit of rain is coming down now. If the temperature holds and the ground doesn't soften up, we could be provided with a rare opportunity. In a way, you see, we have their armies encircled, if only we can move."

Now Kork was hearing other voices, some speaking at once.

Voronov said, "Could you hold for a few minutes, Volodya Kirill? We'd like to come to a consensus here."

Before Kork could say yes, the line was cut off.

Alexeyev eased himself against the desk, his brow furrowed in question.

Kork only shrugged. "They're talking it over."

Under the table the cat had begun to remove the drops of water from its head and neck, carefully pawing off each drop and then licking the paw.

"Volodya Kirill?"

"Yes, Comrade President."

"We're decided now. Minister of Defense Bysotsky will be arriving at your headquarters in a few hours. You're to retain overall command, of course, but Comrade Bysotsky shall be privy to all your decisions. Are you agreeable to that?"

Kork did not pause. "Certainly, sir. I look forward to his arrival."

"Thank you, Chief Marshal."

"Yes, sir."

Kork hung up.

"Who?" Alexeyev questioned.

"Bysotsky."

"Bysotsky? I thought he was—"

"An administrator," Kork filled in, remembering Voronov's description of himself only a few minutes past. "Not a soldier. You see, Vassil, they've come to a 'consensus,' there in their posh office." Kork was suddenly angry. He scraped back the chair and stood. He'd been sitting too long.

The cat darted from under the table, down toward the display boards and the other officers who were monitoring the reports from the battlefield.

"Soldiers lack will?" Alexeyev asked.

Kork looked up at him, the long, scarred face, the bluish-gray, penetrating eyes; perhaps Alexeyev's chances had been ruined as well.

"It's the sole possession of administrators." Kork raised a hand and shook it. "Weaselly little ferrets of Bysotsky's stamp."

The others in the room were now looking at him.

Kork spun around on them. "Get back to work!"

Tuesday, P.M.
West of Uelzen
F.G.R.

Bengsten raised the field glasses. The wind had shifted and was blowing the fog in wisps before the two figures who were standing under the trees of the car park of the supply depot, where he had located his crisis-management center. He had never met the woman he'd been watching, but he'd seen her before in Bonn and where else? SHAPE headquarters, Brussels. Tall, blond, very Prussian in her bearing.

"And the man—how long has it been now, Major?"

"Eighteen hours or so, sir. He showed up right after you

pulled us back here to Uelzen. He flashed a Bundeswehr pass, said his name was Benz, said he was sent to coordinate C&C with the forward German units. Specialist in ECM. He made himself scarce after that. Gallagher only noticed him over there a couple of minutes ago, with her.

"She's a Colonel Kronenberger. Gave us the cover story that she had a message for you from Bundesminister Ludeke. We reached him. No soap. I thought you should know."

Bengsten went up on his toes and set himself down in stages. Eighteen hours. "But before that—"

"Never saw him before, sir. Or her. Him we're having checked out, but the communications being down and with the weather . . ."

Bengsten sorted through what had happened. Could she somehow have stumbled on the seeding operation or the call he'd made to Major Dimauro in Bremerhaven? Even if she had, could she have traced it to him? Bengsten didn't think so. He'd taken every precaution. And she wouldn't have been running a tape on Dimauro's line.

The 12th Panzer-Grenadier headquarters. The conversation with Mackey. Bengsten lowered the glasses and looked down at them, his nostrils flaring. It had been a mistake, there, but he had had to prod Mackey and he probably wouldn't have had another opportunity in private like that.

Well, it was over and done with now, but the major test was still before him. He turned to Cady, wondering if he could count on him. "How long have you been with me, Major?"

Cady was surprised by the question. He was blond with a dimpled jaw and wide cheekbones. Like the rest of Bengsten's staff he had a solid, squared-away look, but his short stature increased the impression. "Counting Vietnam, almost eight years, sir."

Long enough to appreciate power, Bengsten thought, and the kind of work and care it had taken to get it. He stepped away from the dark window and looked down the length of the command shelter where the others were engrossed in the details of the continuing action. "Major, I don't think I can impress upon you too strongly the seriousness of our situation here. Not just"—again Bengsten's eyes flickered toward the others—"not just for NATO but mostly for our country. Do you know what I mean?"

Cady didn't know exactly what Bengsten meant, but he had an idea.

"Major—that man and that woman out there"—he lowered his voice—"are a threat to our country. Now, all we know about the man is that he probably got in here on a phony. Am I right, Major?"

Cady looked away. They really couldn't say that yet.

"And even if not, Major. His . . ." Bengsten searched for a word. "—activities have been suspect."

Cady nodded. "Yes, sir."

"Now, that woman we know about, and I can tell you this—she's got no reason to be here. Her command is what?"

"The Bundeswehr itself, sir. Something to do with internal security, I think. Before that—"

Bengsten raised a palm. "All right. That's established. Now, I'm going to tell you this in the strictest of confidence." Bengsten was tired and he had to concentrate. It all might come back to haunt him later, and he had to stick to the facts. "The situation along the border is deteriorating. The Soviets have"—he paused dramatically—"attacked from Salzwedel in the south and Eldena in the north. Mackey—General Mackey and NORTHAG, well"—Bengsten glanced at Cady—"it doesn't look good, Major. Not good at all."

He straightened up and slid his hands into his pockets. "We're going to have to take over, sooner or later, and respond, and I don't want those two getting in the way. Do you understand what I mean, Major?"

Cady's eyes strayed toward the windows. "I think so, sir."

"Can you handle it yourself?"

"You mean—without the rest of the company?"

"With or without them." Bengsten began turning away. "It makes no difference to me. Those two are a security problem, a threat, and they have to be stopped. I don't care how it's done."

Cady did not button his overcoat. With his second step he could feel the water below the slushy drifts seep into his boots. He snugged his hat down onto his brow. The rain was splashing off the plastic-coated brim. He almost hoped they'd give him trouble.

Both Kronenberger and Hofmann saw the short, blocky officer approaching them.

Kronenberger was resigned to what was about to happen. She knew it was inevitable. Somebody would eventually question her presence or check on Hofmann, and her only tool—her only *weapon*—would be those questions and her own.

She was tired, having driven nearly all night through the snow and then the rain and finally around the evacuees who had become more numerous as she had gotten father east, clogging the highways, snarling traffic.

Hofmann said, "His name is Cady. He's been acting as liaison officer between Bengsten and the artillery batteries, the ones I told you about."

She looked down at Hofmann, who was short and fat. The juncture of his bifocals split his eyeballs into mismatched crescents. The glasses were fogged and spattered with rain. He was soaking wet, his hair slicked flat on his head. "And when exactly did that occur?"

"Hours ago. It was happening when I arrived. Cady passed through security while I was being interviewed. At least it'll be good to get inside." His eyes, which were hazel, flashed up at her. "Do you think there'll be much trouble?"

Kronenberger didn't know, but she was planning on making as much as she could. "You were only following my orders, Hofmann. I'll make a statement to that effect, you have my word."

Hofmann only looked away, at Cady, whose overcoat blew open in the breeze.

He pulled it to. "Colonel. Herr Benz." He removed his right glove and touched the brim of his hat. "General Bengsten has sent me. He'd like you to accompany me back to the security shelter."

"Why, Major?" she asked.

Cady surveyed Kronenberger—her long straight nose, her grayish eyes, the way her cheekbones diminished to hollow cheeks and made her seem haughty. "When you entered the complex, Colonel, you told the officer on duty that you had been sent by Bundesminister Ludeke. He denies it. And then there's some question about Herr Benz's identity as well."

"What question?"

Again Cady looked at her: the high forehead that was

237

visible even under the hood of her raincoat, the thin wisps of yellow hair. Cady did not like Germans, and he'd found their women cold. This one was another bitch, he could feel it. "I'll discuss it with Herr Benz in the security shelter. Please follow me." He took a step toward the shelters.

Hofmann began to follow him, but Kronenberger reached out and stopped him. "We're not going anywhere, Hofmann."

Cady turned back to them.

"If General Bengsten wants to check our credentials, he can do it himself, or is he too busy planning a holocaust? Tell him that for me, would you, Major? Tell him we have him down on tape and before, much before this whole thing"—with the point of her chin she indicated the shelters—"began."

"I'm not going to tell General Bengsten anything and you're not either." Cady opened his overcoat and undid the clasp on the holster of his service automatic, slowly, deliberately. Their eyes were joined throughout the procedure, and hers did not waver.

A hot rush of anger flooded through him—at her, at Germany, at being stuck with Bengsten and staff when the action was taking place only thirty miles away, at the way his boots were swimming, at his soggy uniform, at the rain and the way the little asshole with her looked like a wet, cringing dog.

The butt of the gun was cold. Cady thumbed off the safety and raised it at arm's length, pointing it right at her forehead. "Now, you accompany me to security. If you don't, I'll kill you."

Hofmann's eyes darted from Cady to Kronenberger and then to the gun. He wondered how much experience she'd actually had with soldiers and what she knew about men. Cady was not bluffing. Hofmann had heard the tone before.

"Now, move out." It was low, even, and honest.

Hofmann's hands shot out and grasped the sleeve of Cady's overcoat and thrust it up. The burst of the gun drove them back and Hofmann toppled into Cady.

Kronenberger went down.

Hofmann's knee came up. Once, twice, but his hands slipped from the wet material of the overcoat, and Cady brought the butt down on his head.

They fell back into the snow, but Cady scrambled to his feet.

Hofmann lunged for his legs. Cady only stepped aside and swiped the automatic against Hofmann's ear, sending him sprawling into a snowbank beyond the car.

Taking deliberate steps, Cady followed him. The pain was seeping up through Cady's stomach but he fought it.

He glanced behind him at Kronenberger in the snow. Both of her hands were clasped over her brow. She was not moving. Cady turned his back to her.

Hofmann was reaching inside his raincoat. Cady pointed the gun at his mouth. "Dead man," he said in the same even way, "how does it feel to be a dead man, Herr Benz."

Hofmann's hand stopped. "I'm not Benz. My name is Hofmann." Without his glasses he could scarcely see Cady, only another dark shape that merged with the trees in back of him. He took his hand away from the coat, slowly, carefully. He didn't think he'd have a chance, and why, anyhow? "She's my commanding officer. I was only following orders."

Cady glanced toward the shelters. There was nobody around, and only one window looked out that way.

Cady moved the gun down and fired into Hofmann's leg.

The bullet seemed to lift him right out of the snow. He spun around and fell on his stomach, his hands jerking down to the leg, which was twitching spastically, kicking out at the pain.

The second shot struck the top of Hofmann's left shoulder and tore down through his upper arm, shattering the bone, rending muscle and tendon. It exited from his elbow and, like shrapnel, entered his thigh, where it severed an artery.

Hofmann lay there on his side, his face in the snow, one hazel eye staring beyond Cady, at Kronenberger, who had risen to her knees, her forehead a bright swath of blood. Hofmann was breathing heavily through his mouth, and kernels of snow had caught in the bristles of his mustache, making him appear suddenly old and wise and experienced.

Cady raised the gun once more and took aim at the back of his neck.

Kronenberger pushed herself off the ground, but the soles of her shoes were sodden, slipped in the snow, and she only stumbled at Cady, shouting, *"Nicht bewegen!"* as though scolding a small child.

Cady spun around and the black eye of the barrel winked at her twice—blinding flashes of silver and gold—and she felt her body collide with him. As they went down she heard a muffled roar and felt something hot against her thighs.

But her fists and knees and elbows were flailing, punching, kicking at the snow and the hard thing under her. She was panic-sticken, horrified, enraged. One of her shoes flew off. Her knuckles came down on something that gave way with a snap. The man under her was not moving.

She tried to focus on him but at first she couldn't. Her fist was still in his mouth. Pulling it away, she twisted his head to the side. There was a deep gash that curved from his ear around to the back of his head, the skin yellow at the edges like a ghastly mouth. His head had struck the jagged edge of the dangling bumper of her car.

Hofmann was lying beyond them, watching her.

She turned aside and began heaving, upchucking, nauseated by what she had seen and done and by how she felt, and every throe brought a searing, rending pain in her lower stomach.

Still—she made the side of the car.

"Don't leave me. Please, don't leave me!" Hofmann begged, his voice breaking. With his one good arm and leg he was trying to scuttle through the snow toward the car.

Kronenberger wanted to explain—that she couldn't, that there was something wrong with her too, that— She opened her raincoat and the overcoat below. The whole front of her uniform coat, her pants down to the knees were wet, making the gray-green cloth look black. And what she was feeling in her shoes, the warmth—it must be blood. She'd been shot.

"Please! For the love of God! He'll kill me, I know. Please!"

But Kronenberger was behind the wheel, and the diesel engine, still hot from the long night's drive, started with a turn of the key. She was unable to reach for the door or to depress the clutch far enough. The car spurted forward, the chains she'd had put on in Uelzen biting into the ice and trampled snow of the parking area.

She could see some soldiers near the command shelter now, running toward her. They had carbines in their hands. She didn't know what to do. They couldn't all be like Cady.

Passing down the line of the other cars, she had to tug hard on the wheel to keep it from straying into the others. And she had to apply further pressure as she moved into deep snow toward the woods road that led to the gate and the highway beyond. She had trouble staying in the tracks that she'd made earlier.

Could one of the shots have hit a wheel? No. If it had the tire would be flat and she wouldn't be able to move at all. She'd had trouble like that before, on a skiing trip to Switzerland, but why was she thinking of that now?

"Please!" the shout was agonized, beseeching, a pitiful shriek.

Kronenberger let the car glide to a stop. She shoved open the door and swung her legs out. She managed to get to her feet, but she couldn't straighten up. Spots were appearing before her eyes and carried the green of the pines up into the snow cover and through the slate sky. The ground heaved under her feet.

Like a hook, Hofmann had clasped one hand onto the back of Kronenberger's bumper. He tried to smile. "Thank you. Thank you, Colonel. Thank you, Fräulein. I—"

Kronenberger reached for the arm. From behind her she could hear shouts. The hand seemed stuck to the shiny silver bumper. She tugged at it, lost her footing, and went down. The pain in her stomach—it almost knocked her out.

"Don't leave me. Please don't leave me. I can help you. He'd kill me."

"Fräulein—"

But Kronenberger had succeeded in getting the hand off. She struggled to her feet. It felt as if she had something searing her insides. In a blur, way back behind them, she thought she could see men running down the road. She heard some reports, like pops, but she couldn't be sure what it was, and the hand—Hofmann's hand—had hold of her arm. She couldn't free it.

"Let me go—you'll get us both killed."

"I don't want to die, Fräulein. They'll kill me, you know they will."

"Let go!' Kronenberger hacked at the arm, but Hofmann only smiled thinly and sickly. His face was gray.

Behind them the shouts were growing louder. There were more pops and something tattooed the trunk of the car.

"Here—I'll put you in." Kronenberger began dragging the man toward the passenger side of the Mercedes. She didn't know how she'd get him in, but she was beyond caring. The whole situation, the bleeding, the weak feeling, the way she was seeing—she was sure it was all over for both of them.

"I can help you. Helicopters." Hofmann said.

At the door Kronenberger had to push and heave Hofmann, who shrieked every time he was touched, and the blood from their mutual wounds made the clothing on their arms and legs slick. But Hofmann's short, powerful leg and his hand and arm, which, reaching across the seat, had seized the steering wheel, slid him into the car.

Now the soldiers were closing on them. Seeing Kronenberger, they stopped and raised their carbines to their shoulders. More firing and the back of the car—the trunk, the windshield, the fenders—were riddled by bullets. The trunk lid sprang open. Kronenberger pulled herself over Hofmann and fell behind the wheel.

Hofmann collapsed, his head and shoulders coming down into her lap. She shoved him toward the other door and snapped the gearshift into first, pushing down on the accelerator with all she had.

The car skidded then caught and careened forward.

"The highway," Hofmann said. Propped against the door but sitting up, he was staring straight ahead, the smile still on his lips, almost as though they were out for a Sunday drive. "The trees." With his good hand he pointed to the forest ahead of them. "Stay in them. Helicopters."

But the road broke through the trees into a clearing not far from the low wooden gate and the highway, and there a helicopter was waiting for the lurching, swerving car.

The fire from the machine gun seemed to open up rows of bright blossoms that worked across the hood of the car and burst through the windshield, the dash, the seat, and

242

Hofmann—steel, glass, rubber, padding, and flesh. Dead, Hofmann sat there as before, one hand holding his other arm, and the car managed to reach the edge of the clearing and the highway, a long splinter of the gate jutting from its grill.

There a Bundeswehr convoy was headed east, and Kronenberger steered for it.

Tuesday, P.M.
East of Uelzen
F.G.R.

Adjutant-General Feoklitych was stymied. He didn't know what to do. His tank army had met no resistance until the planes had passed overhead and dropped the minelets— small but powerful antiarmor devices that sank into the snow and slush, disappeared in puddles, and dug right into the mud over a wide area.

He had lost seven tanks and then eleven more of which he had knowledge, and finally he had called a halt. He didn't know how many of his tanks might have heard the order, how many might have blundered on into the minefields, but the devices were everywhere, even behind them. The planes had roared in over the treetops and passed them several times, releasing load after load. The SAMs had knocked down two in his area, but it was small compensation. And it was getting dark again and raining even harder. Already mud had clogged the tracks. The bearing squealed and shrieked and were beginning to burn out.

He sent the mine destroyers forward, older tank bodies on which cranelike appendages with weights and concussion pads had been fixed to dig and tamp the earth before them and set off the mines, but it was slow going and he didn't really have enough of them. And from out of the lowering sky, through the clouds and mist, antiarmor rockets were falling like deadly bolts of lightning. Never a miss. His tanks were being picked off remorselessly. One, now another, two more.

He ordered fire, but it was futile. They had no sighted targets and munitions stocks were running low.

And now, standing in the open turret, he began to hear

other sounds, a buzzing as from gnats but high-pitched, varying, and insistent, in swarms off on both flanks.

"What's that?" he asked the tank commander.

"What, sir?"

"That noise?"

The man pulled up the flap of his tanker's cap and listened. "Those sleds, sir?" He had never heard them himself, but they'd been briefed, just before the strike across the river.

Feoklitych doubted it. Nothing like that could operate over the soupy ground, but it was a sound he had heard before, yet never with such intensity.

Off on the left flank and then on the right fireballs appeared, puffing up into the night sky, and then the unmistakable sound of antitank rounds smacking into armor. Other explosions, automatic fire, and shouts came to them through the rain.

The turret gunner crowded into the hatch and grasped the handles of his weapon.

The tank commander slipped down the ladder and the turbine roared under them.

Feoklitych raised the night-seeing binoculars to his eyes, but all that appeared were little flashes off in back of them and shadows flitting through the flames of shattered tanks, until farther down the line rockets spewed from the woods and closer in and even right up tight on the tanks, the APCs, the mobile SAM and Katyusha batteries.

And the tank wouldn't pull free, only sidled in place, sidewards and down as the tracks churned into the mud and dug trenches.

Feoklitych snatched up the command mike and flicked on the switch. "Abandon the tanks. Fight them on foot. They're on—" He didn't get a chance to complete his statement.

Suddenly from behind a heap of rubble came the blatting, angry bark of powerful two-cycle engines, and a phalanx of six or seven motorcycles veered right for them, the men on the back of each firing rockets at the tanks from point-blank range.

Feoklitych hadn't even time to duck.

The rocket started low to the ground and rose up as though it would miss them, but something—some fire from the turret gun, a fleeing tanker, a vagrant chunk of shrap-

244

nel—struck it and the explosion spewed an arc of metal in front of the tank that sounded like the tinkling of fragile glass shattering on the armor and passed through Feoklitych's soft tanker's cap.

Mackey had mounted the final bike with Werbiskis driving. He had called in airborne and helicopter units once the bikes had struck, and now on a small hill he watched them attacking the tanks, the teams running the line but weaving between the other vehicles in back, aided by the bikes that had flanked the immobilized enemy and now came in from behind.

And even if the tanks were still mobile, Mackey speculated, the rocket teams on the bikes were too agile and they knew where the mines had been dropped. They flitted in and out of the tank and armored columns, using the shadows and the sides of the machines as blinds. And the blatting of the unmuffled engines created a din that had frightened the enemy soldiers who had been caught on the ground. They fled off into the rainy darkness, splashing through puddles, falling, others transfixed where they stood.

Price broke radio silence. "We're at the river, but we're out of almost everything, and I can hear their choppers and what sounds like transport planes. Could they be dropping in troops?"

"Maybe. We are. Just see if you can hold out. We'll be there shortly."

Mackey hit a switch on the radio and an insistent beeping signal was sent to all drivers. They fell off the tanks and pulled away into the darkness, toward the river.

And Mackey called for the helicopters, the ones he'd kept in reserve to evacuate whatever was left of Price's sled force.

But the gap between the two armies was in chaos, both on the ground and overhead. Helicopters hovered behind hills and in ravines, anywhere where the terrain would give them cover from heat-seeking or radar-guided missiles, return fire streaking from their pods to the north and east.

One off to Mackey's right was hit, and then another nearby, lighting up the night sky with billowing washes of fire that fell to earth and kept burning and heavy chunks of hissing metal that were strewn over a wide area.

And through the lethal air, paratroopers of both forces were dropping, becoming tangled, landing together or amidst groups of the enemy, being pierced, penetrated, and severed by the fire and fragments that thickened the dark sky.

Through the infrared goggles that all Mackey's men wore, the eagles on the helmets, the fronts and backs of their field jackets were visible, but Mackey could only assume that the Soviet wore goggles too. He hoped the insignias hadn't hindered the fighting effectiveness of his airborne units.

But still, it was the battlefield that Mackey had imagined would have evolved on the eleventh or thirteenth or some later day when battle-ready supplies had become exhausted and logistics were disrupted, and using whatever was cheap and portable and handy, army faced army. And it was here that he knew the training he had provided his troops would pay off.

The Soviet airborne and helicopter units were late and landing on ground that Mackey's troops had already secured. And they were confused by the noise and the increasing darkness and the number and type of the opposition. Many actually stopped and lowered their weapons when they heard the unmuffled engines of the motorcycles approaching them. And the Soviet helicopters, attempting to land troops, were as vulnerable to the man-portable anti-armor rounds as any tank.

Mackey and Werbiskis, trying to flank the main action, broke into a clearing where a Soviet copter, larger than any in the American inventory, was landing to off-load troops. They could see them in the doorway, ready to hop down and sprint off into the darkness.

Werbiskis turned off the ignition of the bike and they rolled behind a hillock of muddy ground that had been tossed up by the earlier artillery barrage. There they quickly removed two rockets apiece and sighted in the large transport helicopter. They didn't wait for it to touch down or for the soldiers to disperse.

Werbiskis's rocket jetted from the tube and slid off the sighted target to strike just above the doorway of the ship, which heeled over so that a rotor snagged the ground. It bounced back, spilling men from the doorway, and was struck by Mackey's round.

The helicopter flipped over on its side, a sheet of flame puffing up from the doorway. Some of the soldiers could be seen trying to climb through the fire out into the dark night.

Mackey touched Werbiskis's sleeve. They would conserve their other rockets. Nobody who survived the wreck would pose them much danger, and their objective was to get to the Elbe.

There they found that Price had few men left. The snow mask and the right side of his white parka were scorched. He had to extend Mackey his left hand as his men clambered or were carried and lifted aboard the helicopters.

Once up in the air, the copilot of the ship in which they were riding signaled to Mackey, "Got somebody on the radio for you, sir. A woman, a German, but it's not through Bundeswehr C&C. Says her name is Colonel Kronenberger, that you know her, that it's urgent."

The pilot had kept the helicopter low over the water of the river and now was hugging the terrain, knifing down into ravines, using whatever land cover he could find, and Mackey had to use rope stanchions that had been strung along the floor.

The voice was faint, and Mackey didn't think it was because of the signal alone.

"General, I must tell you that I know for a fact SACEUR Bengsten is preparing a nuclear strike against the Soviets within the salient."

Mackey eased back into the cushions of the copilot's seat and felt suddenly very tired and very old. The opportunity to defeat the best part of the Red Army easily and quickly had presented itself, but Mackey had been banking on NATO restraint because of the consequences of such a strike. But Bengsten didn't really have to work through NATO. "On orders from Washington?"

"I don't know, but I can't imagine him—" There was coughing on the other end of the line.

"Colonel, has there been a time set?"

"I should imagine." The voice was weaker still. "It all began hours ago."

"Where is he now?"

"At a base camp near the crisis-management center, eight kilometers east of Uelzen." There was more coughing.

"Well—" Mackey wondered if there was still time to appeal the decision, to show Bengsten and Washington that he and Price had a very good chance of dismantling the Red Army piece by piece, conventionally. "Thank you, Colonel. Where are you now?"

Mackey had to wait before he heard, "Uelzen."

"Where in Uelzen?"

But radio contact had been broken.

When he returned to Price's side, he said, "Bengsten has prepped the nukes."

Price, who'd been resting his head against a strut of the ship, turned only his eyes to him.

"Could he know something about Reiner that we don't?"

Mackey hunched his shoulders. "He'd need something like that to get the go-ahead from Washington."

Price hadn't felt the pain until now, when his fighting was over and he was safe or at least unable to react to whatever was thrown at them. He couldn't tell if it was the vibration from the rotors or his injuries or his exhaustion, but his body was quaking. He had never been more tired in his life. And his face, where he'd been burnt, was searing him.

"I'm going to send you back there, Howard. To Uelzen. Can you handle it?"

Price thought so.

10

Fuel was not a consideration but radar was, and right after takeoff Maher swept the wings of the F-111F to fifty-five degrees and switched on the afterburners, putting the fighter-bomber down into its "hard ride" where at Mach 1.2 it would plunge into the darkness never more than 200 feet above the tops of trees, village spires, and factory stacks, reading the terrain ahead of it as it drove toward the east.

The North Vietnamese had called the -111s whispering death, for the only warning the plane had given was a low hush, like a gentle wind through the trees, before iron and cluster bombs had rained down on them and the plane had screamed overhead, too fast to be seen.

But the newest version of the plane no longer relied on free-fall bombs, rather on a beacon-guided bombing system by which a ground transponder received data from a target- acquisition aircraft and passed the information to the internal electronics of Maher's F-111F. All he now had to worry about were the Soviet air defenses over the military complex at Wittenberge, but he felt confident. At his speed and altitude none of their planes and few of their missiles could touch him, and he knew he would complete the mission that Herder had sent him on.

Bysotsky, on the other hand, was nervous. He was a small man with thick prism glasses that made his eyes look like hazy orbs swimming in a murky medium. He was thin, and the military uniform that he had donned in Moscow was new and smelled of sizing and the tailor's mangle. With the ribbons and medals—even an Order of Lenin that Voronov had pinned on him in the Kremlin only a few hours before—it made him feel clownish. Now he wished he had remained in the plain gray suit that he had worn since the crisis had begun. Being minister of defense was sufficient, he had thought. Voronov said he knew otherwise.

And on seeing the tall, hatless figure of Alexeyev appear in the cone of light at the doorway, the scars on his face shadowed and obvious, Bysotsky knew he was right. There was a soldier, not a messenger, which was the role Moscow had assigned him. Of doom, he could not help thinking.

Was it necessary? he asked himself, and not for the first time. Again the other question arose—had they an option?

Alexeyev did not step out of the doorway because of the rain. He sent two orderlies down the steps as the driver opened the door of the staff car that had met Bysotsky at the airfield.

Bysotsky paused before getting out, and he noted that the light above Alexeyev was the only one on in the vast square that the buildings formed. Along with the rain there was a wind, gentle and soughing from the west. A Zephyros, Bysotsky thought, and he remembered Alexeyev's background, the way Kork had fought the bureaucrats to make sure Alexeyev had received the best of schooling. "A classic education," Kork had said. A wag—or so it was told—had picked the phrase up and repeated it all over Moscow. Alexeyev had served in Peking, Washington, London, Paris, Bonn, and Brussels. Kork had made sure that Alexeyev had gotten around.

Yes, Bysotsky thought, a man with such a background could be reasoned with, made to see that they had no choice, that the gambit would quell the Western Europeans for generations and further erode the U.S. position in Europe. They'd be held responsible. NATO itself might collapse. Mackey's surprise attack would take on the aspect of a Pyrrhic victory.

After having loosed the Rockeye missiles, Maher's eyes caught a pinprick of light about four miles distant, and his hand snapped out and caught the dropstick. He sighted in the target and released a series of three glide bombs that arced in flat, right over the tops of the buildings.

But Maher was far above the targets when the missiles and bombs struck. He had cut straight up, sweeping the wings back to thirty-three degrees and powering quickly through the cloud cover, over, and back to treetop level again, spreading the wings once more to maintain the lower speed and make base.

Kork was showered with plaster and dust. He was down in the strike center deep under the Guards headquarters, and he knew the blast must have destroyed the entire building to have damaged the hardened shelter too. And again the electricity had failed, the auxiliaries filling the air with the strange blue light through which dust was sifting slowly.

"It was indeed fortunate that you evacuated everybody yesterday, Chief Marshal," Tuchin said.

It was only then that Kork remembered Alexeyev, who had said he was going up to see what was keeping Bysotsky. He pushed himself out of the chair, which fell, cracking as it hit the wall. "Get all those men and follow me." Kork began making his way toward the doorway. His face was set, and his eyes seemed swollen.

"What men?"

"Your men."

"But—" Tuchin glanced at his crew who were busy at the monitors.

Kork turned his whole body to Tuchin. "Get them and follow me."

Kork threw open the door of the stairwell, which was filled with dust and—he drew in the thick, choking air—yes, smoke, but not until the doorway into the basement did he find his way encumbered by debris.

There the ceiling had fallen, and, trying to jerk laths and sheets of plaster out of his way, Kork nearly brought the rubble down on his head. But Tuchin and the others were by his side now and had brought electric torches and axes, even a pick. Already they could hear the crackling of the fire and the passageway was filling with smoke.

They discovered Alexeyev just inside the front entryway where the stairs had fallen on him and Bysotsky, crushing the latter, whose hand alone was visible, as if reaching up for somebody to pull him out of the wreckage. Fifty feet of cast iron stair rail had come down on Alexeyev. All but his chest, arms, and head had been caught under it.

The others cleared the way for Kork, who cocked his head from side to side, as though not understanding what he was seeing.

Most of the building was down. The rain hissed into the many fires.

Kork raised his hands and clasped them. He tried to stoop and then went down on his knees and brushed the dust off Alexeyev's forehead. He glanced up at Tuchin, who only shook his head. They couldn't move him. A large slab of the toppled wall was resting on the rail.

He removed his handkerchief from his jacket, folded it carefully, and placed it as a sort of pillow under Alexeyev's head. It was the only gesture he could think of to comfort him.

The hand on the side of Alexeyev's neck told him that there was still a pulse, weak and thready, but all Kork had before his mind was the picture of the tall, skinny boy who had come to him on a cold, wet night just like this, saying all he wanted to do was kill Germans. He'd heard Kork was good at it and could use him.

Kork, who was younger at the time—centuries younger, he now thought—had laughed and had brought him into the tank where the other officers under his command were sharing a couple of bottles after a long, bitter battle.

"What's your name?" The boy had been scared. He took off the steel pot and handed it to Kork. "Vassiliev," the liner read. "Captain Y.T., 32d Tank Group, 176th Guards."

"Do my eyes deceive me," Kork had said, "or has our Yuri come back to us?"

"A reincarnation," another officer declared. "Here, Vassilievich, have a goddamn drink. You must have come a long way."

They all roared with laughter. The kid wouldn't drink, but he ate almost everything they had and promptly fell asleep.

"You've got to be strong to kill Germans," Kork had said, watching him. Only later did Alexeyev tell them what had happened to his family.

And when he had gotten chewed up in Berlin, the tankers had combed the city for a doctor, a scientist, a medical student—anybody who could patch him up. He was like their mascot, their luck. With him along they were fearless because he was fearless. They could see that losing your life was nothing if you had lost everything else.

But not like this, Kork thought, looking down at Alexeyev and trying to keep the tears from his eyes. He placed his hand on Alexeyev's brow, which was cold and damp with sweat. Not after having come so far.

But blinking, trying to clear his eyes, Kork looked up and caught sight of Bysotsky's hand and he remembered why the minister had come.

And Alexeyev had made a sound.

Kork lowered his head to him. His eyes had opened. They were glassy, the pupils contracting in death. "Is that fire?" he asked.

The wind had changed and billows of heavy smoke were pushing their way, driving Tuchin and his men back toward the gap in the rubble and the courtyard beyond.

"I don't want—"

"I know, I know," said Kork, patting Alexeyev's hand. After the burns that had scarred his face and back and had taken whole years to heal, Alexeyev did not want to burn.

"Bysotsky—"

"He's dead."

Alexeyev lowered his eyelids and opened them again.

And to see Vassil like this, crushed again, wrecked, Kork felt the rage rising in him. And after the toll that had been taken on the battlefield, it was more an insult than a necessary strike. But he thought of 12th Panzer-Grenadier headquarters and how he had ordered its destruction. Here was the retribution, and Alexeyev was atoning for Kork's act.

"Your pistol, comrade," Alexeyev said. "Let me have it. Please."

They could feel the fire now, waves of heat that were pushing through a gap in the shattered wall.

But Kork knew Alexeyev's hands were weak, too limp even to grasp the butt of the pistol.

It was better this way, Kork thought, placing the barrel against Alexeyev's temple.

"Chief Marshal Kork," Tuchin called to him from the

253

gap. "Please hurry. The roof up there, it's about to collapse."

And shadowing Alexeyev's body from the bright yellow flickering of the conflagration behind him, Kork said, "I have loved you, my friend." He squeezed the trigger just once.

The head jerked to the side and snapped back. The jaw opened slightly.

Kork tried to lift it back up, to close the mouth, but his palm filled with blood. Kork carried it out into the courtyard, which was ablaze on four sides. He then wiped the bloody hand across the front of his uniform jacket.

Tuesday, P.M.
East of Uelzen
F.G.R.

In the streaks of snow on the muddy fields, the Soviet tanks were highlighted, firing on the move, not so much, Harris judged, looking down from one of the helicopters that had met Price's sled force at the Elbe, because the gunners had sighted targets, but more at the night and their fears and the west.

The pilot veered away from the enemy, through a gap in a stand of pines and along a ravine, careful never to put them up where the ship might become silhouetted on the dusty sky. The supply depot beyond Uelzen was their destination—and a little rest, Harris hoped.

Not to sleep—there had been too much action for that—but to put together his thoughts, to assemble all that had happened, and mostly to savor the feeling of having come so close, so often, and of having gotten through. It was a time Harris had learned to be wary of. He felt impossibly fortunate at such moments, immortal, and that was dangerous.

And like a nightmare from which you awaken and try to drop back into, knowing you'll only end up having to dream it all over again, Harris had before him bits and pieces of the last three days, beginning with the two Soviets on the tank at Eldena squinting up at them in the helicopter, to the strike on the tank park, the flaming, twisted radar tower, the explosion of the fuel dump near the garage, the hovercrafts that they'd destroyed.

And the many enemy he'd encountered—their faces passed before his mind, all looking strangely similar and becoming one to him, like a single Soviet soldier, somebody he could think of clearly, dispassionately, like an abstract. And hate, yes, because of the losses, and fear. Respect? Not yet. They fought much less tenaciously than the Vietnamese and even died differently, like sheep, but Harris supposed it was only a matter of experience.

Harris forced himself to think of something else. His eyes cleared and he glanced down through the open bay door in which a TOW gunner was positioned, strapped against a strut, the sighting grips in his hands.

They were passing down a narrow country road that was crowded with refugees in cars piled high with personal belongings, open trucks packed with people huddling away from the steady downpour, the cold, the encroaching night. The road, like the countryside through which it ran, had been bombarded and was scarred, here and there, with deep depressions in which water pooled. They moved at a snail's pace, and vehicles littered the sides of the road. Abandoned, doors and trunks open. Out of gas or broken down. Maybe walking was faster; like a human cordon, throngs of people lined both shoulders of the road, all moving west.

Some cowered, not knowing who they were, but most didn't even look up. They trudged on stoically. If it came, it came.

Until the firing began.

The pilot of the lead helicopter had had to chance it somewhere, make a break across the open farming areas east of Uelzen, and the road must have seemed the best bet. Without a doubt the Soviets had seen refugees, the Bundeswehr buses on which red crosses on white fields had been painted hurriedly, the moving vans with the doors open and people—whole villages probably—crowded in, and it was obvious the tanks hadn't fired at them until then. The SAMs would follow, and soon.

The pilot didn't have to be told. He veered to the far side of the road and set the ship down behind a bus and a long trailer truck, from which refugees were streaming, slogging out through the mud, into the fields, away from the tank

255

shell bursts that billowed up, orange and fiery into the night sky.

Harris turned to Herz, who was sitting in the co-pilot's seat. If they abandoned the helicopter, their chances were little better than the civilians', and Uelzen was still miles away. And they couldn't put the ship back up; it would be suicide.

"How many rounds we got, Harris?"

Harris didn't have to look. They were low: the helicopter had been sent out to pick them up, not rearm them. "Five or six apiece."

Herz looked away, his face unchanged, the same purse to his small mouth, making him seem bored or tired or both.

Would the Soviets be expecting them? Sure—they'd be expecting anything, everything.

Herz raised his hands to his ears and clasped the phones to his head.

Somewhere og behind them a stunning explosion and a fireball lit up the open fields. People screamed. They rushed by the helicopter, falling into the mud, dragging their children after them.

Herz was up. He pulled off the headset and picked up his helmet. He clambered out of the cockpit into the cargo area of the helicopter. In his grease-smeared face his bloodshot eyes were brilliant, like bright polished glass. "Price and the lead ships got through. That puts us on our own. We can make a break for it on foot or turn and face them. We'll face them."

He snatched up a launcher and began slipping antitank rounds through the loops on his ammunition belt.

The others looked to Harris, who didn't pause. He could still see the civilians but they had scarcely made progress across the long field. And Harris had seen the tanks earlier—there were too many of them traveling too fast. At least in facing them they'd go down fighting.

The bus that had been shielding the helicopter took a direct hit and was driven into the ship, knocking Herz and Harris and three others out the bay door.

They fell heavily onto their backs and side. Looking up, Harris saw a single bus wheel, spinning like a Frisbee, sail up through the cloud of flaming fuel, and then other civilians, their clothing on fire, ran and crawled and threw themselves down into the muddy gully near the ship.

Harris picked himself up and sprinted away from the helicopter and along the side of the road, glancing up under the cars for a gap where they wouldn't be visible, where they could make a break across the road and get down on the other side and away from the tank fire, where they could wait for the Soviets and make sure they scored in close, firing up into the tank bodies.

And there it was, a gap between an odd sort of delivery van that was piled high with furniture and rolled-up rugs, and a low-slung sports car.

Harris paused at the bumper and waved the others through. His hand had come down on something like a decal that was fixed to the shiny chrome.

When the last man passed, Harris turned and looked down at it. A screaming eagle, lightning bolts in its talons. He began to stand. The tank fire, the blazing bus, the cries and shouts of the civilians, but mostly his exhaustion, the way he was now calling on his body to do things it was no longer capable of, had made him feel giddy and displaced, as though he had distanced himself from the event that he was sure would lead to his death.

Now this, as in a dream, like the nightmare he had thought about only a few minutes earlier.

But the number plate was the same too, the deep brown color of the car, the style.

"Harris!" somebody shouted from beyond the road.

But he scrambled up and moved around the car to the driver's side, holding the launcher at his hip, his finger on the trigger.

With his other hand he reached for the door handle. It was locked, but there was somebody sitting in the driver's seat, the window foggy and spattered with dirt and rain.

Harris rapped on the window.

The head moved.

He rapped again, harder. He could hear the shrill whining of the tanks. Several rounds tatooed the side of the road not far to the north, and Harris went down on his knees. The firing was becoming regular now and more accurate.

The window came down, slowly.

It was Mühling. Annette was beyond him, her head thrown back on the seat. In the rear there was another figure, a woman.

"Hello, Harry," Mühling tried to say, but something black spilled from his mouth onto his shirt. His eyes were glassy. He looked away.

Harris glanced to the east and at the needles of tank fire that now pierced the mist, the rounds whistling overhead at targets farther to the west, and he scuttled around the car to the other door, which he opened.

Harris grabbed the arm that was farther from him and gave it a tug, reaching for her thigh with his other hand.

"No more. Please, no more," she said, and Mühling tried to stop him.

"You've got to get out of here," Harris said. "The Soviets. Tanks."

"My mother." Once more the front of his broad chin was covered with black fluid.

"She's dead," Annette said. "I keep telling you she's dead, Karl."

A tank round slammed into the road, and the concussion knocked Harris and the girl down the other side, into the mud and darkness below.

When he could, Harris tried to snatch her up and move toward the bus, the one that had already been hit, the one with the helicopter and gully behind it, but he kept falling. His arms and legs were too weak. He dragged her down into the deepest part of the gully where a large rock shadowed them from the flames. He fell on her.

Annette's entire body pained her, and there did not seem to be a part of it of which she was not aware, especially her back and neck. Both, she realized now, had been injured, perhaps seriously, in the collapse of Mühling's apartment building in Hitzacker.

But more than that, she was exhausted, weary of the turmoil, the fighting, the fear. She wanted only to sleep, and she imagined that there was a place—not heaven, but someplace like it—where she could go and her parents would be there and everything would be as it was yesterday or the day or week before. If she survived, she knew nothing would be the same, and in her present condition she did not have the strength or the courage to face that. She only wanted to continue lying there in the ditch, at the bottom of a depression, in a field miles from anywhere, forever.

But the tanks never appeared, and the firing stopped. Even the roar of the planes deep within the cloud cover had ceased. Harris could still hear noise—the whine of the Soviet armored columns—but it appeared to be diminishing, as if they were moving off, retreating. But why?

Harris raised himself up. "You stay here. I'm going up onto the road again."

Annette said nothing and did not open her eyes. It was quite cold there, and wet, but she did not care. In fact, she welcomed the rain and sleet, the chill that cut through her now that Harris had removed himself from over her. She had let go, quit, and the sooner it was over the better.

Harris had to use his hands to claw his way up the muddy side of the gully. At the car he found that Mühling had tried to get out. He was stopped against the side of the car, and his breathing sounded like wind being drawn through sodden straw.

Mühling was dying and he knew it. It seemed to him so unfair that his chest, which was only one part of him, should have failed while all the rest of him was nearly perfect. But the chest, the lungs, the throat, even his tongue were beyond help, he had realized and long before. Each breath was like tasting fire or acid or hot, searing smoke. And with each breath his desire to try to go on diminished. There was only so much of that sort of pain a person could take, he had decided. He had said nothing to Annette, for, he imagined, she had pain of her own. And so he had carried on, as well as he had been able, but now he could do no more.

Harris could also hear Herz and the others approaching them from out of the dark field to the east.

"Can you move, Karl?"

His eyes only flickered up at Harris. No, he could not, he would not move.

Harris stooped and opened the wet shirt. Something had fallen on Mühling, but long enough ago that his stomach and chest were one massive bruise, blue mottled green and red and swollen.

Boots appeared beside Harris.

"That your car, Sergeant?" one of the troopers asked. "How'd it get here?"

"Place this man under arrest, Corporal."

259

Harris straightened up and pushed by Herz.

"You hear me?"

"What's the charge, sir?" the corporal asked in a tired voice.

"Cowardice under fire."

Harris turned to Herz. "Shut the fuck up."

Harris moved to the shoulder of the road and stared out at the dark field. There was nothing to the east, no fire, no noise. He wondered what it could mean.

Gamsakhurdia knew. He had had to echelon his armor in depth when the motorcycles had appeared. They had stung him, but he placed his losses at fewer than thirty percent and he was rolling. He had covered twenty kilometers in the last hour alone, and it was a breakthrough, he was sure of it.

Then came the call from Wittenberge. GRU had learned that coded messages had been sent out from the NATO fire control center to the 203 mm. howitzer batteries that had been positioned in a crescent beyond Uelzen. They assumed a time-on-target had been scheduled and was running down.

"Their aircraft, Colonel—are they overhead?"

"No, sir. Not for the last ten minutes. We sighted a small helicopter force just west of us, but they appear to be gone now."

"Then that confirms it, Colonel. Disperse your forces as fast as you can."

The Soviet armor wheeled and fanned out in a desperate rush, breaking through the pines that remained standing, into and over the rubble of walls and farms. But given their concentrations, they wouldn't be quick enough. Gamsakhurdia only hoped Moscow's response would be quick and sure and final.

Tuesday, P.M.
West of Uelzen
F.G.R.

Bengsten had just picked up the phone when Price arrived in the crisis-management center. An aide told him, "The

260

SACEUR's speaking to the President now, sir. If you can wait over—"

With a forearm Price moved the man out of the way. If Bengsten was speaking to the President, Price wanted to hear. Already a time-on-target had been established. On a display screen Price could see the seconds running down. An officer kept reading off the full minutes. Seven left. Bengsten was confident of Washington's reaction.

And just outside of Uelzen, at a site where a copse of pines shielded a battery from plain view, Price had asked the pilot to halt for a moment while he watched gun crews raise the long barrels of the eight-inch howitzers. The special, rocket-assisted heavy rounds had been rammed home, the breech blocks turned down, azimuth and elevations selected. Bengsten was ready, and Price thought about the conversation in 12th Panzer-Grenadier barracks three days past.

Now Price stood directly in front of Bengsten's desk, knowing that he was taller and twice as broad as the man, knowing the effect that the scorched snow mask and parka would have on him.

Bengsten was outlining the situation to Harper, updating the information on the Soviet attack: the fact that the enemy was now well within the salient, striking from Salzwedel in a two-pronged attack both south and west.

"Can't you contain them, Harold?" Harper asked.

Bengsten glanced up at Price. The clown, he thought, coming in here like that. Battlefield heroics meant nothing; it was here, at this desk and in his hand, that real power lay. He covered the phone with his palm. "I'll be with you in a moment, General. Please have a seat and make yourself comfortable. I'm speaking with the President."

Price didn't move.

Bengsten tried to hold the gaze of the large, dark eyes in the smudged mask, but he was only wasting time. He glanced at the others who were watching them. He could call the security team, but maybe it was better like this, with Price right in front of him.

He uncovered the speaker. "Staff and I have been watching the situation closely, assessing every option, sir. Elements of NORTHAG have been heavily engaged for seventy-four hours now. Communications are still spotty. The Soviets are throwing their massive reserves across the river. Our tank companies, like some of theirs, have been caught on the ground. But our reserves . . ." Bengsten let his voice trail off. He did not look up at Price.

"And then their counterbattery fire has been extremely heavy. In some cases we've been unable to get close enough to offer a defense. In the last hour the main westward thrust has gained twenty-two kilometers.

"But more than that, sir, and the reason I've called, the reason I want to suggest that we consider options, is that our weapons stocks—TOW missiles, the laser-guided weapons rounds, and even our man-portable antitank tubes—are running down. Way down. I have a report before me—"

In the cubicle off the situation room in the White House, Harper pulled the leg he'd been resting off the other chair and stood. "Forget the report. How low?"

"We're down to twenty-seven percent. It's probably lower than that, now. We've contacted the Bendeswehr, but they refuse to resupply us."

"And they refuse to fight."

"Yes, sir—not until they're attacked."

Harper ran a hand through his hair. Where in the name of hell, he thought, did those bastards think the whole thing was happening, Chicago? Something he had discussed with Meisenzahl occurred to him. "But didn't Mackey predict it—that the Soviets would be where they were, that the Germans would stay out of it, that the weapons stocks would get low? We've got more coming your way, Harold, you know that."

Bengsten tried not to glance at Price. "But not this soon. The Soviets, sir. And not this much. I mean the weapons."

Harper looked up at Meisenzahl, who was sitting on the other side of the table.

The old man cleared his throat. "The toll General Mackey has taken on the Soviets, their losses, are much higher than in any scenario that he or anybody else predicted."

Bengsten was speaking again. "And because of the weather and the"—he allowed his eyes to flick up to Price—"opposition, they've had to mass their forces, canalize their armor. They're just sitting there, Mr. President. A strike right now would be like a *coup de grace*. Without their army they'll be powerless to respond."

"Except in kind, Harold—are you forgetting that?"

"Well, begging your pardon, sir—they can't, *in kind*. And I don't think they'll take this thing any further. By any standard it's still a limited engagement."

Harper didn't doubt that they'd take it at least somewhat further, but he'd heard the argument: just because both sides possessed tactical nuclear weapons didn't make them mutually advantageous. Massed attacks of the sort the Soviets had launched were untenable on a battlefield in which the defense possessed a nuclear capability, but the weapons that the West possessed were clean, surgical, they'd affect the Red Army and perhaps some Western combatants as well, but the civilian population would remain largely untouched. The Soviet devices were huge, dirty, and for the most part could not be precisely targeted. If they retaliated like that, they risked a total-theater escalation and responsibility for the collateral damage that would take years, generations, whole lifetimes to repair, if possible.

If they retaliated, Harper thought. What shape would such a retaliation take?

He began pacing behind the desk, wishing somehow he could open the question to discussion, but knowing that it wasn't his way or the way wars were won and history changed.

Europe. The Soviets wouldn't risk global war with their army gone and with the Chinese—Harper had contacted them a day ago—on their eastern border.

Without their army they'd be powerless to strike, at least until they put together another and equipped it, and, given their technological and managerial backwardness, relative to the West, it probably wouldn't be achieved in a decade.

Without their army it would be a whole new ball game in Europe and elsewhere, perhaps even in Russia itself.

Détente? Understanding? Trust? It had been a charade anyhow, Harper had long thought. The SALT II agreement, and the threats Brezhnev and Gromyko had issued the Senate, had pointed it up. They hadn't wanted it from the beginning. It was all—he remembered a Russian word from the briefing he'd just received—*pokazuhka,* a kind of Russian window dressing designed to lull the West into a false sense of security while they armed themselves to the teeth.

And to Harper world peace was like a happy electorate—a myth. There was always some sort of conflict going on and there always would be. Some people would always have a little more than some other people, and those other people would want it. Boston, Washington, the West, the East, the world—things were too complex and diverse to be equitable, and the iniquity brought contention, hostility, and ultimately violence. To try to pretend it could be made otherwise was stupid.

The point was, then, to provide the United States with peace, freedom, and prosperity, and that—Harper was firmly convinced—could only be built on U.S. strength.

Now he had a chance to destroy the flower of the Red Army, to shove all their years of threats, hostility, and agression right down their throats.

He asked himself what he'd do if it was just politics in Boston he was thinking of, and he had a chance to defeat the opposition, eliminate them for years. He wouldn't hesitate. If he did, the others—those with savvy and instinct—would smell it on him and he'd be a dead letter. It was no different for a country. Look what had happened after Vietnam and was, in a way, still going on: everybody—even little, essentially powerless countries—was assassinating our ambassadors, denying us trade, arbitrarily raising prices, and trying to blackmail us with commercial embargoes.

He thought of Carter and his soft, southern preacher's voice and his trying to teach the American people that they should recognize the diminished position of the United States in the world today. The position *was* diminished, but only because of people like him. *Leaders* like him.

The response would be European, he decided, but he could live with that. The Europeans had been reluctant to defend themselves, and as far as he was concerned, they were responsible for whatever happened. And the Germans, Jesus—they deserved everything they got.

"Have you heard from General Mackey?"

"From his staff, sir. I have General Price standing right in front of me."

"Put him on."

Bengsten smiled slightly and handed Price the phone. He looked around at the others. He had nothing to hide. He knew the man he was dealing with, Harper; and Price, he knew him too.

"Sir?"

"General Price?"

"Yes, sir."

"General Meisenzahl tells me you've been in the G.D.R. How does it look?"

Price didn't understand the intent of the question, but as long as he had the President's ear he was going to lay it all out. "Fine, sir. We completed the link-up and now General Mackey is driving south across what will be their rear, if we let them advance a little more. Once we cut them off it'll be all over. They won't be able to assume the offensive. Here."

"How long will that take?" Time, Harper was thinking. Already the other NATO leaders were getting cold feet, threatening to withdraw their troops, making approaches to the Soviets as "mediators," as it were. And then there was the report from the Germans about some trouble between the Bundeswehr and one of Bengsten's own units. Harper only hoped the Soviets' relations with the G.D.R. Volksarmee were as strained.

"A couple of hours."

"No, no—to complete the plan."

Price thought for a moment, glancing down at Bengsten, who was running his fingers down the line of his jaw, looking off into the command center at the clock that was winding down. By the terms of the NATO security agreement, Bengsten had the power necessary to launch the strike himself, but he was too cautious for that and was playing them all—Harper included—as he had from the first with the weather-modification action. Price wouldn't lie and try to put a good face on the situation. Things were still in flux. "Two days. A week at the outside."

"No sooner?"

"No, sir. There's still too many of them, but we can beat them with what we've used so far."

Time, Harper again thought. If the Soviets had time they might initiate some action in some other part of the world, something that would also be difficult to stop and clean up, and that, for Harper, would be as serious as an escalation. "Thank you, General. Put General Bengsten back on. Please."

"I think it's wrong, sir."

"I understand that."

"It's not really necessary."

"You made your point."

Price lowered the phone and looked down at it. He let Bengsten take it from his hand.

"Harold"—in his pacing Harper had reached a corner of the room; he looked up and stared at the two intersecting beige walls—"if we're going to do this thing, we should do it right with no loose ends."

"Yes, sir."

"You're sure you can accomplish it."

"Yes, sir."

"Harold—they're going to respond. They might use their weapons on you."

"We'll know that before they do, sir. But as we discussed before, it's unlikely. They'd have to use too many with no surety that they were knocking us out. They'd pauper their arsenal and be at our mercy. Any counterattack would leave them with nothing. And even with a mobilization—they couldn't win that sort of war."

"But you think they'll respond."

"Yes, sir—they'll respond, but not massively."

Something, Harper thought, to let them save face. There in Europe.

Harper paused and again ran through the possibilities, the history of the American presence in Europe for the past forty years. Perhaps a Soviet response, such as what Bengsten—and he wasn't alone: Meisenzahl, the chairman of the joint chiefs of staff, the director of the C.I.A., and Harper himself—envisioned might even redound to the advantage of the United States.

"Then do it, Harold, and make sure it's done right. When I talk to them next, I want them"—he searched for a word but only one seemed right—"emasculated."

Price had already left the shelter.

Bengsten said, "We're winding down right now, sir."

But Harper had hung up.

266

11

Standing on the road, Harris and the others saw only a series of brilliant silver flashes, intensely bright and phosphorescent, that pierced the clouds and mist at every point, it seemed, on the eastern horizon. The blast that followed drove them to their knees, but they themselves were well away from the neutron bursts that were rapidly absorbed by the nitrogen in the surrounding atmosphere.

Gamsakhurdia felt only a tingle for about a second, but he knew it was enough. He was dying. Like other field-grade officers, he had to study the effects of an enhanced-uranium attack:

Those armored vehicles directly under each blast had been shattered and fried. Within a half-mile, only 20 percent of the 5,000 to 8,000 rads produced had been shielded by the armor. The rest had been absorbed by the steel atoms and converted to gamma (the standard nuclear-weapon) radiation and was now "shining" through the armor for far longer than the explosion itself. Within five minutes all of them would be incapacitated, but it could take as many as two horrible days to die.

At three-quarters of a mile, doses of 3,000 to 5,000 rads had struck the tanks. Again those tankers only had five minutes before the onset of nausea and fatigue, but their brains, their nervous systems, the linings of their intestines, their blood-producing cells had been severely damaged. And their fate was perhaps worse. In six days, after mas-

267

sive infections and circulatory collapse, they too would be dead.

Even those few Soviet soldiers who had been outside of an armored shell at a distance of slightly over a mile had absorbed enough direct neutron flux to kill them. And more slowly still. They'd linger on for weeks and months, if they weren't cut down by the NATO counterattack that could proceed over the same ground within an hour.

Gamsakhurdia could see that even now the tank commander was trembling uncontrollably. The tank had come up against something hard that stopped it. The engine had stalled, but Gamsakhurdia couldn't raise his head far enough to look out the periscope, and his eyes . . . everything was becoming fuzzy.

Then the gunner fell from his seat to the floor where he began retching uncontrollably, his muscles contracting, seizing up into tight, terrible knots.

And Gamsakhurdia had begun to have trouble breathing. He had thought perhaps they had time to turn the tank and move west, maybe sight in a target and at least fight on. One of them might have absorbed less or have some sort of immunity, and he couldn't be sure of how close they'd been to the blasts, but his hand wouldn't grasp the flap on his sidearm.

Still, he staggered against the body of the tank and leaned on it, letting his knees go for a moment, and the flap came open. He pulled out the handgun and tried to fire it in the direction of the loader who was sitting with his back toward him. He missed and the shot ricocheted at least twice before thwacking into the water reservoir. A thin stream of water, like a silver flame, poured down on Gamsakhurdia.

The man had turned around. Tears were streaming down his face and his eyes were looking in different directions.

Gamsakhurdia staggered toward him and shoved the weapon into the man's chest.

They both tried to stare down at it. Their heads met.

Gamsakhurdia balanced there for a moment before his knees gave way and he toppled onto the gunners on the deck.

And the other Soviet tanks throughout the salient and along the attack axis to the south toward Hannover had begun to operate erratically. Tank fire was only intermittent; direction seemed aimless. Others had simply come to rest. Their engines would continue to idle until the fuel was spent.

Soviet helicopters, reconnaissance and tactical-support aircraft began dropping from the sky, like birds that had faltered in flight. Some attempted to land but the precision was no longer there. Others simply flew into trees, as though still proceeding blithely at altitude.

The Soviet SAM and Katyusha batteries had quieted almost immediately after the neutron strike. The operators, concealed in the lightly armored cabs of the launching platforms or standing out in the open, had been directly exposed.

As had much of the U.S. motorcycle force that had been deployed against Gamsakhurdia's tank groups.

Through the amber glow of an infrared headlight, Mackey peered down the length of a ravine where his helicopter had been waiting. Through the strange, sharp light that made everything seem like a photo negative, he could make out a solitary U.S. soldier who had fallen or slipped off his motorcycle, the rear wheel of which was still spinning as the engine idled. He was holding his stomach and ribs, standing and falling, now trying to climb the steep sides of the gully, but falling back roughly on his face and neck. Something white, like foam, was streaming from his mouth, and although he couldn't hear the man, Mackey could imagine the agonized, retching sounds that he was making.

Although it took all his strength and concentration and will, Mackey turned the ship, grabbed up the handgrip and trigger of the nose gun and dispatched the poor trooper with a long, snaking burst that raced up the ravine and saturated the ground around him.

Mackey then eased himself back in the pilot's seat and set the helicopter back down. He hit the switch that slid open the bay door, and some of the others behind him rolled themselves out. Mackey guessed they had been about a mile from the nearest burst, but it would be enough to kill all of them eventually. Cancers, leukemia, kidney, liver, and heart dysfunctions, neurological disorders—if they had a chance to live that long.

269

With a hand Mackey reached up and knocked first the helmet and then the headset off. The noise, the transmissions—his head felt as if it had been split in two.

He thought about the battle and Bengsten and Harper. He could understand how it had seemed like a good bet, but the strike effectively negated what he had hoped would become a new age of warfare in which armies would fight armies on contained battlefields, both sides tacitly understanding and agreeing that nuclear weapons should not be used.

But—he turned and pulled himself out of the seat and began making his way to the open door; the nausea was upon him now; maybe the fresh air would help—he had known from the start that it was impossible, that because the weapons existed they'd be used, sooner or later.

Out in the muddy ravine, the bottom of which was a rushing stream of brown water, Mackey found that it had stopped raining and the ragged edge of the storm front was passing across the face of a three-quarter moon. The sky beyond was starry and clear, seemingly layers deep. He slumped against the side of the ravine and put his head back.

He thought about Kork and wondered if he was still in command and what shape the Soviet response would take.

" . . . a ploy of possibilities, good and bad luck, which spreads about with all the coarse and fine threads of its web and makes war of all branches of human activity most like a gambling game."

Mackey had lost, he knew it, but he had come very close. So close that, in a way, he was satisfied.

Tuesday, P.M.
West of Uelzen
F.G.R.

Price reached up for the mask on his face and with two fingers of his left hand pincered the bridge between the eye slits. In his right hand he held a laser indicator. He would not do what he planned with anything on his face.

The mask did not come away with a tug or two. Price had to pull it up and away from him. It tore off whole patches of his skin. He tossed it down into the slushy snow near the pines in the parking area of the supply depot. Somehow the skin that had remained on the mask—irregular, bloody and edged with yellow and brown—looked like an infrared, topographical map he'd once seen. Of Europe.

The captain beside him moved. "You sure you know what you're doing, sir?"

Price said nothing, only corrected the aim of the indicator, holding the earphone of the headset to his ear.

A voice came on. "Those coordinates are well within our lines, General."

"Those are my orders, Sergeant. I'm waiting."

Already Price could see two figures in the doorway of the crisis-management shelter. One had pointed to him and was conferring with the other, who had a carbine in his hands.

"If he starts shooting, you go down," Price said to the captain. "And stay there." The cold, wet wind stung his raw face, and up above the pines the stars looked inviting, like places he could go to and would prefer to be.

The men in the doorway started down the steps and suddenly klieg lights at every corner of the headquarters compound were snapped on, the light achromatic and blinding. For a moment Price's vision was blurred.

But then he saw other figures in the doorway, the centermost of whom was Bengsten, hands on hips, blond hair and gray sideburns obvious. He motioned a hand in Price's direction. Price thought he heard him shout something, short and sharp, a command.

The lead soldier raised the carbine.

"Get down," Price said to the captain.

But both looked up. Price and the officer with him had been near so many shell bursts for the last several days that they could feel the rush, like a sudden vacuum, of air being sucked up to meet the terminally guided round, the infinitely slight hesitation, the concussion and fireball, and through it—if you were attentive—the scream that arrived only after the round had exploded. Two-hundred-and-three-millimeter rounds of standard ammunition had been used but had proved sufficient.

And after having heard the last report, Price did not care if he ever heard another.

271

The mobile crisis-management center was gone. In its place was a gaping, steaming crater with only the hulks of two power trailers at the periphery of the clearing still standing. In one a diesel engine was still running, but erratically. It coughed, then wound down. In the darkness.

"Now you can place me under arrest, Captain."

"If you say so, sir."

Tuesday, P.M.
Near Wittenberge
G.D.R.

Kork was in another mobile command center not far from the former site of his headquarters in Wittenberge.

After having put down the phone, he picked up a pencil. On the back of the envelope that contained his resignation, he wrote down his estimate of GSFG losses, both those soldiers who had died and those who would never return from West Germany. Earlier he had watched a few stragglers wandering in and now could no longer bear to look at them.

"147,000." He drew a line through the figure and multiplied by 10, adding a zero and changing the commas. "1,470,000." He drew a line through that figure, then wrote, "Hamburg, Hannover, Brunswick, Kassel."

He was over by at least a million and more, for good measure. He handed the letter to Tuchin. "It's all been cleared with Moscow. Make sure the courier leaves with it right away."

The thin man stared down at Kork's scrawl. He reached up and adjusted his glasses.

"Don't worry. It's my decision. You're only following orders. I'll take care of you."

To Kork the words sounded hollow. He had never been more unhappy. If only he had been less cautious. If only he had struck first.

But could he have? Yes—while the snow was still inconsequential, the moment they had learned of the weather-modification program, the moment after Voronov had asked him for some sort of response. He could have said he misunderstood the call. Explanations were easy, after victory.

They meant less than nothing after defeat.

Tuesday, P.M.
Hamburg
F.G.R.

Frau Professor Doktor Froben was in her office, which she was now preparing for the refugees whom she could see down in the *Platz* between the university buildings. Thousands of them, cold now and crowding into the emergency tents that had been erected there, streaming in and out of the buildings in long lines—the refectory, the baths. The gymnasium, the common rooms, and lecture halls were all filled, and she thought it shameful that the faculty had only just voted to give up their offices.

The clothes of the young man and woman outside the open door were sodden and dripping onto the tiles of the corridor. They were really not much older than some of Froben's undergraduate students, and under the overcoats each had a child, too cold and tired and hungry to cry.

Froben was loading her books onto the wide window sill so the bookcase could be removed and the cots brought in. The office was no bigger than a large closet, really, but it would have to do.

Glancing up, she saw the moon and the stars—cold and bright. Severe conditions, considering what had happened. Not for the first time she thought about Annette Siebenborn and Herr Mühling and wondered where they were and if they were all right. Hitzacker was gone, of course, but maybe they had made it through. With all the refugees—

And she was struck by how quiet the night beyond the city seemed, how usual. The moon and the stars were in their places, the untimely snow was nearly gone, even the rumbling of the guns had stopped. Earlier the chairman of the department said that a Bundeswehr officer had told him hostilities had ceased. She wondered if it would last.

Another stack of books.

273

"Let me help you, Fräulein," the young man said. He handed his wife the other child, who began to cry.

Froben smiled at him. Fräulein, that was nice.

At the window she looked straight up at the moon.

There beyond the penumbra she saw a shooting star—two of them, no, three.

She watched them fall, their progress seemingly retarded because they were moving west, directly at her, from a great distance. Three arcing sparks, there—

It occurred to her what they were, but she placed the books down on top of the others and squared them.

She turned her back to the window and tried to smile.

She pointed a finger to the ceiling.

The young woman, the man, even one of the children glanced up.

EPILOGUE

At first she could not get out of the car, nor look at the eyes, wide and haunting, that were staring out at her from the shadows in the garage. But she decided that this was her home, where she would stay and make her way, whether the Soviets remained, which was unlikely given their losses, or withdrew. She opened the door and with Harris's help got to her feet.

There were soldiers everywhere, Russians mostly, like an army of indigents or drunks, wandering the streets, stopping civilians, asking them in broken German how they could cross the river.

The bridges, the ones the Soviets had thrown across the water, were still there, but most of the soldiers had either forgotten what they'd been told or were too sick to stagger the kilometer to the riverbank. And it appeared that the Soviets didn't want them. There were no provisions, no buses, trucks, or ambulances there to take them to hospitals. They were dying, and Annette was struck by how solitary in their multitude was their agony.

Harris wondered if he would have trouble with them, and getting out of the Porsche, he had held the carbine loosely, down by his side.

But they only watched him from the garage, out of the sun, dying.

Already the dead had begun to reek, bellies bloated, flesh turning green.

And Mühling and his mother—Harris didn't know what they were going to do about them. The other troopers had helped him put the young man in the back seat. There he had died.

Harris had waited for a while to assess the Russians' reaction, but when they didn't move he laid down the weapon and began removing what rubble he could from the area he guessed had been the back door and the stairway down to the sub-basement.

The slabs of concrete, however, were too heavy for one man, and after struggling with them he found he had to tunnel down through the wreckage, hoping every time he moved something that the whole pile wouldn't come down on him. But at least it was dry under there, and strangely warm.

He found the pillow from the little rocking chair he'd given the little girl, Ulricka, three days before. It seemed to him like an eternity ago. And a portion of the dollhouse. He picked it up and peered inside—the kitchen.

When the little light that remained in back of him was obscured, he heard Annette say, "Harry—I want you to come out. There's a Russian here who says he wants to help, and he looks like he's all right."

But Harris heard another sound, another voice, muffled and weak down below him.

"Paul," he shouted.

Again a reply, although he couldn't make out what. ·

Harris had to stop and think to keep himself from pulling away too much too quickly, but in tugging on a timber he pulled too hard and plummeted down toward a small shaft of light he could see in front of him.

Harris landed hard, on his shoulder and the side of his face. A light was shining in his eyes.

"Harry?" Siebenborn asked.

Harris pushed the light away.

"Get him some of that Moselle, Emil. He likes it. He told me so."

Up at ground level, the Russian took Annette's arm and helped her sit on a chunk of concrete. "Are you going back?" she asked him.

He shook his head. "They'll treat us like lepers, and I don't think I'm hurt. To tell you the truth, I've never felt better."

She glanced at his shoulders, his arms that were bulging beneath the tanker's overalls. He was young and strong, something like Mühling, whom she could see in the back of the car, whom she still could not believe was dead, whom she missed now perhaps as much as her parents. He had been, well, everything to her—friend, companion, lover—

276

they had shared their lives together, brief as his was. "Are you afraid to work?"

"No, ma'am. I've always been a very good worker. It looks to me"—he allowed his eyes to scan the yard and the other Russians who were in the shed, out of the weather—"that you'll need some help. I can begin by getting them out."

"Not for a while. They don't have long."

And she was suddenly hungry. She wondered if Harris had any, or had access to, food. Of course he would for himself and possibly her, but could he possibly arrange some means to bring food to Hitzacker? The town would rebuild; it had at least several times before.

"There's a van in the garage," she said to the Russian. "I wonder if you could see how badly damaged it is. Do you think you could manage that?"

"You're in luck. I am—I mean I was a mechanic." He rose and left her, his step heavy, stolid.

"Annette?" she heard a voice behind her ask and for a moment she thought it was her father's.

She turned and looked down into the cavity into which Harris had crawled. "Papa?"

"Annette!" Only his arm appeared and she reached for it and helped him out. "My Annette!"

More Bestselling Fiction from Pinnacle

☐ **41-109-X THE CALLING by Kenneth Girard**
An electrifying story of riveting suspense in which a mysterious cult—
The Illuminati—calls upon forces from hell to entrap unsuspecting
victims.

☐ **41-033-6 SPELL OF EGYPT by Victoria Wolff**
By a strange twist of fate, a vulnerable young woman becomes the
object of tainted desires on an all-male archaeological expedition in
search of buried secrets within Tutankhamen's tomb.

☐ **41-140-5 TOUGH LUCK L.A. by Murray Sinclair**
A prosperous porno king, a ribald prostitute ring, an inept hit-man—
only a few of the bizarre characters that reformed juvenile delin-
quent and sometimes sleuth Ben Crandal encounters while investi-
gating a string of gruesome Hollywood murders.

☐ **41-012-3 TEACHER by Alexandra Bryce**
More touching than *To Sir With Love*, more gripping than *Looking
For Mr. Goodbar*...here is the poignant story of Aggie Hillyer, a lib-
eral schoolteacher who enters the high school jungle and learns
more about the three R's—racism, riots and rape—than anyone ought
to!

All Books $2.50

More Bestselling
War Books from Pinnacle
Fiction

MORE
BEST-SELLING FICTION
FROM PINNACLE